A DESTINY IN ASH

JULIE ZANTOPOULOS

atmosphere press

Praise for the *In Ash* Series

"It's fast-paced, swoon-worthy, addictive, and positively queer."
Madison Fox, Author of *Game On*

"This is the adult, spicy, Fae, witchy, polyamorous, romance, action flick, rom com book we've all been waiting for."
Jessica Williamson

"I haven't been this sucked into a book in a while. Whether you read a lot of Fae books, or this is your first dip into the Seelie and Unseelie courts, this was one of the best and clearest descriptions of how the Fae world works."
Chelsea Palmer

"I finished it in one sitting because I couldn't put it down."
Ashe Grey

*"The communication between lovers was so respectful, honest, and OMG steamy! Have I found a favorite author?
All signs point to yes!"*
Goodreads Review

"APIA is such a whirlwind with so many moving pieces that it keeps you drawn in from beginning to end. Prophecy is such a fitting follow up to Curse."
Goodreads Review

"With incredible world building, an engaging plot, loveable characters, and a swoon-worthy polyamory romance, this series is a must read!"
Goodreads Review

GLOSSARY OF TERMS

Alate: An earth sprite. They can be bark, flower, or plantlike in appearance. Typically very protective of their gardens and glens. Peaceful unless disturbed or molting. Useful for keeping garden pests away.

Dark/Unseelie Fae: Historically, the more "volatile" court. They want change in their favor, even at the cost of lives.

Familiar: Animal companion to Fae with the ability to assist and communicate with them.

Firinne: A council of elder witches that oversees bonds between witches and their Ravdi, as well as with humans.

Light/Seelie Fae: Typically, the more mild-mannered court. They want change through collaborative and mutually beneficial means.

Neapan: The most common type of water sprite. They lure people to the water's edge, strip their flesh, and bleach their bones to wear as prizes.

New Fae: Witches and Ravdi who harnessed the magic of the breaking Veil when it dropped, reconnected with their lost magic, and became Fae.

Ravdi: Human magical conduit to witches capable of harnessing magic and channeling it to witches, through the bond, for the witch to wield. Ravdi are incapable of magic themselves but necessary for magic users.

Sifting: A bending of space and time allowing fast travel through Faerie by Fae only.

Spark: A fire sprite seen as smoke or flame. They are typically destructive and temperamental.

Unaligned Fae: Fae who have chosen or are forced into exile. They live outside the Seelie or Unseelie Courts and therefore have no governing power to protect or rule them.

Veil: The divide between the human and the Fae realms. It is visible to all with Fae blood and some witches, but not to humans. Passing between the two worlds is possible for all Fae during the new moon, stronger Fae at all times, and all humans, witches, and Fae at border checkpoints.

Wisp: An air elemental capable of controlling winds. They can be invisible or take the form of small glowing lights. They're typically peaceful but can be moved to anger.

Seelie Court

☾ **King Kyteler:** King of the Seelie for the past 483 years.

☾ **Queen Branwyn:** Queen of the Seelie, wife to King Kyteler, and mother to Corinna.

☾ **Princess Corinna:** Princess of the Seelie and heir to the Seelie throne.

☾ **Ellasar:** Advisor to the King and Queen.

☾ **Nevan, Regent of the Seelie Court:** Servant to the King and Queen and father of Aisling.

☾ **Aisling Quinn:** Part witch, part Fae, and slated to unite the two courts and realms.

Unseelie Court

☾ **King Tynan:** (Assassinated) Father to Rainer, Levinas, and Ceiren. Ruled for 754 years.

☾ **Queen Moura:** Dethroned Queen of the Unseelie Court.

☾ **Gabriel, Bloody Hand of The Unseelie Court:** Executioner and advisor to Queen Moura. Father to Brynach and Breena.

☽ **King Rainer:** King of the Unseelie Court after dethroning his mother. Father to Beatrix. Widower to wife Brittany (human).

☽ **Princess Beatrix:** First halfling Princess. Daughter of Rainer and Brittany. Eventual heir to the Unseelie throne.

☽ **Prince Levinas:** Second son of the Unseelie Court.

☽ **Prince Ceiren:** Third son to Tynan and Moura. Duties include liaising with the Unaligned.

☽ **Prince Brynach:** Husband to Aisling Quinn, twin to Breena. Named new Bloody Hand.

☽ **Princess Breena:** Twin to Brynach. No "official" role in the royal hierarchy.

CHAPTER 1

Aisling

*"Nobody tells you that fulfilling your destiny may burn down
the world and piss off everyone you love."*
– Aisling Quinn

Quinn! For fuck's sake, a little help would be nice."

She didn't remember the rookie cop's name. Which really wasn't surprising considering over forty new officers had been sworn into Birchwood Falls PD in as many days.

"Someone help the new guy," she called to a veteran, nodding toward where the young man was swatting ineffectually at angry alates.

Aisling's bank account was thriving with all the work she'd acquired since the Veil dropped, but her patience had significantly decreased. It was no wonder, really. Add to her already large list of responsibilities the press conferences, travel, and increased warding of prisons to enable the holding of more Fae, and she was worn out, which left training these rookies as about the only thing she wasn't responsible for.

You'd think having a large majority of your force turned into nearly immortal, strong-as-heck Fae would be a benefit. Instead, the PD was flapping around like a fish out of water, unsure of what to do with itself. Once more, she reminded herself that it was not her fault or her problem. She may have brought down this section of the Veil, but the consequences didn't belong to her. At least not solely.

Checking her watch, Aisling rolled her eyes. She'd been out there for over two hours and didn't have time to get home now before she needed to be at her appointment. And still, somehow, she'd rather have stayed there in the smoke and chaos.

Aisling looked around the once-suburban street and swatted at a frisky sprite flying by her head. The road, once straight through to town, now curved around a chunk of woods from Faerie. Turns out that merging two realms was magically complicated. Areas like this road and shops stayed as they were on the human side of the Veil, but any uninhabited areas were now occupied with bits of Faerie. Geographical displacement of both people, animals, and elementals created more than a bit of conflict.

They were getting better at quelling outbursts like this. The protests were almost to be expected at this point. Her head turned east, and she checked her watch once more. She didn't have time to stop at the New Fae training grounds and see Riordan. The pull to go to him was strong, but Aisling understood her partner's passion for his new role. Riordan was assisting in the transition of magic, strength, and immortality for the newly turned Fae. It was a rewarding role and one she wished she had more time to take part in.

She heard shouts and followed them through the chaos to the deputy in need of help.

"The New Fae are an abomination!"

"Purge the Fae! Keep our children safe!"

"Veilers unite!"

"Witches and Ravdi for the Veil! Stop messing with natural order!"

She shook her head and ignored them. Same fear-based rhetoric, different day. Nobody was happy, and everyone was blaming her. Along with some hard-earned perspective from her mother, Aisling had realized that she could only shoulder so much guilt about creating a world where the people she loved would lead long, healthy lives.

Nobody tells you that fulfilling your destiny may burn down the world and piss off everyone you love.

"Head in the game, Quinn," Loren called as he shook his head. "You know better."

He was right; she did. Getting distracted out here was not a great idea. Not only did she have to assume cell phone cameras were pointed at her at all times, but she had to make sure the police were safe. It was kinda her job.

"You've got me for five minutes. What's the priority?" She jogged into the fray.

"Perimeter protection. Reinforce this line so we can keep these troublemakers at bay," he yelled.

"You know they're just fucking with you, right?" she said as she sprinkled the herb-filled water along the line the fire-fighters had created.

"Just do your job, Quinn," he responded before turning to answer another call for assistance.

She fought really hard to not roll her eyes at her friend's husband. She liked the man, always had, but he'd gotten touchy lately. Not that she blamed him. It couldn't be easy realizing your wife and child would have longer lives than you.

Still, she technically outranked most of the officers here. That's what happens when you become invaluable to the world at large and gain notoriety. Not that anyone on the PD would acknowledge it. They treated her the same as they did when she was a consultant for them. She loved them for it.

Aisling shook her head to clear her thoughts. Walking the line, she placed protections on the ground and the officers. A few spared her a smile as she sprinkled the magic-worked water on them. Before long, her watch's alarm sounded. After a quick scream to the officer in charge, she walked away from the chaos of the front line.

Brynach was meeting her at the conference, so she was sifting alone. She was still a bit nervous about it, but she was getting better each day. Meaning she very rarely fucked up and ended up in the middle of a fountain or someone's private yard.

Aisling called on magic and saw it fold, creating a direct link between where she was and where she wanted to be. Like origami, the world bent, and she stepped through the fold. The pressure still felt foreign, but it wasn't nearly as uncomfortable anymore. Instead, it felt like a tingling across her body. Apparently, when it was her active magic working for her, the unease of the sift lessened.

Aisling exited the fold by the building where she'd be giving a press conference. The shocked faces of the guards who had never gotten used to her sifting in made her chuckle. They recovered quickly and led her through the wards.

"This way, Miss Quinn." They ushered her inside. The older man was very formal and, despite having been her escort for the past few months, hadn't switched to more familiar language. She'd requested he call her Aisling multiple times, not just because she preferred it but because she still hated being called Miss when she was married. But Fae don't take one another's last name, and she sure as shit wasn't Mrs. Quinn.

Once in the small office they'd assigned her, she changed into her "on-air" clothes before her hair and makeup came in. Rating and polls proved the people preferred her as relatable but polished. She'd fought the stylists at first, but then she'd seen a clip of herself without the television makeup. She'd looked horrendous. Cait had been kind enough to send screenshots of some of the more colorful comments about her appearance from social media. Aisling was vain enough to let them do their thing after that.

"Are you ready?" Cathy, her media consultant, entered the room. "Goddess, you stink."

Aisling turned her head. "Have you seen the fires? They're making headway, but their attention is split between the sprites and the protestors. They need help. Maybe we could mention that? Get more volunteers."

The other woman rested her hand on her hip and frowned. "Aisling, you know that we want coverage when you do things like that. You have to tell us so we can get a crew on the scene."

For Cathy, everything was a good press opportunity. Doing something to be nice, or because it was still a part of her job, didn't register for the PR specialist. Aisling respected her tenacity, but the thought of having camera crews around more than absolutely necessary was awful.

"There wasn't time to alert you, nor did I look all prettied up for a photoshoot," Aisling joked. Cathy was not amused.

"That's what we want. Something real. That would have been gold. Next time, please notify us." She sounded put out, but Aisling ignored it.

Aisling sensed her husband before the large Fae walked in. Makeup and hair smartly backed up as Brynach wrapped her in his arms. Aisling was dwarfed by his size and overwhelmed by the strength of his love for her.

"I missed you, too," she whispered into his neck.

"You snuck out of the house this morning. I didn't even hear you go." The hurt was clear in his voice.

"I wanted to help Riordan sift to the training grounds." She took his hand when he set her down. She ran her thumb over the band she'd given him, knowing it would soften him.

Brynach smirked. "He's getting the hang of it faster than you did." Her husband buried his face in her hair. "You smell like smoke."

She shook her head. "You know I worked today."

His hands skirted over her face and body. "I should probably check you over to be sure."

Aisling slapped his hand away. "Don't start what you can't finish."

"Don't be a brat," he warned. "I don't have time to punish you if you're on in less than an hour."

There was a cough from behind her, and Aisling had the grace to blush. She placed a hand on the large Fae's chest and pushed him back a step.

"Get your ass in this chair, darling." Her makeup artist pointed with their brush, and she obeyed.

Brynach leaned against the wall behind her, winking when she caught his gaze in the mirror. When he nodded, she returned her attention to the work her makeup artist was doing. And they were an artist. Aisling had worried at first that they were going to turn her into some kind of New Fae publicity Barbie, but they'd kept her makeup light and her hair a little wild. The "girl next door" had tested the highest with viewers.

Letting them play with her hair and face was easy. The hard part was the scripts they fed her. She understood they had an agenda, a story they wanted to spin, but she'd quickly shut down their attempts to use her as a mouthpiece. Aisling refused to say anything she didn't actively and passionately support. All teleprompt talking points were passed by her, or the guys, each time she went on air.

Her words mattered. There were thousands of New Fae who looked to Riordan, Brynach, and herself for guidance. Not just in Birchwood Falls, but in other towns she'd traveled to and assisted in drops for. With each one, more witches and Ravdi turned New Fae. Each time more people traveled there, waiting for the magic of the Veil to disperse and gift them with their full magic. All those eyes on her meant her words held weight, and that weight sometimes felt like a hell of a lot to carry.

"Where are you, Aisling?" Brynach asked from behind her, hands massaging knots out of her shoulders.

A small moan escaped her lips. "Thinking of you and Riordan."

"Me too, darling." Her makeup artist winked.

Aisling laughed, and Brynach squeezed her shoulders before removing his hands. "Have you looked at the speech?"

"Can you? My eyes are burning a bit," she answered.

Brynach frowned at her, and the makeup artist reached for the eye drops on the vanity. They held a tissue under Aisling's eyes and dropped the cooling liquid into each of them. When she blinked them away, Brynach had the stack of papers in his hands. Aisling wasn't too worried about this press conference. Things were relatively calm at the moment, and the message would be a reminder to maintain order and peace at drops.

She'd remain the face of the New Fae revolution so long as the message the government wanted to perpetuate matched her own. Which was to say, restoring the magic stolen from witches and Ravdi.

Cathy showed at her side. "We want a focus on peace and order along the Veil. Encourage people to be safe in areas scheduled for take-down and encourage them to prepare for the influx of magic. Remind them that centers and phone numbers are in place if they need resources. Help is available before and after the drop to assist those who have transitioned."

Brynach grunted his approval before handing the papers to Aisling. "Don't forget to mention those resources are free, easily accessible, and staffed with knowledgeable professionals trained to help with the mental health consequences of late-in-life changes," he reminded the aide.

"We are getting teams in place at least a week prior to the drop, and they move on to the next only when at least seventy percent of New Fae have either moved to a training facility or reported feeling comfortable with their change," the other woman answered. It was a scripted answer.

Aisling's mother was leading the charge for New Fae mental health services and the accessibility of help both pre- and post-Veil drop. She was incredibly proud of her efforts. It wasn't easy leaving behind all you knew, and a lot of witches and Ravdi had actively moved away from drop zones, afraid of the change. In that way, there was some control, still. It was the large burst of magic from each Veil drop that sparked the change. And with the Veil being as powerful as it was, it couldn't come down all at once, but instead in pieces. That meant that areas had time to allow people to move in and out and prepare for the shift to New Fae or opt out.

"There's an open question and answer at the end. Keep it to three questions max, and please answer carefully. When in doubt, you'll get back to them. Five minutes and you're on," Cathy said before leaving with the makeup artist, giving Aisling and Brynach space.

Careful not to mess up her masterfully crafted look, she went into Brynach's arms. She let him ground her before the cameras and lights were in her face. Teleprompters she could handle, but the reporters hurling questions her way still made her nervous. Having her husband in the back of the room, acting as both her security and support system, helped.

"I'm going to kiss you," Brynach warned before his hand snaked down her back and pulled her close.

He bunched her skirt up, and then his rough palms cupped her ass, squeezing hard. His thumb traced the top of her cheeks while his middle finger toyed with the edge of her panties. His mouth devoured her.

"Bry." She was breathless, clinging to him and spreading her legs wider.

"When the cameras start, I want to know that the flush on your cheeks is from me," he growled in her ear. "I want you up there knowing that when we get home tonight, I'm going to instruct Riordan on exactly how to please you while I watch. Only after you come for him will I take you."

Her belly clenched as she imagined all the beautiful, depraved things she'd be doing later.

"On stage!" Cathy yelled from the hallway.

Brynach pulled away from her with a smile. She wanted to be angry, but she wasn't. It thrilled her to know that Brynach would likely text Riordan, who would watch the news and know exactly why her cheeks had color. Aisling didn't mind at all when they toyed with her like this. She took a moment to reapply the lip gloss that had been left behind and then blew a kiss to Brynach before leaving the room.

Aisling took the stage while the large Fae moved to the back wall. She noted the increased number of security in the room. She saw when Brynach noticed the same thing and his body tensed. Aisling knew that threats had been made against her life, Riordan and Brynach's too. But the idea that she'd be in danger here seemed unlikely to her.

Logically, she understood that what she was doing was upsetting nearly as many people, if not more, than she was pleasing. While none of them were happy about that, they weren't surprised. If anything, they were more vigilant than ever about their safety.

The cameras began clicking as soon as she approached the podium. With a smile pasted on her face, Aisling forced her heart to calm and her mind to clear. The teleprompter flashed a countdown, and Aisling began reading.

"Thank you for coming this evening. As you know, we have a busy schedule of drops coming up. The Veil in Harlisville came down beautifully, and the local police did a fantastic job of protecting the magic workers on the front line. But bringing down the Veil isn't where our work stops. We are proud to announce new tools put in place to ease the transition for the New Fae in drop zones."

She outlined their strategy and ignored the raised hands in the crowd. "We are encouraging all witches and Ravdi in the scheduled areas to reach out to the resource numbers on the screen right now. There are counselors available both pre- and post-drop. I understand the influx of magic can be a shock to the system, but I have seen people flourish with it rightfully restored. Our training facilities are growing better equipped as more New Fae enter with different skill sets."

She paused when prompted.

"Nobody is alone. We are all in this together. With a combined effort, we can make this world what it was always intended to be."

Aisling wrapped up the last two talking points, one on the continued cooperation between the Fae and humans, followed by the promise that Fae and humans were working toward mutually beneficial guiding principles and laws. Then there was nothing left to do but accept questions from the reporters on the approved list the teleprompter provided. The first two questions were easy, which lulled her into a false sense of security. Rookie mistake.

"Miss Quinn," one began. "There are concerns among the human population that they're already wildly outnumbered and becoming more so with each drop. What do you say to those who believe you're effectively wiping out the human race?"

Well, that was a hot ass mess of a take. Aisling did her best to keep her face neutral when she answered.

"First, I'd like to clarify that none of the New Fae were ever human. Secondly, I believe righting wrongs, correcting imbalances, and restoring the world to its intended state are more important than the comfort of people who profit off the oppressed. If that scares humans, that's really too bad. Now that the New Fae understand their full potential, they deserve to see it actualized."

There was a gasp from a reporter, but she wasn't done. "There's no doubt that the world is changing, but I'd like to remind you that the New Fae are the same people you know and love. Your teachers, your handymen, friends, and neighbors. Change can take time to get used to, but we're not going to stop doing what's right in the meantime."

The reporters called out follow-up questions.

"What do you have to say about the rising threat of violence at the drops?"

"Why are the New Fae training in weapons and magic? Are you planning an attack on the humans?"

"The Fae courts have crumbled. Will the Fae now fall under human government rule?"

Aisling ignored them all. She left the stage and was met in the hallway by Cathy. The other woman huffed. "It would absolutely kill you to just stick to the prompter, wouldn't it? For what it's worth, I think it was a great answer. My boss won't."

"Sorry." Aisling shrugged.

"No, you aren't. Don't forget to call in next time you get the urge for community service." Cathy broke off to a hallway on the right as Brynach reached her.

"You were great," Brynach said. He followed Aisling into the now-empty office and waited while she changed into her street clothes.

Her husband's arms wrapped around her, and Aisling let her head fall back against his chest. She turned in his arms, and he dropped his head to kiss her.

"I love you," he whispered into her hair. "And I'm going to show you just how much as soon as we're done with the next appointment."

She took his hand, and they exited the wards so they could sift to a neutral meeting place in what used to be Faerie. Geographical borders between the two lands were a thing of the past. The most "solid" structures of each realm remained post-Veil drop. Where woods existed in the human realm, a Faerie house now stood. Where a store existed in the human realm, it overpowered a glen in Faerie. Despite some resistance, most meetings now took place closer to the old lands of Faerie, where the Fae and New Fae alike felt comfortable.

For now, at least, people were accommodating their requests. And since meetings between Fae, New Fae, and humans were commonplace as they built the new world, Brynach, Riordan, and Aisling attended them as often as possible, if only to show face. Most of the time, they weren't just pretty faces at the table, though. Setting new rules for their world required patience and cooperation. Aisling was in a unique position to broker between the police, the Fae, and the witches. She'd accepted that these meetings got added to her to-do list pretty quickly.

As they neared the meeting area, Aisling saw a dog playing with an animal she didn't recognize. It looked like a cross between a beaver and a fox with three tails. The wildlife had merged more gracefully than the humans and Fae had. Aisling frowned upon noticing the citrus-and-berry scent of Faerie had softened even more since she'd been there last. Aisling missed the concentrated scent of the magic that had once filled the land.

The New Fae, as the newly changed Ravdi and witches had labeled themselves, found themselves in a unique position. They outnumbered the "old" Fae and, with the help of the Unaligned, had overthrown the courts, taking over both palaces and negating the need for their rule. Their rule wasn't the only one to fail, though. The human government hadn't been far behind. Too many politicians ended up being New Fae, and distrust blossomed. Today's meeting was to propose new laws that would apply to all people.

By the time they arrived, the meeting had already begun. She took a seat next to Brynach and tried to catch up on the conversation.

"Tell us again why we'd want to do that?" Marina, a Fae Aisling had met when her husband went missing and she'd been working with Dexter still, said. The mild-mannered Fae had lived across the Veil with her human husband long enough that she'd worked herself into the talks.

Around the table, Aisling clocked the other players. Rainer and Breena; Ellasar, the advisor to the unseated Seelie royals; Theo something or other; a once-witch-lawyer turned New Fae; Governor Settenfield, representing the humans; Pilson, the new chief of police; and a few faces Aisling didn't recognize. She smiled at her mother and Brielle, who also graced the table and rounded out the twenty-some people.

Aisling caught Breena's bored gaze, and her sister-in-law winked at her. She noticed when the other woman met eyes with her twin, Breena brightened and then paled, looking away. Aisling kept her face schooled, but beside her, Brynach stilled. She could feel him vibrating with the effort to not rush to his sister. He hadn't seen her since the battle that killed their brother.

Jashana had sifted the injured woman to the Unseelie healers, but Breena's recovery had taken longer than anyone could have anticipated. With the castle under siege by Unaligned and New Fae, they hadn't been able to gain access to the palace. They'd been able to get messages to one another, but Aisling knew how badly he'd needed to see his sister.

To make matters worse, Breena hadn't seemed all that eager to see her twin. Brynach tried to hide it, but he was hurt by his sister's reaction. Aisling took a good look at Breena and just barely managed to stifle a gasp. Her husband made a pained sound. It was impossible to look at his sister and not know. Of course, they'd already been told. But knowing and seeing it were two different things.

Next to her, Brynach's leg started to bounce, and Aisling put her hand on him. There was no way everyone else at the table was unaware of Breena's situation, but now wasn't the time to talk about it.

"Breathe, Bry. We'll talk to her soon," Aisling whispered.

He reached for her hand, and she gave it to him as Rainer spoke.

"Our release and your cooperation with our efforts benefit us both," Rainer said without a trace of irony.

"You're not in a position to negotiate, Rainer." Marina smirked.

All eyes were on Rainer, who still wore his crown, though it held no power. Kyteler and Branwyn weren't at the table, so she didn't know if they were hanging onto pretense, but she assumed they were. Anything to prove they weren't weak after being embarrassed by their daughter. It had taken them a week to find Corinna after Levinas was killed. Her parents had been so relieved, but Corinna had refused to talk to them. To add insult to injury, she'd chosen to heal at the Unseelie court's hospital ward instead of the Seelie court.

"We can all agree that things have changed in Faerie," Rainer began.

"There is no Faerie," a voice from down the table called.

"The world has changed," Rainer continued, unfazed by the interruption. "We have to change with it; that much is clear. And while some of the New Fae and Unaligned don't want the protection and support of a court, that doesn't mean none do."

"Actually, that's exactly what that means, which is why you're not in power right now. The fuck would we trust you for?" A large New Fae spoke from beside Theo. "Why would we follow the very people who denied us our birth right?"

"A magic set in place long before our generation took power," Rainer reminded them.

"And perpetuated by you. You weren't eager to share, were you?" The man reminded the once-King.

Breena snorted, and Brynach shot her a look. She raised her shoulders in an awkward shirk.

We maintained peace for centuries by offering all Fae the *power*," Rainer stressed the word. "To choose the court they swore allegiance to. The same one you'll be given now."

Theo wasn't impressed. "And we choose to deny the authority of the old courts. Your reign is dead, and the rise of the new court, a united one encompassing all Fae, is the future." The once-witch lawyer had a lot of pent-up anger toward the old Fae.

"How organized is that new court? That new power? How used to threats and politics are they? How safe can they keep you while they struggle to figure out how their system works? The old courts lasted this long because we know how to care for those that belong with us. How safe can they keep you without the generations of magic training?" Rainer was calm as he rebutted the argument.

Aisling had expected a rebuttal. She just hadn't expected it to come from Alex.

"There are plenty among the old Fae who didn't agree with the court's rulings and governing. Those Fae get a choice, too, Rainer. As a people, we've decided the courts have no place in our future. Frankly, you are fighting a losing battle."

"We'll be just fine now that your mother and her lover are out of the picture," someone yelled.

"He's human," a New Fae sneered. "He's no threat to us."

Aisling didn't miss the way Breena's fist curled on the table. Neither did her husband.

"Is he?" Rainer questioned the crowd. "We have reports that Gabriel's magic was restored when the Veil fell."

What was Rainer playing at?

"He's still just one Fae. We took entire castles and toppled ancient political structures. We can handle one Fae, even if it's Gabriel." Theo laughed. Aisling wasn't sure she liked that man, but he had a point.

"I felt Faerie abandon him. The Goddess left him," Aisling assured the table.

"You speak for the Goddess now? Is there anything you can't do, oh anointed one?" Theo spit.

"Watch your mouth," Brynach snarled.

"I stripped a royal Fae of his magic. I brought down the motherfucking Veil. I've touched magic you can't imagine and unwoven the very fabric of it. If you want to measure dicks, I'm pretty sure I'd win." Aisling stared him down.

Breena let out a throaty laugh when Theo finally broke eye contact. She wasn't going to let some smacked ass push her around. There were a few things she'd learned lately, and at the top of the list was she didn't take shit from anyone.

"Like my wife said, when Gabriel's found, she will have the pleasure of either stripping him for a second time or imprisoning him for treason," Brynach reminded them.

"Like hell she will," Pilson barked.

Aisling liked the cop, always had, but he'd become a bit of a hardass as Chief. She'd been happy for his promotion when the prior chief had retired early, tired of the drama and bull-shit. Poor Pilson was woefully unprepared for what he was stepping into.

"We don't want any more damn Fae in our prisons. We can't have 'lifers' there for eternity. Our system can't handle infinite imprisonment." He reminded them.

Aisling nodded. This was something the PR team had already discussed with her. She knew they were taking steps to solve the problem, and so did the chief. They'd strip the worst offend-ers of their Fae magic, and they'd serve human sentences. The others would be sentenced to shorter terms in heavily warded facilities. Regardless, a restructuring was necessary.

She knew Pilson, though. He was just trying to change the subject, and it worked. Soon, they were all arguing over some-thing else.

Brynach's twin pushed her chair back and walked away. Her husband quickly went after his sister. Aisling stayed seated to hear the rest of the discussions. Like most of these meet-ings, suggestions were set to the table and quickly rejected or amended. Nothing would be accomplished today, but each talk created a bit of progress. Breena had pulled Brynach further away, and when the meeting ended, Aisling stood to go join them.

"It's good to see you," Alex said as he came up behind her. When she turned, he hugged her. "You've been busy. Aindrea and I have been keeping tabs on you. We're proud of you."

She waved off his compliment. "I'm flying by the seat of my pants. I don't really have a choice in the matter, do I? You can't start something and then turn away."

"You can. Some do. You haven't." Alex patted her shoulder. "That takes guts, Aisling. I know the threats are getting more serious. Are you keeping safe? Maybe you should slow down some?"

She looked to where Brynach was now nearly out of sight.

"I have a lot of security, and I can't back off now. There's too much to be done. Speaking of which, I heard you're going to be working with Brynach on a big project?"

"Yeah, although there's still a lot of convincing to do," he huffed. "We were hoping to petition Theo and Marina for the use of the palace, but it seems they've given the royals free rein again."

"Just because they're walking around unbothered doesn't mean they're in charge. Just ask. I'm sure they'll see reason on this one." It was a good idea. A necessary one.

"Your husband may still be able to make something work. We'll see," Alex said.

The novelty of having Brynach called "your husband" so nonchalantly still thrilled her. "Well, speaking of my husband, I should go wrangle him. We have a partner who is most likely waiting on us."

Alex nodded. "Tell him to stop by soon. And maybe join him. Aindrea would love to see you."

Aisling was heading toward Brynach when he shook his head. He said something to his sister and then sifted to Aisling's side. She looked back at Breena in time to see Jashana approach her, their heads bent together, and then they sifted away.

"What the hell is going on?" Aisling asked.

"I'll tell you at home."

Brynach took her hand and, before she could argue, sifted them away. She shook her head as her feet settled on the side-walk just off Main Street.

"We've got to talk about it, Bry," she pressed.

He hung his head, dark black hair hiding a face she loved. "Once, a stoirin. I can only do it once. Let's get Riordan first."

CHAPTER 2

Riordan

The groans of the New Fae were loud as they trained but not as loud as the shit-talking they engaged in. The grounds were chaotic even though they did their best to section off training areas. Quadrant A for the sifting practice. Quadrant B for the weapons and physical training, which was where Riordan spent a lot of his time. Quadrant C was probably the most dangerous with magic training. And Quadrant D was for training New Fae with prior police, emergency, or military experience.

Like Riordan, a lot of the New Fae felt it was their obligation to use their new immortality to help others. In truth, it was safer if they understood their abilities. Mistrust between the New Fae and Fae was strong, but having them there to help with magic and sifting was a necessity.

Originally, they'd tried to train with swords like the Fae did, but it was quickly traded for more modern weapons, physical agility, and strength training. Having stronger bodies and quickly regenerating cells didn't make them entirely invincible. The sword training ended when limbs were severed. Even Fae can't grow those back. A throwing knife through the eye socket into the brain, still no bueno. The limits of their magic were clearly outlined and then pushed by those more careless.

Riordan did what he could to keep everyone safe as they learned. He was determined to make these training grounds efficient, if nothing else, to help himself and honor the lives of his family that ended before they could be gifted their full magic.

"Pay attention. I nearly took your head off." Isaac smirked at Riordan.

"As if you could get the drop on me," he joked. Isaac was one of the New Fae Riordan had befriended, and the guy was jacked. He'd been one of those "pick things up and put things down" gym rats pre-drop. Now, he was sheer powerful muscle.

The friendship hadn't been immediate. Riordan was still overly cautious about anyone who approached him. Too many people were curious about him, Aisling, and Brynach. He'd had to put up walls to avoid those who only wanted to get close to him for the clout it provided them. He was fiercely protective of himself and his newfound love and happiness. But Isaac was chill, and he naturally fell into a friendship.

"Too distracted for this, sorry," Riordan offered. "I'm taking a break."

"I get it. I'm intimidating," Isaac teased, turning to find another sparring partner.

Riordan took a deep breath, testing the air. His body thrummed with power, and he fought the sensory overload. He could smell the freshly cut grass from a house three blocks away, hear the swear of the New Fae two quadrants over as he failed to grow a plant, and feel the magic in the ground under his feet. He'd anticipated it being easier after a few months, but it still surprised him that the magic not only came to him but allowed him to wield it. Using magic wasn't something he took for granted.

Alongside his new long life, Riordan felt grounded in the world, tethered to his body and the magic around him. Becoming Fae had done that for him, more than falling in love with Aisling ever had. Of all the mind-blowing situations he'd found himself in since coming to the States, this was the most life-changing.

For the first time in far too long, Riordan felt right. He finally felt at home in his skin. Granted, that skin was more toned and tanned than ever. He had pushed his body further in the past months than ever before. He still had a long way to go to reach Brynach-level sculpted, but he was more muscle than lean and lithe now. He certainly didn't mind the way Aisling looked at his body as it changed.

Riordan called the magic to himself, let it fill his body, and soak into his weary muscles. Feeling fortified, he walked toward his brother. It was Amber who acknowledged his approach. Liam was too busy scowling and cursing as he attempted another sift to say hello. Liam was struggling with the transition to New Fae; Amber wasn't taking to it as naturally, either. There was a theory circling that because Amber didn't have a Ravdi, her New Fae abilities weren't as strong. Similarly, because Liam's bonded was still a witch, he wasn't as powerful.

The Veil was coming down slowly, and only where the Veil fell did the witches and Ravdi transition to New Fae. It would be a while before everyone was at full capacity, but more and more of the Veil was falling each week. Unleashing that kind of magic too fast could be catastrophic to the structure of the world. The merging of the two realms needed to be done slowly, and the transitioning of that many Fae was best done in groups so training facilities like Riordan's weren't overwhelmed.

Liam's girlfriend was in her usual ripped black jeans and black tank top. Her hair was freshly colored blue, and the left half of her head had a close buzz cut. But she didn't look like herself. Her one and only argument against being New Fae was the loss of her tattoos.

"I sure as hell am not going to continue the rest of this immortal fucking life as a blank, boring slate. I'm not kidding, Riordan. We are going to find Hiss and fix this," Amber swore when her cells had regenerated and removed her ink.

Riordan didn't blame her. She'd put a lot of time, money, and thought into her pieces.

"If you think Hiss has settled enough to work on me, I'm down. Set up a time and a place, and I'll be there," Riordan agreed. The large Fae with snake-like physical qualities had once bit through his hand. He wasn't trying to tempt fate. "Just give me enough of a heads up so I can make sure to block my schedule."

Amber rolled her eyes. "You sound like a tool when you say shit like that."

"Yeah, well, it's my reality." Riordan nodded to his brother, who was approaching. "Not going well?"

"We can't all be exceptionally talented New Fae like you," Liam huffed.

Riordan sympathized, he did. Not all New Fae were built the same. While some old Fae had physical characteristics like different colored skin, needle-like teeth, wings, and naturally colorful hair, the New Fae didn't. They maintained their human appearance while they gained Fae capabilities.

Aisling hypothesized that the strength of the New Fae correlated to their strength as a witch or Ravdi. Others thought it was based on the size of the Veil chunk that fell and the magic that was shared. Liam had been an average Ravdi, but his bonded was still human. Amber hadn't possessed much latent magic as a witch. Thus, they were both struggling.

It didn't help Liam's attitude when his "little" brother had bulked up and taken to being Fae with ease. Riordan and Aisling had been strong pre-drop, and he suspected that his bond with Brynach had helped him out, too. Riordan bit back the advice waiting on his tongue. Instead, he offered it to the group at large. His brother could take it or leave it, but others could benefit from it.

"How's everyone doing?" He was jovial when he asked. They weren't as happy when they answered. Groans and mumbles were followed by curses. "I know it's hard."

"Sure, you do." A New Fae he didn't recognize rolled his eyes.

"It's new for all of us, and we're the test subjects. The resources other areas are getting weren't available to us right away. That doesn't mean we can't get a handle on it," Riordan assured them.

"There's no 'we' here, Rory. You have the hang of it." Liam added fuel to the fire.

It was hard to keep himself from snapping back at his brother.

"Go easy on him, Riordan. Sometimes just being near you is a reminder that he's not performing up to his standards."

Riordan did his best not to startle at the voice in his head. Physical changes, no problem. But having a familiar whose voice lived rent-free in your head was a change he was still adjusting to. You'd think with the Ravdi-and-witch bond, he'd be used to it, but having a voice in your head was not the same as sharing intuitive emotions you could block at will.

Maybe it helped that his sneaky familiar had found him early? Riordan had a theory that his bond with Brynach had caused his familiar to notice him before his full change. Valo, the sleek fox who'd been tailing him for months, laughed in his head.

"He's just bitter I got a cooler familiar," Riordan joked. Liam had been a little disgruntled at bonding with a rather precocious raccoon. Riordan thought she was pretty cool, though.

"You know that's not all. You'd just begun your journey as a Ravdi. It was a huge part of his identity, and he was good at it. Now he's lost that and is floundering," Valo reminded him.

Riordan nodded and turned to his brother. "If I can do it, so can you. When have you ever let me master something you didn't?" Riordan challenged him. He turned to the Fae, instructing them. "When you sift, what do you think of?"

"The location I want to go to. I harness the magic of the land, and there's this knowing that falls over me. A promise that the magic I'm holding will do my will. I enter where I stand and visualize a tunnel, then exit where I want to be." They paused and added. "It's being at one with the land and the magic within."

Riordan nodded. "Who here used to be Ravdi?"

He looked around and saw Liam and a few others raise their hands.

"You know how to harness magic already. It's never been more vibrant and available to us than it is now. Pull it to you but start small." Riordan pointed to a large flat stone in the middle of the clearing. "Focus there. Whether it's on top of it or to the side of it doesn't matter. The first former Ravdi to sift there wins."

He watched his brother close his eyes. Riordan could sense the magic drawing toward the group. Then one of the female former Ravdi disappeared. He looked to the stone, but she didn't show there. When he turned back, Liam was gone.

A whoop sounded from behind him, and Riordan swung around to see a New Fae on the rock. Liam was much further out from the rock, looking pissed off.

The Fae who reached the rock sifted back. "That worked! Thank you."

"That's my job." Riordan shrugged off the thanks. "Okay, where are my former witches?"

The rest of the group, Amber included, raised their hands.

"Right. So, you couldn't call magic, and now you can. That's got to feel strange, but you know how to use it once you have it. You also know what the magic feels like once it's built up inside you. So, feel for it. If you had a bonded, then you know how to sense the frequency you worked on. Look for that and pull it to you. The magic won't fight you. It wants to be reunited with those it senses as like, and you're more magic now than ever before. Focus on your destination and trust the process," Riordan paused. "I know you've been taught to be careful with your magic, but right now, you have to let loose a little. Trust it."

The man in front of him nodded, but Amber didn't look convinced. She took a deep breath, and then he felt a surge of magic. She sifted, and he wasn't entirely surprised when she appeared next to the rock, extending her hand and touching it. Even from across the field, he could hear her exclamation.

"Sweet fuck, I did it!"

Liam shook his head and muttered, "I'll never hear the damn end of it."

Riordan turned to his brother. "You're wound too tight. You have to let go, Liam. This is who you are now."

They looked to his girlfriend, who was still by the rock. Amber was waving to them, and he heard his brother's sigh before he tried again. This time he got closer, not quite there, but it was progress.

The Fae instructor moved in next to Riordan. "They hate listening to me," he murmured.

"Can you blame them?" Riordan asked.

The Fae shook his red hair. "No, of course not. All I can do is show them that not all Fae are power-stealing assholes."

Riordan slapped the man on the back. "You are doing great."

His attention was elsewhere, which is the only reason someone was able to get close enough to wrap their arms around him. Slender arms that wound around his hips and then reached up, hands spread across his chest as their front pressed to his back. Aisling's gentle touch and her head resting on his shoulder felt like home. Brynach moved in front of him, looking softly at his wife holding Riordan close.

"How's it going?" His partner asked, turning toward the field.

"Better, I think. I'm still worried about Liam," Riordan confessed as he linked fingers with Aisling and pulled her in front of him. Only when he could look into her smiling face did some of his worry slip away.

"You can't force acceptance on him. But it will happen," Aisling promised.

"I can't pin my happiness on whether he does or not." It felt like giving up on his brother, but he had to protect his own future. "How'd the press conference go? Sorry I missed it."

Aisling leaned in and kissed him. "Don't be. It went fine. Bry was there to make sure I was safe, and the message hasn't changed."

Riordan lifted his hand to her chin, holding her while he kissed her again. "When do you have to leave?"

The question wasn't if but when. He knew she'd have to, and he hated it.

"I've got two days. The Newport Veil is scheduled, and I have to be there. Then I'll be home for a week before I have another trip." She shook her head, her hair swaying behind her. "I can't remember where, but I'm sure my handlers will tell me."

"I hate you being away so much." Riordan looked over her shoulder to Brynach. "Are you going with her?"

The large Fae scowled. Never a good sign. "Not this time. There's too much I've been ignoring here. Brielle will be going with her."

Riordan released Aisling and took a step back. "I don't like it. Talk around the camp is that the threats and attacks are getting more aggressive."

"Have you forgotten the part where I'm immortal and really hard to kill? I didn't bite it when I was human; I'm not about to now. I am more than capable of protecting myself. We can spar right now if that will make you feel better about my abilities." She winked at him.

Brynach pulled her against his chest. "We are going to spar, a stoirin, but it's not going to be in the middle of this field."

Aisling's cheeks flushed, and she sank back into her husband. Riordan loved seeing them together, but even he blushed at the memory of Aisling leaning against Brynach like that. At the time, he'd been between her legs, happily feasting on her while the other man held her open for him.

Moments like this, the lack of his Ravdi bond with them made him ache. He'd had time to learn her body, to feel the way he pleased her, and he missed it. Their quiet communications, the newness of his connection to Brynach, they'd been gifts. He was glad for his new Fae abilities, but he still mourned what had been.

"I have to finish up here, and then I can meet you at home?" Riordan looked from Aisling to Brynach hopefully.

"We'll start dinner, but that's all we will start without you. Don't be too long." His partner ran his hand over the small of Riordan's back before moving to Aisling and sifting them away.

Riordan cursed his sense of responsibility to the New Fae. He wanted to be home with them right now, too.

"Wasn't that sweet?" Liam was grinning from behind Riordan.

The red crept further up his neck to his ears. The damn New Fae and their superior hearing. How many people here had just been privy to their conversation? From the way Amber winked at him, he assumed plenty of them.

"You can take the mickey out of me all you like, but I won't feel bad about it. You shouldn't either. The best way to honor Mom and Dad is being happy. There are still ways to do that without being a Ravdi or part of the Firinne." He put a hand on his brother's back. "You're going to find your place in the new world, Liam."

His brother looked aggravated before his face relaxed into what passed for a smile. "When did you become the wise one?"

"Someone has to be levelheaded here." Riordan joked before turning to Amber. "Take care of him. I have to go make sure the weapons are properly stored before I crack off."

He sifted to the weapons master and told them to start the cleanup. Just because the New Fae were gifted immortality didn't mean they couldn't be killed. Too many had tested the limits of their new healing abilities. He learned the hard way that the weapons got locked up before he left for the day. Which meant all firearms, ammunition, guns, knives, and even the rubber duckies (the fake guns used for training hand-to-hand combat) got locked up.

Isaac pulled up beside him. "Here's the rest from Quadrant B. Should be everything."

Riordan helped his friend rack the weapons neatly and catalog them. He let his mind focus on the task instead of on what he may be missing at home.

"Relax. They're just cooking. Totally platonic if you ignore the ass-grabbing," Valo informed Riordan from back at the cabin.

"Ugh, but I love the ass-grabbing," Riordan quipped, earning a chuckle from the fox.

He left the mental conversation when Isaac shouldered him. "Did you hear anything I just said?"

Riordan shook his head. "No, sorry. My familiar was checking in." He tapped his temple.

Isaac nodded. "I was just saying that tomorrow I want to give more time and attention to Mikal and Heather. They're showing real promise, and I want to encourage them to lean into their strengths."

Riordan had noticed the same inherent skill in them. "I think we should pull in Elias, too."

Isaac made a hum of agreement. "I'll post a note on the board for them to report to us in the morning. Good luck with the leeches." He jerked his head toward the edge of the training ground wards where the press likely waited.

Riordan looked to his new friend. "All a part of the job. You can't alter the very fabric of the world and then walk away to let others handle the mess."

Isaac gave him a sad smile. "Not arguing that, but it would be great if they gave it up already. It's not like you ever talk to them. Have a good night, Riordan."

With a slap on the back, he took off, and Riordan snapped the lock into place on the cabinet. Riordan felt the magic draw up from the ground, through his booted feet, and into his hands. Once warm, he placed them around the lock and filled it with intention. He left his magical signature on it, ensuring that only he would be able to open it come tomorrow morning.

He took a deep breath and prepared himself for exiting the wards. Aisling had been a genius to suggest them, keeping the trainees from injuring anyone with magical outbursts. The extra bonus was it kept photogs and reporters away. Riordan had been a media darling once before and had no desire to repeat the experience.

Liam had escaped attention. Riordan suspected it was because he left with Amber, and she, like Brynach, didn't encourage conversations or confrontations. And while his partner had offered to meet him after training, having Brynach pick him up after work seemed a little needy. As expected, when he walked beyond the border, the reporters swarmed him.

"How's Aisling?"

"Do you worry that the threats against your girlfriend have gotten more detailed?"

"How many New Fae are currently training?"

"Have you seen the Oracle? The Seers owe us answers!"

Riordan did his best to school his face, but it was impossible to tune out their words. He hated people being this informed about his personal life. The reminders that Aisling's life was in danger put him on edge.

"Just sift away. Don't listen to them," Vola encouraged.

Riordan knew he was right. He couldn't give them information about Aisling's security detail. Lettie and the "Oracles," or "Seers," as the media had begun addressing them, weren't something he could speak to, either. They never got answers from Riordan, but it didn't stop them showing up. Any New Fae who did provide them with information were quickly dealt with. As always, they'd leave without sound clips or a story. Maybe one of these days, they'd learn.

Instead of lashing out, like he wanted to, he turned away. What faced him was no better than the reporters. A team of wisps and a few particularly gnarly looking bark-covered alates swarmed. The sprites were more abundant now that the Veil was gone. At first, Riordan had reacted poorly to every sprite who crossed his path. Eventually, his reaction dulled. Just like people and Fae, sprites weren't all assholes. The ones he had beef with hadn't shown their faces in a while.

Riordan sifted to the edge of their land and walked through the ward Aisling had crafted. The soft waterfall sensation of her magic welcomed him home. He loved that Aisling had protected their haven. Nobody got to their front door unless the wards recognized them. It was the only way Aisling had convinced them they didn't need some form of witness-protection housing.

As he stood in their yard, he let his shoulders fall, and he took a deep breath. He was home.

CHAPTER 3

Brynach

The sound of Riordan's boots on their deck had Brynach closing his eyes with a smile. He always felt better once they were all inside Aisling's wards, safe. Besides, he'd promised to ravage his wife, and that would be a great distraction from the swirling thoughts occupying his brain.

Brynach lifted his phone and sent his brother a text message. He'd been surprised to not see Ceiren at the meeting earlier, but one perk of not having a Veil anymore was the ability to communicate with him at the court. As the go-between of the Unseelie and the Unaligned, he'd been ever present as they transitioned into this new world. So, what had kept him away today? In fact, Ceiren had been strangely silent lately.

> What's this bullshit about Gabriel?
> Is Rainer talking out his ass?
> I need to see you soon.
> Keep an eye on Breena for me!

I'll keep two on her as often
as I can, but she's okay, Brynach.

You're avoiding answering my question ...

Can't answer something I don't know.
Rainer believes it. That doesn't mean it's true.

If their father was Fae again, Breena would be in even more danger than before. Dread settled in his gut when he remembered the very human aura surrounding his twin. Logically, Brynach knew she couldn't have, but he swore she'd aged since he last saw her. A few short months shouldn't have made a difference, but how many would it be before it showed? Before she aged? Died?

He'd give anything to think about something other than his sister's mortality. As soon as the thought entered his head, he felt guilty. Breena couldn't just turn off the truth. Couldn't look to her lovers and soothe her fears.

Aisling was smiling into a book, a glass of wine in her hand. Riordan walked into the house, and the air changed. It was full of potential. The other man met his gaze, and his teeth tugged on that full bottom lip. Fuck. A part of Brynach looked forward to the few days Aisling was gone. There were things Riordan and he needed to work out.

"Get changed and join us," Brynach instructed when Riordan lowered his eyes. The other man nodded and moved to their bathroom.

A warmth settled in his chest at the way Riordan listened to him without question. He didn't take that trust for granted. Aisling snuck up behind him, and her arms circled his waist. Those tiny hands spreading across the surface of his stomach, her nails turning in and applying slight pressure. The minx knew exactly what was in store for her, and she was letting him know she was ready.

"Watch yourself, a stoirin. We won't let all that food go to waste just to satisfy your other hunger," he tsk'd.

"But I need it, Bry. I want you stamped on my body before I leave. I want to carry the ache and memory of you with me when I go," she crooned against his back, her hands traveling south to the band of his sweatpants. They were all he was wearing, and if she kept it up, he wouldn't be wearing them for long.

"You'll wait and love every desperate aching moment. By the time we carry you upstairs, you'll be soaked and begging for release," he promised before removing her hands and turning around. He was onto her games, but she wasn't going to rush their night.

"Already am," Aisling said with a flip of her hair. She settled on the sofa and lifted her glass of wine again.

"Even I have to admit that's not fair, Bry," Riordan said with a laugh when he came into the room.

Brynach turned to Riordan, and the newly awakened warmth in his chest overwhelmed him. The way he cared for the other man surprised him. He understood lust, but staring at Riordan, the sexual tension was the least of what he felt. Instead, he felt admiration, respect, love, and protectiveness. What he felt for the other Fae mirrored what he felt for his wife.

Riordan's head quirked as he stared at Brynach. "Why are you looking at me like that?" He ran a hand over his bare chest and moved to pull up the basketball shorts that rode low on his hips.

It was difficult to pry his eyes away from the V of muscles and the hair disappearing into the shorts. The man was gorgeous. Becoming Fae suited him.

While Brynach's hair draped over his bare shoulders, Riordan's was still tied in a bun. Aisling's was still styled from the press conference, and he couldn't wait until it was a tangled mess after they took their pleasure together. They needed to talk, and then he'd let their touch heal him.

"Go sit down, both of you. I'll bring the food over," Brynach said, less of a command than wanting them to be comfortable. Riordan gave Aisling a slap on the ass when she rose. Her laughter filled the home as they walked to the table. Their conversation and soft music filled the space.

How long had he wanted a home? Not to rest his head but to house his heart. Somehow, he'd managed it two times over. Whenever it felt like his world was caving in on itself or rage and guilt overwhelmed him, he reminded himself of that. But there was still this small part of his brain that warned him they may decide he was too much work and walk away. It wasn't a logical part of his brain, he knew that, but it nagged at him all the same.

"What do you want to drink?" Brynach called out to Riordan.

"Beer, please. You need help?" he answered.

"I got it." He placed an unopened bottle of beer in the pocket of his sweatpants and hoped they stayed up ... or maybe he didn't.

With the plates in his hand, he gestured to his pocket. Riordan reached into it and removed the bottle with a thank you. The way the other man embraced physical intimacy with Brynach thrilled him. Aisling caught his eye and gave him a knowing wink. It didn't escape his notice that his wife found pleasure in the way they cared for each other.

"I expect all this to be finished." He sat down and dug into the chicken, roasted potato, and broccoli.

"Nobody told me I'd be ravenous as a Fae." Riordan piled food onto his plate.

Despite the teasing they'd all done earlier, nobody rushed the meal just to get to the bedroom. There was a comfort in knowing it would happen and in the knowledge that they had an eternity to explore one another. In the last months, their relationships and communication had opened dramatically. Now that Riordan was a part of their forever, both Aisling and he had let themselves fall deeper for the man.

Brynach had insisted upon conversations clarifying their sexual comfort levels. Coaxing his two partners to share their desires was both rewarding and incredibly erotic. He loved Aisling's desire to submit to him and Riordan's willingness to explore his attraction to Brynach.

And while the discussions about sex were essential, they had many more discussions about the dynamic of their relationship and satisfaction levels within their home. Recently, their talks had centered around feelings of jealousy and making sure everyone felt heard and cared for. The fact that leading these conversations and sexual situations made his partners feel better was a happy side effect. In truth, Brynach needed to take this role. It made him feel more loved and understood than any other relationship he'd ever been in. This, at least, he could do.

He'd failed to protect his sister. Brynach had failed Aisling and Trent when he didn't see through Ollie's double-crossing. Riordan had been wronged when he'd lost loved ones who may have been safe had they been in possession of the true breadth of their magic. He knew it wasn't logical to lay all that at his feet, but he carried it anyway.

He'd keep them happy, and by doing so, he'd keep himself sane. For all his shortcomings, he knew they could redeem him. If they could love him, forgive him, and accept him, then maybe he could do the same for himself.

"Bry?" Aisling's hand on his thigh brought him from his thoughts.

"Sorry." His grin was sheepish.

Aisling squeezed his leg. "Share your worries."

He ran his hands through his hair. "It's Breena ..."

Aisling picked up the thread. "She looked good. She was her usual eye-rolling, snarky Breena."

"That's good, right?" Riordan asked. "I mean, that she healed. That she was at the meeting."

Brynach lowered his hands. "Apparently, the doctors Rainer had on staff are the only reason she's alive. The wound missed vital organs but got infected."

Riordan spoke between bites, saying, "But now she's back in business."

Aisling frowned, and he leaned over to kiss her forehead. "Breena needed physical therapy, but yes, she's okay. Jashana hasn't left her side since she sifted her to the palace. I'm glad someone can be there for her."

"We can, too, now. They opened the courts," Aisling reminded him.

"Yes, and I'm very thankful for that. But there's something else." He took a deep breath. He knew his wife was smart enough to have sensed Breena's mortality, but the reason was still lost on her. Aisling was going to beat herself up over this. "When the Veil fell and magic dispersed, things changed. But Breena and Levinas, they weren't just by the Veil; they had fallen into it. And when you pulled the last thread of magic from the Veil. When it broke ..."

Aisling's eyes were wide. "When the Veil broke, what?"

"It stripped them." The ache in Brynach's heart was surreal. "It's why her sword killed Levinas. It's why her injuries were so serious."

"No." Aisling's hand left his leg and covered her mouth. "I didn't pull from her. I was careful. I didn't take from anyone."

He shook his head. "I don't know how, Aisling, but that's what happened. She doesn't blame you. She's just, well, she's Breena. She's angry."

Riordan was quiet. Brynach turned to him. "Say something."

"I was gifted a long life. I don't take that for granted. But it's new. Breena has lived hundreds of years knowing she'd live hundreds more." Riordan looked horrified.

The table was quiet. Earlier, Brynach had tried to put himself in his sister's place and immediately rejected the notion. Not just because he couldn't stomach losing Aisling and Riordan now that he'd found them but because mortality was a foreign concept to him. His sister's pain had felt visceral when she'd explained how she'd been stripped.

"I don't care if she didn't mean to do it. She did! And she damn well better find a way to give it back. They're stripping Fae of their magic instead of life sentences in jail now. If they're able to do that, there has to be a way to give it back." Breena threw her hands up. *"I can't stand this, Brynach. I feel like I'm going crazy."*

"You know that if there's a way, we'll find it. She'll do it. You know that, right?" He heard himself beg.

"I don't want promises. I want action." Breena had charged away from him.

"It's okay. I'll fix it. If we can strip, there has to be a way to restore, right?" Aisling asked.

Bless her for always being so positive. Through all their ups and downs, she always saw the bright side. "No, a stoirin. That's not how the gifts from the Goddess work."

She shook her head. "It was an accident."

Brynach reached out and cupped the back of her neck, rubbing along the length of it before cradling her head. He leaned down, resting his forehead against hers. "I'm not telling you because I need you to fix it. There's nothing for you to feel bad about. This isn't your fault."

He felt the tension leave her, not all of it, but some. Enough that she was able to take a deep breath, unconsciously mirroring his own. Slow. Steady. When she nodded against him, he sat back.

"What can we do to help you?" Riordan asked.

"You're already doing it. Before, that information would have burrowed into me until it caused a spot of rot." Vulnerability came almost naturally to him now.

Beside her, Aisling's phone dinged, and Brynach nodded to it.

"Check it."

"It can wait," she assured him.

He lowered his voice, slowing his speech and focusing on her. His shift caused one in her. It was his signal that she was to submit. "Check it."

She picked up the phone. "It's your sister."

"Breena texts you now?" Riordan asked.

"Sydney. She wanted to confirm our visit to the precinct tomorrow," Aisling answered as her fingers flew over her phone.

Brynach loved hearing Aisling call Sydney his sister. He liked the New Fae. Her mother and brothers, not so much. His wife had noticed her aimlessness and put in a good word at the precinct for her. With Aisling's media positions and travel for drops, she couldn't perform the warding and protections for the PD. Sydney could. His sister had been thrilled at the opportunity to help.

"And this is how you help. You do things that make those close to me happy. You care for yourselves and our family. It's more than I could ever ask for," Brynach professed.

"Bullshit. It's the bare minimum, big guy. We're happy to do it." Riordan shook his head, and Brynach wondered if he had any idea how much he was loved.

After dinner, they sat out on the patio and watched the world turn orange and then grey.

"I hate leaving you," she murmured, and he felt himself soften.

"I hate you leaving us. I didn't wait this long for you just to be parted from you," Brynach agreed.

She bridged the gap between the chairs and took his hand. He linked their fingers and gave them a squeeze.

"We trust you to take care of yourself until you're back." He knew she'd do it regardless of his request, but he wanted her to know that they needed her. Riordan exited the house and moved to them.

"All cleaned up," he announced.

He settled into the chair on the other side of Aisling and took her other hand. Fireflies lit up their yard, and the sprites wove through the trees. Within their wards, Aisling had ensured that any sprites were ones with good intentions. Brynach didn't understand the specifics of her magic, but he knew that Riordan hadn't been hounded at their home.

From within their woods, he heard the call of an owl and the thrum of insects. Night noises that soothed him. On their deck, those sounds dulled, and the beating of his partner's hearts rang in his head.

"You're quiet," Aisling commented.

"I have a lot on my mind," Brynach answered.

"You're always telling us we have to share. It's good advice. Maybe take it, big guy," Riordan jibed.

He shook his head. "Smart ass."

The New Fae nodded. "We carry a lot on our shoulders, Bry. With us, at home, you need to be able to lay that burden down."

That was it, wasn't it? With them, he could leave the weight of his mistakes at the door and walk in as the man he wanted to be for himself and for them.

"I love you," he said.

Their answer came in sync, "I love you, too."

He closed his eyes and thanked the Goddess. When they opened, he turned to Aisling with a fire in his eyes. She squealed and leaned closer to Riordan. Brynach lifted his lips in an approximation of a grin, baring his teeth and snarling.

"You can run, wife. I don't mind chasing you." The idea of it thrilled him.

It took a moment before she sprinted off the deck and into the woods. Brynach looked to Riordan, who shook his head.

"That's all you, man. Go get our girl."

Brynach sifted off the deck and into the woods, surprising Aisling. She yelped and sifted away. He stilled, his heart thudding in his chest, and listened for the crushing of leaves in their woods. He sniffed the air loudly, a growl growing in his chest. She'd hear both, and it would fuel her fear.

Now that his wife was Fae, he didn't need to be as gentle with her, and he was hardly gentle to begin with. This game was infinitely more fun now that she had a chance of evading him. She wouldn't, of course, but he did love when she tried.

Before he ran after his wife, he looked up to Riordan again. Their partner sat with his legs stretched out and crossed at the ankles. There was a smirk on his face as he adjusted himself and blew a kiss at Brynach. Fuck, he loved that man.

"Run all you want, a stoirin, but you can't hide from me. Being my prey excites you." He pulled air into his lungs. "You're wet for us already."

He moved further into the woods, actively hunting her. This type of play let Brynach unleash something animalistic in himself and let Aisling be vulnerable in a safe way. The beast lurking beneath his skin craved the taste of Aisling's fear. He wanted her pulse racing beneath his teeth as he drove into her.

"When I find you, I'm putting you over my knee, and you're going to count out one strike for every minute you hide from me." He heard Riordan's chuckle.

The threat wasn't empty, but it wasn't a punishment either. Aisling loved a spanking, even more so when Riordan held and caressed her while she was paddled. Brynach was hard just thinking about it. If the whole world burned down around him, he'd still be hard thinking about his wife.

He looked to the deck, and Riordan nodded toward the side of the house. Brynach winked and sifted, surprising Aisling so much that she forgot to sift away. Instead, she ran from her hiding spot and tore branches out of her way. Her red hair was a beacon in the woods. He kept his stride steady. Let her hear him coming and anticipate his touch.

To keep it fun, he let her stretch the gap between them before he lunged at her with a growl. He caught her around her middle and brought her to the ground, his arms cushioning her fall. Once she was resting on the grass, he let his weight settle onto her. She twisted her body, hands scrambling.

Aisling arched away from him, and he dropped his mouth to her neck with a feral growl. "Stop fighting me, Aisling."

When she continued to wriggle under him, her soft body rolling against his hard cock, he sank his teeth into the soft flesh of her throat. She stilled immediately, the most beautiful moan escaping her. Her hips rose to him, and her hands gripped the earth under her.

He left his teeth there, the constant pressure a reminder that he owned her. And he felt her go still beneath him, her breath panting out. She loved it. The scent of her arousal mingled with the damp earth she was clawing. His hand stilled her hips, and his tongue lapped at the indents his teeth left when he released her.

"Naughty girls don't get to demand friction," he scolded, pressing her hips down.

She whined, pushing up against his hold. Testing. Aisling was belly down on the earth, her face held up by his grip on her hair. Aisling, needy woman that she was, tried to push up on her knees and press her ass into him. She was strong. He was stronger.

Brynach ground his hardness through her ass crack and thanked the Goddess for leggings. Leaning down, he spoke low and slow. "Behave, or I'll make you."

Her eyes closed on a sigh and her body went loose. She never looked more beautiful than when she gave herself over to him. Brynach bit his lip, high on the way she shut off her brain and gave her trust and body to him.

He took advantage of the moment to stand and toss her over his shoulder. She laughed and shoved her hands down the back of his sweatpants, cupping his cheeks. He delivered one sharp slap to her leggings-clad ass and then ran with her up the steps to their door, which was held open by Riordan.

Then he made good on the promise to carry her to their bed with her begging for them. By the time they reached the bedroom, he was holding her hips down as she squirmed. The needy minx was trying to get off on his shoulder.

Riordan spoke from behind them, "Oh, kitten. We all know that's going to get you in trouble. You come when we let you come."

"Tiger!" Aisling protested, but it lost its heat when it ended with a groan.

Brynach tossed her onto their large bed and followed her down.

"Riordan, how many?"

"Five for running. Five for attempting to get off on your shoulder when she knows that's our job. Ten for not coming out when you called her. Sound fair, kitten?" he asked. Brynach hid a smile at his teasing pet name.

Aisling pouted from her place on the bed, hair splayed out behind her, but then raised herself to kneel in the middle of the mattress.

"It's hardly my fault you didn't catch me fast enough. And you've been teasing me all day, so I took matters into my own hands. If you fail at your job, then somebody has to take over." Her hands went to her waist, and she tilted her head at them.

She knew exactly what she was doing when she bit her lip to hide a smile. Riordan added five more. Brynach was going to enjoy this.

"Assume the position, wife," Brynach said, sitting on the edge of the mattress.

He waited to see if she would continue to brat, but she was wound too tight to delay her gratification any longer. She crawled across the mattress and spread her body over his lap.

Aisling wiggled against his length, tormenting him. His hand came down sharply on her ass. "You already have twenty-five. Do you want more?"

"No," her voice quieted.

Brynach settled himself and focused on Aisling. He didn't like hurting her, but he loved being what she needed. He'd be her escape from her thoughts. Brynach looked to Riordan, and he moved down to the ground in front of Aisling, taking her face in his hands.

"You're going to count for us, aren't you? Real nice and loud so we don't lose track," he instructed.

Aisling nodded, and Brynach made sure his attention was solely focused on Aisling and her body's reactions. She could safeword if she needed to, but his goal was never to make her. Bringing her to the edge, testing but not toppling her resolve, was a balance he had learned. Riordan would calm her, wipe her tears, and kiss her sweetly. He knew the other man would care for her while Brynach made her stunning ass red hot.

He rubbed his hand over her leggings-covered butt, gripped it in his large hand, and listened to every hitch in his wife's breath. Each gasp sent a bolt of lust straight through him. He gave no warning when his hand came down on her ass, a sharp crack through their home.

"One," Aisling counted.

She continued counting through the first five, voice loud and body still. Their woman was so strong. But some of that bravery slipped when Brynach put his hand under the waistband of her pants.

"Lift your hips for me, a stoirin."

She pushed herself up on her toes but stayed over his lap while he pulled her pants and underwear down her legs. He barely contained a groan at how pretty her ass looked, pink from his hand. He put an arm around her stomach and lifted as he leaned down and bit the bright skin.

Aisling cried out, and he soothed it with his tongue before lowering her to his lap once more.

"Ready, Ash?" Riordan asked. Before she could answer, Brynach's hand came down on her naked ass cheek. First, the right, then the left, and back to the right again before he gripped the flesh in his hand. Aisling counted nice and loud.

He let her catch her breath and then brought his hand down in a quick count of five rapid strikes. Aisling's body was shaking by the time she counted out the number thirteen. She was halfway there, and Brynach wasn't letting up. Full Fae Aisling wouldn't even be red in the morning. She could take this. He moved his hand to her pussy and stroked her, just once. Enough to know she was soaking wet. Aisling moaned, and then his hand cracked down in quick succession until she reached twenty.

Beautiful tears streamed down her face, and she was making a mess of his sweatpants. An idea came to Brynach, and he slowed the scene a moment to make sure Aisling understood what was changing.

"My wife, my love, do you want to come?" he asked.

She nodded her wet face. "I want whatever you want, husband."

Brynach made a soft huffing sound. "I'm going to reposition you. You will continue to count. You will come before I reach twenty-five, or tonight will be a full night of edging where we feast on and fuck you, but don't let you finish."

Aisling cried out in frustration, and Riordan smiled. "She's complaining, but I think she may enjoy that."

"No," she insisted.

"I sure would," Riordan promised.

"Think you can handle that, my heart?" Brynach asked as he let his short nails scratch over her red cheeks.

"Yes. Yes, please, yes. I need to come," she begged.

She was perfect. Absolutely perfect. Brynach lifted his hips and his wife until he could push his pants to the ground. Riordan moved and helped him kick them all the way off, removing Aisling's fully, too. Brynach paused to smile at the man and then repositioned Aisling so her legs were split, one above and one below his lap. He slid her back until her hot core was pressed against the inside of his thigh. Instinctually, she moved herself to gain friction against him.

Aisling was wound so tight she may just finish before he began spanking her again. He couldn't have that. Her arms wrapped around his calf, and she held on, rocking against him and moaning. Brynach brought his hand down hard on that red, writhing ass.

"Twenty-one," she panted.

He did it again, keeping to the same asscheek. If she was going to finish, it would be through the pain. He centralized the strike, and she moaned out number twenty-two. Brynach's leg was slick with her arousal as she slid across him. With every shift of her body, she brushed against his cock, but he did his best to ignore the sensation. This was about Aisling.

His hand came down again, and Aisling cried out, "Twenty-three. Fuck. Please. Please."

She was hanging so beautifully to the edge of pain and pleasure. He waited a moment, paying attention to her body. Her breathing became ragged. She was almost there. Brynach gave her one more moment to slide that hot pussy against him, and then his hand came down once, twice, hard and fast.

Aisling cried out her numbers, and on the tail end of twenty-five, she absolutely fell apart. Stunning. Brynach needed her in his arms. He picked up her shaky body and placed her ass in the space between his spread legs, bringing her head to his chest and holding her close. He kissed her tear-stained cheeks and rubbed her back. Riordan was stroking her leg and holding onto Brynach's knee. He was comfortable giving them their space and time for scenes like this. Both Brynach and Aisling appreciated that.

"You did so good, a stoirin. So perfect for me," Brynach praised as his fingers massaged her scalp until her breathing evened.

Riordan sensed the shift in the room and nudged Brynach's leg. He spread them further for the man, lifting Aisling as he did. Sitting on the floor, Riordan was level with Aisling's beautiful cunt. He lifted her leg over his shoulder and leaned back on Brynach's leg to pull her to his mouth. Brynach supported her weight while Riordan feasted on Aisling. She shook in his arms and sought his mouth.

Brynach kissed her hungrily while the other man sat at his feet and lapped at their lover. He felt Riordan lift her and angle her so his tongue could trace the handprints on her ass. Aisling gasped into his mouth, and he smiled.

"Does it sting, love?"

"Yes," she moaned.

"I'll make it better, Ash," Riordan promised and resumed stroking her with his tongue.

"Does his tongue feel good on your sensitive clit? You made a mess of my leg. Our perfect desperate wife," Brynach spoke into her ear.

His words stoked her. He kissed her again, demanding, as his hand cupped her breast and rolled her nipple between his thumb and forefinger. Aisling's small hand dropped from his chest. He pulled away from her in time to see her nudge Riordan out of the way and wet her hand with her arousal. Riordan sucked on her fingers, adding to the moisture. Aisling groaned and dove at Brynach's mouth again, and then her wet hand gripped him. She caressed him in broad sure strokes. Squeezing, twisting, and palming his crown.

The wet sounds of her hand and Riordan's sucking at her filled the space. He felt positively feral with the need to sink into her. They could do this all night long, likely would, but right now, he was damn near desperate.

"Riordan," he managed. "I need to be inside her. Where do you want to be?"

The other man hummed from between her legs, and with a pop of suction, he released her clit. "Her mouth. I want to fuck that pretty mouth."

Aisling moaned, her hand tightening around Brynach's cock. He knew just how he wanted his wife. He wanted to see that red ass and slam his hips into it from behind while watching her suck Riordan's beautiful cock. He stood easily with Aisling. Riordan rose from the floor and followed them as Brynach set his wife down on the bed.

"All fours, love," he instructed.

She hurried into position, and Brynach gripped his cock, stroking it while staring at the marks he'd left. Already they were beginning to fade, but they were beautiful. He fit his hand perfectly into one of the handprints and palmed that sweet cheek. Aisling gasped and rocked forward.

"There's no escaping us, a stoirin," Brynach laughed.

"Who's running?" Aisling asked. "I learned my lesson."

Riordan moved in front of her and lifted her chin until she was looking into his eyes. "There's nowhere you can go that we won't find you and bring you home. You are ours. We are yours. This is where you belong. Go where you must, but you come back here. Always."

"Always," she swore.

Brynach slid himself inside his wife, biting his lip at the way she clenched around him. Her soft warmth pulled him in. The gasp that left her mouth as he bottomed out inside her was so satisfying, but not more so than seeing her lean forward and lick Riordan's cock. His hand flexed on Aisling's hip as he began to move, eyes never leaving her mouth and his partner's erection. The way she nuzzled her cheek against it, kissed, and cherished it.

He had to admit, as cocks went, it was worthy of worship. When the crown disappeared into her mouth and she pulled the back of his thighs, bringing him further into her mouth, Brynach growled and drove into her. Riordan stroked her cheek and buried his hand in her hair.

"You should see yourself, full of our cocks, and still wanting more," Riordan said when her free hand dropped to her clit and began rubbing herself. "You're so fucking sexy with your cheeks hollowed around my cock, eyes still red from Brynach's spanking. Our messy girl begging for it."

She moaned, rubbing herself faster. Brynach pulled back, angling against her front wall, hitting right where she needed him as she strummed that pretty clit of hers. Aisling pulled back from Riordan's cock and screamed their names as she came. Riordan gripped her hair and dragged her mouth back onto him, pushing his hips forward and his cock down her throat.

"Fuck, Ash. So hard for you. Are you going to swallow me, kitten?" he asked, and she nodded as much as she could.

Brynach deepened his thrusts as soon as her pulsing walls allowed him to move, lost in the feel of her. At least he was until Riordan's words broke through the lust-filled fog of fucking his wife.

"Or are you going to hold my load on your tongue and then kiss your husband? Let him taste me, too?" Riordan's eyes were on Brynach as he asked, a challenge in them.

"That's exactly what she's going to do," Brynach said. "Don't you waste a single drop."

Brynach cursed when she moaned around Riordan's cock and threw her hips back into him. Fucking hell. She let him slide in and then squeezed down on him when he was pulling out, driving him wild. He met Riordan's eyes again, and the man winked at him. He damn near blew his load at that look alone.

"If you don't stop squeezing me like that, wife, I'm going to finish too fast," he warned.

She clenched around him harder, and he threw his head back with a groan. Riordan chuckled and gave a light tap to her cheek. "That's not nice, kitten."

Her hand wrapped around his thigh, and Riordan cursed as her nails sunk into his ass.

"And we think we're in charge," Brynach chuckled. He knew damn well Aisling held the power in the bedroom. Absolutely nothing happened there that she didn't want. Which is why when he leaned forward and gave Riordan his thumb, the other man smiled before taking it in his mouth. He maintained eye contact while he sucked on it the way Brynach imagined

Aisling was sucking on his cock. He swirled his tongue around Brynach's digit and grazed it gently with his teeth.

"Fuck," Brynach growled. He pulled his finger free and moved his hand to Aisling's ass. His wet thumb pushed gently at her asshole. It swirled and coated the sensitive area with Riordan's saliva. Aisling moaned around Riordan's cock and pushed back against him.

"Breathe, a stoirin," Brynach told her, and she came off Riordan long enough to moan his name as his thumb slipped past the tight ring of muscle and pushed deeper. He left it there a moment, one knuckle in, before pulling out slowly and pushing back in further.

"Fuck. Fuck. Oh, sweet heaven on earth," Aisling cried out. "More."

Brynach nearly spilled his load right then. He could not wait to have both he and Riordan seated fully inside her body, cocks rubbing one another through the wall of her. He gave her what she wanted, spitting onto her once more and stroking into her.

"Back to me, Ash," Riordan coaxed, and Aisling's mouth moved to his cock while Brynach started to thrust in time with his thumb.

Aisling pushed herself back on him as he thrust forward, asking for more, for harder. With his thumb deep in her ass, he pounded into her pussy. She got messy on Riordan, letting him slide out of her mouth while she cried out, only to have him slide deep into her throat again.

Seeing her lose control was damn near the sexiest thing Brynach had ever experienced. All that poise and power reduced to a body full of need. No thinking, just nerve endings and passion. He pulled his thumb all the way out, and she cried at the loss, only to groan as he pushed his pointer finger against that tight opening and slid inside. He watched her ass swallow his thick finger and teased her by placing the tip of his middle finger against her, too. The nervousness made her tighten around both his cock and finger.

Brynach plunged into her, leaving his second finger as a steady pressure but not entering her. Aisling spoke around Riordan's cock, but he couldn't make it out.

"Use your words," he reminded her.

"More! Damn it, give me more," she cried before sinking her mouth back over Riordan's cock.

Brynach nodded to Riordan. "Some help here."

Riordan leaned over Aisling's back and dripped his spit onto her ass crack, then used his fingers to spread the saliva across Brynach's middle finger and Aisling's asshole. He stayed there a moment while Brynach pressed, pulling out his pointer to the edge and then adding his middle finger slowly.

"Push a little, love," Brynach instructed, so she'd open for him.

Riordan groaned, "Fuck, Ash. You have no idea how hot this is. You're sucking him in."

She moaned, and Riordan moved back, stroking her face and talking softly to her. Brynach now had both fingers inside her, and he moved them gently, stretching her slowly until he could slide both deep inside her.

He didn't fuck her with them; he left them buried deep and fluttered them. He rubbed his cock through her thin wall, and Aisling felt the friction and absolutely shattered. Her legs gave out, and Brynach scrambled to hold her up with his free hand.

"Easy, Aisling. We're not done with you yet."

He stroked into her as she shook. He wanted another. Could get another. She'd had multiples before. "Again, love."

She shook her head, but he moved those fingers in her ass, and she moaned.

"Her eyes are rolling back in her head. Whatever that was, do it again. Fuck, she's sucking me senseless," Riordan moaned. "I'm close, Ash."

Brynach fluttered his long fingers and stroked deep inside

her, the arm holding her up, angling so his fingers could strum her clit. Aisling was moaning, her whole body shaking. If the sound of her wet cunt was any indicator, their woman was about to experience something new.

She bucked against him, driving his fingers and cock deeper. He applied pressure on her clit and gave himself over to the feel of her. His balls tensed, his whole-body electric as he spilled into her hot pussy. Fuck. He stilled his cock, seating it deep as he continued to spasm while moving his fingers in her ass. Then he pounded her relentlessly with his still-hard cock. She was almost there.

"It's too much!" Aisling protested. That wasn't her safe-word. He wasn't stopping.

"Don't you dare hold back, wife. Give it to us." Brynach demanded. "Be a good girl and come for me. Now."

He ground his hips into her hot ass, and Aisling screamed, fluid releasing from her in a torrent across his hand, splashing onto his belly as he fucked into her. Perfect. Beautiful. Free.

"Did she just ..." Riordan asked, awe filling his voice. "Fuck, Aisling, get your mouth back on me."

Her whole body was shaking, but with Brynach slowing his strokes and holding her up, she managed to get her mouth around his cock. Riordan groaned and came moments later with Aisling's name on his lips. She hummed around him, sucking him through it until he pulled himself free. Gently Brynach eased his fingers out while stroking her so the plea-sure overrode any discomfort.

"Share, Ash. Don't be greedy," Riordan reminded her.

She tried to rise on shaky legs but struggled. Brynach lifted her, pulling her up so she could wrap her legs around his hips as he stood at the end of the bed. She was sweaty, wrecked, and beautiful. He kissed her, mouth closed and sweet.

"I love you," he told her. Then she took his face, and he opened for her. She swept her tongue over his, silky and rich with the taste of Riordan. He groaned, gripping her ass and pulling her closer. Her mouth above his, she let Riordan spill into his mouth, and he swallowed before returning to Aisling's kiss.

"I love you, too," she said when they parted. "I can't believe I made that mess."

"It was the hottest thing I've ever seen. I loved it," Brynach told her.

"I damn near finished without you touching me," Riordan agreed, jumping up. "Shower?"

Brynach shook his head. "Damn New Fae and their endless energy."

CHAPTER 4

Riordan

Guy time wasn't so bad, even if they did miss Aisling. He and Brynach had indulged in loud music, beer, and gaming without feeling bad about ignoring their woman. Brynach had worked late one night, and Riordan had invited Russell and Isaac over to hang out. Which he could have done with Aisling home, but the vibe just felt different with only the guys. It was nice to just sit around, belch, and talk shit.

When Brynach had gotten home that night, he'd stopped to put a hand on Riordan's shoulder. He'd reached up to cover the other man's hand instinctually. Riordan loved that there was still a sense of intimacy, a comfort of being home with someone who loved you. It was different without Aisling, but no less important to him than that he had that time with Brynach.

She'd gotten back into town that morning after both the guys had left for their days. As much as he wanted to run home and spend the day wrapped up in her, he couldn't. The horrors of adulting called, and they all had work to do.

Training the New Fae wasn't his only responsibility. Rainer had promised that Aisling, Brynach, and he would be the face of the new world, and he'd held them to it. So, today it was his turn to show his face in meetings.

He hated it. Every single second of it.

This was not where he felt most competent, but he'd learned to fake it well. At least, that's what Brielle promised each time they met in the conference room. Unlike a lot of the meetings Aisling and Brynach took, these were conducted indoors. State secrets and security plans weren't for the open air. Men and women sat in uniforms with pins and stripes he'd never understand, next to Fae like Rainer. When he'd arrived, he'd been greeted by Alex, who was new to meetings like this but said he had a complaint to lodge.

So far, the meeting had been the same old debates and whining. More documented threats, reports from Liam of cyber surveillance on radical groups they were watching, and more concerns over the number of New Fae officers and military. Today's uproar regarded the latest signing bonus to encourage New Fae to enlist. Almost like they were building some super-hero squad. Thing was, they weren't the only ones with New Fae. Across the globe, other areas were dropping sections of their Veil. It made things a little more tense globally. Countries hurried to increase their number of Fae, afraid of some hostile New Fae takeover.

Rainer growled a few seats down. "Before, we couldn't join your politics or security, and now you clamor for us. You're just as hypocritical and short-sighted as ever. Why these New Fae agree to help you at all is a mystery to me."

It was Alex who spoke. "Maybe because it was you who kept them castrated, and they feel more loyalty to those who embraced them than those who repressed them." Brynach's best friend sighed. "Fucking idiot."

Brielle chimed in before the two men could start arguing too much. "Regardless of the past, we have a future to ensure. The goal is to secure the safety of the American people, both Fae and New Fae, the remaining witches and Ravdi, and humans.

If you're unwilling to contribute to that discussion, then see yourselves out."

"Says the traitor Fae." Rainer shot the tiny warrior a scathing look that had Riordan bristling.

"Because I was smart enough to walk away from your court? Is that it, King Who Never Was?" Brielle mocked.

Riordan was ready to step in as the others around the table sat uncomfortably and unsure of what to do. This was getting out of hand, and it was unlike Brielle to feed into Brynach's brother's nonsense.

"All I'm saying is that you should watch yourself. Without a court, with a wobbly system you're fighting to balance, bad things happen to those who aren't protected." Rainer pushed up from his chair and faced the table. "They'll come back to us. Just you wait and watch. People want to be governed by those they see as stronger and more capable of decision-making than they are." He gestured around the room. "That isn't any of you. The courts will reign again."

Like that, voices erupted, and Rainer walked unfazed from the room. While they guffawed and turned red with indignation, Riordan turned to Brielle.

"Are you okay?"

She shook her head. "Of course. Takes a hell of a lot more than that to bother me."

"Right," Riordan said. "Well, I'm still sorry."

"Don't be. You're not Rainer, nor do you need to make excuses for him. Besides which, you never have to apologize to me. Not after ..." her voice trailed off.

"Brielle, don't. Nobody blames you. You have to stop blaming yourself." Riordan knew she was remembering Trent, and while it never got easier to remember he was gone, nobody thought it was Brielle's fault. She was put in an impossible situation. Not even a Fae would have been fast enough to alter the trajectory of a sword with force like hers behind it.

Everyone knew her real target had been Ollie. Trent's boyfriend had turned on them, trying to attack Aisling. Only after his passing did it come to light that Ollie was part of a radical group of Fae who opposed the dropping of the Veil and the unification of human and Fae. Pure bullshit seeing as he'd spent decades on the human side of the Veil. But apparently, he'd really committed to being a mole for his group.

"This is a shit show. I'm leaving." Brielle stood, and Riordan moved with her.

As they walked outside, he turned to her. "I'm going to hang with the guys. Do you want to come?"

"No, Riordan, but thanks."

Brielle may have been one of the toughest Fae he knew, but she still hadn't gotten over being responsible for Trent's death. They'd keep inviting her and proving they cared for her until she could forgive herself.

"You know you're always welcome. We'd like you to come," he told her.

"I appreciate it, but I can't. Maybe one day." She frowned and walked outside the wards to sift away.

Riordan shook his head and blinked out of existence, feet landing on the pavement outside Trent's old apartment. He acknowledged the pang of pain at being there without the tattooed skateboarder and let it pass. After years of therapy, he'd learned not to ignore emotions but not to dwell on negative ones, either.

"You going to stand out here all day?" Sean's voice sounded from behind Riordan. "Don't tell me I got the drop on the super-Fae."

Riordan laughed off his friend's teasing. "I was thinking. What are you doing out here?"

"Just dropped Lettie off at home." Sean walked past him and into the stairwell that led to what was once Trent's top-floor apartment.

They'd been shocked to learn he owned the whole building. Though nobody was surprised to learn that when the older woman who lived downstairs fell on hard times, he allowed her to stay rent-free. It was in the paperwork that she could stay as long as she lived, but the building now belonged to Sean, who had reluctantly moved in.

"I invited Kareem over. He should be here soon," Sean told him as they ascended the steps.

Despite practicing with Brynach now and then, Riordan hadn't gotten much better at gaming. Kareem and Sean were going to absolutely destroy him.

Riordan followed Sean inside, still surprised to see how much the apartment had changed. Aisling hadn't come over yet, and he didn't blame her. A lot of Trent's tech equipment had been taken to Liam's for use by their team. The walls that once held pictures of Trent's modeling campaigns were bare now. Eventually, Sean would make the space his own. For now, he settled on just having it be less Trent's. The reminders had been too hard on him. On all of them.

"Where are you coming from looking like that?" Sean asked, gesturing to Riordan's jeans and dress shirt.

With an eye roll, he answered, "A security briefing."

"And they let you in armed?" Sean eyed him funny as Riordan took the horizontal holster off his belt and set it aside.

"I mean, yeah. Kinda the whole point of me being part of the security team. I wouldn't suggest you try it," he advised.

"Yeah, 'cause I have so many weapons," Sean's sarcasm was obvious. "You saw Brielle." It wasn't a question, so Riordan didn't treat it like one. "You told her ..."

Riordan nodded. "I did. Again."

Sean gave him a sad look. "It's open!" he yelled when a knock sounded through the apartment. Kareem walked in and dropped his bag.

"Being the only one still fucking going to classes sucks. You guys really blow, you know that," he complained. He flopped down next to Riordan, put his arm across the back of the sofa, and kicked his legs up onto the coffee table.

Riordan gave him a raised eyebrow stare. "Um, hi."

"Yeah yeah, hi. I swear, the resentment I have for you two is unreal. You get to be some immortal badass Fae now, Sean is pretty much promised a job in some fucking government spy program, and I'm still taking fucking calculus." He drank from his water bottle and took a deep breath. "Okay. Done bitching now."

"You sure, dude? Cause it sounded like you still had some left in the tank," Riordan asked.

Kareem shrugged. "I mean, it's my choice, right? Just seems like I should finish if I'm this close. Besides, I'm pretty sure my parents would literally kill me if I dropped out. But homework? Really? You guys are saving the fucking world, and I'm writing papers. You have to admit, it's kinda bullshit."

Laughter burst from Riordan's chest. "Man, I missed you."

"Same, brother. Though at least I can see you on the news. You have to get up close and personal to see my mug," Kareem joked.

"Don't remind me." Riordan slumped further into the sofa.

Sean turned on the gaming system. "For right now, let's just ... not."

Riordan picked up his control and clicked aimlessly until Sean took pity on him and pointed to one of the multiple screens where his player stood, jumping like a jackass waiting. Kareem laughed at him, and they all entered the RPG game.

Hours later, Riordan put down the controller and thumbed a message to Aisling in response to her text. She'd sent several throughout the day, but this one marked the end of his free time.

"Sorry, guys, I have to go get my girl from work." Riordan stood and strapped his knife back onto his belt. He tested the release to the wide-eyed stare of his friends. "What?"

"You have a knife strapped to you, man." Kareem shook his head.

"I have people constantly threatening me and the people I love. Trust me, I've trained enough to be safe about it," he assured his friend.

"Still fucking strange. Tell Aisling we say hey and we miss her," Sean said.

After promising to deliver the message, Riordan jogged down the steps and sifted to the precinct. Being there hadn't gotten any easier after Dexter was suspended. The other cops were vocal in their distaste of his interference within the department. Fuck them.

He ignored the glares shot his way. He got it. Internal investigations and talks of crooked cops made even the decent ones look bad, but that wasn't his fucking fault. Riordan continued unfazed toward the cells where Aisling was working.

"You son of a bitch," a man shouted from behind him.

Outbursts weren't uncommon, but Riordan recognized the voice and spun just in time to avoid a punch to the back of the head. His hand shot out, snatching the forearm of the man who had just attempted to sucker-punch him. Behind him, officers watched and waited while a few brave souls stepped forward, trying to grab at the other man's back.

Dexter spit in Riordan's face. "You've got balls, showing up here."

Riordan shoved his arm away and braced his feet, his hand slipping back to his belt. He didn't release the knife. Yet. Aisling was in this building. His blood boiled as he realized he'd been gaming while she was this close to danger. Fuck, he hoped she stayed back at the cells.

"I knew you were a stupid fuck, Dexter, but this is ridiculous. Look at where we are." He gestured to the room full of cops. "You want to do this here?" Riordan smiled and shook his head. "I'd be happy to lay you out, believe me."

"You fucking wish." Dexter's hand shot to his hip and a weapon that was no longer there. He seemed to realize it, and his fingers formed a fist at his side. "You won't always be this lucky."

The laugh that left Riordan's throat was unhinged, even

to his ears. "You know the advice you give women? Travel in groups. Stay in well-lit areas. Don't drink too much. Careful what you wear. Be aware of your surroundings. You're the prey now, Dexter. Take your own advice."

"You can't threaten an officer of the law!" He spat, red-faced. Dexter's head swung to look for backup, and while a few officers looked more than willing to have a go at Riordan, nobody took a step forward.

Riordan smirked. "It's not a threat, and you're a civilian right now. Good luck."

He turned his back on the man, smirking at the way he heard Dexter sputter behind him. Riordan's only goal right now was getting to Aisling and getting her out of there. He didn't make it far; she was striding down the hallway, her magic crackling around her.

Her eyes were on fire, and he assessed his options quickly. No way was Dexter out of the building yet, which meant he wasn't letting Aisling past him. He stopped her forward momentum and pulled her into an open interrogation room.

"Breathe," he instructed.

"I heard you," she said, eyes looking over his shoulder. Her fists were clenched, the smell of magic strong. "Where is he?" she asked and tried to step around him.

"Not happening, kitten. You stay right here with me." He held her in his arms. "Hey, eyes on me." He'd learned more than one trick from Brynach. Step one, get her attention. Step two, hold it. Step three, promise safety.

Her eyes met his, and before she could open her mouth to argue, Riordan narrowed his eyes and shook his head. "Don't, Ash." His voice dropped, his speech slowing so each word mattered and held her attention. "It's handled. I know you can handle yourself, but we can't afford a public fight. For me. Stay here."

She cursed and took his hand. "I have another cell to ward. Come on."

Riordan followed after her and watched as she centered herself and resumed her work.

"That man has to be held accountable," she said as she lifted a smoking bowl in her hands and walked around an empty cell. Magic pooled around her, creeping outward and draping itself around the space. It filled the gaps in the bars, the cracks in the walls, and any other spaces another magic user's spell could penetrate. It was as effective as cementing a person underground. Nothing was getting past his girl's wards.

Aisling's rings caught the sun coming through the window. The dark blue wedding ring Brynach had given her, and the lighter amethyst Riordan had gifted. Her charm bracelet chimed softly as she moved through the space. Riordan reached to his chain and gripped the rings that hung there. He couldn't wear them when he was training, but on days like today, they comforted him. Somehow, he had to come to terms with his parents being gone and even with Maggie's passing. He wanted to let go of his anger and the hate burning in him. It didn't serve him and the new life he was building.

"He will. No matter what happens with the trials, they'll all pay. The Goddess will see to it," Riordan assured her.

She blew out the small flame inside the bowl. "Just have to clean this stuff up, and I'm good to go." She walked toward the back room where she stored the essentials for the wards and protections.

Riordan followed her and listened for voices in the other room while she straightened up. He knew she was doing the same. He took out his phone and sent Brynach a text letting him know about the confrontation and to be extra cautious.

"All done." Aisling wrapped her arms around him. "Are you going to tell me what happened out there?"

He kissed her forehead. "Not worth your time. Let's get out of here."

She nodded. "I wanted to pick up drinks and dessert. Think we can make a few quick stops?"

Brynach had already texted to come straight home, but Riordan knew that would upset Aisling. "Of course." Riordan put his arm around her shoulder and led her toward the door. He was hyper-vigilant, but Dexter was nowhere to be seen. As soon as they were outside the doors and far enough away that he could take a deep breath, he stopped her.

Aisling smiled at him and leaned in for the kiss she knew he wanted. And how he wanted it. The moment their mouths met, he was lost in the taste and feel of her. The silky slide of her tongue against his lips as he opened for her. The feel of her hands fisted in his hair as he pulled her closer to him grounded him. It felt like both forever and not long enough before she pulled away.

"Welcome home," he said and put his arm back around her. "Let's get our errands finished before Brynach gets growly because I'm hogging you."

Instead of sifting, they walked the streets. Fae and their familiars walked alongside humans and their pets. Sprites settled into gardens and manicured lawns, some covered with signs protesting the drops, others supporting unity and equality. It was just as common to see people smiling and calling hello as it was to see humans crossing the street to avoid Fae. It hurt to see neighbors with open disdain for each other.

Aisling and Riordan were called out to or waved at often, usually from New Fae. Most humans who remained near the dropped Veil were friendly enough. Those who strongly opposed the New Fae had moved away from the area. Still, a few people gave them scathing looks. It hurt Riordan to see anyone turn away from Aisling.

"She's strong, Riordan. It will get easier," Vola assured him.

His familiar was wise, but Riordan didn't have the same confidence. *"She shouldn't have to be this strong. Nobody should."*

"We don't always get what we should, but we can choose to make the best of what we're given," the fox advised.

"Have you been digging in the trash for fortune cookies

again? Who are you, and what have you done with my smart-ass familiar?" Riordan teased.

"I'll see you at home. Try to enjoy the walk." The fox scampered off, and Rin flew away overhead.

"They're getting along," Aisling commented, watching their familiars leave together.

"How could they not? They're both awesome." Riordan dropped his arm and took Aisling's hand. "Come on."

"Riordan Campbell, we meet again," an alate rasped in front of him.

His ears rang, and his vision threatened to go black as he focused on the image that had haunted him for far too long. The alate smirked, if such a thing was possible on its hideous face. Riordan had made peace with sprites, but never this one.

He pulled for his magic. The alate had just a moment to register the attack before Riordan had him caught in a ball of water from a nearby fountain.

Aisling started, "Riordan!"

She was precious about anything magical. Riordan loved her for her soft heart, but there was no place for it here. He wasn't going to show mercy to the sprite who had been the last to talk to him before the murder of his aunt. If it was dumb enough to approach him, he didn't feel bad for it.

"You made a mistake, alate. You should have stayed far, far away from me," he snarled.

Riordan felt Aisling's hand on his arm. "Talk to me," she begged.

"This is the fucker who threatened me right before they blew up the bakery," Riordan answered but didn't take his eyes off the alate. It was thrashing inside the water, desperate for air.

He heard Aisling's sharp intake of breath and then the sound of rushing feet. A calm voice spoke next to him as Dawn joined them.

"I'm not sparing it," he told both women.

"Alright, Riordan. That's within your rights, but don't you want to know what it has to say?" Dawn asked.

Riordan had always liked the witch and had been thankful for the apartment he'd rented above her shop and her kindness to Aisling. But even that wouldn't stop him from taking this sprite's life.

"No," he bit out. "Anything that leaves its mouth is poison."

From the trees swarmed other sprites, and their collective magic overpowered Riordan's. The alate was released from the bubble and landed on the pavement. Its waterlogged wings couldn't support it, and the alate struggled to stand on its weak thorny legs. Riordan raised his foot, ready to end the pathetic creature's life.

Aisling's hand on his arm stopped him. "This isn't you, Riordan."

"Like hell it isn't, Ash." But he lowered his foot without crushing the alate. "What do you want?"

The raspy voice coughed up at him. "I didn't start any fires, Fae. It's not my aim to hurt anyone. But I owe someone service, and so, I have a message for you."

Riordan sneered. "Let's hear it."

Dawn and Aisling moved closer to him. He hated that they were seeing him like this. His toe moved over, pinning the alate's wing to the ground. "Speak."

"You're being cautioned to drop the charges. If you want to keep yourself and those you love safe, walk away," it said before ripping itself free of Riordan's boot. Its wing tore, and one of its hideous brethren swooped in and lifted it, flying away while Riordan stood there stunned.

Aisling put a hand on his arm and whispered his name. "Don't let them get in your head. You know we're not doing that. We can keep ourselves safe."

Riordan turned on her. "And if we can't? We have no idea what they're capable of, Aisling. How will we know when they're going to strike? We aren't protected every second of every day.

You weren't even safe at the police department. Dexter clearly sent that fucker, and he was just in the building with you. Did anyone warn you he was there? No. You were back in the cells alone. What if he'd made it back there? Don't you get it? We're not safe."

Damn. He hated when he yelled at her. "What does it really matter, Ash? They're all still dead. People sitting in a jail won't change that." He hated how dejected he felt. "Can we just go, please? I want to get these errands done and get home."

He saw the look Dawn gave Aisling and the way she shook off the older woman's concern. Instead, she took his hand, and they walked quickly to the corner store. Unable to relax, he stood by the door while she shopped. With their arms weighed down, they sifted home.

Brynach opened the door for them. "Thought I heard you."

The Fae's smile was tight as he took the bags from Aisling and left Riordan with the cases of beer. Brynach winked at him, and Riordan grumbled.

"Come on, you gotta use all that new muscle," the larger Fae teased.

He saw Aisling shake her head at Brynach, and Riordan groaned. "Don't start tiptoeing around me. I'm fine."

"No, you aren't," Aisling said.

He turned to Brynach and filled him in. "I'd really like to forget about it now, please," he finished.

The larger Fae shook his long black hair. "Riordan, you have to tell us what you want. We can keep ourselves safe regardless of your decision. But if you're pressing forward with all this because you think it's weak to back off, we should discuss that."

Aisling nodded. "Nobody would think that, babe. If it's keeping you from moving on, from finding peace, you don't have to do this."

"I don't think I can sleep at night knowing they're just living their lives and my parents aren't. I want to move on, I do, but Dexter being free feels wrong," Riordan acknowledged.

Brynach nodded. "That's that, then. We move forward."

Riordan set the cases on the counter and began unloading bottles and cans into the refrigerator while his girlfriend kissed her husband. He grinned when Brynach lifted Aisling by the ass, and she wrapped her legs around his hips. Their mutual moans as they said hello to one another were music to his ears.

"You were only gone two days," Riordan joked as Aisling began to slide herself against Brynach's hard abs.

"Kill-joy," Aisling cursed but lowered her legs.

Brynach sighed. "I should tell Brielle that Dexter is fucking around again."

Riordan nodded. "I want to reach out and warn Liam."

Aisling threw up her hands. "Did you two even miss me?"

Both men laughed. Riordan spoke, "Of course we did. But we don't just keep you around for sex. Come on, kitten, you can wait a little."

"If I'm waiting, you better get making with the feeding. I'm hungry," she whined, and Riordan thought it was adorable.

"Food is still in the oven," Brynach said, looking at the timer. "We have fifteen minutes. Let's make our calls and be responsible adults. No time for sexy stuff, so keep it under control."

Aisling cocked her head to the side. "You really think that's going to work?"

Brynach's face got serious. "Oh, it will because I said so. Do we need to welcome you home with punishments, wife?"

Riordan saw the shiver run down Aisling's spine.

"Don't give me those eyes, a stoirin, and stop licking your lips. It won't be a punishment you like." Brynach's voice had lowered, and even Riordan responded to it.

"Fine, but just so you know, I haven't met a punishment I didn't like." Aisling tossed her hair.

Riordan unbuttoned his dress shirt, ready to be in more comfortable clothes. Aisling's eyes heated as she took him in.

They followed his hand down his chest, past his newly formed abs, to the buttons on his jeans. He coughed, "My eyes are up here, love."

She threw her arms up and growled the cutest kitten growl. He laughed and tore the rest of his clothes off, dumping them in the hamper before pulling on shorts.

Brynach had his phone to his ear, most likely talking to Brielle. Aisling smiled, and Riordan kissed her. Her hand snaked down to his ass and gripped him.

"He'll know," Riordan warned.

"How?" she whispered, her tongue licking his neck until she was gently sucking on his earlobe.

"Wife! Don't you dare!" Brynach called.

Aisling removed her hand from his ass and rolled her eyes. "Damn him."

"Heard that," he yelled.

Riordan laughed and found his phone to call Liam.

"What is the point of having a hot as fuck husband if he won't let me have any fun?" Aisling moaned as she drank him in.

"Have I ever left you unsatisfied?" he asked before giving her a slap to the ass.

"You are right now," she answered. "I'm not wearing a bra or panties. Try enjoying your meal, knowing you could have had me as the main course instead."

She swished her hips away from them and called over her shoulder. "No sex until you apologize."

Riordan raised his hands to his partner. "Don't look at me."

Brynach shook his head. "She's going to be the death of me." He pulled at his hair. "You both will. Put on some fucking clothes." Then he stalked away, leaving Riordan laughing.

CHAPTER 5

Aisling

Aisling had to schedule time with her mother now. It wasn't all her fault, though. Her mom was busy with New Fae counseling and services. Combine both their schedules, and free time was nearly impossible to find. She walked into the diner they'd agreed to meet at and found a quiet booth near the back. When her mom got there, and she began talking, it was hard to stop the soft whine that entered her voice. Something about talking to her mom let her admit she was feeling spread too thin.

"Sweetie, you have a lot on your plate. Anyone would be overwhelmed," her mom reminded her.

"I know, and I'm lucky. The guys don't ask me to be okay all the time, and I know I can lean on them," she assured the worried-looking woman. "I'm more worried about you."

"Don't be." Her mother waved off her concern.

Aisling wasn't buying it. The lines around her newly Fae mother's eyes were deeper than ever. She was adjusting to life as a New Fae while also helping others through the transition. Aisling worried her mom hadn't taken the time to fully process all the recent changes in their world. She sure as hell hadn't properly dealt with kicking out her husband.

"Mom, I know you're an independent woman who doesn't need a man, but it still has to sting. Have you thought about downsizing? It can't be easy being here. You're busier than ever at work, but how often are you seeing people in the home office? You're really good about asking me to check in on myself, but have you checked in with yourself?"

Her mom sighed, "Honey, I don't want you worrying about me. I am handling things fine. Maybe I should be more broken up about Patrick, but I'm not. The fact that he's not around hasn't changed much for me. The thought of moving on top of everything stresses me out. I'm fine in the house."

Aisling nodded. "Have you talked to Nevan?"

She watched her mother stiffen. "No. I've been to the castle and looked for him. I was refused access. Not because the Unaligned blocked me, because he wouldn't see me."

It helped knowing she wasn't the only one her father was avoiding. Aisling cursed. "He can't hide forever."

"No, he can't," her mother agreed. "But if he's smart, he'll hide as long as he can. Once I get my hands on him ... oh, Goddess, I can't wait."

Aisling managed a smile. She would pay to see her mother clock Nevan. The fact that he'd avoided meetings and public appearances this long bothered her. He'd never been a present parent, but this was ridiculous. Eventually, he'd have to own up to his part in the lies of the royal Fae.

"How are the guys?" her mother asked.

She couldn't help the smile that split her face at the mention of them. "They're amazing. Brynach is going to be in touch with you soon. He's got a fantastic idea for the young New Fae. And Riordan is leaning into his new role."

Her mother nodded. "They seem to be getting closer."

The comment hung in the air, and Aisling knew it wasn't made with judgment. She closed her eyes and answered. "Yes, they are."

There was only joy in her mother's eyes when she looked at her. "How does that make you feel?"

Aisling bristled. "Thrilled, of course."

"Honey, it's normal to feel jealousy, even within a structure like yours," her mother assured her.

"I know that. But I'm not. Really. I'm happy for them, and it would be selfish of me to be upset since they're understanding of my relationships with each of them."

The look her mother gave her made Aisling want to slink back in the booth.

"There's nothing logical about emotions." Her mother studied her face.

"Fine. It's different. Hard. I'm gone, and they have this time together. But I rarely get alone time with either of them. I'm happy for them, and I love seeing them fall more in love with each other, but I do feel left out sometimes." She took a deep breath. "Everything I do, I do with both of them now. There's a transparency to my relationships with them that I'm worried won't exist between their relationship and me."

Her mother shook her head. "Have you talked to them about the way you're feeling?"

"No." Aisling worried her lower lip. "They're still figuring out how they feel about one another. It's mostly gone unspoken. I'm afraid if I bring this up, they'll back away from what's growing. I'd never forgive myself."

"Promise me you will before it festers." Her mother reached over and squeezed her hand.

"I promise."

They were wrapping up their breakfast when her mother brought up the one thing Aisling didn't want to discuss and yet couldn't avoid. "Are you ready for today?"

"Not really, no. But I won't be alone. Lettie will be there, and it has to be done." Aisling winced. "Forever is a really long time to be without him."

Her mother hugged her and kissed her forehead before

Aisling got into her car. It was all the comfort she'd be able to accept without falling apart.

The day may have started in the arms of two men she loved and quality time with her mom, but it was about to go downhill. Picking up her best friend shouldn't have made it onto a "dread scale." Nothing about the Moore household should make her anxious, but here she was, anxiously heading their way. She loved Lettie, but there was no denying things had been strained between them lately, and Aisling didn't know how to fix it.

The past few months had been rough for them; losing Trent had left a hole in their already rocky relationship post-curse. The last few months had been busy for Aisling, and she'd been shit about checking in with Lettie. She knew it hadn't been easy on her friend getting media attention or being called a Seer and prophet of the new world. The magic surrounding the Hive had only strengthened when the people that had woven the curse became New Fae. Their heightened magic fed the threads inside everyone linked.

Aisling had reinforced Lettie's protections, along with anyone else local who needed help, but there was only so much she could do. Her friend hadn't asked yet, but Aisling was already looking into stripping Lettie of the magic left inside her. If she was being honest, though, she didn't trust herself to do it. Yet.

She'd lost Trent, and there was no getting him back, but Lettie she could do something about. Aisling was determined to fix what was broken. Today would be hard, but maybe it could unite them again.

She parked her car and walked up the steps. She had never knocked on the door before her, not once, but now she raised her fist. Aisling shook her head. No matter how rough things were with Lettie, this was a safe space for her. Bracing herself, she pushed open the door. The television was loud. Loud enough that nobody heard the door. Aisling could have called out a hello, but she didn't. Instead, she spied on them like a creeper from the entryway.

"Isn't that Ash?" Gracie asked.

Aisling nearly called out then, but the words got caught in her throat when she heard Lettie's mother.

"Yes, sweetie. Sit down; we're listening," Mrs. Moore shushed the youngest of her kids. The family was gathered in the living room watching Veil drop coverage from the other day. News stations often criticized and picked apart her performance. Multiple parties would debate whether she was doing good or evil. From what Cathy told her, it was ratings gold. Aisling had never watched it. In fact, she actively avoided any media involving her.

She hated the thought of the Moores gathered around to listen to that toxic crap. Logically, Aisling knew they would see the newspapers, the tabloids, and the interviews. She also knew they loved her, which made them hearing negative things about her even worse.

"Is she breaking things again? Tanya said she was really screwing things up," Gracie commented.

"Grace Anne, that's not appropriate language, and you need to stop hanging out with Tanya," her mother scolded. "Aisling isn't breaking things; she's fixing them."

Aisling crept closer, observing them without being seen.

"She's really strong, huh?" Cait whistled as Aisling floated on the screen.

Nothing about the scene on the television felt real. When she worked that magic, she felt like a conduit for the Goddess and less like herself. Seeing her body without a concrete memory of the moment was surreal.

"Incredibly," Lettie agreed.

"I wish I had magic," Tate said, his brown eyes on the television screen.

"How come we don't?" his twin brother asked.

"Because we didn't have magic before the Veil fell, and only those who already possessed magic got more," their father explained. She doubted it was the first time they'd discussed it.

"But how come we didn't have it before? It would be so much cooler if I did. I wanna be like Thor," Brayden exclaimed and held his fist up in the air like Thor's hammer.

"Yeah," Tate agreed. "And Lettie got magic."

"Alright. I think that's enough screen time. Don't you two have a room to clean?" Mrs. Moore shut that down.

Aisling heard them complain as their footsteps echoed on the stairs. She should announce herself, but this was probably the most honest anyone not romantically involved with her would be.

"It's okay, you know. They can ask questions. It's not like I can hide it from them," Lettie said. "Better they get their information from me than from people like Tanya."

"It really is phenomenal what Aisling is capable of," Mr. Moore said. "I just wish we could keep her safe."

"She keeps herself safe, Papa," Lettie reassured him. "Ash is kinda hard to break now."

Mr. Moore shook his head. "Doesn't make me want to protect her any less. You either."

Aisling backtracked and knocked loudly on the door before shutting it dramatically. "Hello," she called.

"Aisling, is that you?" Mrs. Moore walked down the hall and wrapped Aisling in her arms. "It's good to see you, sweetie."

"You, too." Aisling let her go only to be embraced by Lettie's father next. "Woah. Hi," she laughed.

"Are you girls sure you don't want us to come with you?" Mrs. Moore asked. "Nobody your age should have to do this. My heart absolutely breaks."

"Mom," Lettie warned, her face screwing up.

The older woman held her hands up. "I'm sorry, but I will always want to protect my girls. Get angry if you want, but I'm not going to stop offering to be there for you."

Aisling jumped in. "My mother said the same thing. He was like a son to her, too. It's tough, but this is something we need to do."

Mrs. Moore nodded, but tears were forming in her eyes. Her husband moved to her side and put an arm around her shoulders.

Mr. Moore said, "No point delaying the inevitable, yeah? We love you. Both of you."

There wasn't much else to say, so Lettie grabbed her bag, and they left. She couldn't imagine how hard it was living at home with your parents and siblings as all this happened around you. Aisling was married. She had a husband and a lover. She had support, space, and understanding. And yes, Lettie had Sean, but it was different when your parents loved you so much it felt like a weighted blanket on your shoulders.

Aisling had hoped that when Sean moved into Trent's old apartment, Lettie would go with him, but she couldn't face the space Trent used to occupy. Not yet, at least. As they pulled into the parking lot of the office, Lettie wiped at her face.

"I'm not sure I can do this, Ash." It was the first thing she'd said directly to her.

Aisling unbuckled and reached across the car to take Lettie into her arms, holding her tight. "I'm right there with you. We'll get through this, and then we can fall apart."

Her best friend looked up at her. "How many times?"

"What?" Aisling didn't understand the question.

"How many times can we fall apart before we can't be put back together?" Lettie asked.

"As many as we have to, L. The pieces may not fit perfectly, and the finished product may not look the same, but we keep mending ourselves anyway." She stroked her friend's hair, which was longer than it had been in years.

"I'm not alone, right? You feel it, too? It's like this hole inside me that nothing fills. Not Sean, not being home again with my family, not even having you here. There's something missing, and I don't think I'll ever feel normal again."

Aisling wiped away her friend's tears and only realized she was crying when Lettie did the same for her.

"You're not alone." It was all Aisling could say without falling apart completely. The pain associated with thinking of Trent was too intense. And she knew it wasn't healthy to avoid it; her mother had told her that on more than one occasion, but it was the only way she could get through the day.

"Okay. Let's go." Lettie got out of the car, and Aisling followed her. They linked fingers and together went to face the reading of Trent's will.

Luckily, they were quickly led to a room and not made to sit in the waiting room, crying. Both asked for water and handed over their IDs when prompted by the receptionist. While they were alone in the office, Aisling unapologetically moved her chair flush against Lettie's and took her hand. There was no doubt there was a strain between them, but they'd silently agreed to put it aside for the moment. Her friend leaned forward, took the box of tissues from the desk, and placed it in her lap. They looked at one another and managed a little smile.

"He'd have a field day if he saw us right now," Lettie's said. "I can hear him saying we look like little old ladies."

Aisling smiled because Lettie was right. The door opened, and her friend squeezed Aisling's hand so tight the bands of her rings bit into her skin. She must have made a sound because Lettie relaxed her grip but didn't let go as the executor rounded the table and sat.

"Hi, ladies. I'm so sorry to be meeting you this way. Trenton told me a lot about you," he began.

"Trent. He hated Trenton," Lettie said, her voice quiet but firm.

"My apologies. Trent thought highly of you both. He was a responsible young man. Not many his age set up wills with such specificity, but he was adamant about keeping his up to date." He picked up a pen and toyed with it.

Aisling fought to keep her breathing steady. Her magic had changed, stabilized, but she worried about spikes when her emotions rioted.

"He didn't have much of a choice, did he?" Aisling said in response. Talking about Trent in the past tense felt like a dagger to her heart.

"No, I suppose not." He shuffled some papers and opened a folder. "You ladies are aware of the purpose of this meeting. Mr. Eastham left things to each of you. I have to read the will as it is stated, and if you have any questions, we can discuss that afterward. Sound good?"

None of it sounded "good" to either of them. Aisling gave Lettie a squeeze and nodded. The man's face and tone remained steady as he began reading. His words slid over her. She wanted to pay attention, but her chest was tight, and it all felt too surreal.

She vaguely heard him mentioning trusts for Trent's brothers and one for his mother under the stipulation that she left her husband. Trent had left her enough money to never have to depend on a deadbeat piece of shit again. It was more than she deserved, but it was a very Trent thing to do.

Next, he discussed Sean's assets, which they already knew about. He'd braced himself and had his visit much earlier. It made sense for Trent to bequeath him the tech equipment and the building. The passwords and accounts for Trent's social media had gone to Sean as well, in case he wanted to maintain them. Sean still hadn't decided what to do with them outside of posting an update about his passing.

The social media buzz around his death had been beautiful to see. So many people admired and were inspired by him. An out and proud skateboarder in the pro circuit was important representation. The funeral had been something to see. Pro athletes, models, photographers, local friends, and family. But it all added fuel to the hate for her, the best friend who got him killed.

Aisling came out of her thoughts when she heard Lettie's name. Beside Aisling, she choked out a sob. He'd left Lettie his car and enough money to pay off student loans, finish her degree without financial worry, and probably keep her comfortable for a considerable chunk of her life.

He turned his head to Aisling. "For Miss Quinn," he began. "Trent has left you the house he purchased in Scotland."

"He what? I didn't know he'd purchased a home there," Aisling interrupted.

The man nodded. "Just last year, yes. As I was saying, the home is yours, and all international legal fees for switching over the paperwork to your name have been covered." The man looked down at the paper, and Aisling saw him swallow. "In his words, it's a wedding present, and he intends for you to, quote, 'defile each room with your men.' I'm sure you understand what he meant."

Lettie choked out a laugh, and Aisling felt like she blacked out for a moment. A home in Scotland was too much. He should have been here to enjoy it himself.

"In addition to the monetary gifts, Trent had letters for you." He removed two sealed envelopes, and the dam broke.

Aisling let out a strangled sob at the sight of her name in Trent's blocky handwriting. She cradled it to her chest and let the tears come. Lettie handed her a tissue, and she took it, dabbing at her face.

"I wish he was here right now. I'd curse him out so hard," Aisling tried to laugh through the tears. "What the hell was he thinking?"

Lettie shook her head. "Such an asshole. He knew this would break us."

The executor gave them a small smile. "Are you ready to hear the rest?"

"No," they answered together.

"Let's get it over with anyway," Lettie finished.

"Alright. Trent would like this read word for word, so please excuse any profanity or lewd comments."

Aisling laughed, "Goddess, Trent."

The older man blushed and then began, "Listen, ladies. I

have no idea when or why you have to hear this crap, but here we are. Sucks, huh? I update this every year, so if you're hearing this version, at least I left a hot fucking corpse behind. That said, I'm probably going to angrily haunt you both because it's too early to say goodbye."

Aisling held onto Lettie tighter as they let the tears flow unchecked.

"I'm not sure there'd ever be a good time for goodbyes, though. Even if we were old and crotchety, it would still be too soon. I hope you know, and never forget, how much I love you. Not past tense. Wherever I go, whatever is next, I'll love you there as fiercely as I do here. Don't roll your eyes at me, Ash.

"You saved me. I may have provided the good looks and the talent but none of that matters without heart. The only reason I have any heart left as I write this is because both of you restored my faith in love and family. I could keep blubbering on, but I know you're both ugly-crying, and nobody needs that. Still, it's really important to me that you know none of it matters. Not the money, not the houses, and not the followers. It's all bullshit without the two of you. I'm so sorry I'm not there. I wanted to be. I'd never leave you willingly, so I'm sure I did some stupid shit. Or maybe I died in a buff man orgy. I suppose it doesn't matter how it happened, huh? Fuck, this is hard. Says the dead man while his friends grieve.

"Look, I don't want you being sad. I know you will be anyway, but if I was there, you know I'd tell you to knock it the fuck off. So, be sad and cry for me today, but then I want you to move on. Aisling, you have so much ahead of you, so much greatness, and those men—gimme a moment! Lettie, babe, I don't know who it is you end up with, but make sure they're worthy of you. Fuck that; nobody is worthy of you, not even Sean. Though I'm glad I lived to see the start of that."

Lettie let out a sob, and Aisling turned in her chair to put an arm around her. They both blew their noses noisily and tried to gather themselves.

"There's not much left," the man promised.

"Please finish," Aisling said, her voice thick with emotion.

"I hope I hugged you the last time I saw you. I hope we weren't fighting, or I hadn't said something bitchy to you. But if I did, I'm sorry. I'm nasty sometimes, but I have never once wavered in my love for you. Not even when you mocked me for making out with a grandfather."

Aisling managed a small smile, and Lettie hiccupped a cry that was part laugh.

"You couldn't get rid of my annoying ass in life, and you won't be able to in death, either. I won't ever leave you; I promise. But it will get easier—maybe—I mean, probably. I hope so. When you think of me, I hope you do it with a smile and the knowledge that you're the baddest bitches I know, and I'm so lucky you were mine. So, finish crying and get back to your lives. Oh, and *Top That* is still better than *Dance Magic*. Ha! Can't fight me on it anymore. I get the last word, bitches!"

Aisling couldn't help the laugh that broke free of her, but it quickly turned into a sob.

"He's still wrong," Lettie sobbed and held Aisling tight.

She was vaguely aware of the executor telling them he'd give them some time. The door opened and closed.

Aisling sobbed, letting the pain sink deep. It felt like her bones were breaking, her throat burned, and her nose ran. Even in death, he loved so big. Everyone thought it was Lettie who had the big heart, and she did, but Trent's capacity for love and forgiveness was unrivaled. They were the lucky ones who got to see it.

"If that's what he said publicly, what the hell is in these letters?" Lettie wailed. "What an asshole."

Aisling blew her nose. "I can't read it yet."

"Me either. Hell, I don't know when I'll ever be ready to."

"If you want me there when you do, I will be," Aisling offered.

Her friend shook her head. "No. I should do it alone."

When they calmed enough, they took a sip of water, threw away their balled-up snotty tissues, and opened the door. The receptionist alerted the executor, and he came back with their identification and some details on the next steps. Neither of them registered a damn thing he said.

They squinted at the bright sun as they left the office with red, puffy eyes. Aisling pulled the sunglasses from the top of her head and hid. They hurried to her car, and Aisling pulled a shaky breath into her lungs.

Nobody warns you that grief can be a physical thing. There's never a mention of how it feels crippling to your actual body. Lettie slumped into the passenger seat, silent.

"Do you want to go home? To Sean? What do you need, L?"

"I need Trent back." Lettie sighed, "Just take me home."

Aisling could feel the wall going back up and didn't know if she'd survive it. "I know things have been weird lately. I'm sorry I've been so busy, but I will always have time for you, L. We don't have to do this alone."

Her friend sniffed before she answered. "Did you know my parent's home number got doxed? They had to change it. The other day a reporter tried to stop Gracie to talk to her about her Seer sister as she left school."

Aisling hadn't known, and she hated herself for it. "Lettie, I'm so sorry."

"Why?" she asked. "You didn't do this, Ash. You're busy. You have a new life, literally. I get it. But so do I. I think we just have to acknowledge that things have changed. It's never going to be like it was before. Before Trent. Before the curse. Before the Veil drop. Just ... before."

"So, we figure out how to move forward as our new selves. But I don't want to do it without you, Lettie," Aisling told her. She held her hand out and practically held her breath until Lettie linked fingers with hers.

As they neared the Moore household, Aisling saw the signs she'd missed before. Signs both praising and cursing the Oracles. Candles burned and effigies were laid along the roadside. Lettie cried out for Aisling to stop the car. When she pulled over, Lettie stormed out and ripped the signs out of the ground.

"No matter how many times we take these down, they're there again." Lettie balled her fists at her sides.

A fanatical group of people had learned about the Hive's ability to connect to one another and started a strange worship of them. They believed that their group would be able to foresee a way to save the world from the pain of the split and the transition of the joining.

Some people thought they'd help them push the Fae back to "their side" of a Veil that no longer existed. Others thought they were messengers from a higher power sent to assist the world through this shift. A new breed of magic for the "humans" and a way to balance out the powers of the New Fae and retain a place in the magical world.

The majority of the Hive wanted nothing to do with worship of any kind. But some of them were exploiting the belief, setting up fundraisers and collections for their talents and advice. It didn't surprise Aisling.

In times of change, it was normal for humans to seek reasons, blame, and salvation. The humans? When had she stopped counting herself among them? She rubbed Lettie's back.

Aisling took her phone out. "I'm going to have Brielle put some of her people on surveillance. You won't know they're here. They stay out of sight, sometimes just familiars checking, but they'll run these guys off. Eventually, they'll get the message."

Her friend sighed. "Worth a try."

"We'll be okay. Not today and maybe not tomorrow, but we will be," Aisling reassured her.

"Doesn't feel that way." Lettie kept walking. "Literally nothing is the same. You, you're going to live forever. I'll be alone."

"Woah, Lettie. We can't start thinking about that." Aisling held up her hands.

Her friend frowned. "You don't have to! Don't you get it? It's all I think about. I'm going to get old and die ... and you'll be. Fuck you for being so pretty."

Aisling laughed and hugged her friend before leading her back to the car. "Shit is weird, Lettie, and different for sure, but we're going to make it work."

"Girls' night soon? Tara, Kara, you, Me, Amber, if she wants to come?"

"Absolutely." Aisling pulled out her phone and sent out a group text, including Sydney. The answers were nearly immediate, and all were yes. Not wanting to let it go without solid plans, she sent out a date and time and told everyone to meet at her condo.

CHAPTER 6

Brynach

There were a few short hours before Aisling left for another drop, and he sure as shit didn't want to spend it like this. Still, this meeting was too important to miss. Having both Riordan and Aisling there for support, championing his cause, bolstered him, though. Plus, he really didn't want her entering the Seelie court alone, and she wanted to see Corinna. First, he'd get through this meeting.

Before him, Theo sat with a smug look on his face, but Marina was smiling gently. He liked her. Outside the make-shift meeting room's window at the Seelie court, he heard the shouts of young Fae. He would make this work for them. Alex smiled at him, and Brynach took a deep breath before pitching his idea.

"You're both parents to young New Fae, yes?" He didn't wait for them to answer. "As each section of the Veil falls, more and more children are becoming New Fae. I don't know how versed you are in the ways of Fae, but young aren't as common for us as they are in the world you came from. We are training the adults in magic use and adapting to their new strength, but I can't help but notice the human realm schools struggling to help our New Fae youth. They need specialized care."

Marina nodded, but Theo bristled. If he had to guess, it was because he hated someone else pointing out something he should have realized as a father.

"We're all overwhelmed and overworked, and children are resilient. It's easy to say they'll be okay because they have peers and adults to guide them, but I'm afraid that's not enough. They need Fae instructors to maintain safety as they learn to use their magic. They deserve the same benefit Fae children have to navigate their newly formed relationships with familiars. And that simply won't happen in their current academic settings." Brynach paused, and Aisling took his hand. He smiled at her before continuing.

"It's not going to be easy or smooth at first, but I've already spoken to some experts who are ready to step in and take on this project. Mrs. Quinn is prepared to help hire counselors. Alex is an expert in working with Fae youth and would act as a headmaster of sorts, and his wife is prepared to help with staffing for housekeeping, food prep, and dormitory aides." Brynach finished up with, "You're sitting on a massive building that's largely unused. The children need somewhere to learn where they can be surrounded by those who understand them. We offer the school to all New Fae, housing for those who want it, and provide a service our youth desperately need and deserve."

There was silence, and Brynach did his best not to wipe his sweaty palm on his pants. He desperately wanted this to work.

"We will need to set up classrooms for different ages, preschool through high school. Fae all but stop aging in their early twenties; until then, they need guidance. Housing needs to take familiars into consideration, also. There's a lot to consider." Brynach knew it was a lot, but he also knew they could make it work.

"I assume you have a formal proposal, budget, and timeline?" Marina asked.

"Of course. The royal vaults are largely unnecessary. That money can be spent investing in the future of Fae. We can discuss this in more detail, hopefully very soon, but I wanted to bring this to you as soon as possible." Brynach met both their gazes. Theo held his before lowering his eyes.

"It's a good idea. We will need to iron out details, of course. No way are we sending children into the Unseelie castle. There are pitfalls and death traps hidden all over that place. We'll re-home the Seelie royals to that court and start converting for classrooms and housing." The other man hung his head. "Fuck, it's gonna be a big project. You're taking this on? You and Alex?"

Brynach nodded. "We can come back tomorrow with the paperwork. I'll bring Gemma, Aindrea, and Lydia with us, along with a spokesperson from the children's current school district, to discuss their core curriculum."

Marina sat back. "Alright. Let's go over the specifics and plan how to move forward on the fastest and safest timeline. If we do this, we do it right. The children deserve the best, not a trial run."

"I couldn't agree more," Brynach said. "Until tomorrow."

The three of them walked out of the room and down the hall before he let out a large breath. Aisling's hand squeezed his, and Riordan put an arm around his hips.

"You did great in there, big guy," his partner assured him. "You're going to lose hair over this. Do Fae go grey?"

Aisling laughed. "I wish. That would be sexy as fuck."

Brynach growled softly. "You couldn't handle me any sexier. And don't worry about my hair. I did good, right? This is going to help those kids. That means something."

His wife went up on her toes and pulled his face down to hers. She kissed him lightly. "You did a fantastic thing today, Bry. Those children are lucky to have someone like you looking out for them. You're saving countless young Fae from a childhood much harder than they need to have."

Brynach rested his forehead against hers. "That's all I ever wanted."

Riordan patted him on the back, and they moved down the hall toward Aisling's old room. He worried that being there and seeing her old friend would be too much for her, but he had to trust her.

Once she'd gathered a few personal items from her room, Brynach watched her look around and shake her head.

"I don't ever want to come back here."

"Then you won't," Riordan assured her. "Come on. Let's go visit and get you out of here."

Together, they walked toward the princess's rooms. She'd left the Unseelie hospital and gone back to her rooms, but apparently, things were tense between her and the King and Queen. When they neared her room, Brynach and Riordan paused while she knocked and walked in.

"The gang's all here," Corinna joked, but he could tell she was nervous. The royal Fae had her wings tucked in behind her back, and her pale skin flushed.

"Corinna," Aisling greeted her. "I'm glad to see you well."

"Thanks to you." She made no move to get up. "I'd still be in that pit if your friend hadn't told my parents where I was. It's more than I deserved. I'm so sorry, Aisling."

"I know you are." Aisling moved to her side. "We all do stupid things for guys. I mean, you have spectacularly shit taste, but I get it."

The princess laughed, and Brynach marveled at his wife's capacity for forgiveness. When Corinna looked past Aisling and met his eyes, Brynach gave her a small smile.

"Hello, Dark Prince." She paused before looking back to Aisling. "I want you to know I'm not staying here. I'm going to the Unseelie court. Breena said there are rooms I can use. I can't stomach being near my parents."

He couldn't hide the shock on his face. "You're telling me my sister invited you to stay at the Unseelie court? Breena?"

Corinna huffed. "Is that so hard to believe? We got to know one another while we were healing up. Turns out we both fucking hate Levinas."

Riordan laughed deep in his throat. "No shit," he murmured.

Aisling shot him a look before turning to Corinna. "I think that's a great idea. I have some insider knowledge that you'd be moving there regardless. Better to get set up now."

The younger Fae's black eyes went wide, but Aisling didn't offer any more information. "We have to get going. I have another drop I'm leaving for, but I wanted to stop in and see you while I was here."

Corinna lifted an arm but lowered it before she touched Aisling. "I'm glad you did. Maybe we can talk again soon?"

His wife nodded. "Yeah, we can arrange that. Take care of yourself, okay?"

"I'll try," the princess promised.

Riordan turned for the door first, but Aisling and then Brynach caught up quickly. "Well, that wasn't so bad," he commented.

"No, I guess it wasn't. I don't forgive her, not all the way, but I don't want to hate her. Does that make sense?" Aisling asked.

Before Brynach could answer her, Aisling stopped short. Over her head, Brynach saw Nevan take a step toward his daughter, only to stop when Aisling's hand dropped to the hilt of her blade. She didn't pull it out, but Brynach could tell from the rigidness of her shoulders that she was thinking about it.

"Aisling?" Nevan sounded unsure of himself.

Good. He should be.

"Don't you dare." She shook her head, her hand still on her blade. Those hazel eyes with the potential to hold so much love pinned the older Fae down. "You don't get to be excited to see me, or hug me, or even smile in my direction."

Brynach noticed the subtle shift in the older Fae. His shoulders dropped, and his typically rigid posture slumped under the weight of his daughter's words.

"Whoever you think you knew, she's gone. And the woman I am now isn't one interested in a relationship with you. But I will have answers."

One of the new guards behind him chuckled and clapped lightly. Riordan turned and shot him a look. The noise stopped.

The snarky Seelie guard didn't know when to stop. "How's your family faring, Dark Prince? I heard word your sister is worse for wear," the Fae sneered.

Brynach's vision narrowed to the man's smug face. The urge to feel their blood slippery on his hands nearly overtook him. A touch on his lower back brought him back to the moment. He looked over, expecting to see Aisling, and instead saw Riordan next to him. Sweet man.

"Your pathetic verbal sparring only further proves you're not in a position of power anymore. Still sure this is who you want to swear allegiance to, Father?" Aisling said with venom.

"Aisling, you don't understand," Nevan began, but he never got a chance to finish.

His wife pushed on, "Oh, I understand perfectly. I understand that you magically castrated your own child. I understand that you were complicit in purposefully withholding the birthright of both witches and Ravdi so you could maintain a perceived dominance over them."

With each word, her father withered a little more. Brynach would have felt bad for him if the words hadn't been true. But he deserved each and every one of them.

"I love you," Nevan said. One sentence. Three words with a world of hurt and lost opportunities behind them.

"Even as a child, I understood that those words held a different definition for you than they did for me. I forgave you for not being the father I wanted or deserved. I brushed aside my own pain at your distance to better understand what it was you needed for your own happiness." Aisling held her hand out, and Brynach and Riordan walked to her.

"I have men in my life who understand my worth and who love me unconditionally. They don't make me wait for scraps of affection or question whether I'm worthy of their time. That should have been a role you filled, too." Aisling was losing steam.

"You've sharpened your claws. It doesn't become you," Nevan said.

Aisling shrugged. "Turns out I learned from the best. An entire lifetime you pretended to care for me before stabbing me in the back. I figure I'm just the person you helped raise me to be."

Her father shook his head and turned, walking away down the hall. Aisling waited until he was out of sight to turn and run. Riordan and Brynach pivoted and followed her. As soon as they reached the courtyard, Aisling sifted away. Brynach knew where she'd go. He took hold of Riordan and went after her.

"Where are we?" Riordan asked when they settled out of the sift.

"Aisling's place. She always came here when she was upset as a kid," Brynach walked toward a clearing in the brush. He'd purposely sifted outside of her space so she would hear them coming.

"It's not far from Alex's place, and you know she feels better by water," Brynach explained as the sound of the stream met their ears. In a minute, they'd see Aisling dangling her bare feet in the water.

"Oh, a stoirin." Brynach walked into the water in front of her. He pulled her close, and her body shook as tears ran down her face.

"I knew better than to let myself believe that would go any other way. But I let myself think maybe," she admitted.

"That's not your fault. You've always thought the best of people. It's one of the reasons I love you." Brynach stroked her hair.

"That doesn't mean it doesn't hurt to see you like this," Riordan offered, settling onto the tree next to her and putting an arm around her shaking shoulders.

"You'd think I'd be all cried out," Aisling said, wiping at her face. "How can anyone do that to their child? How could they knowingly keep what belonged to us? How could anyone be that cruel?"

"Aisling, not everyone operates out of love the way you do. And the Fae got too used to power and influence to share it. The same dynamic exists in human politics and injustices. It just hits differently when it directly impacts you," Riordan answered.

She sat up straighter. "You're right. Goddess, I'm a mess. It's not about me, and here I am sobbing because I couldn't control the moral compass of people who never had one in the first place."

She started to stand, and Brynach pulled her into his arms. "Oh no, you don't. Not yet. Come here."

He held her close and kissed her. A splash behind them let Brynach know Riordan was in the water. Then, Aisling's hands were in his hair, tugging at the base of his scalp, centering him.

There was a jerk on Aisling's shoulder, and Riordan pulled her to him. She leaned into his arms and kissed him, accepting the comfort they were giving.

She was stunning all the time, but she never looked more beautiful than when she gave herself, mind, body, and soul, to the two of them. Riordan stood from his position over her and then leaned back in to kiss her cheeks and her forehead.

"No more tears, kitten," he instructed.

"Tiger," she said softly.

Brynach laughed and then walked from the water with his wife in his arms and set her on the grass. Aisling pulled on her shoes and looked up at him.

"Breena before we go home?"

"Yes, a stoirin," Brynach confirmed and sifted to the Unseelie court, knowing the two of them were following. Before Aisling left, she wanted to see his sister, and so did he. The last thing Aisling needed was more guilt or hurt, but she needed the closure of talking to Breena.

"*You're going soft,*" Kongur commented.

"*Only for her. Always for her,*" Brynach agreed.

"Ready?" Aisling asked, taking his hand.

"Yes," he answered.

A New Fae guard stopped them when they approached the door. "Welcome, Dark Prince. Can I help you?"

Brynach all but snarled, "I know my way around."

They huffed a laugh. "Right. Well, your sister will be on the tower roof, and Rainer is in his quarters. Trixie is currently in the gardens out back, and Ceiren is in talks with some of the New Fae. I can let him know you're here, and I'm sure he'll find you."

Brynach didn't miss that they'd used the opportunity to remind him his family was no longer in control of the palace. It was both a warning and a display of power.

"Since the others seem occupied, we'll go to the tower first," Riordan answered.

They walked away, and Brynach patted his shoulder, thankful that he'd decided for the group. Brynach hadn't wanted to show his hand by running to his sister. Riordan was more intuitive than anyone gave him credit for.

They took the stairs two at a time, even Aisling, who pushed to keep up with the men's longer strides. He loved her all the more for the quiet show of strength and compassion after such a difficult day. He'd reward her later for putting his need for his sister before her own discomfort in the moment.

He crested the top of the stairs and pushed through the doors. Brynach's hair whipped around his face, and before he could wrangle it, a body slammed into his.

"Brynach!" Breena wrapped her arms around his waist.

He held her close before he pushed back, holding her at arm's length. "Are you okay?"

She groaned. "I'm fine. Don't look at me like that."

Brynach could see she was okay, her cheeks rosy and her body seemingly whole. He also knew she wasn't the same, would never be the same again. He put his hands on either side of his twin's face and stared into her eyes. They were forever a mirror of his own citrine orbs.

"I'm still the same person, Brynach. Don't start treating me differently," she warned and pulled away to punch him in the arm. "I'm glad you're here." Breena finally got a look behind him and grinned. "And you brought your harem."

This time it was Brynach's turn to punch her in the arm.

"Ouch. Fuck! Damn it, Brynach, that was full force. I'm fragile, you asshole." She clutched at her arm and hopped around.

Jashana laughed from behind his sister. "Don't believe her. She's been sparring with me for weeks now. She's no less strong; she's just a little more breakable, even if she doesn't understand that yet."

"Well, you better," Brynach said. "If you get hurt, I'll never forgive you."

Breena turned on Aisling, and there was something in her feline eyes that startled him. Brynach surged between the two of them.

"She didn't do it on purpose," he called out.

"I know that." Breena waved him aside. "Relax, brother. I just have a question for her."

Aisling moved forward and hugged Breena. Brynach noticed his sister's tense frame relax slightly the harder his wife squeezed her. "I'm sorry. I know it wasn't my fault, but I'm still sorry."

"About that," Breena started. "I heard that dear old Dad got his magic back."

"Excuse me?" Riordan's voice was higher than normal.

Brynach turned to Riordan with a wince. "Sorry. I think we forgot to tell you that part of the meeting the other day."

Riordan glared at him, which was what he deserved. He stored away a more personal apology for later.

"Right, and I'm sure you can find him and strip him again. Blah blah. That's not why I brought it up," Breena rattled, excitement and fire coming back to her eyes. "If Gabriel got his magic back when the Veil fell, then I could, too. If I go with you and I'm in the Veil when it goes down, I could be Fae again."

Brynach looked to Aisling, who bit her lip. "I don't know. Only witches and Ravdi are given any magic; it's not changing humans into Fae. And you're human now."

"So was he!" she yelled.

Jashana rested her hand on his sister's forearm. It was a gentle touch, but Brynach saw the hidden meaning. It was a comfort and calming. It was the way Riordan and Aisling touched him when he was getting too hot. As such, it was innately intimate.

"We can try," Aisling offered. "I just don't want you getting your hopes up. I don't know why it worked for Gabriel, if it even did. It shouldn't have."

"I get it, Quinn. Do your best, but make it work." Breena cocked a hip and glared at his wife.

Brynach would always support Aisling, but he silently seconded his sister's words.

CHAPTER 7

Riordan

S o, they just let you walk in and walk right the fuck back out?" Isaac was still processing the events from the court trip. "It could have been a trap. Didn't you consider that?"

"Only about a thousand times," Riordan answered, landing a kick to sparring partner's shin.

"Well, I'm glad you're back safely. Nobody else can keep up with me," Isaac joked as he knocked away Riordan's jab.

"Please. You're not that good. I'm pretty sure that Mikal put you on your ass last week," Riordan laughed.

"Pure luck. I was distracted by Heather. She was looking especially hot that day." He turned red when he said it.

Riordan hadn't noticed the New Fae, but he hadn't noticed anyone like that in a long time. Looking was fun and all, but the real thrill came in knowing that you *could* pull someone if you wanted to, and that had lost its appeal when he fell in love with Aisling.

Or Brynach.

He allowed himself to admit it in his head. He couldn't, and wouldn't, lie to himself. He loved the big, hulking Fae. Not only did Brynach take incredible care with Aisling, but he showed

Riordan in countless ways that he was important to him and to their dynamic. Never once did he pull rank on Riordan. Repeatedly, he'd reassured Riordan that they were a team and all three of them were necessary for their collective happiness.

That in and of itself was priceless to him. But Brynach also made him feel cherished and safe without threatening his view on manhood. He'd never experienced anything like it, never imagined that he would. But now that he had it, he wasn't going to let it go.

A kick caught the back of Riordan's leg, and he cursed, "Goddess, Isaac. Really?"

"Pay attention." Isaac circled him, and Riordan countered. "She's gone right now, right?"

He didn't need to ask who "she" was. "Yeah, for a few days."

"So, it's just you and the big, black-haired baddie hanging around the house?" Isaac winked. "How does that work?"

"Well, you see, we start out the night with whip cream blowjobs. Then we sit around naked, drinking beer and playing video games. And then we get into bed, and he rides me like I'm a racehorse toward the finish line." Riordan slammed his fist into Isaac's chest. "Don't ask stupid questions, man."

The other Fae held up his hands. "I don't know what the fuck you thought I was asking, Riordan, but it wasn't like that. I don't give a fuck what you do at home so long as your head is in the game here."

Riordan dropped his arms to his side. "That's not what it sounded like."

"Maybe you're projecting your own shit, man. I just wanted to know if you were okay without her. Like, I'm sure you guys miss her. But also, it has to be nice to get a little guy time. That's all, I swear." He looked hurt. Guilt struck Riordan hard.

"Fuck, man, I'm sorry." Riordan ran a hand through his hair. "I must be letting the tabloids get to me. They keep harping on our personal relationship, and it's wearing on me."

Isaac nodded. "I bet. But I swear that's not where I was going."

"Sorry," Riordan repeated. "Uh, yeah. It's tough. We miss her, of course. I guess things run pretty much the same as when she's here, just, you know, she isn't. In an ideal world, she wouldn't have to leave, but we understand why she does."

"And we're all pretty fucking grateful she goes." He waved around the field. "I never would have known this was possible if it wasn't for the three of you. I know you think what you did was just another random Thursday evening. Some fulfillment of a prophecy or an experiment to see if you could do it. But I'm glad you did, and I know I'm not alone. So, you know, if it gets hard, just remember that there's more of us grateful you did it than not."

Riordan held out his hand, and Isaac clasped his forearm in a traditional Fae greeting. They held one another's arms and looked into each other's eyes. "Thank you."

"Sure." Isaac shrugged and let go of Riordan's arm. "So, they're really going to combine the two courts? I may not have paid attention pre-drop, but even I know that's not going to end well."

They began to circle one another again, Isaac trying to disarm Riordan and gain control of his weapon. Riordan blocked a grab and nodded.

"Frankly, they'd be doing everyone a favor if they did take one another out. But yeah, everyone is moving to the Unseelie court." Riordan laughed. "I can't wait to see that stuffy bitch of a queen fall into one of the random hallway traps."

Isaac connected with a particularly hard blow to Riordan's forearm, but he kept his grip tight. He clenched his teeth and kicked out at his sparring partner. There was a knife in Isaac's hand, edges dull, but it would still hurt like hell. Riordan flipped his fake handgun around, using the butt of it to come down hard on his friend's knuckles.

"Mother fucker," Isaac cursed, and his hand opened, dropping the knife.

Riordan grinned. "Gotcha."

The other man leaned down and picked up the knife, holding it out to Riordan, who traded weapons with him. "Again."

"You're a real sucker for pain, aren't you?" Riordan teased.

"You know I have younger sisters. They're getting bullied at school by human mini torturers. Children are evil. If what you say is true, I'm making sure they're among the first signed up for the school." Isaac was panting as he circled Riordan and dodged the blade. "My mom is going to be thrilled. My father took off years ago, and she has no idea how to help the girls, being fully human."

It still shocked Riordan to hear himself referred to as anything but human. "Yeah, well, that's the point. The kids need a safe space, and I think Bry and some other older Fae want to make amends for the crap their older generations did."

Isaac scoffed. "It's a start, but fuck. They really screwed us over. I still can't wait to see the drama unfold. No way Branwyn and Rainer play nice for long."

"If at all," Riordan agreed. Of all the things he loved about his partner's plan, this part had the highest chance of going to shit. Lifetimes of resentment and animosity didn't just disappear. "They make the move ... what the fuck day is it?"

"It's Thursday. You gotta get more sleep, brother." Isaac kicked out, and Riordan just barely avoided the shot to his knee.

"Tomorrow, then. They move tomorrow, so we'll see sooner than later, I guess." Suddenly, he was staring up at the bright sun, all the air knocked from his lungs. Before he could curse, his friend was on him, knees pinning Riordan's arms to the ground, and his hand ripped the gun away. "Damn it, Isaac."

Above him, his friend grinned and popped up. He held out a hand and helped Riordan to his feet. Damn, that guy was like a freight train. He moved gingerly to pick up his water bottle and check his phone.

" 'Bout time someone put the pretty boy on his ass," a newer trainee growled as he passed.

Riordan bristled. "Something you want to say to me?"

The man walked toward him, large but nowhere near intimidating with all that fake bravado. His hand went to his hip and the weapon strapped there. Riordan placed him now. He was a New Fae who used to be a part of the police department, a co-worker of Dexter's.

He refused to back down; nothing good would come of showing weakness right now. Instead, he stood his ground, Isaac at his side.

"Yeah, I do. Stay out of my fucking way." The guy leaned into his space.

"Buddy, I can't stress enough that you came over here. Seems like you're a smidge obsessed with me, which is flattering and all, but you're not my type." He knew he was pushing his luck. Nothing like calling out a cop's sexuality to get them angry.

"You fucking wish. Do yourself a favor. Don't look at me. Don't even breathe my way," the guy warned.

Riordan nodded, holding his thumb up. "Got it, pal. Now if you and your 'roid rage could go elsewhere, that would be swell."

Isaac laughed, and the red-faced man stalked off.

"Keep an eye on him. I didn't trust some of those cops as humans, let alone Fae. I want a closer watch on the weapons training that the service member New Fae are running," Riordan muttered to his friend.

"You got it." Isaac still hadn't taken his eyes off the large man as he moved across the grounds. "We can kick him out, you know?"

"Better to keep him here and keep an eye on him. For now, anyway." Riordan looked at his phone again. "I've gotta call it a day. I have somewhere to be. Will you be okay?"

Isaac grinned and shrugged a shoulder. "Of course. Get out of here."

Like that, his friend took off, and Riordan gathered his things.

Before he left the training ground wards, his phone rang, and when he saw his brother's name, he quickly answered.

"Liam, what's up?"

"You want the good news or the bad news?" his brother asked.

"Um, the bad?" Better to rip off the Band-Aid.

"They flagged Stavos at the Canadian border."

Riordan could feel his heart beating in his head. The last of Peggy's kids was in custody.

"Rory?" Liam's voice broke through his thoughts.

"I'm here," he answered. "How is this bad news?"

Liam sighed. "Because they flagged him only after he was through. He's in Canada somewhere now."

"Fuck," Riordan cursed. "How in the hell did that happen? There's a fucking APB out every-fucking-where for him."

"Turns out the Mounties missed the memo," Liam responded.

Riordan ran a hand through his lengthening hair. "Is it wrong if I don't have the energy to care anymore, Liam? Maybe it's enough that he spends the rest of his life looking over his shoulder."

His brother was quiet on the other side of the line, but Riordan waited him out. "No, Rory. I don't think that's wrong at all. I think it's okay to let it go."

The sigh that left him was soul deep. "Okay, tell them to call off any official search. It's a waste of their manpower anyway."

Liam made a grunt that Riordan knew meant he agreed. "But remember that good news? Dexter was arrested last night."

"Wait, what?" Riordan paced. "Why are we just learning about it now?"

"Because the charges are bullshit. Honestly, this should probably be added to the 'bad news' category," Liam explained.

"What are the charges?"

"D&D, indecent exposure, destruction of public property, resisting arrest, and a host of other bullshit charges. Basic frat boy drunken bullshit." There was a pause, and then Liam tacked on, "He posted bail already."

"Are you serious? Liam, how is this remotely good news?" Riordan was getting more frustrated as the minutes ticked by.

"He has a court date and an order not to leave town. I think they did it just to make sure he couldn't slip away. It will give them time to continue building the case," Liam clarified.

Well, when he put it that way. "Okay. I mean, that's something."

"The case is coming together against him. I don't think he's getting away again. This might be it." The hope in Liam's voice stabbed through Riordan's chest. Finally, there might be justice for his aunt. After all this time, the people responsible could be held accountable.

"Is there anything I can do?"

"No, Rory. We've got it covered. I just wanted to keep you up to date. If I learn anything else, I'll let you know," Liam promised before he hung up.

His phone chimed a reminder, and Riordan made his way through the ward. When he reached his motorcycle, he threw a leg over, lifted the kickstand, and started her up. He took a longer wooded road to give himself time to think. The trees around him were a blur as he tried to outpace his speeding thoughts. Turns out that being Fae didn't cure you of anxiety or depression, but it made your dangerous behavior less deadly. As the wind ran its fingers through his hair, Riordan let the roar quiet his internal monologue.

Before his ride was over, he had to let the weight of responsibility for the New Fae drop. He was constantly worried his incompetence would end up injuring someone. What if he rushed a training, didn't notice destructive behavior before arming someone? That would be on his head.

It didn't help that large numbers of New Fae were in need of training with each drop. There were other training facilities set up, but none as seasoned as his. Before Aisling left, she asked him to consider going ahead of her to the drops and helping set up their training grounds pre-drop. It made sense, but the idea of piling more on his plate didn't appeal to him.

But like Mrs. Quinn had told him in his last session, he was developing better coping strategies. For the first time in his life, he felt in control of how things might turn out for him. There was power in being able to say no and doing it for the right reasons.

That's what he was telling himself as he parked his bike just inside the wards of their home. The smell of cooking meat wafted on the breeze, and Riordan's mouth watered. It may not be important to everyone, but knowing Brynach was planning a nice dinner for them made getting home on time a priority.

He called out his hello and then closed himself in the bathroom to shower. His long hair took effort to untangle after his helmetless ride. He handled it and then dressed in a pair of shorts. When he walked out, a glass of Fae wine rested on the end of the counter. He picked it up and looked out the back window to where Brynach stood by the grill. Like Riordan, his hair was down, a breeze stirring it.

His phone buzzed, and Riordan answered a video call.

"Hey, babe. Whatcha doing?" Aisling's voice was bright, her smile even brighter.

"Just getting home. The big guy is cooking," Riordan told her and flipped the camera around.

"Ugh, I'm so jealous. I had room service all alone in this big bed." She sprawled out across it and winked at him.

Riordan licked his lips and took a sip of his wine. "Don't be a tease, Ash. We miss you."

He walked outside and let Brynach say hello to his wife.

"How's it going? Everything running smoothly?" Brynach asked, giving her his full attention.

"Yeah, it's all going fine. Same old. No problems. Stop worrying about me," she complained.

Brynach growled. "A stoirin, did you just roll your eyes at me?"

Aisling sat up and shook her head. "No. I mean, I didn't mean to."

Riordan laughed. She was skilled at getting herself in trouble. Brynach took the phone from his hand.

"I have to go and make dinner for the partner that doesn't cause me heartburn. I love you, wife. Get home safe." He handed the phone back to Riordan.

"Love you," he told her and accepted the kiss she blew him before ending the call.

He settled against the railing, glass in hand. On the grill, steaks, corn, and potatoes were cooking. His mouth watered as he took a sip of his wine.

"The hard stuff tonight?" Riordan asked.

Brynach shrugged. "Figured we could eat, drink, and have that talk you've been avoiding."

Brynach was right. He'd been running from this for too long, and it would be easier to discuss when Aisling was gone. With a deep breath and then another large sip, he nodded. "Thank you for cooking."

"You know I like doing it," Brynach answered, brushing off his thanks.

"It's still nice having a big, buff house husband," Riordan joked.

Beside him, the larger Fae froze before turning to him and locking his intense gaze on him. His voice dipped, and he practically purred, "Is that what I am to you, Riordan?"

Oh, no, you don't. Riordan shook his head. "You have to wine and dine me before I start answering questions like that."

That elicited a laugh from Brynach, who turned back to the grill. "I thought that's what I was doing."

"You want to eat out here or inside?" Riordan asked. "I'll set the table."

"Out here would be nice," Brynach answered, and Riordan set his glass on the small table. Walking inside, he brought back two of everything, steak knives included, as well as the bottle of wine.

"A little liquid courage?"

Riordan shrugged. "You know it isn't the conversation that makes me nervous or doubt about our relationship, right? Sometimes, I'm not sure what I want. Or what I want changes so much I'm afraid I'll overcomplicate things."

Brynach nodded. "And you know that your answers can change. Relationships are fluid, Riordan. We have forever to let this grow, but we need to continue to talk to one another. Try and enjoy the meal; there's time for the rest."

Riordan refilled their wine glasses, sat with his hand buried in Valo's warm fur, and enjoyed the view while he waited for the food.

"*He loves you,*" Valo told him. "*Whatever you say, he's going to be okay with.*"

"*I don't want to disappoint him. I know what he wants, and I feel like a dick tease,*" Riordan admitted.

"*Look at him. Does he look unsatisfied or unhappy? Is either of you lacking sexual or intimate touch and affection? Has he even once expressed that voicing your comfort level upset or let him down?*" Valo called him on his bullshit.

Riordan was quiet because he knew his familiar was right. He didn't know what he was so afraid of. He loved Brynach. He'd never felt safer, happier, or more loved than he did within these walls with Aisling and Brynach. They provided everything he needed in partners. In a home. All he had to do was allow himself to take the love that was offered to him. Denying himself that connection felt like the dumbest thing he could do.

There wasn't another man who made him feel the way Brynach did. Riordan was positive there never would be again. He was scared. That much he could admit to himself. This was a big leap for him.

Brynach placed the plates on the table and turned to Riordan. His handsome face open, the pride in being here and providing for him was evident. The other man's chest was bare and sun-kissed. His long black hair caught the last rays of the sun. Maybe feline Fae eyes should have been disarming, but on Brynach's face, they looked right. And the way they were looking at him right now ...

Riordan stood. Brynach's expressive eyebrow rose as he watched him step closer. There was an excited flutter in his stomach that he leaned into instead of ignoring. Brynach didn't say anything; his eyes locked onto Riordan's as he stopped in front of him.

His hand rose and brushed Brynach's hair behind his shoulder. Riordan's newly rough fingers grazed the muscled skin of his neck. The other man's body shivered, and he wasn't sure if it was his new Fae hearing or his imagination, but Riordan swore he heard Brynach's heart hammering in his chest. Riordan wove his fingers into the silky weight of his hair and felt his partner relax under his touch. Riordan's lips lifted at the corners.

One slow blink of the larger Fae's eyes.

The wetting of lips.

The quiet gasp of breath between them.

Riordan's hand squeezed the back of Brynach's neck.

Still, he waited. Letting Riordan decide.

It was one of the easiest decisions he'd ever made. With the smallest of pulls, Brynach's head dipped down and met Riordan's rising mouth. Unlike other times they'd kissed, it was full of promises. It was an offering, and though the words would come later, Riordan knew Brynach understood exactly what this kiss was saying.

Being able to render the other man breathless as he opened for Riordan was a thrill. Hearing the gentle moan Brynach let slip as Riordan pulled him closer by his hair sent blood rushing to his cock. He knew he'd have to be the one to break the kiss, but he wasn't ready yet. Especially not when Brynach's control snapped, and he began touching Riordan.

A large hand slid up his chest to his neck until Brynach

cradled Riordan's face. His thumb swept across his jaw and, between kisses, slid over his wet lower lip. That small distance between them was too much. Riordan groaned before he nipped at the man's thumb and moved to recapture the kiss. Brynach allowed it.

Kissing Brynach was nothing like kissing Aisling. The stubble on his face, the sheer bulk of him, made it impossible to pretend it was anyone but another man. If that didn't prove it, the hard length of Brynach's cock against his stomach as he moved his hips toward his partner made it all the clearer. Riordan couldn't help the whimper that left his mouth as he moved against the other man.

How had he gone from hating Brynach to trusting him, to this? To the other man's tongue driving him wild as his hands held him tight. Right there in his arms, he knew he was safe to explore whatever he was feeling. This was right. He wanted more.

"Shhh," the Fae crooned softly. "I'm not going anywhere."

Riordan took a deep breath before he opened his eyes. Brynach was staring at him with such open wonder that he felt dizzy.

"I figured we'd enjoy the food more if we both knew the general direction of the conversation," Riordan whispered and took an unsteady step back from Brynach's large chest.

The larger Fae was looking at Riordan with such tenderness that a blush crept up his cheeks. Brynach's black hair shook with his head. "Let's eat before it gets cold."

Riordan sat across the table and dutifully picked up his knife and fork. He was too hungry to argue about eating, but something still gnawed at him. He wouldn't enjoy the food until he let it loose.

"I love you," Riordan blurted. "I am more than a little nervous, Bry, but I want whatever this is between us. I can't promise to know what I'm doing, and I'll probably fuck up a time or dozen, but I'm all in."

The silence terrified him. If Brynach didn't talk soon, he'd probably start to babble more nonsense.

"I'm glad, Riordan. Thank you for sharing that with me." The other man's eyes pinned him to his seat.

Riordan bit his lower lip where he could still taste Brynach and closed his eyes. He knew Brynach loved him, too. Why wasn't he saying it? There was no way he read this wrong.

"I want to make something clear to you. What I feel for you isn't rooted in physical attraction." His voice was low and clear.

Ouch. That fucking stung. He wasn't built like the other man, but he wasn't repulsive.

Brynach laughed. "Oh, don't worry. I want you. Badly. But that's not all this is for me. What I'm trying to say is I love you. All of you. I can be patient. We'll take this at your pace, okay? Whatever you're comfortable with. No pressure. I need you to understand that our relationship satisfies me as is. I don't need it to be physical. I want it, but I don't need it. I'll take as much as you're willing to give."

Riordan swallowed before answering. "Even if that takes time? Or never happens?"

"Even then." Brynach smirked. "But I don't think you can resist me much longer. Not the way you just kissed me."

"Cocky son of a bitch," Riordan muttered and resumed eating.

CHAPTER 8

Brynach

When Brynach shifted from sleep to waking, he couldn't stop the purr that vibrated in his chest. Riordan was snoring on his shoulder, a leg thrown over him. Being sought out, even subconsciously, made Brynach smile. Then again, after that mind-blowing kiss and their talk at dinner, he wasn't so sure it was subconscious anymore. Hearing that Riordan loved him and wanted a more physical relationship was more than he had given himself permission to hope for.

Brynach was so proud of his partner for coming to terms with what he wanted and allowing himself to have it. They'd agreed to speak to Aisling about the change in dynamic. They were both sure she saw the change and knew she wouldn't object to them having a romantic relationship without her, but communication was key. Personally, Brynach couldn't wait to explore what that looked like with Riordan. He'd have gladly started testing boundaries right then, but he had obligations in Faerie today. Plus, he was too distracted. Today, Aisling was bringing down the Veil in a small Ohio town and potentially restoring magic to his sister. Brynach knew the chance of success was slim, but he clung to hope all the same.

"What time is it?" Riordan's voice was raspy with sleep as he stretched against Brynach's side.

Fantastic. Now he had raging morning wood that would likely terrify the other man. He shifted to prevent it from being overly obvious.

"A little after seven," he answered.

"Are we going to talk about the elephant in the room?" Riordan rose on his elbow and looked down at Brynach, gaze traveling from his face down his body.

Brynach laughed. "It's rude to discuss people's uncontrollable erections."

Riordan winked at him. "If you say so. Today's a big day for you and the new school. I have to get to the training grounds, but if you need me or you get news from the drop, let me know."

Brynach nodded. "I hope I can convince Rainer to enroll Trixie. I think it will ease the worry of other parents. I'll keep you posted. Be safe today, okay?"

Riordan rolled his eyes and stood up, stretching his newly muscled body. "I'll be in a heavily warded dome of amped-up New Fae. I'll be fine. You're the one traveling to a court occupied by two feuding royal families. You be careful." At the look on Brynach's face, he held up his hands. "I'll be careful. Promise."

"Thank you," Brynach said. He stood and moved to the other man, pulling him close and kissing him. A light press of lips, the slight grip on his hips, and then they parted, both smiling.

They dressed, grabbed a handful of granola bars each, and left together to sift to their respective destinations. He was in no way looking forward to talking to his brother, but if enrolling his niece helped the Unseelie feel more comfortable with the school, he'd do it. Besides, Brynach knew Trixie would thrive among other children after being starved of peers for so long.

Inside the palace, he found his brother exactly where he expected, in his suite, surrounded by his yes-people. There had been a time when he'd trusted his eldest sibling and believed he'd make a good king. Now he was no longer a king, and he'd broken Brynach's trust when he used Aisling as a pawn.

"Brother, come for a visit?" Rainer greeted him.

"Send them away." It wasn't a request.

Rainer scowled at him, but with a nod, the room emptied. Only when they were gone did Rainer let the mask drop and his anger show.

"Don't for a second think you can come in here and start ordering me around. Those damn New Fae and Unaligned bastards are already taking too many liberties. I hear I have you to thank for our new house guests. Really, Brynach? The Seelie living under our roof? Have you lost your mind?" His eldest sibling was pissed.

"Things have changed, Rainer. You can either shift with it or get left behind. This isn't a seat of power," Brynach pointed out.

Rainer shook his head. "People need direction. They want to be led. They'll be back looking for stability, and I'll be here when they do. I won't abandon my flock."

"Do you even hear yourself?" Brynach asked. "This is your chance to put away all the bullshit and be a father to your daughter without the burden your father left for you. Take it."

His brother's face contorted in a way he'd never seen before. "I wanted this, Brynach. I waited patiently while our mother let your father lord over my people, our people. I didn't ask for this, but I can be good at it. And my daughter has a father. She's awarded safety and respect she'd never have without my position. Don't tell me how to raise her, and don't tell me to give up what's rightfully mine. I know we had different experiences growing up. I'm not ignorant of the fact that your allegiance to the Unseelie isn't as strong as mine. I had hoped that making you Regent would bring you a sense of pride in our Fae." Rainer's voice held barely contained annoyance.

Brynach fought to keep his voice low and even. "That's not what you did, Rainer. You used Aisling and me. You wed us in secret and used her show of strength to bolster the Unseelie. Then you declared me Regent when I couldn't turn you down. That's not how this shit works, brother."

The King rose. "You're the one who decided to strip Gabriel! Don't turn this around on me. There was no way to do that without Aisling harnessing some of your magic. I did you a favor. Did I use that favor to benefit me? Yes, but it didn't hurt anyone."

"Wrong." Brynach let his voice get loud now. "It hurt me. It hurt her. My wife mistrusts my family, but she trusted you! She fucking trusted you, and it made me so damn proud that she could. If you wanted to use her ability as a show of strength for Faerie, you should have come to us first. She'd have done anything for you."

"I didn't have time. I regret that I hurt her, but it was unavoidable," Rainer admitted.

"How long have you known what the Veil really was?" Brynach held his breath, waiting for the answer. He'd fallen in love with a witch and Ravdi, two people deeply hurt by the secret kept by Fae. He needed to believe his brother wouldn't have continued such a harmful cycle.

The look on Rainer's face told him all he needed to know.

"How long?" Brynach's voice was tight.

"Not until after I took the throne. There were certain documents that weren't available to me until afterward." Rainer had the grace to look guilty.

"And you didn't tell me? You didn't immediately make plans to bring it down?" Brynach felt the throbbing of blood in his temples as his anger rose.

"I did," Rainer said, taking a seat again. "I married you to Aisling. Twice. If your prophecy was correct, that should have brought down the Veil. But I couldn't very well scream it from the rooftops. I didn't want to be responsible for the downfall of the Fae, and I knew this would happen. Knew the Unaligned would use the opportunity exactly as they have. Knew it would increase mistrust between humans and Fae. I did what I thought was right with the information I had."

"You should have told me," Brynach insisted.

"Maybe. I have to live with the weight of my decisions, as does any ruler. But I promise you, brother, I did try." Rainer's eyes begged Brynach to believe him.

Brynach shook his head. "I officially reject your offer to be Regent. I didn't ask for it. I didn't want it. Consider this my resignation."

"Brother, don't," Rainer's voice was desperate.

"I can't. Not just because I don't want to but because doing so hurts the people I love and have sworn my life to. I won't add to their pain, Rainer. They mean more to me than a court that no longer exists." Brynach chose then to push. "If you want to do something positive for Fae, for your daughter, for your people, then I have a solution. Enroll her with the New Fae children. Show your support for it. Encourage people to protect our future generations."

Rainer was quiet for a moment. "Security?"

"The school will be staffed with New Fae, Fae, and located in the Seelie court. It will be secure," Brynach assured him.

His brother nodded. "Consider it done."

Brynach stood. "Thank you."

Before he could reach the door, Rainer called out to him. "Stop and see her before you go. She misses you. She's usually in the gardens."

The hallways were busier than he'd seen them in a long time, louder, too. The Seelie guards, staff, and royals were certainly creating a buzz. Of course, he wasn't lucky enough to make it through the gardens without incident.

"You sorry son of a bitch," King Kyteler called out as he passed an open room. The older Fae hurried out into the hall.

"How dare you? It wasn't bad enough to shred the very fabric of our world; you had to incite this madness, too?"

"You'll not hurt me insulting my mother," Brynach informed him. "As for your new housing situation, the new generation of Fae is more important than an outdated and power-hungry one."

He looked over the King's shoulder to where the Queen was standing. "I don't expect either of you to understand the importance of Fae youth. You certainly didn't for your own daughter. But I suggest you do nothing to stand in my way. You won't like the result."

"You don't scare us, Dark Prince," the Queen snapped.

Brynach cocked his head. "Don't I? Because at a mere suggestion from me, you were sent from your home. Imagine how quickly I could remove you from this one as well."

With that one last threat delivered, he turned and walked away from the displaced monarchs. He didn't stop again until he was under the bright sun. Brynach lifted his face a moment, then let the sound of children playing lead him toward the low maze of shrubs surrounding a fountain. His eyes went wide as he neared. The fish were all on one side of the fountain while the children played on the other. "Who is using water magic on the fish?"

An adorably plump girl of about eight raised her wide brown eyes to Brynach. "I am, sir. I swear it's not hurting them. I didn't want them getting squished!"

He smiled at her. "I'm not upset. That's impressive control. Are you New Fae?"

She shook her ringlets. "No, sir. Unaligned."

He nodded. "Well, thank you for protecting the fish. They've been here longer than I have, and some of them are friends of mine."

"They are?" she asked, eyes wide.

"He's playing with you," Trixie answered and threw her wet body against his. "Hi, Uncle Brynach."

He lifted her easily, and she squealed as he kissed her cheek. "Think I can steal you away for a few minutes?"

Trixie looked down at the kids, already back to playing, unbothered by her absence. "Sure."

He set her on the ground and took her hand. "I missed you, Bug."

"Missed you, too. And Aunt Ash and Uncle Riordan. Breena's not as much fun as you," she stated simply.

Brynach's heart clenched at her calling Riordan her uncle. It was the first he'd heard it, and he loved that she felt it was the right thing to call him.

"How has it been with all the new people in the castle? You know I can't have an unhappy Trixie on my hands," he reminded her.

"Do you know the kinds of sneaking around I get away with now? It's been awesome!" She skipped beside him.

He laughed. Of course, she'd use the siege of a castle to her own benefit. "If you ever need anything, you can ask me. Just tell someone, and they'll sift you straight to me or deliver a message."

She rolled her eyes, and it was the cutest thing ever. "Uncle Bry, we both know all I need to do is walk to the stables, and Kongur will let you know. Can I go play again?"

"Of course," he answered, and she turned and ran back to the fountain. Before he could leave the court, he reached out to his familiar.

"*Want to go for a ride to the Seelie? Stretch those old legs?*" he asked.

"*Oh, now you have time for me?*" he answered. "*Yeah. Okay.*"

Brynach wasn't surprised by Kongur's surly mood but knew he wouldn't say no. As he walked toward the stables, he pulled out his phone and sent Aisling a message, knowing she wouldn't see it until later. Brynach was careful about his wording, so she knew he was thinking of her and not just if Breena was Fae again.

Missing the hell out of you.
Rough days are always
better when I have you to
come home to. Love you.
Hurry back to us, wife.

He slid the phone back into his pocket so he'd feel it vibrate if she answered, and he entered the stables.

"Your partners keep their familiars close. Would it kill you to build a stable for me closer to your home?" Kongur complained.

Brynach climbed onto the sizeable draft horse, and they exited the building. He leaned his head back and let the sun shine orange through his lids. Then the horse took off, and he clamped down with his thighs and enjoyed the ride.

"And make you leave your lush accommodations? You don't want to slum it over there. You need a team to look after you, your highness," Brynach teased.

"You're right, but you could visit more."

"I'm doing the best I can, Kongur. You know that, right?" he asked. *"Besides, I've been thinking lately that you'd be a great ambassador for the familiar program we are launching. You and me, educating the masses. What do you think?"*

"I think you've gone mad," The horse huffed under him as he sped through the woods. *"I guess it's a good thing you don't need me as much anymore. I always was your escape from a life you hated."*

"Not just that, friend," he promised, although it wasn't entirely untrue.

"It's alright, Brynach. I never expected you to need me as much as you did as a kid. I didn't want you to. Frankly, the peace has been nice."

It was a lie, but it did ease Brynach's guilt a bit.

"Close your eyes, Brynach. Let yourself just breathe for a bit," his familiar suggested.

Brynach lowered his chest to the horse's neck, hugging him tight like he did as a kid, and let the wind knot his hair. He couldn't remember the time he'd felt this relaxed, this free.

Before long, Kongur was pulling up at the Seelie gates. Brynach prepared to jump off and offer his hand for the blood-letting before remembering he didn't need to. That would have to be reinstated once kids were housed here. As it was, he stayed atop his familiar and rode into the Seelie stables.

"Aren't you majestic?" a silver-haired Fae said by way of greeting as Brynach dismounted.

"Why, thank you." He gave them a winning smile.

The Fae waved a hand at him and shook their long hair. "I was talking about your familiar."

Kongur's laughter rang in Brynach's head. Well, that was one way to humble a guy. Brynach held out his hand and introduced himself.

"Semele. Well met. Anyone who earned the trust of a spirit like this is someone I'm happy to meet." They stroked Kongur's side, and his familiar reveled in the attention.

Before they could turn away, Brynach called out to them. "Are you well versed in animal husbandry?"

They huffed a laugh. "You could say that."

"How do you feel about children?" Brynach asked.

The Fae cocked a hip and tilted their head at him. "That's an odd question to ask a stranger. It was my understanding you were spoken for."

Brynach backed up. "Oh, gosh, no. I mean, no offense, but what I meant was I'm building staff for a school here at the court, teaching the New Fae youth. They need someone to guide them in caring for their familiars. Is that something that would interest you?"

They nodded. "I see. Well, I'm not an expert on all animals, but I'm well-versed in most. I'll not stand by and let any get mistreated, so if I can be a help, then yes."

He smiled at them. "Thank you, Semele."

Without saying anything else, they led Kongur away, and Brynach walked toward the meeting with one more instructor secured. Alex and Aisling's mother were waiting for him in the hallway outside the room. Alex greeted him with a hug, and Lydia followed suit.

"Where's Aindrea?" Brynach asked, looking around the hallway.

"Joeigh wasn't feeling fantastic, so she stayed behind. I have all her notes," Alex assured him.

His friend looked tired. "You sleeping okay? You look a little stressed."

"Gee, thanks," Alex smiled, but it didn't light up his face the way it usually did. "There's just a lot on my mind. I want to make sure this goes according to plan."

"It will. We'll see to it," he promised.

Mrs. Quinn smiled and shook her head. "It's normal to worry, but it's important to note that things will go wrong, and that's okay. Plans will change, shift, and grow. You'll adapt."

Alex stiffened. "If we lay the groundwork, I see no reason things won't play out the way we want."

Brynach laughed. "Alex, you have children. You know things change. When did you become stuck in your ways?"

His friend shrugged. "The new world is unstable. How we proceed may be a sign of how the world, in general, proceeds. We have to get it right."

He patted Alex's shoulder. "And we will. Don't let it keep you up at night. We're going to be okay."

Before the other man could argue, Mrs. Quinn clapped her hands. "We ready to do this?"

With a nod, the three of them walked into the office and sat down with Theo, Marina, the school board representative, and a Fae that Brynach recognized as one of the former castle guards. After introductions, Brynach got down to specifics.

"I know this is a large undertaking, but we can all agree that this is the correct step for the children and for the world we are creating for ourselves. While the conversion and structuring of something this large will take time, I believe that with a collaborative attitude, we can have it running within three months."

As voices called out, Brynach held up a hand. "Mrs. Lauder, you have extensive knowledge about curriculum and the academic needs of children. You have resources within your district that could be diverted to our school; is that correct?"

The human woman nodded. "We do. And we also have an abundance of New Fae teachers who are excited about the idea of starting fresh without prejudice from some more vocal parents on the board. I'm sorry to not see your wife here," she addressed Alex. "However, I have a food services expert, a custodial expert, experienced teaching staff, and resources like desks, textbooks, and laptops that we can arrange for your use."

"At what cost?" Theo asked, clearly skeptical of the offer.

Mrs. Lauder shook her head. "You misunderstand. It is a gift. We have a budget for our schools, and with the New Fae children leaving, our need for resources will decrease by more than half. It's a transfer of resources, not a sale."

Marina's eyes went wide. "That's generous of you."

The other woman smiled. "It's the right thing to do. Now, I can't speak to whether or not I can fully staff or provide for the classrooms, but we'll certainly do what we can."

"That's more than enough, thank you," Alex said.

Aisling's mother spoke next. "The children are experiencing changes, transitions, and an upheaval to their lives unlike any we have seen before. It's a lot to process for the adults, and for a child's developing mind and worldview, it's even harder. My goal is to have a counselor available for every fifty children. Not all will want to use the services, but I think some group sessions and discussions are necessary for the mental and emotional well-being of the kids."

Around the table, nobody argued her opinion, and she sat

back in her chair with a deep breath. She'd clearly expected pushback.

"I spoke to a Fae named Semele in the stables just now. They agreed to help with the husbandry of familiars. I'm sure we can staff for special subjects like magic use and sifting from within the Fae community, as well," Brynach added.

Alex spoke next. "And my wife and I are dedicated to the physical well-being of the children who stay here. I'm happy to oversee the conversion of the castle into something suitable for the kids, and my wife is excited to work with the dormitory staff to ensure a homey atmosphere for the children. A Fae nurse will also be employed on a live-in basis for the health and safety of all children."

It was a lot of information, but it was all positive. There was just one topic that had yet to be discussed, and that was money. The funding was the hardest part, but it wasn't impossible.

"While we would love to treat this as a public school, that means government money, and we may not have time for that. I suggest that we ask for donations and then use the royal coffers to fund the rest. Both the Seelie and Unseelie vaults have money we can use to get the school off the ground while we apply for state funding. We're in new territory here, so we'll have to figure it out as we go." Brynach knew it wasn't ideal, but it could work.

"And you plan on getting that money how?" Theo asked.

"My brother is enrolling my niece. He'll donate to the school. Following his lead, we hope others do, too. As for the royal vaults, well, it seems those are in your control now. Am I correct?" Brynach raised a brow.

Marina shook her head as she answered. "Technically, yes. Do we want to make enemies of anyone by pillaging them? Not particularly."

"It's for Fae. For the benefit of Faerie. If ever there was a reason to use money from the Fae courts, this is it," Alex pointed out.

Around the table, heads nodded.

"Looks like we have ourselves a school," Marina confirmed.

CHAPTER 9

Aisling

She checked her phone one last time and saw the message from Brynach. Aisling read between the lines and understood he wasn't just missing her. His concern for his sister was valid, and he'd done nothing to make her feel responsible for the outcome of this drop, but she felt it all the same. He'd eventually lose Breena. Maybe not today or tomorrow, but he would. Before being gifted a lifetime with Riordan, she'd also faced losing someone she loved. Hell, she still was. Lettie would grow old. Sean would age alongside her.

Aisling closed her eyes and took a centering breath, letting the magic around her ground her. She'd feel better outside, and even more so when she connected with the magic of the Veil. It was hard to describe how she felt when she was wrapped up in all that power, and she'd never tell anyone anyway. But being a part of a magic that old felt like touching something sacred.

Did it matter that she was destroying it? No. Holding it for a moment before releasing it to those who were owed it was an honor. She knew people didn't understand or feared it, but if only they could feel it.

The idea that witches and Ravdi were fleeing drop zones made sense to her, though. Not everyone wanted immortality and Fae magic. Some people feared change too much to accept the gifts they were offered. For people like Breena, who desperately wanted that gift, or Riordan's parents, who would still be alive if they'd had it, it felt more than a little unfair.

"Are you ready, Ms. Quinn?"

She turned and offered the officer a smile before taking one last look at her phone and nodding. "Yup."

Aisling plastered on her public-relations smile and exited her holding room. Brielle met her in the hallway, her white-blonde head not even meeting Aisling's shoulder. She smiled at her friend and then got serious.

"There's a lot of people here. Nothing we haven't seen before and nothing you can't handle. But the guys would have my head if I didn't tell you to be careful. My team has scanned the neighboring buildings, the usual measures. The threats are still there, though, Ash. I need you to be careful."

Aisling continued to walk out into the open sun. "You've always got my back, I know that. This isn't my first rodeo. We've got this."

The local police were lined up and as ready as possible for the event. Seeing something on the news and experiencing it first-hand were not the same thing. Large numbers of Ravdi and witches had gathered, waiting for the drop and their magic to find them. Some cried, and a lot held one another, savoring the last moments of their bond. It was important for the healing and grieving process.

The strongest of the local witches approached her and shook her hand. He was an older gentleman, and Aisling gave him a fast rundown of the procedure, even though he'd likely heard it a dozen times. She had one last thing to do.

Breena's eyes, so like Brynach's that it hurt to see them filled with such fear, met hers.

"I'm going to warn you one last time. Being in the Veil

when it drops may not have the results you want. In fact, I'm not sure that it won't hurt you further." Aisling had to at least try to keep her safe. She didn't have a good feeling about this.

Breena stared at the gathering of witches and Ravdi. "It can't be worse than this."

Aisling shook her head. "You're still alive. Being human is favorable to being dead."

She could see the anger in the woman's eyes. "You have no idea what you're talking about. I'm over two hundred years old, and now I can feel time, Aisling. Do you have any idea what it's like to feel this body dying each day? To be viscerally aware of each breath and passing second?"

Aisling's mouth opened and closed.

"I didn't think so," Breena cursed. "I can fucking feel it, and it's terrifying."

Jashana moved toward her, a slight shifting of her body. Breena turned on her. "Don't! Don't touch me." She asked Aisling, "Where do I go?"

Aisling frowned before pointing. "This way."

Together they walked toward the group of magic workers at a Veil invisible to Breena for the first time in her life. "I don't think you should be in the Veil when it comes down. Being near it should be enough. Your father wasn't in it when it dropped, and nothing good happened when you were," Aisling suggested.

"Fine. Whatever. If this doesn't work, we can try again with me in the Veil." Breena gestured around her. "This doesn't seem like that many bonded pairs."

Aisling looked around the park. "It's enough. With each drop, the Veil gets a little weaker. I'm more than capable of handling this. I'll check on you after the drop."

Before she was out of earshot, she heard Breena whisper to Jashana that she was scared. She saw the Fae warrior take Breena's hand and twine their fingers, pulling her close.

Aisling called instructions to the witches, who moved forward while the Ravdi stayed in place. Slowly, she gathered the magic of the Veil and instructed the witches and Ravdi to do the same. As the magic flooded them, a few of the witches in the line fell, their Ravdi moving forward to assist them. Aisling stood and continued to call out to them.

"Don't stop. Continue to focus your intention," she yelled into a strange wind.

Two officers stepped up to her side and called magic to them. They were New Fae. Interesting. She spared them a look, but they were concentrating on the Veil. One cast their eyes to the side.

"It's our duty to serve and protect. That's what we're doing." They nodded, and Aisling gave them a small smile.

Even weakened by other sections of the Veil falling, this still wasn't easy. Aisling called to the wild magic, promising that her intention was to heal, not harm. It swirled and flowed toward her, and she drew it into herself, feeling it fill her. She was a part of the Universe, a vessel for a higher power, and also fragile. The wild magic sank into every crevice and empty spot in her body. She'd come to grips with her natural urge to keep it for her own. But with each drop, it got easier to relinquish the power.

When the Veil was at its weakest, she thrust the magic from her body and made room to pull more. There was a moment, a single moment, where they all stood on the edge of something huge, and then it happened. The balloon popped, and magic flooded the area. Around her, some fell, others gasped and clutched at their chests, and some simply stood crying.

As soon as she felt in control of her body, Aisling sifted to Breena. Jashana had Brynach's sister's face in her hands, searching her eyes.

"How do you feel?" the warrior asked with tears in her eyes.

Breena closed her eyes, and the two Fae waited and hoped.

Tears streamed out of the raven-haired woman's closed eyes. Breena wipes at her tears, then turned her back to them.

Aisling wasn't sure if they were tears of joy and relief or sorrow. She hoped for both Breena's and her husband's sakes that it was the former.

"Why didn't it work?" Breena rasped.

Aisling's hand rested on her shoulder. "If I had to guess, it's because there will never be a dispersing of magic quite as powerful as that first chunk of the Veil. You were hit with the largest blast of magic the world has seen since the Veil went up," her voice was soft.

Someone called Aisling's name, and she knew she couldn't ignore them. The cameras were pointed at her. She needed to be public-relations Aisling right now.

"Breena," she began.

"Go," she told Aisling. Then she turned to Jashana. "Take me home." The Fae sifted them away. With a heavy heart and a big sigh, she straightened her back and walked back into the crowd.

It was another hour before she was able to go inside and sit down. She dropped her head in her hands and wished she weren't alone. She'd sent Brielle to assess the local training ground after the crowd dispersed. In the quiet moments like this one, at night and emotionally spent, she missed the guys the most.

She reached for her phone on the coffee table and saw messages from each of them. Logically, she knew they missed her, too. But Aisling couldn't stop the surge of jealousy that they were together, and she was the odd man out when she traveled. They'd spoiled her, making her the focus of their attention, and she was struggling a little to share it. More than ever, she loved Riordan for accepting her relationship with Brynach. It wasn't easy sharing people you loved but seeing them loved doubly was worth it.

> Can't wait to get home to you.
> Love you. Be back soon.

We're waiting.

Brynach's response was immediate and warmed her heart. She knew he must be dying to ask about Breena, but she couldn't tell him through text. Damn it. She should have called him already. What if Breena needed him right now?

"A stoirin?" he answered on the second ring.

"I know you want to ask, and you won't. Bry, it didn't work. I should have told you sooner. She might need you. Jashana took her back to the palace." She heard the pained sound he made, and it broke her heart. "I'm so sorry. I really tried."

"Of course you did. It's okay. I'll check on her," Brynach reassured her.

"I'll be home tomorrow morning. Are you sure you want to move forward with the party?" she asked. Riordan would understand if they canceled his birthday celebration.

"Absolutely. Don't worry, I've got it handled here," he assured her before hanging up.

Aisling sent Riordan a text to let him know how the drop went so he'd be prepared when he got home. She gathered her bag and walked from the building, ready to go to the hotel, shower, and fall into bed. Her flight was early the next morning. Brynach absolutely refused sifts of this distance, and honestly, Aisling was too afraid to try them.

A reporter standing with a newly minted New Fae called her over when they saw her. Aisling went with a smile she didn't feel plastered on her face.

"Here's the woman of the hour. You successfully brought down the eleventh section of the Veil today. How do you feel?" she asked Aisling.

"I think the better question is, how are the New Fae feeling? This is a big day for them," Aisling diverted. "I'm just doing my job and helping connect those who deserve it with the magic that's been kept from them."

The New Fae beside her beamed. "I feel amazing," he said.

"As a witch, I was able to use magic, but to feel it all around me, to sense it in the very ground I stand on, it's beautiful. I wouldn't have known this without Aisling's help. We owe her a lot. All of the New Fae do."

She shook her head. "You did this for yourself. You and all the other bonded pairs and solitary witches and Ravdi who helped today. The magic returned to you today was yours already."

"And what do you have to say to those who believe what you're doing here isn't natural? Do you have a message for the groups who believe what you're doing will be the downfall of our civilization?" the reporter asked.

Aisling didn't get defensive. She'd learned the difference between those who asked questions like this maliciously and those who asked to give her a platform to defend herself and further her cause.

"Change is scary. I can respect the desire to keep things continuing on the path of least resistance. But I believe that righting wrongs, correcting imbalance, and restoring the world to its intended state are more important than the comfort of people who profit off the oppressed. These New Fae didn't ask for their magic to be kept from them. If that scares humans, that's really too bad. Now that the New Fae understand fully what their potential is, they deserve to see it actualized. With or without me, the Veil will continue to fall. I may have been the catalyst, but there are more than enough people to take up the call. It's within the right and power of each witch and Ravdi to do exactly what we did here today."

Cathy was going to have a field day with that sound bite. She wanted Aisling to be the face of the New World, as they coined it. But the truth was, Aisling wasn't necessary at the drops. She came because it gave people the impression that the drops were controlled by "experts." She was just a showpiece.

"How are you responding to the threats against your life? I don't see either of your partners here today. Don't they worry?"

The reporter was starting to veer to areas Aisling didn't like.

"Scared people make rash and illogical decisions. It's my hope that those people will educate themselves, talk to their New Fae neighbors. I have faith in the goodness of people. I won't let intimidation tactics influence my decisions. As for my partners, they know I'm capable of keeping myself safe and are very supportive of me." Aisling smiled. The media loved Brynach and Riordan. She winked and then sifted to her hotel. She was sure that would make for a fantastic teaser for the eleven o'clock news.

S he looked ridiculous trying to shove the massive bundle into her car. Aisling was pretty sure it wasn't legal to drive with this many balloons obstructing her view. But she wasn't about to risk sifting with enough helium to lift her body.

There was a cake on the front seat and a batch of Dawn's moistest brownies on the floor of her passenger side. Brynach was handling the rest, whatever that meant. She'd left a lot up to him while she was at the drop and felt bad about it. But she was home now and determined to make the most of Riordan's birthday.

It was his first without Maggie, his first since becoming a Fae, and she wanted to celebrate with him. Brynach thought it was silly to keep track of birthdays as a Fae, but they hadn't been immortal long enough to not count the years passing. Perhaps one day they would, and she'd look forward to that day. An eternity with the two men she loved sounded perfect.

Her phone rang, and she scrambled to shove the last of the balloons inside the car. Breathlessly, she answered the phone and slid into the driver's seat.

"Are you okay?" Lettie asked. "You sound like one of your guys just gave you a workout."

Lettie's voice came through the receiver. She'd missed that teasing tone so much. Their sleepover was still on the horizon, and Aisling couldn't wait.

"I wish. It was just latex," Aisling answered.

"Sex toys this early in the day. Get it," her best friend joked.

"Haha. Balloons for Riordan's birthday," Aisling clarified. "You're still coming, right?"

"Sean's picking me up around five," Lettie confirmed. "I'm still too nervous to drive very far. The condo, right?"

"Yeah. Brynach's worried that too many people in and out of the wards may weaken them. It's a lot easier to secure the condo. Plus, the house is a mess, and some stuff just can't be put away that easily," Aisling explained.

"You have a sex dungeon there, don't you?" Lettie squealed. "Please tell me! It's a swing, isn't it? A giant sex swing and a wall of beautiful floggers. Oh god, leave me to my imagination."

Aisling laughed, "It's not quite that scandalous."

"You'll never convince me you don't have a St. Andrew's cross set up in your living room," Lettie laughed.

"You've been to the house, Lettie. You know that's not true," Aisling reminded her.

Their teasing was as natural as breathing, but something was missing, a third voice that would have been adding to the joking joyfully.

"I know, Ash. I feel it, too. Enjoying life doesn't mean forgetting him," Lettie reminded her. "I'll see you later."

Aisling hung up and focused on driving. Roads that had once run straight now curved around areas where Faerie overlapped. Distances that had been walkable were now probably best suited for driving. When she finally pulled into her parking spot, she'd missed two texts from Brynach and one from Sydney. She shot her sister-in-law the address for the condo for the third time and then texted Brynach that she was there so he could help her bring everything up.

"Damn it, Bry!" she yelped when he sifted in front of her.

He laughed and leaned down to kiss her. There was no better way to be welcomed home. "I'll wrangle the Goddess-forsaken balloons. Can you get the cake, brownies, and case of water from the front seat?"

"You know I can," he answered and moved around the car. "How was your trip?"

"Exciting. Sad. Exhausting." She wrapped the string for the balloons around her wrist tightly, locked the car, and followed her husband up the steps.

Once they were inside, Brynach put everything down and untangled the balloons from Aisling's hand. They bounced on the ceiling when he released them, but Aisling was looking at Brynach, nowhere else.

"I'm sorry I wasn't with you. Riordan is, too. I know it had to be hard for you." He brought her close and held her.

"Harder on Breena. How is she?" Aisling asked.

"Not great. She's stubborn. She's looking for areas of high magical concentration so she can attend those drops. I don't think she can give up on it yet." Brynach sounded so sad. "But enough of that. Tonight, we celebrate Riordan. Tomorrow we can relax and be together. We both took off." He took her face in his hands, and she lost herself in those deep citrine eyes.

"A whole day with nothing to do?" Aisling sighed. "I don't remember what that feels like."

Brynach kissed the top of her head. "We'll remind you."

The door opened behind them, and Riordan walked in with two cases of beer stacked in his arms. He'd gotten so strong. Once upon a time, he'd have cursed Brynach for being brawny enough to do that, and now his corded muscles rivaled Brynach's.

"Snuggling without me?" He winked and set down the beer before moving to them. Riordan turned her head and kissed her before saying hello to Brynach. "Have you told her yet?"

"About our day off tomorrow?" Aisling grinned. "I've heard."

Riordan smirked. "Yeah, sure. That's what I meant." He

walked away. "I have to clean up before everyone gets here."

"Hey! Wait," Aisling called after him, but he didn't turn, just laughed as he walked down the hall to the master bedroom. She felt Brynach's chest vibrating with laughter. "What the hell does that mean?"

Brynach disengaged. "Nope, it's a surprise. That guy has a big mouth."

Aisling shrugged. "I like his mouth." Her snark earned her a smack on the ass. "Just saying. Now, can you pull those balloons back down?"

"After I get my kiss." His lips swept over hers, and she opened for him. His smell surrounded her, and some of the tension left her shoulders.

Brynach broke the kiss and easily reached up to hand her the balloons. Aisling began creating an archway above the doors to the patio. A warm breeze blew in, airing out the unused space. Rin flew in and settled on her shoulder, nipping at her ear.

"Nope. It's a familiar free zone. I'm not housing a damn zoo along with all the people." She waved him away.

"*You know, I liked it better when I didn't have to talk to you all the time,*" Rin teased. "*It's fine. We have our own things to do.*"

"*Harassing sprites isn't a thing,*" Aisling scolded.

"*For your information, we're having a little meeting with the New Fae familiars. You damn Fae aren't the only ones adjusting. These poor animals aren't used to whiny Fae in their minds,*" Phlyren admonished her.

"*Sorry, friend. I know you've been doing a lot of work. Thank you for taking the time to help them.*"

"*I'm not doing it for you.*" He poked at her shoulder. "*I'm doing it for them. Have fun.*"

"He was in a hurry," Brynach commented as he filled a metal tub with ice and beer. Aisling moved to the kitchen and put the cake and brownies on platters. Sean and Lettie were getting the pizza on their way.

"He had to tell me off and make me feel like shit." Aisling shrugged. "I can't get anything right anymore."

"You put too much pressure on yourself." Brynach rubbed her shoulders, and Aisling groaned. "Goddess, you're tight."

"I am doing everything, but nothing well, and I hate it." She shook her shoulders out. "Enough of the pity party. They'll be here soon, and I have to change. You have this?"

Brynach nodded, his long hair swinging in her face. She laughed and walked back to her room, where Riordan was getting dressed. He took her breath away.

"I missed that ass," she murmured, and her lover turned with a smile.

"Damn right you did. Come here." He hooked a finger, and she went to him eagerly. When he kissed her, he claimed her. His mouth was hot on hers, his chest wet under her hands, and his hair dripping down his back.

"You're beautiful." Looking into his face, she felt the tears start. "I love you more than you can possibly know."

"Hey." He kissed her tears. "Shhh. It's okay."

"I know." She buried her face against his neck and let his strong hands on her back soothe her. "It's just that sometimes it hits me all at once. The fact that I get to come home to you. To Brynach. To the life we've built for ourselves, and it over-whelms me."

Riordan pulled her tighter into his firm chest. "We're solid, Ash. Eventually, you are going to have to accept that life really is this amazing. At least within our walls."

She laughed. "Let it burn down around us, huh?"

"If that's what has to happen, yes," he assured her. "I'm going to get dressed, you're going to change, and then we're going to have fun. Sound good?"

That night, they tested the limits of the condo with the number of people they invited. Riordan had wanted everyone there, and they'd all come. Isaac, Sydney, Lettie, Sean, Cait,

Kareem, Russell, and Breena, with Jashana, who had surprised everyone by bringing Corinna, were all there. There were a few other New Fae that Aisling didn't recognize, who popped in throughout the night.

It took longer than she'd have liked to calm Brynach down after Brielle had been a no-show. She was supposed to work security around the condo but had never made it. He'd called in old Unseelie guards to do the job instead.

"I'm sure she just got held up at the training grounds," she told him when he continued to text her friend. "Relax. She'll be here."

She understood he was nervous about Dexter potentially deciding to target them. They'd been keeping an eye on the disgraced cop since he posted bail, but Dexter was lying low. Lettie and the Hive were watching for any visions about him. Aisling hated that it had come to that, but she was happy to have their help.

Liam had hugged her tight while Amber stood off to his side. "Thanks for doing this for Rory. He's lucky to have you."

"Of course," Aisling answered. "How are things?"

Riordan's brother tilted his head. "With work? With life? With magic? Pick your poison."

"With you. How are you? The rest doesn't really matter, does it?" she clarified.

Liam and Amber exchanged a look before she answered. "We're okay. Just trying to figure out where we belong."

"You're not the only ones. There's been a lot of change for everyone." Aisling lifted her glass to her lips and took a large sip. Liam and Amber mirrored her and then excused themselves to go talk to some other people.

Then Cait was there, an arm around Aisling's shoulders. "This is what I needed! Thank you for inviting us."

Aisling hugged her closely, and they moved toward Lettie. With music loud and Fae wine singing through her blood, she danced in the living room with her friends. She spun with her hands above her head and body twisting with Lettie laughing beside her. The romper she was wearing was strapless, and the shorts were barely there. The looks Riordan and Brynach were giving her made her belly flutter and heat gather. They looked absolutely rabid for her. She loved it.

"Remember when I made you dance with me to get Elijah's attention? That feels like ages ago." Lettie smiled and shook her head.

"It was." Aisling laughed. "A whole other life ago."

"Where are Tara and Kara?" Lettie asked. "I miss them."

"They're still figuring out their comfort level with Fae. They weren't ready for this. But they're coming to the girl's night." Aisling understood, but it was hard missing so many of her friends right now.

"Your men look like they want to eat you instead of the cake." Any other time Lettie's voice would have gotten lost in the music, but surrounded by Fae, Aisling knew everyone had heard.

She grinned. "Isn't it great? I'll let you in on a secret; they're probably going to."

Lettie grasped non-existent pearls. "What will the people say?"

Aisling's head fell back as she laughed. Their conversation was cut short when Riordan called across the condo.

"Get your sweet ass over here so we can cut this cake."

With a shake of her head, she went to stand by the guys, and then everyone sang happy birthday to her partner. Looking out at the group of friends, Fae and humans alike, she realized how lucky she was. There was zero chance these people would be in the same room if not for her partner. The eclectic mix was refreshing. This is what she'd created. A world where people coming together looked like this.

Royal Fae with wings and purple skin or with catlike eyes, New Fae just learning their new bodies, and humans she'd known and loved her whole life. The diversity made her smile.

This is how it should be. Joy-filled and understanding.

After the singing, Aisling cut and handed out the cake with the help of a less-surly-than-normal Breena while Riordan opened some gifts.

Cait and Kareem had bought him a stunning art piece from a local gallery they'd visited. It was abstract and grungy and would look amazing in the cabin. Russell looked on sheepishly when Isaac presented Riordan with a beautiful set of leather guards for his forearms.

"I didn't know we were bringing gifts," he mumbled to Aisling.

She gave him a side hug. "We weren't. It's fine. We're glad you're here."

Lettie and Sean gifted Riordan a second amp so he didn't have to travel back and forth with his when he played. And Brynach and Aisling would wait and give him theirs later, in private. It was after one o'clock in the morning by the time the last guest left. Aisling was exhausted and so thankful when Brynach pulled her into his arms and sifted her back to the cabin.

By the time she washed her face and brushed her teeth, Riordan was already lounging on the bed. "I miss being casually tipsy," he whined.

Aisling huffed. "Now you know how hard I had to work that first party to feel anything but sober."

"You really went hard. I'm not sure I could feel a buzz if I drank a whole keg."

Brynach came toward them, naked, a towel drying his hair. "Please don't try. You may be immortal now, but your body won't thank you for that."

Aisling nearly choked on the water she'd been drinking. "Have I been gone that long? You just free ball through the house now?"

Riordan laughed, "Babe, it's nothing we haven't seen before. Are you uncomfortable?"

"No. Hell no," she babbled, and Brynach winked at her.

"Then I see no problem," Riordan said. "That's part of what we wanted to talk to you about."

"Part of? How much is there to talk about?" she wondered.

The two men shared a look. If she wasn't completely off-base, both of them had extra color in their cheeks as the two men looked at one another and then at her. Riordan bit his lower lip. Aisling wanted to lean forward and pull it from between his teeth with her own. Instead, she waited for whatever it was they had to share.

"Brynach and I have decided to pursue a relationship. One that will exist when we're all together, but also separate, like you have with each of us." Riordan's voice was steady as he looked at her.

She grinned, her heart so absolutely full. "Really?"

If they were messing with her, she was going to be crushed. She looked to Brynach, who, to her surprise, wasn't looking at her. Instead, his eyes were locked on Riordan. Okay, that might take some getting used to, but she'd learn. When she looked at Riordan, he was staring at her, concern etched on his face.

"Why are you making that face? You can't actually believe this would upset me." A laugh bubbled from her throat, and she threw herself at Riordan. "I am so happy."

She looked to Brynach, whose mouth tilted into a smirk. Beside her, Riordan said, "I'm glad because I kinda love the guy."

"Well, of course you do. About time you admitted it was more than platonic love that bound the two of you. This is fantastic." Aisling couldn't wipe the smile from her face. "So, just no-holds nakedness now. Noted."

Brynach lowered the towel he'd been using and hung it on the loft railing. By the time she ripped her eyes away from her husband's abs and looked at Riordan, he'd shed his shorts. Both men stared her down, and heat flooded her body. Aisling hurried to tug her romper down her body. If the guys wanted to be naked, she was all in.

Brynach climbed into bed, leaving Aisling standing.

"What's the matter?" Brynach asked, the concern clear in his voice.

The two of them looked absolutely stunning, and, as always, she was drawn to them. But she couldn't drum up the energy for more tonight. That had never induced dread, but it did now. If she turned them away, would they turn to one another instead? Would they shut her out?

"Aisling, talk to us. Are you okay?" Riordan asked.

"It's just that I'm exhausted. I'm sorry; it's been a long couple of days. Is that okay?" Her fingers found her bracelet and worried over the charms while she waited. They loved her, she knew that, but she'd been away, and usually, they reconnected physically.

Riordan took a deep breath before answering, "You don't need to apologize or explain yourself. I will never want anything inside this bedroom or out of it that you're not comfortable with. It's more than enough being close to you." He turned to Brynach. "Both of you. Now get over here before I have Bry turn your ass red for even thinking that would upset us."

Aisling was once more struck by how lucky she was. It was nothing more than a good partner would have said, but it soothed a worried part of her she hadn't realized needed reassurance. She tried to hide the choked sob by coughing. Neither of them bought it. Their arms shot out toward her, both men moving fast and pulling her onto the bed.

"I didn't mean to make you cry." Riordan calmed her with his words while Brynach brushed her hair with his fingers.

A thought came to Aisling, fully formed and vibrant. Before she could think about it too much, she opened her mouth and let the words spill out.

"Marry me, Riordan."

CHAPTER 10

Riordan

He'd heard her wrong. He must have.

"Say something," Aisling begged.

He sat stunned with her in his arms. "I, uh, I wasn't sure if you were being serious."

Aisling stared at him and took a deep breath. He didn't know what was about to fall from those beautiful lips, but he really hoped it helped make sense of things.

"I know I'm married already. Don't look at me like I'm crazy. Our Ravdi and witch bond, our recognized bond, doesn't exist anymore, and it feels wrong. Something has felt off lately, and I think that's part of it. I know I gave you the ring." She took his hand and toyed with it. "But I want something more official."

"Right," Riordan drew out. "But like you said, you're married already. I thought us being openly polyamorous was a lot to ask our loved ones to accept. Multiple husbands, that's a lot to swallow."

"Do you care? I don't. If our loved ones don't accept our relationship, that's their problem." Her cheeks were flushed. He could see her shields going up. He wasn't saying this right.

He hadn't meant to put her on the defensive.

"Ash, there is nothing I'd love more than to be your husband. I love you. I want to tie myself to you in any and every way. I'm just not sure this is possible," he pleaded with her to see his side of things.

Brynach coughed, and they turned to look at him. "Technically speaking, Aisling isn't married."

Riordan wasn't following. "Brynach, I may not be the smartest in this bed, but I'm pretty sure I remember an entire ceremony and joining of courts, yadda yadda. There are crowns in our fucking closet. Pretty sure you got married, big guy."

His partner smiled and shook his head. "That did happen, yes. But technically, she's still free to marry you."

"Explain, please." Riordan's head hurt.

"Fae marriage isn't the same as a legally binding human one. You two could technically wed legally in a more human marriage." Brynach finished his sentence and looked away. "But depending on what the two of you want, it's actually very common to have handfastings with multiple partners in Faerie. It recognizes you as a life partner and is respected within our culture."

Riordan's breath caught when the other man's citrine eyes pinned him to the bed. "In other words, you and I could also be bound. It would tie all three of us together."

Aisling shifted beside them, slowly removing her strapless bra and underwear she'd still been in. The guys laughed, and the tension broke a little.

"Sorry." She blushed. "I just wanted to get comfy."

"I'm not asking for anything you don't want to give. I know our relationship is new. If you want to handfast with Aisling and not me, that's okay. We can wait. Or we can never have it, and I'll still love you," Brynach told him.

"No. I mean, I want to be bound to both of you. I miss our bond, too," Riordan told the Fae and turned back to Aisling. "You mean it? This is what you want?"

She nodded. "More than anything. You're both mine. I'm yours. It doesn't feel right only being married to Brynach."

He sat with that for a minute. "Holy crap. Okay. I mean. Yes. Yes, of course, I will."

Aisling's smile split her face, and then she threw herself at him. Her arms circled his neck, and her mouth met his in a frantic and messy kiss. He found himself laughing as Brynach took his face and kissed him, too. Aisling yawned, and Riordan pulled her close. "Time for bed."

Brynach turned off the light and joined them, the three of them tangled and staring at the stars through their skylight. The warmth of his lovers on either side of him. How could anything top this?

T he smell of breakfast meat waking him in the morning turned out to be the answer. Riordan peered over the loft wall and saw Brynach and Aisling making food, stark naked. He laughed, and they looked up at him.

"We're really leaning into this no-clothes thing, huh?" he called down.

"Do you have any idea the risks Brynach is taking cooking bacon naked? I do not want my husband getting grease burns on his bits and pieces. And apparently, seeing me make pancakes in the nude gets him all excited, so the risk is higher," Aisling stated.

Riordan cracked up. When he got downstairs, there was a box in his hand, and his heart was pounding. "You left this on the bed. Is it mine?"

Aisling nodded. "Happy Birthday."

Brynach turned off the stove and wiped his hands on the towel Aisling handed him. Together they waited while Riordan found a gap in the tape, which wasn't easy, and tore into the package. The box was plain brown, no hints. He dug at another layer of tape to peel back the flaps.

Aisling rolled her eyes. "Bry wrapped it."

Riordan grinned and looked down at the now open box. Inside was a jeweled cuff that reminded him of the one Brynach had worn to his wedding.

"Did you raid the vaults?" he asked, eyes on his partners.

"No." Aisling smiled. "We had it made. It matches our wedding jewelry."

Riordan looked back at the cuff as Brynach spoke. "It's made to look like a crown."

Aisling kissed his cheek as he gazed at the brushed silver cuff fitted with deep sapphires set inside the gaps of trinity knots. "You're my Prince, too."

"May I?" Brynach asked, nodding to the box.

"Please," Riordan answered when he found his voice. The larger Fae lifted the cuff and locked it around his wrist.

"Do you like it?" Aisling wondered.

"I love it," he answered honestly, fingers stroking the cool metal.

"It was Brynach's idea. I gave you the ring, but he wanted you to have something from him, from us," Aisling explained.

He shook his head and grinned. "Possessive Fae. Thank you, both."

Riordan kissed them and then stole a piece of bacon before Brynach whipped the towel across his ass.

"Don't be an animal. Sit down, and we can eat. There's a surprise on the way, and I'm pretty sure we should at least put robes on before they get here." Brynach shooed them to the table. Aisling picked up the pancakes, butter, and syrup while Riordan carried the juice, and Brynach got the bacon and scrambled eggs.

Together they had a morning feast fit for three ravenous Fae. Out of some unspoken agreement, nobody brought up the Veil drop, training, the courts, Breena, or anything else that could cause distress. Instead, they laughed and talked about how they were going to gorge on food and have sex all day.

Which was perfect because his brain was still buzzing with the idea that he was going to enter into a polyamorous handfasting. Every time he thought about it, his heart raced and he had to fight a stupid grin.

"Told you it would be worth letting go and allowing yourself to be happy. Good things happen when you don't fight the joy that comes your way," Vola reminded him.

"Yeah, yeah. You were right. Happy now?" Riordan stuck his tongue out at his familiar, who was sunning himself on the deck.

"Very. But also, you realize your home is comprised of nearly all windows, right? Like, we can all see you," he reminded Riordan.

He laughed out loud, and his partners turned to him. Riordan explained, "Vola is reminding me that our home has a lot of glass and that not all wildlife appreciates our new no-clothes policy."

They finished eating, and Brynach brought out three plush robes and instructed them to put them on. They lounged on the sofa, watching television, until there was a knock at the door. Aisling's wards had alerted them to someone crossing their border, so she was ready to greet the troop of people with tables and travel cases of Goddess knew what.

"What is all this?" she asked.

Brynach grinned as he moved the sofa Riordan had abandoned. "I booked massages and facials."

Riordan groaned, "Sweet Goddess, yes. My body needs this."

"Mine, too!" Aisling agreed. The team set up the massage tables and used their countertop to lay out massage oils and assorted other bottles.

"Thank you, Bry," he said to the large Fae, who was grinning.

"I did good?"

"Hell yeah," Riordan told him.

After that, there was a lot less talking and a lot more groans and moans as every knot and tense muscle was massaged and deep-tissued into submission. It was Riordan's first massage, and he was pretty sure he was addicted now. Sitting with their face masks on, Riordan told Brynach as much.

"I'll book monthly visits," Brynach said casually.

"Yeah, 'cause we have that kind of money. I'm getting paid at the training facility, but I'm not making bank. I'm sure the royal vaults aren't exactly sharing with you anymore," Riordan said and then immediately regretted bringing real-world issues to an otherwise stress-free day.

Brynach just chuckled. "Hey, we're committing ourselves to an eternity together. What's mine is yours, and what's hers is ours. And I gotta admit, she's carrying us right now."

Aisling puffed out her chest. "I'm your sugar mama? I like it. Look, I happen to know that Bry is loaded. We're going to be just fine."

After their faces had been steamed and buffed, the team packed up and left. The three of them sat in a relaxed heap on the sofa and drank a lot of water, as instructed. Hydration was apparently very important after a massage.

"Movie?" Riordan asked and picked up the remote.

"Crank for old time's sake?" Aisling joked.

"Absolutely not," Brynach objected. "There's only one option."

Riordan thought for a moment and came up with nothing obvious.

Brynach grinned ear to ear before announcing, "*The Lord of the Rings.*"

Aisling looked at the clock before complaining. "Bry, those movies will take all day!"

"And we have nothing else to do, do we? Come on, they're amazing, and we have this great new system to test." The larger Fae stuck out his lower lip in a mock pout, and Aisling laughed at him.

Brynach had splurged on surround-sound speakers mounted in all corners of their A-frame house. The sound bar mounted behind their heads alongside the additional speakers created a very immersive experience. Riordan couldn't lie; it would be pretty cool. He cued up the first movie, and they got comfortable.

Brynach was sprawled down the long lounger, Riordan in the recliner at the other end, and Aisling crisscross between them. All of them were still naked under their robes, oiled and relaxed. In other words, they were perfect.

Before the quartet of hobbits reached The Prancing Pony, they'd made popcorn, and Aisling had her head on the pillow next to Riordan's hip while Brynach rubbed her feet. Their girl was happily napping while the guys finished the movie.

"You ever want to pinch yourself and make sure this is really your life?" Riordan wasn't sure why he felt the need to verbalize his thoughts, but he knew they'd be respected.

Brynach looked at him and nodded. "Every time I look at you. Or her. Or I walk through those doors and know I'm home. I didn't say it the other night, but I'm really proud of you. I know what's happening between us isn't something you would have been comfortable with a year ago. It's difficult changing world views as quickly as you have."

"You two make it pretty easy. It was either let this thing happen or choose misery. Because once I knew I could have her, have you, that's what I would have felt if I turned you away," Riordan admitted.

He knew Brynach well enough to understand his looks, and the soft look in his eyes had most definitely turned to heat. Riordan licked his lips, and his hands in Aisling's hair stilled.

"Bry? You have that predator-stalking-prey look," Riordan warned.

The Fae nodded. "Smart man. The question is, who do I want to eat?"

Riordan's heart stuttered in his chest and then sped. "Umm ..." Brynach hadn't looked at Aisling once during the exchange. "Are we waking her up, 'cause I kinda feel like I should be running right now?"

Brynach clicked his tongue and shook his head. "Silly man, you know what happens when my prey runs from me. Are you sure you want to do that?"

"No, but I haven't seen a man look at me like that before. You're activating my fight or flight. Either you tone that down, big guy, or I'm going to fucking flee," Riordan told him truthfully.

Brynach placed Aisling's feet down softly. She didn't stir. Slowly, the other Fae stood and walked down the length of the sofa. He'd done as Riordan asked. The softness was back in his eyes, and Riordan let himself draw a ragged breath.

"Bry," he whispered.

"Yes, Riordan?" He settled himself on his knees at the arm of the sofa, eyes level with Riordan's.

"I don't know what I'm doing here," he admitted.

The other man smiled and stroked Riordan's cheek. The rough pads of the other man's thumb caught on Riordan's scruff. "Do you trust me?"

Riordan nodded, words escaping him.

"Good. Then for right now, let me worry about how this goes. Sound good?" Brynach asked, his eyes never leaving Riordan's.

He nodded again. Apparently, he was a bobblehead now. His throat was dry, and he struggled to swallow. His tongue slid out to wet his lips. When it did, Brynach caught the tip of it with his thumb.

The Fae's breath caught in his throat. Riordan had done that. Brynach's gaze dropped to the erection that had made its way through the gap in Riordan's robe.

"Is that because of the way I'm looking at you?" Brynach asked.

Riordan managed a shaky yes.

"Riordan, that's just my eyes. You have no idea what's going on in my head right now," he whispered.

"Tell me," Riordan asked, hungry for the other man's words.

He wanted to know just how crazed Brynach was for him. The high he got from Aisling unraveling for him was stunning, but this large, powerful man on his knees for him undid something in Riordan.

"Promise not to run?" Brynach asked and only continued when Riordan nodded. "I've tasted you second-hand on Aisling's tongue, and I nearly came from the flavor of you alone. I have watched you sliding into her mouth, seen the way your newly toned body moves when you fuck her, and wished so desperately that it was me you were moving around. You are a feast to a starving man, and I want to indulge in you."

Brynach ran a hand along Riordan's chest, parting the robe as he went. His heart was going to pound right out of his chest.

"The way I want you scares me, Riordan. Aisling craves my dominance, the hunger and barely restrained violence I have pent up in me. But I never push her too hard. What you see with her is soft. The way I want you isn't gentled with a lifetime of affection the way it is with Aisling. Our relationship was born of fire and spite, of rivalry turned to love. The things I want to do to you, the cries I want to wring from your spent body, aren't gentle, Riordan. But I know you can take it. I've seen your body sculpt itself with hard work and training." Brynach's hand deftly undid the tie around Riordan's waist.

The other man's words rolled over him, his cock hardening almost painfully. Aisling was asleep mere inches from his now fully exposed erection. Brynach's eyes hadn't left his as his hand played along Riordan's stomach so close but so far from where he needed it.

"Can you handle that, Riordan? Will you be able to withstand the way I love you, like a storm crashing over you?" Brynach asked.

"I trust you," was Riordan's only answer.

The moan that left Brynach was primal. Those three words meant more to this beast of a man than any *I love you*. And while words were great, he wanted to back them with action. "Bry, I need you to touch me. Please."

There was no shame in begging. Riordan knew his vulnerability and honesty would be rewarded within these walls.

"You're going to be really quiet so Aisling can get the rest she needs, and in return, I'll give you what you want. Understood?" Brynach asked.

"Yes. For the love of all things sacred, touch me," Riordan cried.

Brynach's thick fingers ran up Riordan's thigh, around his hip, to his stomach, and rubbed circles on him. Every time he got close to Riordan's cock, he skirted around. Riordan bit his lip to avoid crying out. The Fae just laughed.

"I'm not doing this dry. I need to gather all this lovely massage oil from your body, handsome," Brynach told him. He held up a shiny hand. "Think this will do."

Riordan nodded, reduced again to wordless bobblehead status.

Brynach leaned in and placed his mouth on Riordan's neck, kissing and licking his way from his collar to his ear. When he got there, he tugged the lobe into his mouth and sucked on it. Then he whispered in Riordan's ear, "Don't forget to stay quiet. Can't wake Aisling."

Yet again, Riordan nodded. He'd do anything right now so long as there was relief for the pressure building painfully between his legs. There was a flare of heat in the other man's eyes, and then his mouth claimed Riordan. It was rough, teeth on lips and soft growls. Riordan angled his head back, giving Brynach access to his neck when Brynach's mouth moved there, and he finally gripped his cock. Riordan's hips rose off the sofa, and Brynach pushed them back down with a *tsk*. He fought to stay still as that large hand squeezed and stroked. There was nothing dainty about the way he was jerking Riordan off. There was a knowledge of just how much a man could take. And right now, Brynach was jerking him off the way

Riordan would if he was in the shower trying to purge himself of ridiculous levels of lust, rough and hurried. Desperate.

"I told you; I won't be gentle, but I will be kind," Brynach said as his mouth trailed Riordan's chest to his nipples. Brynach sucked one tight bud. Riordan put a fist to his mouth to stop the cry from escaping, and Brynach rewarded him by palming the head of his cock and running his thumb along the sensitive underside.

"Fuck," Riordan breathed quietly.

"Do you want my mouth?" Brynach asked in a gravelly voice Riordan had, until now, only heard him use for Aisling.

He did. Oh, Goddess, he did. "No, Brynach. I *need* your mouth." Riordan knew he'd want the words, needed the words. He forced his hips to stay still despite the way he longed to thrust himself into Brynach's hand.

The other man lowered his head over the arm of the sofa, his warm breath cascading over Riordan's cock. Fuck. Riordan was torn between awe and shock. Both marveling that it was happening at all and thankful it was.

"Honesty gets rewarded, Riordan." Brynach's hair tickled his thighs as he looked up at him, his tongue extended toward his cock. Those citrine eyes staring into Riordan's.

"Wait," Riordan gasped. "I. Fuck. I don't think I'm going to last. Please, before you do it, tell me where I'm finishing?"

Brynach licked his lips. "I'm going to swallow down every beautiful drop. And I don't care how long you last, Riordan, so long as you're satisfied. Understood?"

He nodded, and Brynach gave a slight dip of his head before he lowered his mouth. Riordan saw stars. There was nothing gentle about the way Brynach went down on him. It was hard and fast, as if the other man was just as hungry for him as Riordan was desperate to find relief.

Riordan kept his eyes open, staring at Brynach's mouth closed around his cock, his hand pumping him. He cherished every moan that vibrated in the back of the other man's throat.

Every hum of satisfaction when Riordan moaned or gasped as his skilled mouth played over him.

He moved Brynach's hair out of his face, stroked the other man's stubble, and felt his entire spine seize up when those intense yellow eyes locked on his. Brynach was relentless. This wasn't a seduction; it was an owning. He was stamping himself on the deepest recesses of Riordan. Brynach's dark lashes lowered to his cheeks as he sucked Riordan deep into his warm mouth, teeth gently teasing as he pulled back. He was beautiful.

The larger Fae moaned as he lifted his mouth, "You're perfect."

Riordan ran a thumb over the other's man's plump lower lip and groaned when he sucked gently on it. He removed it and guided his head back to his lap. "Take me deep," Riordan begged.

Brynach didn't object to the instruction, lowering himself on Riordan's cock until his nose was nestled against his thigh. He held himself there, tongue working the underside of Riordan's cock while his throat squeezed him. Riordan lost track of time as the other man held him within those warm walls. The large Fae lifted enough to breathe through his nose and looked up at him. In that animalistic gaze was a command, an order to come. His mouth stroked Riordan's cock until there was nothing left to do but obey.

The way he came wasn't suave or restrained. He grunted his release as his body locked up and let loose. The other man's mouth didn't let up. Like promised, he took everything Riordan gave him and then continued to suck on his sensitive cock. Brynach was fevered, his face heated under Riordan's hand. His mouth slowed but didn't stop its hot wet slide over him.

"Bry, stop. Goddess." His whole body shook. The sensation bordered on pain.

The other man wasn't relenting. A hand in his inky hair, Riordan yanked until his cock was free of the other man's mouth. But he didn't stop there; he continued to pull until Brynach's mouth met his. Their kiss was wild, teeth and fingers biting into one another's flesh. When they broke, they were both panting.

"If she hadn't asked you to marry her, I would have," Brynach vowed.

"Such a greedy man," Riordan teased and kissed him again. "Thank you."

"I know you aren't thanking me for a blow job." Brynach's eyes narrowed in warning.

Riordan shook his head. "Thank you for your patience with me. For letting me get to this point on my own. You never pressured me, but you let me know exactly what you were offering. Your vulnerability let me feel safe enough, brave enough, to accept this kind of love from you."

Brynach started to speak, but Riordan stopped him. "I'm serious. This wouldn't have been possible between me and any other man. It had to be you."

The larger Fae closed his eyes, and Riordan could see his body trembling. He understood on some level how undeserving Brynach felt of happiness, love, and acceptance. He needed words like that to feel valued. Riordan gave them easily because they were true. It didn't matter how rough Brynach was in the bedroom or how feral he was when others threatened those he loved because Riordan got to see him in moments like these.

Riordan lifted his face and placed a hand over Brynach's hammering heart. "Only you."

"Wake her up, Riordan." It was more growl than words. The air vibrated with the intensity. "Wake her now and get your asses upstairs."

The Fae stood and stared down at him, his erection breaking through the robe. Fuck. Riordan reached over and stroked Aisling's face. "Ash, love. It's time to wake up." He gently shook her shoulder and smiled at her when her eyes opened, unfocused and sleepy.

"I fell asleep," she stated the obvious.

"You did. It's time to get up," he told her.

Aisling moved to sit up. "What's wrong?"

Riordan gestured over his shoulder to where Brynach towered. He knew the moment she registered the look in her husband's eyes because her cheeks flushed. The nipple that had broken free of her robe hardened, and her breath quickened.

"Oh," she said softly.

Brynach's dark laugh sent shivers down Riordan's spine.

"Five," he counted.

Aisling's wide eyes swung to Riordan, and together they stood hand in hand and ran.

CHAPTER 11

Brynach

How do you end up exhausted after a day when you don't leave the house? He grinned at the memory of exactly how they'd spent their day off. The massages had been fantastic, but afterward ...

As much as he wanted to drown in the memories of Aisling and Riordan naked and pressed against him this morning, he couldn't. He had a certain husbandry expert to see, a tiny soldier to yell at, and some cranky royals to visit. The first stop was the Seelie stables; the rest he'd take care of at his old court. Luckily, Semele was right where he'd expected to find them,

"Back so soon?" they said when they spotted Brynach walking through the stables.

"Couldn't resist you." He tried for charm and got an eye roll and a huff. It made him smile. "I had a proposition for you. I'd like to team up. You teach the husbandry, and I'll teach the communication and other aspects of familiar relationships."

Semele stopped their work and turned on him. "You're going to teach the children?"

He couldn't help but be mildly offended. "I happen to be

great with kids." He gestured to himself. "I'm just one piece of play equipment."

The other Fae chuckled. "Is that what your partners call you?" they mumbled.

Brynach gasped. "Did you just make a joke?"

"Guess I did." They resumed cleaning out the stall. "I'm not the one in charge here. If you want to co-teach the class, who am I to say no?"

"Um, the expert? I'm not going to force myself into a working relationship against someone's will," Brynach informed them.

"So dramatic. Is that the royal in you?" They waved him away. "Yes. That'll work just fine. Now get out of here, and let me get back to my work. That damn construction is upsetting my horses."

Brynach could hear the banging and shouts from workers and could see how that would be an issue. Hopefully, it would be fast work, but there was no way to know. From Alex's update, he knew the classrooms were easy. Just a clearing of rooms in the castle and the moving of things from the school into the new classrooms. The dorms were a bit harder. They had to source a lot of beds for the once-opulent Seelie bedrooms. One whole section of the far east wing now housed the displaced furniture.

Almost as soon as he sifted to the Unseelie court, he could hear the shouts. Branwyn was ranting about their meager accommodations and threatening violence.

"Ma'am, I don't give a flying fuck what you want or how you feel, but you will get out of my face." The New Fae guard stood his ground, and the once-Queen huffed and turned around.

Brynach walked toward them and held up a hand with a grin. The guard returned the look and gave him a high five. About time someone put that woman in her damn place. "Do you know where I can find Ceiren? Tall, lanky, long blonde hair, quiet but smug?"

"I know who he is." His lips tilted up at the corners. "Last time I saw him, he was still asleep in my bed. Your guess is as good as mine."

Brynach gave a nod. "Right. And Brielle, tiny platinum-blonde killer?"

They shook their head. "Know who you're talking about but haven't seen her. Give your brother my regards."

When the other Fae turned away, Brynach mumbled, "Nice to meet you, too." With a shake of his head, he went to find Ceiren.

"You're a hard man to find," Brynach commented when he finally found his brother.

"On purpose," Ceiren replied. "Why are you looking for me?"

Right to the point. "The school. I want you to be a part of it."

Ceiren shook his head. "I hate kids unless they're Trixie."

There was no stopping the laugh that broke free of Brynach. "I'm not asking you to be a dorm mom. I want you on the board. You know the Unaligned. You're used to brokering conversations between people at odds. I want someone even-tempered to smooth things over. You can be as involved as you like, but the meetings, the decision-making, I want your voice. Not to mention that one kid you care about, she'll be there."

His long blonde hair shook. "Damn it, Brynach. You have to bring logic into it. And I really don't have to play hopscotch or anything?"

"I'd pay to see it, but no," Brynach assured him. "I wouldn't ask if I didn't think you'd be doing good, Ceiren."

His brother looked up to the sky and groaned. "Fine, but you get me on the board. I'm not going to campaign or any-thing."

"Done," Brynach promised him. "For what it's worth, I decided to teach."

Ceiren laughed so hard he bent over. "Is this what married life looks like?"

"You tell me. I ran into a guard in my search for you who

had the pleasure of sharing your bed last night." Brynach nudged his shoulder.

Ceiren nodded. "We're not all looking to settle down. Don't start looking for connections that aren't there."

He held up his hands. "Not looking for anything but a representative for the board. Thank you, Ceiren. I have an appointment I have to make, but I'll be in touch."

His brother waved him away, and Brynach hurried out of the palace. He was just about to sift when he heard her. Pulling out his phone, he saw he had a few minutes to spare and turned toward the sound of Trixie's voice.

Trixie had a wooden sword in her hand, play-sparring with a little boy about her age. He caught her attention, and she lifted her hand in a wave, which gave the young boy the opportunity to land a hit with his practice sword.

Trixie winced and turned on him, bringing her sword down on his head. Brynach stifled a laugh and walked over to where their instructor was now scolding her. She looked up, waiting for him to come to her defense.

"Just because you lost your focus doesn't mean you get to lash out at your sparring partner. You are supposed to be building skills and trust with your peers. That wasn't an appropriate reaction," Brynach reiterated.

"But it hurt, and I didn't mean to stop paying attention," she whined.

The young boy looked terrified as he stared up at Brynach. He looked at his niece and nodded toward her sparring partner.

"I'm sorry," she said, sounding genuine.

The little boy ran off, and Brynach picked his niece up.

"Uncle Bry! They'll think I'm a baby!" She wriggled in his arms.

"I'm sorry." He set her down, trying to ignore the pang in his chest at his niece being embarrassed by him. "How are you?"

"It sucks not being able to leave the grounds." She covered her mouth.

"You won't be here too much longer. We are building a school for young Fae just like you." Brynach had never been prouder than he was at being the reason for the joy that split her face.

"I wanna go! Can I?" She bounced and took his hand. "Please!"

He laughed, "Of course you can."

She looked worried. "I'm not a princess anymore. That's what Thomas said. I don't get to do whatever I want."

Brynach stilled. "Thomas is right, but that wasn't nice of him. You're still a princess to me, kiddo, and in this situation, you still get what you want. Any young Fae is welcome at the school."

She grinned up at him, a toothless gap in her mouth.

"You lost a tooth!" Brynach whooped and swung her into his arms. She laughed and didn't argue this time about being held.

"I let Thomas tie it to an arrow and shoot it. It went flying, but we found it! It barely hurt." She poked her tongue through the gap.

"You're such a brave girl. But maybe no more arrows attached to body parts, yeah?"

She giggled, "Okay, Uncle Bry."

B rynach usually avoided official meetings, but today he was determined to get to the bottom of Brielle's silence. If that meant going to one of the horrible security meetings, he would. Besides, he needed to discuss the re-instituting of the wards around the Seelie court, anyway. If it meant he got to stare at Riordan and unnerve him while he worked, that was an added bonus. He walked into the building, his jeans, boots, and tight t-shirt out of place among the suits. He gathered his long inky hair and tied it back, at least attempting to not look as wild.

He caught his partner's eyes and smirked, hearing Riordan's sharp intake of breath. He moved across the room, eyes locked on the chocolate brown he had grown to love. Brynach loved how his undivided attention made Riordan squirm. His hand moved to the chain around his neck, playing with the rings there before dropping his hand self-consciously. What Riordan didn't realize he was doing was thumbing the band of the ring Brynach and Aisling had given him instead. It was adorable.

"Hello, Riordan," he purred when he drew up close. The memory of the other man's taste in his mouth flooded him. Fuck. He couldn't get hard right now.

"What are you doing here?" Riordan asked and then heard himself. "I mean. It's good to see you, but why are you here?"

"I came to pin down Brielle. She's still not answering my calls." His head swiveled, and he took in the room. Notably missing was the tiny Fae that resembled a certain winged Disney character. "Though it seems she didn't make it here, either."

They were both looking at the door when another Fae walked in. A large blonde curly-headed Fae. Brynach recognized him as both someone Brielle hung with and a Fae who was vocal about his extreme views. With a squeeze on Riordan's arm, he moved toward the large man.

"Hello." Brynach paused.

"Walker." The Fae held out his hand, and Brynach clasped his forearm.

"I've seen you around the house with Brielle before, right? I came here looking for her. She's not answering my calls." He looked over the man's shoulder. "Is she here?"

"No." He shook his head. "Haven't seen her in a few days. Figured she was off on some secret mission."

Brynach frowned. "Not that I know of, and I'd know about

it." He turned and looked at Riordan, who also looked worried. This wasn't like Brielle.

"Everyone, please take a seat," an official called. With a groan, Brynach did as instructed and took a seat next to Riordan and Liam.

The meeting started, but Brynach was elsewhere, wondering where the hell that tiny menace was. He'd known her for decades and liked her more than a solid majority of the people he'd met in his over two hundred years. It wasn't like her to not show up for work or answer. She was capable of taking care of herself, but Brynach felt protective of her still.

"... in Carnlough." Liam's voice broke through his musings. "The Firinne, as they were, are still looking into the claims that Peggy was behind the attacks. More and more, it's looking like a credible claim. With the help of cyber defensive experts, we have located a cloud backup that Firinne Durstin didn't think about. I believe it's enough for a conviction."

That was news to Brynach, and the way Riordan stiffened beside him, told him it was a surprise to his partner, too. That was shitty of Liam to drop on him in a meeting. But the older brother didn't look Riordan's way. Instead, he kept going. "We have also uncovered some dark-web discussions and threats that we believe to be credible against the training grounds and those actively participating in bringing down the Veil."

The fuck? "You mean your brother and my wife? And this is how you're telling us?"

"Bry, don't." Riordan put a hand on his arm.

"No. That's shitty."

Liam gave him a withering look. "It's my job. The particular intel just came to us. Between briefing government officials and you, I chose this, knowing my brother would be here. Any other complaints?"

Brynach sat back with a huff, definitely not enjoying being put in his place. Maybe he was a little jumpy. Riordan rubbed his leg under the table, but even still, he was pissed. Direct threats against the people he loved were no joke. Yes, they were Fae, but that didn't mean they were unkillable. Less likely, harder to kill, yes. But not impossible. That small margin was too large of one for him.

There was one thing he was sure of. The world did not want to see what he'd turn into if either of them were taken from him.

CHAPTER 12

Aisling

Brynach had warned Aisling that the meeting had been rough on Riordan and that they had some logistics to discuss when they got home. She did her best to not be nervous. She hated when the guys hurt, even more so when they worried over things outside her control. The fact of the matter was there was too much in the world they couldn't control. People looked to her and saw someone who was reshaping reality, but she still couldn't stop the men she loved from hurting. She hated it.

Aisling grounded herself, bare feet in the grass, and closed her eyes. "Goddess, hear my intentions. Let this house be free of harm and heartache. Fill this space with love and positivity. Let any hard times fall away inside these wards and ease the mind of those who are troubled." She emptied the jar of rice by the door, burying it outside her wards and refilling it to trap ill intentions before they crossed her threshold.

Then Aisling walked the perimeter of their space, reinforcing her wards. She dropped protective herbs, setting down protective crystals at the four corners of their property and reinstating her intentions of safety and peace.

When she'd admitted to Brynach that she didn't always know how to help Riordan, he'd told her to love him. Just love him like only she knew how. Doing this was her way of loving them. With their home safe, Brynach could let the weight of their safety slip from his shoulders. Riordan could rest knowing the people he loved were safe from harm. She was still lost in thought when she rounded the corner of their home.

Maybe that's why she didn't immediately see the purple-haired Fae waiting for her on the other side of her wards.

"Corinna!" Aisling started. "What are you doing here?"

Corinna stood, wringing her hands. Her lips were folded over her pointed teeth, her wings tucked close to her body. It was clear to see she was nervous. "I can feel the magic you have protecting you here. I couldn't get in."

Aisling understood the other woman's mood now. "Oh, Corinna. Here." Aisling let her hand trail through the newly reinforced ward and nodded for the princess to step through.

"I don't mean you any harm. I promise!" she hurried to say.

"I'm sure you don't. It was specifically warded against you and a few others. Until I was sure," Aisling mumbled.

Corinna nodded. "I deserve that. Thank you for letting me in. I know we talked the other day, and I still don't understand why you're being so nice to me, but I wanted you to know that I didn't know."

"You're going to have to be more specific than that." Aisling kept walking and warding, knowing Corinna would follow.

Her friend laughed. "Fair. In this particular instance, I'm referring to the Veil. I didn't know, Ash. As for Levinas, I suspected he didn't actually care about me, but I wanted to believe he did. I know you won't understand, but I thought being with him made me more like you."

Aisling turned and saw the deep purple blush on her cheeks. "Corinna, what the hell are you talking about?"

"I saw how Brynach treated you. I saw how happy you were, not just with him but with Riordan, too. I wanted that.

And my parents kept such a leash on me, but they didn't mind me seeing him. I understand why now. I know they were working with him to try and keep you and Brynach apart, to keep the prophecy from breaking the Veil and sharing magic they'd kept for themselves." She paused. "I know they used me. All of them. And I let them because it felt good to be loved, even if it was a lie. It's not easy, you know, realizing everyone you care about never gave a shit about you."

Aisling wasn't sure how it would be received, but she reached forward and hugged her old friend. "I understand a bit about that. Seems we both have at least one crap parent."

"I know I hurt you, and I hate myself for it. I sat in Levinas's dungeon and told myself I deserved every blow, every harsh word." She kept babbling, "I was wrong. I was naive. The weakness was mine and not in my appreciation of your friendship." She wiped her hands on her pants. She never wore pants. "I moved out of the palace. Well, I mean, we all did. I didn't go with my family to the Unseelie court. I claimed an empty dwelling."

Aisling was genuinely happy for Corinna and told her as much. "I think that's a fantastic move for you. Be sure to talk to Jashana and Breena about some security. I don't think anyone is out of the woods yet, and we don't want anything else happening to you."

"I'm not sure I deserve your forgiveness, but I'm happy to have it all the same." Corinna smiled at her and looked more like her old self than she had in a while. "I won't take up any more of your time. I actually have to meet someone. Well, actually, your friend Lettie. She's helping me with some of this Hive stuff."

Aisling tried to ignore the pang of hurt. "Tell her I said hello and thank you for coming, Corinna. Let's just let the past be the past, okay?

The Fae hugged Aisling close and nodded. "Thanks, Ash."

She watched as Corinna turned and walked away. Aisling

completed the circle around the property and walked up their back deck. Riordan sat there, a knowing look on his face.

"You heard all that, didn't you?" she asked.

Her lover nodded his head. "You're amazing, Ash. You know that, right?"

She shrugged. "What am I going to do? Stay angry forever? You know how that wears on you. Corinna didn't mean to hurt anyone. She was taken advantage of. I think she more than paid the price for that already."

When Riordan held out his arms, she went into them, resting against his body. Aisling breathed in his distinct scent. She had no idea how the smell of ocean air still clung to him, but she loved it.

"Are you alright? Bry said it was a rough day for you." She held his face and looked into his eyes. When he nodded, she let her lips touch his.

He kissed her back. "We're no stranger to the hard days. We always get through them. The big guy worries too much."

Riordan's head snapped up. "Do you smell that?"

She was already off his lap and running down the stairs toward the edge of their property.

"Don't go out!" Riordan called.

Aisling pulled her hand from her ward. The smell of magic faded, and the tang of coopery blood wafted in. "Crap! Riordan?"

"We don't split up," he told her and then walked through the ward. Together, they followed the scent carried on the wind. Her heart hammered in her chest. Their woods weren't remote. They were close to the old Veil but removed from other Fae homes. It wasn't unusual to catch the scent of other Fae, but she hadn't smelled blood like this since the original fighting at the drop.

"I'm scared," she admitted.

He took her hand and pulled her close. Then his free hand reached behind him to where his knife was harnessed. Aisling cursed her lack of weapon before remembering her mother's gift. She dropped Riordan's hand and ripped out the two sticks that held her bun in place. They were meant to look decorative but were sharpened into deadly points.

"You are the sexiest deadly thing I've ever seen," Riordan mused as he took in her fighter's stance.

"Focus." The scent was getting stronger. They were closing in.

Riordan angled her slightly behind him as they rounded a felled tree. He groaned, and she peeked around him to see what caused such a reaction.

"Oh, gross." He scanned the area around them.

A lump of bloody flesh rested in the brush. Aisling moved closer, and when realization struck, she turned and covered her mouth. She tried, she really did, but the bile burned up her throat, and she ran to empty her stomach.

"Ash?" Riordan ran to her, knife still in hand, and put his free arm around her. "Are you okay?"

She shook her head, her brain struggling to process what she'd seen. As soon as she thought about it, she dry-heaved again. Fuck.

"You're scaring me." Riordan sounded on the edge of panic.

"*Breathe, Aisling. Get more information,*" Rin tried to calm her.

"*Did you see anything?*" If anyone had, it would be her familiar flying above the woods.

"*No.*" She could hear the regret in his voice. "*I was ... I was chasing an alate.*"

"*Damn it, Rin. You gotta stop doing that!*" she scolded.

"*It pulled out one of my tail feathers!*" he argued. "*Focus, child.*"

She spat onto the forest floor and wiped her mouth with the back of her hand. She wound her long hair up and secured it with one of the chopsticks, keeping one in her hand just in case.

"I'm okay," she told Riordan.

"Bullshit. What is it?"

Aisling nodded her head toward the source of the smell. "A scalp."

"What!" Shock registered on Riordan's face before he turned back to the offending clump. "Are you sure?"

She walked back over, breathing through her mouth. Aisling was careful not to touch it as she studied it. The hair was short, straight, and a shade of white blonde that she recognized. "Riordan. Please tell me that's not what I think it is, or whose I think it is?"

She felt him at her side, heard the sharp hiss of his breath. "Fuck," Riordan cursed.

Riordan had his phone in his hand, making a call. "Hey. I'm going to need you to sift to us, the south side of the house about one hundred yards into the woods. Careful where you step. Sift, listen for us, and come right here. Don't stomp around." He hung up. "Bry will be here soon. Until then, let's just get you breathing right."

She hadn't realized she wasn't. But she acknowledged she was panicking. Aisling closed her eyes and breathed in slowly through her nose and out her mouth.

"There you go. That's better. Keep those eyes closed," Riordan instructed her. She heard the thump of her husband sifting in nearby. "Here."

Within moments Brynach had his arms around her, cradling her head to his wide chest. Riordan must have directed his gaze because he cursed, and she felt his arms tense around her. "Is that what I think it is? Whose I think it is?"

Aisling nodded into his chest. "It's Brielle."

A growl surged through his body. "Fuck!"

"Easy big guy. We need to keep our heads." Riordan brought everyone's attention back to him.

"What do we know?" Brynach rubbed her back and let her go.

"Nothing. I was warding the house. Corinna came to visit.

Then we smelled blood and found this," Aisling filled him in.

"Corinna was here?" He looked around the woods.

"She didn't do this, Bry. She doesn't have it in her," Riordan said.

"I know that," her husband answered. "But I'm confused. You didn't hear anything? No shouts or a fight? No way someone got the drop on Brielle, and she didn't get some shots in."

Riordan shook his head. "Nothing. And she's been MIA for days, Bry. Look closer. There's no blood around the area. This wasn't done here."

Aisling forced herself to calm down, grounding her feet in the earth, and opened herself to magic. She let her vision slip the way she did as a witch but didn't see any magical signature.

"This feels personal. It's too close to our home. This has to be a message." She voiced her fear. Neither of the guys argued with her.

Brynach moved closer to the scalp and reached back for her thin blade. Aisling handed it over, and he carefully moved the hunk of flesh and hair around. Her stomach flipped, and she fought not to be sick again.

The look in his eyes when he glanced up at her made her blood run cold. "What?"

"I recognize this," he said.

Riordan threw his hands out. "We know. It's Brielle."

"No. Who did it," her husband answered.

"Care to share with the class?" Riordan asked when he didn't elaborate.

With a curse, Brynach stood and cleaned the blade on his shirt. Aisling groaned and shook her head when he tried to hand it back to her. He nodded and held onto it.

"This has Gabriel written all over it."

"Fuck," Riordan cursed and ran a hand through his hair. "What do we do?"

Brynach pulled out his phone and spoke into it before returning it to his pocket. "Jashana is on her way. I don't trust anyone else. Riordan, take her home."

Aisling was about to argue when Riordan put his arms around her and sifted.

"Damn it, Riordan. That wasn't cool." She stomped into the house.

He followed her. "I'm not sorry for protecting you, Ash."

"We weren't in any danger," she argued.

"You don't know that! You heard Brynach. If that was his father's work, we can't have you out there unprotected. Within your wards, you're safer. We were sitting ducks out in the open like that. It was stupid to stay there that long," Riordan complained.

Aisling closed her eyes and lowered her shoulders when she felt him behind her. She didn't know why she was being so bitchy. Logically, she knew getting back to the house was a wise thing to do.

"I don't know what's wrong with me," she said, turning to face him.

Riordan's hands came up to frame her face, and he leaned his forehead against hers. "Ash, the amount you're asked to handle is unreasonable. You're overworked and stressed. And there was a violent attack close to our home right after you warded it. Gee, I wonder why you snapped at me?"

She groaned, "When you put it that way."

Aisling sat on the sofa, feeling suddenly numb.

"Can you have Vola patrol the woods for us? Rin is keeping an eye on things, too. I'll feel better knowing we have extra eyes," Aisling asked Riordan.

He nodded. "He's already on it. Says he doesn't smell anything strange. Other than. Well. He didn't notice anyone enter the woods."

When Brynach entered the house with Jashana and Breena at his side, he walked past her to the kitchen. He returned with a bottle of water. "Drink it."

Aisling didn't think twice before opening the bottle and

taking a large sip. Her husband winked at her.

Jashana rolled her eyes. "This isn't just someone getting the drop on Brielle. They want you to know they have her. But there's no note and no ransom. Why?"

There was silence as everyone thought.

"Send a message to us?" Riordan hypothesized.

"Threaten Aisling," Brynach said.

"Eliminate your number-one security team member?" Jashana wondered.

Brynach tensed, his hands fisting at his side. "We have to find him. If we don't, he'll keep doing shit like this. I don't want her coming back in pieces. Why isn't he making demands?"

Jashana shrugged. "Probably because he doesn't intend to give her back; he just wants to hurt you. Scare you."

"Mission accomplished," Aisling answered.

Maybe she should have stayed silent because Brynach turned on her, citrine eyes on fire. "Nobody is going to hurt you, a stoirin! I'll hunt him down myself."

Jashana shook her head. "Like hell, you will. You're domesticated now, Brynach. Besides, if you go running around after him, he'll get what he wants. You separated from them, and all three of you nervous and scared. You'll leave it to me and focus on the school, drops, and training as always. I'll keep you in the loop."

"She's my friend, too, Jashana. I want her home. Now. Yesterday. Any more harm comes to her, and I'll never forgive myself," Brynach instructed.

Aisling agreed, but it wasn't a healthy way to think. "Brynach, we can't control Gabriel's actions or protect everyone we love around the clock. She'll be okay. She's a fighter."

Jashana gave her a satisfied nod. "I'll check back in. Right now, everyone stays here. Keep within your wards."

Riordan stood from her side and walked the woman to their door while Brynach moved to her. She didn't complain when he wrapped her in his arms and dragged her onto his lap. Aisling knew that holding her would make him feel better. As soon as the door shut, Riordan was on the sofa next to them.

"Well, today's been swell," Riordan commented and put his head in his hands.

"Oh yeah, a real winner of a day," Aisling joked right back.

Brynach didn't say anything. She tightened her arms around him. "Hey, we're okay. We're safe."

Her partner let out a yelp as Brynach's arm shot out and gathered him closer. "Not safe enough. Not if he was that close. Not if he could get the drop on Brielle."

She didn't know what to say to that. Truth be told, she had felt pretty invincible. She'd convinced herself that the three of them were damn near untouchable. But if there was anyone more equipped to handle themselves, it was Brielle. And yet, she'd just stared down at a hunk of her scalp and hair. The image in her head turned her stomach.

Outside, the sky was darkening, and Aisling pulled out of Brynach's arms. "Come on." She held out her hands to both the guys and tugged them to their feet. Then she led them outside and up the side steps to their outdoor bathtub. "We're safe here, and I could really use the steam."

With groans of approval, Riordan got the water started in the giant outdoor tub. Brynach switched on the lights that hung above them, and Aisling dropped in some oils. Then the three of them sank into the steaming water. Aisling was pulled between Brynach's legs and rested her head on his chest while Riordan sat in front of her, his head cradled on hers.

She let herself relax between the two men she loved and felt their muscles relax under the starry sky. Their chests rose and fell together, hands soothing and playing along one another's limbs casually. Behind her, Brynach purred, and in front of her, Riordan sighed as she worked a knot in his shoulder.

They sat there long enough that the water began to chill, but none of them complained. If she could end every horrible day like this, remembering all she had to be grateful for, all she fought for, she could handle the hard times.

Her husband's lips lowered to her shoulder, and she tilted her head, letting his lips travel the expanse of her neck. Riordan's hands ran up and down her thighs before pulling them to wrap around his waist. Aisling closed her eyes and did her best to stop her spiraling thoughts.

"Stay with us, a stoirin," Brynach whispered in her ear. "Keep that beautiful brain focused right here."

"I'm here," she promised. "Just thankful that this is how my days end."

Riordan chuckled from in front of her.

"What?" she asked, immediately defensive. "I am!"

Brynach ran a hand down her arms and squeezed. "We know. He's laughing because you think this is how your night will end."

Before she could question him, he lifted her and settled her into his lap, his hand cupping her breast. Brynach's large thumb rolled her nipple into a hard nub.

"Oh," she sighed.

"Are we ready to head inside?" Riordan asked, lifting her legs off him.

He stood and, backlit by the moon, held out a hand to her. Brynach guided her with a hand on her lower back down the steps and in the back door.

"*We can still see you*," Rin groaned.

"Look away, pervert," she said aloud, making the guys chuckle.

"*I know I encouraged you to let yourself love them both, but you have a bed, you know*," he joked. "*It's clear out here. Go enjoy yourself.*"

As they entered the house, she let Brynach know the woods were free of threats. He stepped ahead of her and rounded the sofa, sitting down and pulling her toward him. In one swift motion, he lifted her thighs onto his forearms and curled the entirety of her body toward his mouth.

"Holy shit!" She scrambled for purchase. But there was only air and not a damn thing to hold onto. "Bry!"

He was tall enough that his shoulders met the back of the sofa, which meant her calves hung over the back as her husband pulled her to his mouth.

"Oh!" she gasped as his tongue stroked her. Aisling dug her hands into Brynach's hair and engaged her core to rock herself against his mouth.

The moan that sounded low in Brynach's throat told her she was doing exactly what he wanted. He held the bulk of her weight and dedicated himself to feasting on her. The lewd sucking and slurping noises colored her cheeks. Riordan stood behind the sofa, his cock in his hand.

His eyes met hers, and he licked his lips. "Beautiful." His hand stroked up and down his shaft, slow but firm.

Brynach's hands splayed up her back, rocking her against his face. She marveled at the strength he was displaying as he sucked her clit and stroked her pussy as if she weighed nothing at all. Her hips rocked, and her thighs closed around his head.

"Fucking smother him with your delicious cunt," Riordan demanded, walking around until he was out of sight behind her. Which would have been fine if her husband hadn't jolted under her, making her scream and grip his hair tighter.

"What the fuck?" she cried out. Brynach groaned against her folds, and she tried to turn her body to see what was happening, but she couldn't without threatening to topple herself.

"I'm stroking Brynach's cock, Aisling. He's long and thick and so hard from eating you out. But that's not fair to him, is it? He deserves to get off, too. And since he was nice enough to blow me the other night, I thought now would be a great time to repay the favor." Riordan's voice was husky. It drove Aisling crazy!

Brynach moaned against her and tried to speak.

"What?" Aisling asked and moved her hips back to give him air.

"I need you to come, Aisling," he begged. "Please come on my face so I can watch Riordan stroke me."

Aisling nearly burst from the raw need in her husband's plea. Brynach pulled her close and doubled his efforts, strumming his tongue over her clit and sucking on it feverishly. When he pulled it into his mouth and moaned around it, she almost lost her balance.

"He feels so good in my hand, Aisling. Do you think I should taste him," Riordan asked.

Aisling's legs tightened on her husband's head, and her hips bucked as he fucking screamed against her. "Stop distracting me, Riordan! Fuck. I want to see you."

She felt Brynach's whole body shift.

"So does our lover. His hips are thrusting that thick cock through my hand. What if I just lick the tip?" Riordan asked.

Brynach went absolutely feral on her pussy, his hands gripping her so hard she knew she'd have bruises. Her stomach shook from engaging her core and riding his face. She was close, so close. Aisling closed her eyes and screamed her release, her body quaking. Only Brynach's sheer strength kept her from falling.

Even though her limbs felt liquid, she needed to see what was going on. Aisling raised her hips, and Brynach lifted her up and over his head. She was ready for it, landing on her feet behind the sofa and immediately spinning.

Riordan was on his knees in front of her husband, cock in his hand and the tip in his mouth. His tan cheeks hollowed around Brynach's cock and had her quivering pussy clenching on nothing. Fuck, that was hot.

"Riordan, you don't have to," Brynach ground out through his teeth.

"I want to." Those chocolate brown eyes begged for permission from between the larger man's legs. A simple nod of Brynach's head, and Riordan lowered his mouth onto him.

Brynach cursed, and his hands fisted against the cushions. Aisling leaned over the sofa, stroking his chest and sucking on his neck.

"Is it good?" Aisling asked.

"So fucking good," Brynach confirmed.

She ran her nails up her husband's arms, and he shook. She could see the muscles in his thighs as he fought the urge to thrust into the other man's mouth. She watched as she kissed Brynach's neck and whispered dirty things in his ear.

"The first man. The only man to have those lips wrapped around their cock." She bit his ear. "Look at him gag and his eyes water, trying to please you."

"Stop, Aisling," Brynach growled.

She licked his neck. "I don't think so, husband. Look how well he takes you."

"I am, damn it. And I'm trying not to come. You're not helping." He cursed.

Aisling could see Riordan grin, proud of himself and the way he was making Brynach feel. She decided he could use some more praise. "You look so strong between his legs, Riordan. I love watching you fuck him with your mouth. Isn't he delicious? Are you flicking your tongue under the head of his cock, Riordan? Licking up through his slit? I know how much you like that. Have you tried it on him yet?"

His eyes met hers, and he hummed as she saw his jaw and tongue work on Brynach. The larger man cursed, and Riordan lifted off his cock as Brynach came across his own stomach.

Aisling waited for the jealousy to settle in. The small voice saying that maybe they didn't need her anymore now that they had one another. But it didn't come. Not when Riordan's eyes left Brynach's and met hers.

"You and your filthy mouth," he smiled.

"Oh, Riordan, you made a mess," Aisling tsk'd. "Guess I'll have to clean it up."

CHAPTER 13

Brynach

B ye!" Riordan called, rushing out the front door and sifting to the training grounds.

"Love you." Aisling kissed Brynach before following after Riordan, sifting to a briefing before the next drop. He'd argued for her to stay in bed, but she'd refused. His poor wife hadn't slept much. She'd been determined to try and dreamwalk with Brielle, but she hadn't been successful.

Brynach wanted to go with her, especially with elevated threats looming, but they were exactly the reason he couldn't. His priority for the day was security, not just Aisling's, but also the school's and Brielle's. He needed to face Rainer and, once and for all, find a way to end Gabriel's reign of terror. By the end of the day, he'd make damn sure everyone was safer, somehow.

He was tackling his list with the easiest task first. He needed to check on Alex and the school's wards. Brynach was shocked at how quickly it was coming together. By the end of the week, they'd be operational on a small scale. In a meeting room, Mrs. Quinn, Gemma, Aindrea, and a few other people were discussing menus and extracurriculars for the children.

The women were more than capable of determining the best thing for the kids, having all raised children themselves.

He paused for a moment to listen and nod to Aisling's mother when he caught her eye. Meanwhile, Ceiren, who had accepted the board seat, sat in on the meeting, looking like he wanted to end Brynach's life. He wiggled his fingers in a wave and moved on. He trusted the experts to make sure the specifics were handled. He wasn't going to start micromanaging people.

It wasn't until he was nearing the room Alex had designated as his office that his smile dropped from his face. An Unaligned known for causing trouble exited his friend's office. What the hell was he doing in there? The other Fae kept his head high but avoided eye contact as he walked past. When he reached the door, Brynach rapped with his knuckle. Alex was sitting at his desk, a cup of coffee in his hand. His normally bright face was fixed in a scowl, and it wasn't until he saw Brynach that he plastered on a smile.

"Was that Walker?"

"It's been a busy morning," Alex commented, which wasn't an answer at all. Alex looked at his watch. "I have about twenty minutes before I have to meet with the PTA."

Brynach squinted at his friend. "Alex, why was Walker here?"

Alex waved him off. "He's just making sure that everything at the school is on the up and up. The Unaligned want to be sure old court politics won't play a part here before enrolling."

The radical-leaning Fae wanting to ensure kids they sent weren't swayed toward the old rule made sense. Brynach still didn't like it. The man was known for having next to no remorse for his actions so long as they served his needs.

"We have to reengage the sentinels at the gates. No more sifting onto the grounds. It's not safe for the kids. Can that be done today?" Brynach asked.

Alex nodded. "It's on my list." He tapped the notebook in front of him. "Why the rush?"

"There was an attack near our house. I don't have details yet, but I suspect my father is sending a message. Trixie will be here, and I'm sure he'll have heard this is my project. The school could be a target." It would be Brynach's worst nightmare to see harm come to the kids.

His friend nodded. "I'll see it done immediately."

"PTA?" Brynach asked, changing the subject.

"The New Fae are hesitant to give up their old customs. They like being involved, and the fundraisers could come in handy." Alex shrugged. "The limits to their decision-making powers and influence have been clarified. If they don't keep themselves in control, I'll step in."

Brynach had no doubt he would. Alex was used to dealing with people who thought they knew better than him. But nobody he knew had more experience with what children needed than Alex. A group walked into the conference room, and Alex greeted them. After telling them to take a seat and help themselves to a beverage, he turned to Brynach.

"I have to take this meeting. We can catch up soon, yeah?" He patted Brynach's back in clear dismissal and moved to close the door.

Brynach scratched at the scruff on his face. Well, that wasn't what he'd expected. He knew he was taking a more passive role in setting up the school, but Alex looked like he'd aged. That was saying something when you're Fae. Brynach couldn't remember a time he'd looked that stressed. He made his way toward the exit but was waylaid by a herd of girls who looked to be Trixie's age.

"Wow. You're huge!" One little girl cried out.

"You have eyes like my cat!" another called out.

Brynach smiled. "Well, hello to you, too. Have any of you seen Trixie, Beatrix? She's about your age."

A brunette child, her face dotted with freckles, tilted her head up and gave him a stare that would wither most grown men.

"We know who she is." Her hip cocked out to the side, and

she placed a hand on it. "And she's not with us."

Brynach looked over the children. "Yes, I see that. Do you know where she is?"

"Probably with the boys. She is always with the boys," a round-faced girl answered. "They're gross."

"Boys are fine, but Buttrix isn't." The brunette sneered.

"Excuse me," Brynach said, getting down on one knee to stare the girl down. "What did you call her?"

"Butt. Trix. She's one of the bad Fae. We don't play with the bad Fae." She was not intimidated by Brynach at all.

A gasp rippled through the girls, and then they took off running. Those little shits! He didn't have time to check in on his niece; instead, he sent Breena a text.

Keep an eye on Trix.
These kids are ruthless!

Already handled it.

How?

Taught her to throw a punch
Those assholes will get what's coming

Breena! You better not have!

I may be human, but you're soft.
She's got to stand
up for herself, Brynach!

Before she'd gone missing, Brielle and a troop of her soldiers had moved into Alex's abandoned house. He and Aindrea had moved to the court, and they trusted Brielle. He couldn't imagine what it looked like now without her. More than that, he didn't understand why more people weren't looking for her. He'd have to stop over there, but first, Rainer and Jashana were getting a visit.

The Unseelie court had never felt like home; it felt even less so now that there were Seelie wandering the halls. His brother still had his cronies outside his doors, though. Brynach could already hear his yes people yammering on inside. He didn't pause as he threw the doors open.

"It's a closed meeting," his brother dismissed as soon as he saw him.

"Looks open to me," Brynach commented. "I won't take up much of your time, but I think you'll want to listen to me."

Rainer gave him a look as petulant as his daughter would but then nodded. "Take a seat, and let's get this over with. What horrible offense have I committed now? What have you come to scold me about, baby brother?"

"I'm sure there's something, but that's not why I'm here. There's a situation I'm dealing with right now, and I need all information you have on Gabriel. Now."

Ranier steepled his fingers and crossed his leg before answering. "I don't know anything, Brynach. I spoke on speculation without proof. It was effective, and I don't know for sure it's not true, so I wasn't lying. I do know he's been out to see Mother. She didn't tell me, of course. One of her guards remains loyal to me and reported his appearance."

"Is he still there?" Brynach asked, but Rainer shook his head.

"No, he didn't stay even a night. He was there and gone before I could order him captured." Rainer had the good grace to look upset about that.

"But they had to notice something. Did he sift in? Did he use magic?" Brynach asked.

His brother shook his head. "I don't know. They didn't say anything. You might try talking to Mother."

Brynach laughed. "Yeah, she's a big fan of mine. I'm sure she'll be happy to talk."

"Since when have you given her a choice?" Rainer asked.

"I'll consider it. For now, I want you extra cautious. The Seelie court is reinstalling their sentinels today. You should do the same. If Gabriel is trying to strike out against me, he may come for Trixie, knowing it would upset me." Brynach knew it was a long shot, but it wasn't impossible that his father would stoop so low.

Rainer stiffened. "I'll fucking kill him."

"You'll try." Brynach may be pissed at his brother, but he didn't want him hurt. He sure as hell didn't want Trixie in harm's way.

"I'll see it done. I expect security measures at the school to be top-notch, Brynach. I won't send her otherwise," Rainer threatened.

"They will be. Nobody is taking risks with our children," Brynach assured him.

Before Brynach had exited the room, Rainer was giving orders to better protect the palace. Satisfied, Brynach went to find Jashana. No doubt, she'd be with Breena somewhere. He rounded a corner and was proven wrong. Jashana was arguing with a New Fae in the hall but stopped when she saw him and walked his way.

"You look awful," Brynach said by way of greeting. The normally put-together Fae had her hair in a tangled mess, and her clothes looked like they were days old.

"I was up all damn night chasing down leads, and your sister never lets me get any sleep." She blushed. "I didn't mean ..."

He laughed. "Yes, you did. What did you find out?"

"Absolutely nothing," Jashana said, taking his change of topic and running with it. "I went to the house she's been staying at. Nobody's heard from her, and they haven't received any demands for her. But Brynach, as far as I can tell, the last person to see her was your wife. Nobody has seen or heard from her since she left the drop."

"Fuck. That doesn't look good, considering where we found

the scalp." He locked eyes with Jashana. The woman was fidgeting.

He looked down at her. "Jashana. I'd like to think we're friends."

"I'll allow that belief." The deadly Fae nodded.

"As friends, I prefer not to be lied to. There's something you aren't telling me. Out with it."

Jashana frowned. "Are you sure you want to know?"

"Stop playing with me," he warned.

"I'm not playing with you, Brynach. It's not going to be easy to hear," she explained.

"Tell me."

"Your father was spotted at his old house. He was in and out before we could breach the ward again. With Faerie a little weaker and your sister's help, we got through pretty quickly, but he'd already left."

"My sister?"

"Sydney. Keep up," Jashana continued. "He wasn't there, but the room Aisling described, the one in the library ... he left the door open. We didn't need to go in to know what he'd done. Across the doorway, he'd pinned Brielle's wings. He took them off above the flesh, but it would have been painful nonetheless."

Neither Jashana nor Brynach had wings, but both of them straightened their backs. "It was a bloody messy job. Once we got inside the room, we noticed more than a few weapons missing from his walls. He's armed with his faves."

"Fuck," Brynach cursed. "Did she survive it?"

Jashana flinched. "The fireplace in the library was still smoldering. My bet is he cauterized the wounds."

"And we have no idea where he went next?" Brynach wondered.

"Not yet, but unless I'm mistaken, he's going to continue leaving pieces of her across Faerie until we find him." Jashana's voice was flat, resolute.

"Fuck."

"Yeah, you said that already." Jashana closed her eyes again.

Brynach looked around the halls. "I know you still have connections. Do you have a tracker you trust?"

Jashana sighed. "Gael, but he agrees the trail is cold." She pointed toward a large Fae with white, braided hair and thighs the size of tree trunks down the long hall.

"Goddess," Brynach gasped.

The Fae warrior was unfazed. "He's quiet, keeps to himself, but he's good."

Brynach was contemplating how to tell Aisling her friend was hurt even worse than they thought when the shouting started. Jashana was moving in an instant, and he followed her toward the yells. Inside the room, he saw everyone scrambling to gather weapons and tie-on battle gear.

"What's happening?" Brynach asked.

"Attack on the training grounds," someone shouted.

His stomach dropped. "No."

Riordan.

He had to get to his partner.

He didn't say a word as he ran for the front door. He heard Jashana call out to him and paused just long enough for her to toss him a long sword. Brynach didn't bother thanking her. He got outside, thankful his brother hadn't acted fast enough to stop sifting in and out of the grounds yet. He stepped out of a sift to the border of the training grounds. Which was a problem because the border of the training grounds didn't exist. The wards had been broken, and smoke and screams filled the air.

"Riordan!" Brynach bellowed, his lungs filling with smoke.

Flames rose from a pit in the ground. From what, only the Goddess knew.

Jashana showed at his side. "The smoke will make telling friend from foe difficult."

"And getting to the injured," Brynach added. "If you find

Riordan, bring him to me."

He ran into the chaos, still calling out his partner's name. It was too much to hope he'd have gone home already. Brynach knew he stayed until the day was done, and it was hours before then. Riordan was there somewhere.

Not only was his vision limited to about a foot or two in front of his face, but his senses were overwhelmed with the smell and sounds around him. Shots rang out, and they seemed to be coming from every damn direction. Brynach moved in a weaving pattern, but he doubted even the shooters could see through this smoke, which meant they weren't targeting anyone specific; they just wanted to cause harm. It was pure chaos.

Brynach needed a clear head right now. He couldn't afford to panic. Precision in crisis saved people. Still, worry over his partner buzzed in him, making him reckless. He wanted his arms around him, sifting home, making sure he was safe. Literally nobody else here mattered to him right now.

"Riordan!" he shouted. Again, there was no answering call. He ran blind, cursing when he stumbled over a body on the ground. He stopped long enough to make sure it wasn't his partner and to establish that the Fae on the ground wasn't mortally wounded.

"Stay down! Crawl toward shelter. A tree, a rock, get behind something." He didn't wait to see if the woman took his suggestion.

Brynach snagged the arm of the next person who ran past him. "We need a wind to clear this smoke. Call on Faerie. You've been training. You can do this," Brynach encouraged. "Get rid of their cover, and the cowards will retreat."

"Got it!" the man screamed as he rallied those around him, and a wind started to clear the haze.

He turned, excited for a better line of vision, looking for Riordan. It wasn't his partner he saw, though. It was the flash of a muzzle as a bullet fired. A hot searing pain lanced through his thigh. Fuck, the asshole had gotten him.

Brynach sifted in the direction of the shooter and startled the man still firing blindly into the crowd. He didn't waste time with questions or mercy. Brynach snapped his neck and threw his body to the ground. No amount of tactical gear, which he had in spades, could save him from that.

Human. The assailant was human. Brynach stalked the perimeter, looking for both Riordan and other attackers from this new vantage point. A woman with a crossbow lifted her weapon and took aim at a huddle of New Fae working to clear the smoke bombs. Brynach saw some in the group shielding them, but they were distracted. He knew it wouldn't hold. With a growl, Brynach sifted to her and brought his arm up under the bow, sending the arrow sailing high into the sky.

Brynach squeezed her wrist until bones broke. Her screams continued as she dropped the weapon, and Brynach moved behind her. She had time to plead, just once, for her life. He ignored her. Before she got a second chance, he snapped her neck.

He paused for a moment, scanning the crowd for his partner. What he saw instead made his heart stutter and his stomach drop. Red hair trailing behind a tall slim figure, darting through the chaos.

Aisling.

She couldn't be here.

He caught another flash of her red hair and sifted. She was already gone. His heart hammered in his chest. Damn it, where was she? He couldn't split his attention right now. Not with active shooters attacking the camp.

Just once, could they stay the hell out of the fight? He stood still, searching for her. Which meant he was a sitting duck. Another bullet grazed him, and he cursed. He couldn't scream her name, couldn't draw attention to her being here. It wasn't lost on him that this might be a ploy to draw her out.

There! Brynach sifted, landing in front of Aisling. "Go

home," he growled.

Maybe not the best approach. He yanked her into his arms, shielding her. "You can't be here. It's not safe. Please. Please go home. I'll meet you there soon."

She pushed away from him. "Is Riordan still here?"

When he didn't answer, she shook her head. He loved her fierce eyes, but not now.

"Let go of me, Brynach." She kept her voice low, controlled. "I'll never forgive you if you try to stop me."

Aisling fought against him. His arm and leg burned from the bullet wounds. "Just once, will you please listen to me?" he screamed.

The speed with which her arm shot out and her hand connected with his cheek was impressive. Damn it, she was strong now. He didn't let her go, though, and she pounded on his chest. When her hand came away sticky with blood, her eyes shot up to his.

"I'm fine," Brynach assured her. "I'm begging, a stoirin. Please, go home."

Aisling's jaw clenched, and he sighed. She wasn't going to leave.

"You stay right next to me. I swear, if you so much as think about leaving my side, I'll make it impossible for you to sit for a week." He was going to do it anyway.

"We're wasting time."

Aisling spun to stand at his back so they could look in all directions for Riordan. With Aisling as safe as possible at his side, he felt renewed fear for his partner. He'd burn the world down if he'd been hurt. Around them, the injured moved to safety with wounds that would absolutely need treatment. Fae healing would help, but bullets and arrows still needed to be removed.

Aisling's voice called out for Riordan, and he slapped a hand over her mouth. "No, a stoirin. Everyone knows your voice."

She clawed at his hand until he lowered it, but Aisling didn't call out again. They picked up their pace, running through the crowd, silently sifting, searching for Riordan. Police sirens joined the other noises. Ambulances with lights spinning and sirens singing. Still, no Riordan.

"Isaac!" Aisling ran from his side.

Damn her! He raced after her to the New Fae's side.

"Riordan. Where is he?" she asked, clinging to the man's arm.

His golden curls shook. "I don't know. Last I saw him, he was near the weapons locker arming anyone staying to fight."

"Is Liam here? Amber?" Aisling asked.

Shit. He hadn't even stopped to consider that their other friends would be here. But Isaac shook his head, and Aisling let out a long breath. Aisling grabbed his arm.

"Rin has eyes on him," Aisling cried. She sifted them to her familiar. Her head pivoted, searching for Riordan. He called out for their partner.

"Bry?" Riordan's voice answered.

At the sound of his voice, Brynach took the first full breath since arriving. Riordan ran toward them, his hair pulled free and wild around his face.

Riordan crashed into Aisling. "You shouldn't be here," he said, holding her face.

"Fuck both of you! Of course I should," Aisling cursed. "I'm so glad you're okay." She kissed his dirty face frantically.

Aisling pushed him away and looked him over. "You are okay, right?"

Riordan nodded, but Brynach had already scanned his body. He was bleeding, and he could see a hole in his shirt. He'd been shot in the shoulder.

"Riordan," Brynach warned. He didn't push, though.

The other man shook his head. "I'm fine."

Aisling noticed the blood then and choked out a cry. He pulled her close with his good arm, and she tucked her head into his chest.

"I need to get you both out of here," Brynach told them.

"I'm responsible for these New Fae. I'm not going anywhere." Riordan's stance widened, ready for a fight.

"Okay," Brynach relented, but only because the shots had stopped ringing and the screams had lessened some. The three of them stood together and took stock of the scene before them. Smoke still lingered high in the air, and people were still running or talking frantically into phones. More were sifting in and out, which had to be a police and safety nightmare. Still, it appeared the immediate threat had passed.

Aisling took a deep breath. "I'm sure I'll be needed for a press conference. You will, too," she said to Riordan.

"They'll have to wait until I check on the injured." Riordan ran a hand through his long hair.

"You do nothing until we get your shoulder looked at. If it heals too much before the bullet it out is out, it can cause real damage."

Riordan lifted his shirt and showed Brynach the front and back of his shoulder. "It was a through and through. I said I was fine. Plus, you're one to talk."

"Just a graze," Brynach assured him.

The other man wasn't fooled. "On your arm, sure. How about that leg?"

Aisling let loose a choked sob. "What?" When she turned and saw the blood pooling by his feet, she screamed.

"Medic, right now!" She pointed toward the flashing ambulance lights.

"Fine," Brynach relented. "Riordan, see to your charges. Aisling, you sift directly to the captain by the barricade, understood?"

His wife nodded.

"I'll get checked before I speak to the police about the mess I left," he growled. Before either of his partners could object, he walked away. He grumbled to himself as he neared the medics. He was not going to enjoy having this bullet ripped from his thigh.

"Sir, sit down," a paramedic instructed him.

He sat and tried not to growl when they cut his pants. He'd liked them. They sterilized the wound to see it better and then offered to take him to the hospital for imaging before poking around for the bullet.

"Just get in there and grab it." He could practically feel it in there. It couldn't be that hard to fish it out. The medic shrugged, numbed his leg around the bullet hole, and began digging. Brynach distracted himself by watching Aisling near the cameras. Even with smoke-stained tear marks on her face, she was stunning.

"You won't let me stitch this, will you?" The medic asked. She dropped the bullet into a metal dish and pointed at the wound.

"Smart woman," Brynach said and stood. It took less time than he expected to explain to the police why two of the attackers had snapped necks. It probably helped that he'd sought out Loren, who had a softness for him doing whatever it took to keep Aisling safe. Other than getting his name, they didn't seem all that angry the intruders had been taken care of.

Aisling had the bright light of cameras on her, finishing her on-the-spot interview. He watched her, scanning the area with hypervigilance. That's where Riordan found him.

"This is a shit show," Riordan commented.

"Any idea who is responsible?" Brynach asked.

"The terrorists in custody aren't talking. But there's been official statements from the usual contenders. They all say it wasn't them and that they condemn violence." Riordan was fidgeting with the rings on his chain.

"We'll figure it out," Brynach promised. "Someone will talk."

Riordan turned his face up and frowned. "Does it matter? We lost five New Fae today. They were friends. There are eight more in the hospital who will pull through but won't ever forget the fear. I just want to make sure it never happens again."

Brynach understood, but there was value in knowing where

threats were coming from. If he couldn't handle that right now, Brynach would do it for him.

"You've got Aisling?"

Riordan nodded, and Brynach made his way over to Jashana. She stood in a large group, some of which he recognized as Brielle's friends. He was surprised to see Walker among them, talking with the others. He eyed the other man until he nodded his acknowledgment.

"Any injuries among you?" he asked.

"No, but this is a mess, Brynach," Jashana sighed. "We may have captured one of the attackers before the police could."

"And?" Brynach wasn't feeling particularly patient.

"And they're human but not claiming allegiance to any of the usual suspects. Not the Anti-Veil, the Pro-Veil, the Anti-Fae, or the radical religious groups." She shrugged. "As far as we can ascertain through our very persuasive means, they are mercenaries. Paid to bring their own weapons, horribly coordinated, and rushed. They got orders just yesterday, worked almost entirely individually, and their only instruction was chaos."

Brynach took it all in for a moment. "And the person who paid them is anonymous?"

Jashana rolled her eyes at the dumb question. "All contact was digital. They were approached individually online and given a location to be during the attack. Other than that, it was a free for all."

He pulled out his phone and sent a text message to Liam.

Riordan is okay! Ash & me, too.

Thank the Goddess. That thick
headed asshole hasn't answered
my texts. I was going crazy.
They won't let us sift to the grounds.

No. Don't come here.
I have a job for you.

Good! I need something to do with
these nerves. Give it to me.

The mercenaries were hired
by someone anonymous online.

No such thing as anonymous online.
I'll find them.

Brynach made his way back to Riordan.

"Your brother would appreciate you checking your phone in emergency situations," Brynach informed him. "I already talked to him. He knows we're okay. I have him looking for whoever organized this."

"You have a lead already? The police are clueless," Aisling said as she moved into Riordan's open arms.

He nodded. "Jashana doesn't have to deal with red tape. Are you done?" The question was directed at both of them.

They nodded. Brynach gathered them into his arms and sifted them to their porch. They moved from his arms, and Brynach noticed Riordan wince. His wife caught it, too. As soon as they were inside, Aisling reached for his shirt and lifted it. She gasped when she saw the bruises peppering his skin.

"Riordan!" She let her fingers trail the dark patches and then lowered her mouth to kiss some of the higher ones. "I thought you got checked out, both of you."

Brynach answered first. "They removed the bullet in my leg, and it already feels back to normal."

"They cleared me. One of the attackers tried to breach the locker, and we fought. It looks worse than it feels," Riordan promised.

"Let me help you." She moved to him and undid the buttons on his pants, and pulled both them and his boxers down his legs.

Brynach moved behind the New Fae and grabbed the hem of his shirt, gently working one arm out before slipping the shirt over his head and down the other arm. Aisling sucked in a breath at the patchwork of bruises down his side.

"Riordan, your ribs have to be broken," she noted.

"They'll heal fast. Come on." He walked into the shower, and they followed. Without words, they washed themselves and exited to get dressed.

Aisling and Riordan settled onto the sofa. Brynach watched their heads lean together as they held one another. The fear that had been squeezing at his chest all day loosened a little. If only he didn't have more bad news to tell them.

CHAPTER 14

Aisling

Aisling looked at her phone and groaned. Sleep hadn't come easy for any of them after the day they'd had. She truly hadn't thought it could get any worse, but then Brynach knelt in front of them and told her about Brielle. Her stomach had threatened to empty and probably would have if she'd had anything in it. Her poor friend.

She knew Brynach had a soft spot for the orphaned Fae, and Riordan had befriended her. Aisling could close her eyes and remember her friend flying up to the tree house while she climbed the ladder on warm summer days. She'd learned about her magic alongside the young Fae. She had a decade on Aisling, but they'd always been peers.

"I don't have the energy or desire to get out of this bed today," Aisling declared when the sun broke through their curtains. Riordan groaned beside her.

"Then we don't," Brynach declared.

"That's not an option for me. I have to get back to the training ground." Riordan started to get up, but Aisling pulled him back down.

"Not yet. Give me more time." She ran her hand over his

shoulder where his skin was already healed. She had been so terrified when she'd learned about the attack. Aisling hadn't anticipated the chaos she'd arrived to or the terror of not being able to find Riordan.

Brynach smoothed a hand over her back. "You're spiraling, wife."

"Can you blame me?" Aisling asked.

"No, but it might help if you talk to us," Riordan encouraged. He was on his phone checking on the New Fae at the hospital.

"I'd rather be stabbed, kidnapped, bitten by massive wolves over and over again than ever have to face fear like that again," she admitted. "And you're Fae now. You had to deal with all that before I was fully Fae."

She felt the tears gather. The two men shook their heads and pulled themselves closer to her. Brynach kissed the top of her head, and Riordan kissed her mouth.

"I wish you'd never had to experience that, Ash. But we're all okay," Riordan assured her.

"For how long? Every drop, every public appearance we have, every time we go out into large groups, we're targets. Always." Aisling was so angry.

"Ash, there are never any promises. Not for my parents or Aunt Maggie. Not for Trent or for us, either. But we are uniquely equipped to handle trouble, aren't we? We're too stubborn to kill. We do everything in our power to protect ourselves. That's all anyone can do," Riordan told her.

Brynach's phone dinged, and he reached for it. "It's Sydney. She's heading to the training grounds to reinforce the wards and protections."

"I should go," Aisling said.

"Like hell, you will." Brynach pulled her tighter to his side. "She can handle it. That's why she was given the job."

"I have to go." Riordan kissed Aisling. "But don't get out of bed on my account."

Brynach grinned from the bed. "Oh, we won't. Hurry home."

Riordan got himself dressed in his typical wardrobe, tight jeans, a T-shirt that used to fit him but now looked like he could burst through, and boots. He sat at the end of the bed and laced them up. Aisling watched the muscles of his back rippling and the way his now-long hair curled at his neck.

He leaned down to kiss Aisling before he left, pausing as he looked at Brynach. Her husband turned his cheek, and Riordan rolled his eyes before leaning in and kissing it. Her heart flipped in her chest. They were adorable.

Riordan fingered the necklace he'd hung on a nail by the stairs. It wasn't safe to wear while training, but he touched it each day like a good luck talisman.

"I love you! Don't get hurt," Aisling called downstairs.

"Love you, too," he called as he closed the door.

"Will I always worry this much?" she asked her husband as they heard his motorcycle rev.

Brynach turned her so she faced his bare chest and kissed her. "It's the price we pay for loving deeply. What do you want to do with our day?" Brynach asked.

"You pick," Aisling answered.

Her husband sat against the wall, pulling her between his muscled thighs, her back against his chest. She let out a small cry at being manhandled but secretly loved it. A quick button-push on the remote and the windows opened, letting in fresh air. Brynach leaned over and picked up their books. He was reading a non-fiction book about teaching practices. She thought it was about the cutest thing in the world that he was so nervous about classes starting. Aisling was reading a new urban fantasy that was starting to feel too real.

"You want to read naked in bed?"

He nodded. "That okay?"

"Absolutely." She settled against him. The sound of pages turning and Brynach's free hand lazily caressing her hair soothed her.

Phlyren flew in and settled on a high beam. "*Isn't this cozy?*"

"*Haven't I earned this bit of peace?*"

"*You have. I just wanted to let you know that Riordan got to the training grounds okay, and the wards are back in place. They need additional reinforcing, but he's safe,*" her familiar informed her.

"*Thank you, Rin.*" She smiled up at the beautiful racket-tailed roller. "Riordan is safely behind the wards again," she told Brynach.

Some of the tension in her husband melted away. She turned to him. "How quickly can we plan the handfasting?"

"Fast. Who do you want there?"

"It doesn't matter so long as you and Riordan are there. My mom, Lettie, Dawn, Loren, and Eves. I suppose not my father anymore. But honestly, I just need to know we're tied to one another." She wiggled herself closer to her husband.

"We already are, a stoirin. But I understand."

She was quiet for a moment before speaking. "I've been thinking that I want to change my last name. I know the hand-fasting isn't legally binding, but I want to file to have my name changed to Campbell."

Brynach was silent behind her. She turned so she could see his face and was relieved to not see anger or jealousy. Instead, her tough Fae had glassy eyes.

"Bry?"

"I know it will mean a lot to Riordan. That's incredibly sweet of you, wife." He kissed her. "Do you think ..."

His voice trailed off, but Aisling could guess where he was going. "I think he'd be honored."

He nodded, his hair hiding his face. She brushed it back. "I love you." Aisling ran a hand over Brynach's chest. She felt incredibly small when she was in his arms but so powerful.

"If you keep stroking my chest, we're going to be doing something more than relaxing, a stoirin," he purred.

She changed her fingers to nails and scratched across his

nipple lightly. "Is that so?"

With a growl, Brynach pushed her onto her back and caged her in with his body. His hips ground down into her, and he bared his teeth. There was only a moment to register his intention before he lowered his mouth and bit her shoulder.

Aisling cried out in pained ecstasy. This man unleashed things in her she never knew existed. Apparently, biting did it for her. Her hips arched, her nipples pebbled, and her breath hitched until his teeth released her. Then she groaned at the gentle pain that was his large tongue licking the teeth marks he'd left behind.

"Don't toy with me," Brynach warned. His mouth lowered to hers, and he demanded she open for his tongue. She gave in to him happily. Her hands traveled his back, clinging as he lifted her torso so he could savor the kiss.

"And if I want to play?" Her hand slid between them. She found him hard and stroked his length.

"My wife gets what she wants," he answered and lowered his hand to stroke her. "You're soaked."

"Always for you," she said, looking into his eyes. Then she moved her hips and guided him to her entrance. "Please."

"Use your words, wife. What do you want?" Brynach taunted her, his thick thumb sliding through her folds, gathering moisture, then coming up to circle her clit. Aisling's hips rose to meet his touch, needing more pressure.

His muscular arm crossed her hips and held her down while his thumb toyed with her. Brynach's mouth skimmed her neck, kissing and licking his way to her ears, where he drew the lobe into his mouth.

"Try again, Aisling," he encouraged. "Last chance."

His thumb pressed hard on her clit, and her body bowed as she cried out. "I want to come on your cock."

His answering growl was enough to have her heart racing. Brynach's mouth claimed hers as his hips moved, lining himself up with her pussy. She tried to move herself onto him, but he held himself just out of reach.

"Beg for it," he demanded into her mouth.

She wanted to brat. To point out that he wanted her just as much. "Maybe I should make you beg for it instead."

"A stoirin, I will kneel at your feet and worship you for the rest of eternity. You want to me to beg? I'll beg. But, if I'm lost for you, you will be just as lost for me." He strummed her clit harder.

"I am," she panted. "I'll forever be lost for you, Brynach."

"Husband. Call me your husband," he growled in her ear.

Her orgasm slammed into her as she screamed his request. His hips drove forward, and she wrapped her legs around his hips, pulling him closer.

"Fuck, you feel so good." His hands thrust into her hair, gripping her and dragging her up to his mouth. Brynach bit at her lip. "So perfect for me."

She never wanted this feeling to end. She clawed at his ass, trying to bring him deeper into her body. The way he thrust into her was punishing, sharp snaps of his hips. Brynach was big, and even when gentle, there was a line of pain he toed. But now, like this, it bordered on unbearable. If it wasn't for his mouth on hers, his fingers on her clit, she'd be crying different tears.

"That's right, Aisling. This body is mine, and I'm going to take my pleasure from it." He slammed into her again. "This is for not listening when I told you to go home." He did it again. "And for constantly putting yourself in danger."

His teeth sank into her neck, and she cried out. All Aisling could do was cling to him and let him take out his anger on her body.

"Do you want me to admit how fucking obsessed with you I am? Is that it? That I want to lock you in this house, naked and filled with my come, and never let you out? Because I do, and I would if I thought you'd let me." His breath was hot on her face as he fucked her.

"I'm sorry, husband. Punish me. I deserve it," she panted.

"That's right, Aisling, you do. And to say you're sorry, I want you to finish again on my cock." She clung to him as she crested and fell over the edge into an orgasm so strong spots danced in her vision. She was so lost in her own sensations that only Brynach's growl broke through. The sharp lines of his neck strained as he released into her.

She gathered him to her, his weight a comfort, as he settled.

"Promise me this won't go away," Aisling whispered.

Brynach moved her hair out of her face, those citrine eyes locking onto hers. "Never. Why are you even worried about it?"

She shrugged a naked shoulder. "You and Riordan have one another now. I love that. I do. But I've gotten used to being enough for both of you. Through our relationship, I was being shared, not sharing. It's stupid. You two did it, so I know I can. What if I'm not as gracious about it? If I still have jealousy? I don't want to ruin this."

Her husband kissed her eyes and followed the tears down her cheeks with those lips. "I won't tell you that there won't be times you still struggle with jealousy or uncertainty. But we're not going anywhere. We will always be here to remind you just how much we need you. Our love, yours, mine, Riordan's … it's not going anywhere; it's only growing. You promised me eternity, and I intend to hold you to it."

Aisling nodded. "Good." She wanted to believe him. The feeling would pass.

"Are you decent?"

They both startled at the sound of Breena's voice. That woman was a menace. How had she snuck up on them? Brynach pulled the covers over them a moment before she came bounding up the stairs to their loft.

She stood with her hip cocked on the railing of their stairs. Her red-painted lips quirked up, and then Breena waved an exaggerated hand. "I'm not even Fae, and it stinks in here.

Come on. You're needed at court."

"What? Why?" Aisling struggled to catch up.

"They're doing some stupid shit, and I think it would be wise if you two got your asses over there before things get out of hand." She looked at her nails, totally unbothered.

Brynach growled. "Breena, this had best be important. You can't just barge in on people."

The raven-haired woman shrugged. "Can't sift. You'll need to get up and take me back anyway. Time's a-ticking."

Her husband grumbled, "Get out of here so we can get dressed."

"Five minutes," she offered before heading downstairs and out the door.

They rushed to get dressed, and Aisling sent Riordan a quick text message. This better be fast. She really hadn't wanted to get out of bed today. Brynach pushed his way out the door and rounded on his sister.

"Care to give us any more information?"

"They're trying to reestablish a ruling system. Figured the two of you practically built this new world, so you should be there," she offered.

Double fuck. Brynach grabbed them both and sifted to the Unseelie court, where all the ex-royals were cohabitating horribly. They entered into an already loud room and barely warranted a turned head, though Rainer scowled at Breena. She didn't miss the way that Brynach situated his body between the crowd and her.

Theo's voice broke over the others. "We need to find and persecute whoever was responsible for the attack on the training ground."

Brynach nodded. "We are looking into it. I have a team already investigating leads. We'll find out who it was."

Rainer sat back in his chair. "The death of any Fae is a tragedy that can't go unpunished."

Aisling stepped forward with a growl. "Oh, shut up." Brynach chuckled behind her.

"Excuse me?" Rainer lifted a brow at her, and it hurt how much it reminded her of Brynach. But this man was nothing like her husband.

Aisling walked up to Rainer, and nobody stopped her. She'd have liked to see them try. When she reached him, she didn't hesitate to slap him across the face, his crown tumbling with a loud clang to the stone floor.

There were a few gasps, but nobody moved. What were they going to do? He wasn't King anymore. The crown meant jack-shit. They had two of those in their closet, too. They were just metal.

Brynach moved to her side and took her hand, glaring at his brother. "You deserved that," he told him.

Rainer nodded his head. "You get away with that once."

Aisling rolled her eyes. "Novel words for someone who allowed the death of countless witches and Ravdi on the other side of the Veil. Be quiet; the adults are speaking."

She watched him seethe. Rainer may not be as ruthless as Gabriel, but he was still an Unseelie royal and entirely unused to being treated like that. Aisling waited him out, refusing to lower her gaze. Eventually, he looked away. Her husband gave her hand a subtle squeeze, and she let herself breathe again.

When she looked to Ceiren to see how he felt about her attack on his brother, he gave her the smallest nod. Nobody else around the room seemed to object to her outburst, so he decided to keep the discussion going.

"I believe it's premature to start governing a people while they're still finding themselves," Ceiren contributed. "Clearly, the New Fae don't approve of our systems, and it's rather obvious the human government structure doesn't work, either."

"They can't be left to their own devices. Things will break down," Rainer responded.

Ceiren stood. "Will they? Because since the fall of the courts, I've seen a school started, a people coming together to learn about their new magic, and a sense of community that hasn't existed in Faerie so long as I can remember. It seems like they're doing just fine."

Around the room, there were nodding heads, but Aisling didn't miss that none of them were from the former leaders. She let a smirk settle on her face at the idea that they'd been made irrelevant by the drop of the Veil. Aisling might regret a lot in her life, but reuniting the two sides of the world was not one of them.

"Look at the training ground! You call that community?" Ellasar's gruff voice sounded.

"I call that the actions of a scared, angry individual or party. That doesn't represent the whole," Ceiren answered.

"Without leadership, people will devolve into chaos," Kyteler claimed.

Alex shook his head. "If anything, the continued attacks prove that you have no interest in protecting people unless they bow to you. You could, you know? If anything, the continued harm and threats prove that you are doing nothing at all to embrace and bring into the fold all of the New Fae."

Aisling stood stunned. As long as she'd known him, Alex was a quiet observer, and now he was getting into heated political debates. Sure, he'd back Brynach or protect the kids, but he didn't bother himself in larger matters.

At the silence, he continued, "In fact, I've heard no official statement of apology to the witches and Ravdi or New Fae. No offer to officially welcome them. No attempt to offer them protection. The only safe spaces they have are the ones we are creating now."

She waited for someone to argue.

Nobody did.

T he screaming and disagreeing continued for another few hours, with everyone talking in circles. Eventually, when it was clear absolutely nothing was being decided that day, they left. At home, they filled Riordan in and listened to him talk about the cleaning up and warding of the training ground. They did all this while Aisling set the table, Brynach poured them wine, and Riordan put the finishing touches on the fish and chips he was making. She'd convinced him to play music for them outside later that evening. For now, she was going to enjoy sitting with them.

Maybe she didn't get her whole day relaxing in bed, but this was pretty amazing.

"While we're all sitting here, there's something I'd like to talk to you about. That we would like to talk about." She could hear the nerves in Brynach's voice.

Aisling saw Riordan's shoulders tense and offered him a smile. He nodded, and Brynach continued.

"We'd like to have the handfasting soon. Like, immediately. We were thinking to keep it small, but if you want something different, we're happy to talk about it."

Riordan looked between the two of them. "Small and soon sounds perfect. The sooner, the better."

Aisling lost herself in those warm brown eyes. "There's something else I wanted to ask you. I wanted to know how you'd feel about me starting the paperwork to legally change my name?"

Riordan looked confused. "You don't have to ask me if it's okay to take Brynach's name, Ash."

Aisling smiled at him. "I'd like to be Aisling Campbell."

The New Fae's eyes went wide, and he made a choked sound. "What?"

"It's okay if you'd rather I not. It's just that I'm married to Bry, and the handfasting is amazing, but I want to be tied to you more securely," Aisling explained.

Riordan's eyes were wide as he looked between Aisling and Brynach. If he was waiting for the other man to argue, he'd be waiting a long time. At her look, he shook his head. "No. I mean, yes. Of course, I'm okay with that. But are you sure, Aisling?"

She leaned over and kissed him. "I'm positive. Besides, it has a nice ring to it."

"Aisling Campbell," Riordan tasted the words and grinned.

Brynach cleared his throat. "You know I can be a jealous man," he began.

Riordan held up his hands. "I'm not going to cause a rift in our relationship. I love the idea of her having my name, but not if it means upsetting you."

The large Fae shook his head and smiled, his hand moving to Riordan's shaking leg and stilling it. "That's not what I'm jealous of. I think Aisling Campbell is a beautiful name. I also think Brynach Campbell sounds particularly spectacular."

Aisling watched her partner realize exactly what Brynach was saying. His chest rose and fell in a quick, shallow rhythm.

"We're your family now. We're yours. Will you let us be Campbells?" Aisling asked.

He was crying. Tears sliding down his face as he nodded. "You have no idea what this means to me."

"We have some idea," Brynach said before pulling Riordan into his arms.

CHAPTER 15

Riordan

I t'll be nice to see everyone. I feel like I haven't seen your brother or my mom outside of work in forever," Aisling admitted, moving around their closet.

"He's been so busy tracking down internet leads that I don't think anyone's seen him. But he's making progress. He got through a few firewalls and found a couple IPs. It seems like each vigilante was messaged from a different one. No doubt, run through a scrambler. It's making things harder, but nothing is impossible for that man," Riordan said with pride. His brother really was something else.

He'd been avoiding his brother, knowing full well that once they sat down to talk, Liam would break his heart. The writing was on the wall. His brother wanted to go home. Riordan didn't blame him, not really, but the thought of his brother leaving hurt.

Riordan put the idea out of his head as they finished getting dressed. Brynach pulled on linen pants and a loose shirt. His thighs stretched the fabric, and Riordan had to tear his gaze away. Aisling was no safer to look at. She'd gone braless under a sundress and pulled her leather jacket over the thin straps. Meanwhile, Riordan stood in boxers, staring at a wall of clothing.

"He loves you. He's just struggling," Brynach reminded him. His large arm reached past Riordan and grabbed the black dress pants he'd worn to Aisling and Brynach's wedding. "These. They make your ass look amazing."

Riordan shivered at the other man's words. But then Aisling's soft curves were at his back, kissing his neck and reaching around him. "I love you in this shirt." She pushed the fitted hunter-green shirt against his chest.

He began to pull the clothes on, and Aisling moved to the bathroom to brush her hair and put on makeup. Her head popped out of the doorway when he finished dressing. "Imagine how much happier he'll be once Stanley is Fae. He'll be stronger. Just watch. I'm sure of it."

Brynach's hand slid across the countertop to touch his. Riordan's heart raced. He was marrying Aisling *and* Brynach today. People he loved, respected, and desired. And he was doing it as a Fae. The joy in his heart proved it was exactly where he wanted and needed to be.

"You okay?" Brynach whispered.

Riordan turned to him. "I'm great. You? Not getting nervous, are you?"

The large Fae leaned down, and his hot breath stirred the hair by his ear. "Do you remember how I celebrated marrying Aisling?"

He felt his cheeks go hot. "Yes," he said on a soft exhale.

Brynach's lips grazed his neck. "I plan on giving you the same treatment. I want you crying my name when you come tonight."

Sweet Goddess. Riordan's cock hardened in his pants as Brynach crowded him.

"Is that okay with you?" Brynach asked, his lips skimming Riordan's jaw.

His head bobbed.

"Good." Brynach kissed his cheek and straightened.

Aisling exited the bathroom, oblivious to what had just taken place. "Everyone will be here soon."

A quick look to the clock on the wall showed they had all of fifteen minutes tops before friends and family arrived in their backyard. There was already a small team of Fae and New Fae decorating a quickly constructed arbor with flowers. There were no chairs; it was a standing-room-only event, bare feet required, and casual dress.

"We have to bring down the ribbons," Aisling reminded them.

Brynach held up a box. "Already have them."

Aisling leaned forward and kissed Riordan. Brynach pulled her to him next, his large hand threading between her curls and holding her close. When their kiss ended, Riordan looked at the larger man and blushed before pulling his head down and swiping his tongue into Brynach's mouth.

"Ready?" Riordan asked when they parted.

Brynach chuckled. "Later, I'll show you just how ready, a chuisle."

His head swung to the other man. Aisling sighed happily next to him, but Riordan kept his eyes locked on Brynach's.

"Do you not like it?" he asked, softly.

"I. No. I like it just fine," Riordan answered. "It just surprised me."

Brynach smiled. "I've been tormenting Aisling by calling her a stoirin for so long. She's my little treasure, and you are my pulse." He held them both close. "A chuisle."

Hearing the Irish term of endearment, *a koosh-leh*, from Brynach's lips, sent his stomach flipping.

"We should go," Aisling said softly.

Both men turned, and Riordan winked at her. "After you, darling."

"Perverts, the both of you," Aisling sighed but put an extra sway in her hips and flicked up her skirt so they could see her panties.

"She pays for that later," Brynach growled.

"Can't wait," she called over her shoulder before her mother swooped in and embraced her.

Riordan and Brynach broke off to mingle with friends and family before the ceremony started. He was used to his brother's exuberant hugs, but this one was positively painful. Liam swung him around in a circle and whooped in a voice so loud everyone in the yard stopped what they were doing to watch.

"Liam! Damn it, put me down," he gasped.

He was placed back on his feet. "Sorry. I'm so just happy for you. This is fantastic, Rory."

"*He's right, you know,*" Valo commented. Riordan turned to see his familiar sitting at the edge of their woods. They'd agreed they wanted their familiars here. Rin was currently sitting atop Kongur, looking much more comfortable than Riordan had ever been on the massive horse's back. "*You balance one another.*"

"*I prefer when you're being a sarcastic shit,*" Riordan quipped.

"*I'll be back at it tomorrow, promise. For now, let everyone remind you how lucky you are.*"

Riordan greeted Russell and Kareem and then joined Sean, Lettie, Cait, Breena, and Jashana near the drinks and snacks. They were talking and laughing together happily. He joined in the conversation, accepting congratulations.

"Are you taking a honeymoon?" Russell blushed. "I'm not sure how this works, to be honest."

"Me either. But no, not right away. Eventually, we will," Riordan answered. "I want to show them Ireland, and Ash really wants to see Scotland."

Lettie gave him a sad smile. "To see Trent's place?"

He nodded. "Yeah. When she's ready."

She shook her head. "I still can't believe he's not here for this."

Cait wrapped her arm around her sister, and Sean moved closer to her. Lettie had support, but he knew it was hard.

Every time something like this came up, he missed his parents and Aunt Maggie. Sometimes, life just wasn't fair.

Aisling called his name, and everyone moved into a half circle around the archway of flowers. Riordan joined his partners under it and basked in the glow of their smiles.

Aisling spoke first. "Thank you for coming to our handfasting and commitment ceremony. Your love and support mean more than you know or my words can convey. Today, my partners and I give ourselves to one another."

"Our love is not tiered; it is a relationship born of respect and admiration for one another," Brynach continued.

"And today, in front of our family and friends, we swear to continue that love and partnership through the rest of our lives. Thank you for joining us and blessing our union," Riordan finished.

There were whistles and claps, and then everyone quieted. Aisling's mother stepped forward and pulled a gold lace ribbon from the wooden box with a tree of life carved in the top. All three of them placed their left hands between them and maintained eye contact as her mother bound their wrists in the soft fabric.

"Gold represents longevity, wealth, intelligence, and energy. I wish that and so much more for the three of you," she kissed each of them on the cheek before moving away.

With their hands tied now, it was Liam who removed the blue leather strap and proceeded to wrap it around their wrists, linking them tighter. "Blue is a symbol of devotion, peace, and sincerity. If there's one thing I've learned about your relationship, it's that you share the most pure of loves. May you continue to be as dedicated to one another's happiness for the rest of your lives as you are today." Liam hugged them each and moved to Amber's side.

Riordan was fighting back tears by the time Breena approached them. She removed the brown vine. The three of them linked their fingers, and Brynach's sister finished tying their hands together.

"This brown vine represents a grounding. If anyone deserves a home, a haven, it's the three of you. May you always find comfort and safety in one another's arms." Breena's voice was low and soft. She smiled at each of them before stepping away.

Riordan straightened, eyes meeting Aisling's and then Brynach's. The love reflected there made his knees weak. He'd never been happier. And this was just the start of a lifetime of days like this.

They turned and raised their joined hands. Everyone clapped and cheered, and like that, it was done. They moved around the yard, talking to family and friends, still tied to one another.

The crowd greeted them, offering their congratulations and well wishes. The first toast of the night was offered up by Lettie and Sean, and then Aisling's mother helped them untie themselves. Dawn took the ribbons and cords and braided them before winding them back into the box. They had decided to find a way to display them in the home. But that was only after Aisling vetoed them being used to tie her up that night. He closed his eyes and listened to the voices of their loved ones.

Unlike Aisling and Brynach's wedding, there would be no political bullshit. And unlike their bonding ceremony, there would be no Dexter harassing them. Today was going to go smoothly. Which is why when Alex approached Brynach and started discussing the school, Riordan stepped in and shut it down.

"Not today, friend." Riordan put a hand on Brynach's arm and smiled at Alex. "Talk business another day."

The other Fae nodded. "I'm sorry. It's a habit now. Congratulations, all of you," he said, bending to kiss Aisling's cheek.

"Thank you." Aisling grinned and hugged Riordan's side. "Now, if you don't mind, my partners and I are going to enjoy some of that delicious food over there."

Brynach led them through the yard to a table heavy with food. It was simple barbeque fare, but that was perfect. With their plates full, they made their way to the table set for the three of them.

"What do you want to drink?" Brynach asked after setting down his plate.

"Beer for me. Ash, champagne?" Riordan turned to her, and at her nod, the large Fae moved to get them.

"When he gets back, will you stand with me? I want to say something to everyone," Aisling asked.

"Of course," he answered. "Everything okay?"

"Perfectly." She leaned over and kissed him. Brynach approached and handed them each a drink. Aisling stood with the men at her side. Behind Aisling's back, Riordan reached for Brynach's hand.

"If I can have everyone's attention for a minute," Aisling began, and the small crowd quieted. "I want to thank you all for coming today. You are our dearest family and friends, and today was made more special because of you."

She kissed both men in turn.

"I think I can speak for the three of us when I say that this is the happiest we've been. Had you told me a few years ago that I'd bond to a powerful, stubborn Ravdi or marry the surly Dark Fae, I'd have laughed in your face." Aisling smiled at each of them.

"Our relationship may not look conventional, but Brynach and I have decided that we'd like to keep one tradition alive. If there was ever a person who deserved a family surrounding him, it's Riordan. Which is why, this morning, Brynach and I filled out paperwork to become Campbells."

Liam stared at them in wonder. Mrs. Quinn wiped at her eyes. Around them, their family and friends were grinning and congratulating them.

"So, from the Campbells to our friends and family, please eat up." Aisling lifted her glass, and they tapped their bottles against it before drinking.

Riordan hadn't been expecting that, but he loved that they'd announced it to everyone. After all he'd been through, all the heartache and loss, it felt impossible to be this happy.

Each time he started to worry this, too, would be taken away, he felt the reassuring press of Aisling's hand on his leg or Brynach at his side. They reminded him good things can last.

Soft music played, and a few people started to dance. Riordan stood with his brother on the outside of the circle.

"They took your name," he commented.

"They surprised me by asking not long ago." Riordan looked at his brother. "You don't mind, do you?"

"Not at all, Rory. The opposite. I love it. I'm glad you have them." Liam paused a moment. "I have to go home."

He nodded. "I know. It's alright, Liam. I'm okay."

His brother clapped him on the back. "Of course you are."

They changed the topic, and eventually, Liam and Amber drifted away as others came up to say goodbye to the trio. Aisling's mother was one of the last to leave after insisting on cleaning up leftovers and gathering trash.

Aisling stopped her. "Please, as a gift to us, just leave it."

"How is it a gift to leave messes for you to straighten?" her mother complained.

Brynach and Riordan shared a look, and Aisling stifled a groan. Her mother caught the look and blushed. "Oh, Goddess. Right." She kissed her daughter. "Goodnight. I love you," she called with a wave over her shoulder before sifting.

Riordan slumped into a deck chair. "I thought she'd never leave."

Brynach laughed. "I like that you're so eager for me, a chuisle."

Aisling sat on Brynach's lap and began kissing his neck. Their husband had a fire in his citrine eyes as he slid his hand up Aisling's bare leg. "What should we do tonight, a stoirin?"

Their wife squirmed in his lap with a pout on her face. "You know I hate decision-making."

"I think you'll like this one," Brynach promised. "Go to the closet and get the two gold-wrapped packages in my bottom drawer."

Aisling leapt up and ran into the house. Meanwhile, Brynach kept his eyes on Riordan and licked his lips.

"Your safeword, Riordan," Brynach encouraged.

"Um, I don't have one. I haven't needed one before." He was confused.

His husband smirked. "You might tonight. Pick one."

Aisling exited the house with two boxes in her hand. One slim and long and the other wider and shorter. She sat back on Brynach's lap, but he lifted her and made her stand. Carefully, he reached up her leg and pulled her skirt up. Only when Riordan was staring at her underwear-covered ass did he slowly hook a finger into them and pull them off her body.

Their wife stepped out of the scrap of lace and squealed when Brynach turned her and pulled her into his lap, positioning her legs on the outside of his. She was spread wide, her skirt rising so Riordan could see her. Aisling rocked herself on his thick leg.

"Riordan, choose one," Brynach reminded him.

"Ravdi," he blurted, and his partner nodded.

Aisling leaned her head back on Brynach's shoulder and pulled his face to hers, kissing him while she rocked on him. The larger Fae moved his hand down to her spread legs.

"So needy," he purred as he stroked her clit. Aisling moaned into his neck when he pulled his hand away and spanked her pussy. She jumped, her cheeks red. "Pick a box."

She chose the larger, longer box. Brynach's face split in a grin, and Riordan didn't know if that was a good or bad thing. He reverently took the other box from Aisling and handed it to Riordan.

"Happy handfasting, my loves. Aisling, you first," he instructed.

Their girl tore into the package, gasping at something Riordan couldn't see until she lifted a flogger with three colors of fabric, maybe leather, braided together to make up each of the falls. The gold, blue, and brown wove together like the ties that bound them earlier in the day.

Aisling moaned. "Husband?"

The dark Fae's lips curled into a smile that managed to look threatening. "Do I mark you as my own, or would you like me to show you how to mark Riordan?"

Her eyes went wide. "I couldn't."

Brynach gripped her jaw and turned her face to his. "You can do anything your heart desires, Aisling. Anything. Tell her, Riordan."

"I'd let you," he answered in a voice deep with lust. He couldn't lie; he was curious to learn what was so enticing about the pain Brynach inflicted on her.

She nodded. "Mark me. I won't do that without practice. I want to get it right, and tonight is too important."

He corrected her. "Anything you do or want is right. But I won't push you."

She sighed and went back to slowly moving over his leg. Both their eyes landed on Riordan, who, with shaky hands, unwrapped his box.

Inside, like a crown jewel, was a set of glass butt plugs on a satin liner. Riordan paled. They weren't huge; in fact, the one was quite slim, with a curve to it before a mushroom head.

"Which means Riordan gets the butt plug. There's a his and a hers, but I think you'll especially like the prostate-massaging one. I've already cleaned them, and there's lube in your box."

Riordan considered it a moment and nodded. He didn't want to safeword, but he hadn't considered bottoming with Brynach. He'd always assumed he'd be the one fucking him.

The growl that left Brynach when he didn't object was damn near feral. "Inside or out?"

Aisling looked to Riordan and shrugged, making it clear the decision was his. Riordan looked around their lit yard, the arch of flowers they'd celebrated under, and saw how it could play out. He stood, not saying anything, and moved down the steps and across their yard with his box in hand.

He didn't have to look to know they were following him.

The stool their handfasting box had sat on remained, and he lowered his gift to it. Riordan removed his clothing and stood under the blooms, lit by the small lights strung in the arch.

Brynach paused. "Fuck, you're beautiful."

Aisling lifted her dress over her head and walked to him naked. His hand wound in her hair, and he kissed her before pulling back to whisper against her mouth.

"Shall we run?"

She shivered in his arms and gave the slightest nod. He held tight to her hand, and together they took off. Brynach snarled behind them.

"Oh, you're in trouble now!" There was mirth in his voice as the two of them ran through the yard, not really trying to evade him. They made a game of it, him letting them get away before chasing them again. Brynach called out threats, and they laughed, hand in hand, and ran naked through their yard.

A hand clamped around Riordan's waist, pulling him back against a hard chest. He stilled, this body thrumming as Brynach used his free hand to reach down and grip his cock.

"It's all fun and games until someone comes by and sees what's mine," he growled into Riordan's ear. "Aisling! You better get your sweet ass over here, or you're going over my knee with that second plug in."

She popped into existence in front of them, flushed and panting. Riordan stared at her, still pinned to Brynach's chest with the other man's erection pressing into his back.

"You're going to be a good girl for me and open your mouth," Brynach ordered.

Aisling stared into Riordan's eyes when she opened for Brynach. He lifted his hand from the other man's cock and held three out to their wife. Mouth open, tongue out, Aisling took his fingers into her mouth. Her eyes watered as Brynach fucked her throat with them. Only when Aisling was drooling down his palm did the large Fae remove his hand and return it to Riordan's cock, using her spit as lube to stroke him.

"Oh, fuck," Riordan groaned. Brynach moved him just to the side, where he continued to jack him off.

"Bry, please," Riordan begged.

"Please, what, beautiful man?" He looked away from Aisling to give him his full attention.

"I won't last like this, and I want to."

"Hmmph. You're just as greedy as our wife. Is this about what you want or about what I'm willing to give you?" he demanded.

Riordan wasn't sure what the right answer was, so he gave him the honest one. "Both."

Brynach smiled and ran his thumb over the crown of Riordan's cock, picking up the precome leaking from the tip. He brought it to his mouth and sucked it between his lips.

"Go get the lube and pick your toy."

Riordan nodded and stepped to the box, bringing back the curved prostate massager and the bottle of lube. Aisling was on her knees, sucking Brynach deep into her throat while the large Fae fisted her hair and degraded her.

"Such a pretty little whore for me with your mascara running down your face," he said as he stroked her cheek with his other hand. "That's enough." Brynach pulled his hips back, and Aisling pouted.

He took the toy and lube from Riordan and spun him. Using his large hand, he pushed on Riordan's back until he was bent over, hands in the lattice of the arch.

"Hold tight, a chuisle." He caressed his back. "Aisling, I want you on your knees for Riordan. Suck him and make him feel good while you play with yourself and I get his ass ready."

She didn't say anything; she simply ducked under Riordan's arms and knelt before him, obeying. The distraction was wonderful, and the stimulation overwhelming as the cool lube dripped between his cheeks and Brynach spread him.

"You trust me to make this good for you, Riordan. If it becomes too much, let me know," Brynach told him.

"Okay. Fuck. Aisling, damn it, that's too good," Riordan groaned.

Brynach chuckled. "Don't you dare let him finish, wife."

She pulled off him with a whimper. "I can't help it if I'm good at what I do." The hand between her legs had her squirming.

"Nice deep breaths, Riordan," Brynach instructed and pushed a lubed finger against the tight ring of his asshole.

Aisling went back to work with her mouth on his dick, stroking a hand along his thigh while the other moved over her pussy. From his position, he could only see the back of her head and her sweet ass. Riordan wanted to touch her, but his grip on the wood was resolute.

Brynach's finger pressed and slid past his ring of muscle, and he cursed. It burned a bit, but it faded quickly to a fascinating sensation. Aisling doubled her efforts on him, and Riordan tried to focus. The pressure in his ass was impossible to ignore.

"Wife," Brynach called, his finger thrusting inside Riordan. "Are we finishing inside or out?"

Aisling chewed her lip. "Inside. I have a request."

Both men turned their gaze to her. "I'm going to need you to use your words, wife. Tell me what you want, in detail," Brynach's voice dipped deep, walking the line between seductive and threatening.

Riordan heard Aisling swallow before speaking, "I want you to fuck me. Both of you. Together. Tonight. Finally."

The growl that left Brynach's throat had Riordan's cock dripping. "In the bedroom. Now."

They raced to their bed, more than ready for what came next.

"Before anything else. Riordan, your toy." Brynach held out his hand. Gently, he guided Riordan onto his belly and used the bedside lube to get the toy ready. Slowly, he used the cold glass to lube the ring. His finger entered again, and Riordan hissed. Experimentally, he rocked back on Brynach's hand.

"More," he panted. Aisling lifted his face and kissed him as Brynach added another finger.

"Oh fuck," he groaned. "How do you do this, Ash?"

"You okay?" Brynach asked, kissing his back.

"Yeah. Doesn't feel bad, just different," Riordan answered. Aisling kissed him again, and his husband removed his fingers, replacing them with the head of the toy.

"Relax and let me in, Riordan," Brynach encouraged.

He did his best to let his body go loose. He wanted this. Wanted not only to please Brynach but to know what this could be like. Patiently, Brynach stroked his cock as he inserted the toy. Overwhelmed with sensation, Riordan didn't even realize it was fully seated in him until Brynach twisted and thrust it a few times.

"You did so good, Riordan." Brynach kissed his back. "Fuck, that's hot. Now, I'm going to finish in our wife's pretty pussy, but I want you to fuck her a little first," Brynach instructed.

He didn't have to be told twice. Aisling scrambled onto her hands and knees, and Riordan moved behind her. He wasted no time sliding home.

Brynach moved in front of Aisling and grabbed her abused jaw.

"My heart, can you take more?" he asked her.

"Always for you, husband," she answered and opened that pretty mouth of hers.

The extra weight of the toy in Riordan's ass was strange. It hit spots inside him that shot electricity up his spine when he flexed his ass and thrust into Aisling. He snaked an arm around his wife to circle her clit, further shifting the toy to a new position that had him cursing. With a laugh, Brynach grabbed him by the back of the neck and pulled him close. He kissed the other man, knowing this had to be as good as it got. He was wrong.

Brynach's long arms circled Riordan's hips, and his hand cupped the flared end of the toy. The way his fingers pulsed on the toy in Riordan's ass had him ready to come. The other man's mouth moved to his ear, and he spoke in a husky voice just for him.

"You look so beautiful right now. So perfect as you take care of our wife. And still, all I can think about is how badly I want to bury my cock in your tight ass." Brynach let go of his ear and kissed his mouth hungrily.

"Oh, crap. Not going to last," Riordan cried.

"That's enough of that, then." Brynach moved away from both of them, leaving them moaning. "Sadly, I won't be inside your ass tonight, Riordan. But that's only because you're going to be too busy inside Aisling's."

Riordan turned her head and kissed her. "I love you."

Brynach kept Aisling on all fours and positioned Riordan's leg until he was lying below her. With carefully placed pillows Riordan comfortably licked at her pretty pussy. Aisling cried out immediately following the sharp sound of the flogger against her skin. Brynach landed hit after hit of their braided flogger against her pale flesh. Riordan did all he could to make her feel good while Brynach brought her pain,

He tried to stay out of his own head. Goddess knew the taste of Aisling was enough to overwhelm the senses, but all he could think of was fucking her ass. Not only was he absolutely into it, but knowing how badly Aisling wanted it made it that much hotter. The idea that he'd feel Brynach's cock slide along his through her body thrilled him.

Right now, he wasn't about to dissect the way Brynach wanting to fuck his ass made him wild. With steady pressure and speed right where Aisling needed him, she was crying out her orgasm as Brynach rained down strikes. Her pussy pulsed around the tongue he plunged into her, desperate to drink her in. He squeezed her thighs and then slid out from under her so she could settle all the way down on her shaky legs.

Their husband dragged Aisling into his arms. Brynach kissed Aisling hard. Tears were streaming down her face, but she was kissing him back as if she needed the pain to breathe. When Riordan reached her, he gripped her jaw and pulled her face away from Brynach.

Aisling cried out but didn't resist when he kissed her just as hard. In fact, she moaned and pressed her face harder into his fingers. "Where do you want her?"

"You remember your safeword, Aisling?" he asked, stroking a hand down her spine.

She nodded. "Yes."

"No matter how we've prepped you, it's going to feel different, being stuffed full of both our cocks. Are you sure you can handle it?" Brynach followed up.

"I'll take them," she promised.

"Of course, you will. You're my filthy princess." He splayed his body out on the bed, his head propped up on pillows. "Ride me, a stoirin."

Aisling didn't need further instruction. There was no gentle adjusting to his size; she lined him up and impaled herself on his dick. Watching her bounce on him, seeing his face darken with lust, made him feel drunk. Riordan moved behind her, straddled Brynach's legs, and held her tits. He moved with her, his eyes locked on the larger man's.

"Get the bottle and prep her," he instructed.

Riordan reached to his left and squeezed lubricant onto his fingers. He slid his hand down Aisling's back, groaning when she moaned and leaned forward on Brynach. His finger found her asshole and rested on it, pulsing until she slammed herself down on Brynach's cock and impaled her ass on his digit.

"Fuck, yes!" she cried out.

Slowly, Riordan added another finger, prepping her like Brynach had taught him to.

"I need you," she begged.

Brynach's hand reached up and pinched her nipple. "You don't make demands here."

"Sorry, husband."

His laughter followed. "You won't get out of this that easily."

"I don't want out of anything. I want more in me," she teased.

"Give our wife what she wants, Riordan."

He applied lube to his cock, generously. Then he slicked his fingers with more and circled her asshole again.

"Come here," Brynach said and pulled Aisling down against his chest.

Riordan pushed his slick cock against the tight ring of muscle. His hand was choked up, a finger along the head, pushing into her. He slid as she moved. "Stay still a second, Ash," Riordan instructed.

Brynach soothed her, his hand stroking her back. "Lightly push against him. Relax and open, love. Let us in until we're the only thing that exists."

Riordan felt the moment her body eased, and he slid into her. Fuck, she was tight. The first inch of him pressed into her, and he paused.

"More," she demanded.

The further in he slid with his shallow thrusts, the tighter she got. She was practically strangling his cock. Riordan poured more lube down her ass crack and around the remainder of his shaft, slid out, and then back in again. With patience, he eventually bottomed out inside her ass.

"Oh fuck. So full," Aisling cried. She reached back and caressed Riordan's thigh. He was terrified that he was hurting her, but she wasn't asking him to stop.

"You're taking us so well." Brynach kissed her sweating face. "I'm going to move now, and Riordan's going to stay where he is for a bit."

Riordan clenched his jaw so hard his teeth squeaked. He fought to stay still as he felt the larger man's cock slide in and out of Aisling's body, stroking along his own. Damn it, that was hot.

"Oh, Goddess!" Aisling wiggled between them, and Riordan nearly blew his load. "It feels so good."

Slowly, and because he couldn't stay still anymore, Riordan began to move alongside Brynach. The sensation was intense for him; he could only imagine what Aisling was feeling. He pushed down on the small of her back, making her arch more. Her clit pushed against Brynach, and with her ass presented to him, he was able to slide even deeper into her.

Brynach's eyes rolled back, and he called a stop. "Don't move, Riordan. Aisling, I want you to fuck us. Make yourself come on our cocks."

Aisling braced her hands on either side of Brynach's head and pushed herself back on their cocks. As gentle as they had been with her, easing her into the sensation of both of them at once, she was not. Aisling was voracious in her search for an orgasm.

Riordan leaned forward, kissing her back. "I love the way you look like this, Aisling."

Not to be outdone, Brynach got vocal. "I can feel Riordan's cock stretching that pretty little ass. Watching him fuck you while you pant in my ear and your pussy clenches around my dick may be the sexiest thing I've ever seen."

She slammed back on his cock, and Riordan cursed. He wasn't going to last. Aisling seated herself on both of them nestled deep and rolled her hips, making it good for herself. Her breathing changed, and he knew she was close.

"Come for us, Princess," Brynach encouraged, sensing the same thing.

When Aisling came, her entire body shook, her muscles contracting around him. He stroked into her, Brynach doing the same. The slide of themselves through her pulsing channels was too much. Then his husband's hands circled Aisling and pulsed against his plug. Lightning shot up his spine, and Riordan emptied himself inside Aisling.

Even as wrecked as they were, Aisling laid a hand on Brynach's chest, and Riordan mirrored her image as they watched the man they loved fall over the edge. Riordan fought to keep his weight off Aisling, but his body was worn out. He didn't want to hurt her now that the pleasure had passed. The worry that they'd pushed her too far slammed into him. Had he been too rough?

Aisling shook under him, and it terrified him. "Aisling?"

Then her laughter rolled over them. "I will never be the same."

Brynach chuckled. "We're so proud of you. We love you so much."

Riordan kissed her shoulder, and Brynach claimed her mouth. He felt the slow slide of Brynach's hips as he moved Aisling's body and slid out of her. Immediately, Riordan felt less constricted. She sighed at the loss of him, but Riordan knew he'd have an easier time pulling out without the added pressure of Brynach's cock.

Aisling's body tensed a little as he pushed back on his ankles and left her body. "Are you okay?" he asked as she fell boneless against Brynach's chest.

"I'm a noodle," she giggled. "No bones. Just gooey limp goodness."

"Mission accomplished," Brynach murmured and stroked a hand down her back. "Riordan, can you get the shower running?"

He left, giving Brynach time for aftercare with Aisling. Only when the bathroom was steamy did he show with Aisling cradled in his arms. For the first time in their relationship, Riordan was a part of Brynach's aftercare.

"Husband," Brynach spoke softly and stroked his cheek. Riordan looked into the man's citrine eyes, his long hair a mess around his face, and sighed.

"Yes?"

"Come here and kiss me," Brynach instructed, his voice still low and soothing. The larger man held him tight, kissed him softly, and gently removed the plug. "You did so good for me, Riordan. I love you," the other man praised.

Then Brynach turned to Aisling. "So perfect for us, wife. I'd be lost without you."

His voice had gone so serious it gave Riordan pause. Aisling raised a hand to his stubbled cheek and smiled up at him. "No more than we would be without you."

The three of them exchanged quiet words. Promises that the only people they'd ever need lived within these walls. And when they dried off and fell back into bed, Brynach held them as if they were his entire world.

CHAPTER 16

Brynach

He could ignore one ringing phone. Two were suspicious. But when all three of the phones vibrated and rang, Brynach knew something was wrong.

"What the fuck is happening?" Riordan grumbled.

Aisling was already up, with the blanket pooled around her waist, exposing her breasts, which still bore marks from his teeth. Brynach barely contained the growl rumbling in his chest at the sight of them. He ripped his gaze from Aisling's pale skin to his phone with a curse.

"Get up. Get dressed," he ordered. Neither one of them argued.

Riordan grabbed his phone as he hurried downstairs with Aisling hot on his heels. They dressed quickly, and then Riordan saw his messages.

"Fuck!" he cursed. "Let's go!"

They sifted into a riot of activity. Guards and police screaming and patrols scrambling. Alarms blared, and it was clear the prison was on lockdown. But even outside the walls, they could hear the inmates screaming and rattling bars. The news crews jumped out of their vans and began to set up.

It took time to work their way to where Chief Pilson was standing with a very pissed-off warden.

"How the fuck does something like this happen?" Brynach raged.

The warden shook her head. "The cameras are obscured. We're working blind. There's one guard on the inside, but they took their coms. We are working to get eyes."

Riordan pulled his phone out and began speaking into it. "Sean, we need you, buddy."

Brynach turned to Pilson. "We'll get your eyes, but you turn the other way and don't pay attention to how."

The older man gave him the smallest of nods. "Just get us in."

"Give him a few. He'll call back when he's through," Riordan told them.

The warden and chief shared a look and then turned his way. He didn't like that at all. Beside him, his partners moved closer, and he braced himself. "What?"

"It's not just that Turstin's ward is open, but that they've barricaded themselves in and taken hostages," the warden began.

"You said that already," Riordan pointed out.

"Among the hostages are a guard and a civilian that was warding the cells," she continued. "Sydney is in there."

"Fuck!" Brynach drew his hands through his long hair. "With Peggy?"

Aisling cried, "She'll kill her. We need to get in there right now!"

Brynach put a hand on her arm. "If they can't see in there, you're not going in. Sydney will be okay. She survived her mother for a long time. She knows how to navigate her. We wait until Sean does his job."

The warden looked at them. "Even if we get eyes, you're not going in there. There's a whole block out of their cells."

"Try and stop me," Brynach snarled.

"We have professionals trained for situations like this. Riot gear. Weapons training," Pilson reminded them. "Let us do our job."

He shook his head. "We're standing around, and my sister is in danger. Forgive me for not trusting you to do your job when this happened in the first place."

He saw the warden bristle, but she held her tongue. Riordan's phone rang, and everyone turned toward him as he answered. He made a humming sound and hung up. "Cameras are online."

A scream came from the door to the prison, "Warden! They're back."

The three of them grinned at one another and followed her into the prison. Brynach took Aisling's hand and leaned to her ear as they walked. "You will not go in there, Aisling. Pilson is right. We're not the experts here."

She looked up at him. "Then none of us go in."

Riordan nodded. "I like the sound of that. I'm in no rush to go into a cell block of criminals."

If he had his way, Brynach would be going in to rescue Sydney, but if it meant his partners were safe, he'd sit it out. They were escorted with the warden into a control room where video footage of the riot was streaming.

"That's happening right now?" Aisling whispered. Tables and chairs were overturned and barricading the doors to the block. Inmates were fighting, and more than a few were strewn across the floor, clearly dead or injured. Brynach had no basis for comparison, but that didn't look good.

The warden was talking with a heavily armored man with a shield at his side. More officers dressed just like him lined the hallway. He listened to the woman outline their plan. They needed to break through the blockade and gain access to the block.

Over the intercom system, the warden instructed the inmates to get back in their cells or face the riot police. As he watched, many did just that. While she spoke, the guards made their way down the hall toward the block. While the chaos inside the square room had lessened, there was one thing that hadn't.

Peggy stood in the middle of a group of inmates, Sydney in her grip, a knife in her side. The others around her seemed to be shielding her. Brynach's eyes never left his sister. She winced and struggled but couldn't move with that weapon lodged in her.

"She's New Fae, Bry. She'll be okay," Aisling reminded him.

He nodded his head. "How'd she get a weapon?"

The warden turned and shook her head. "We sweep the cells, but weapons are made and traded in a prison."

"That doesn't look like a prison-made weapon," Riordan commented.

"We'll do an in-depth review of all prison footage leading up to the riot. But right now, my priority is regaining control of that block and the safety of my guards and your sister." She turned away from them.

Together they watched as the cells locked and the guards started breaking into the block. Peggy called out, but they couldn't hear what was said. The warden turned to them briefly. "If I play sound, will you stay calm?"

Aisling squeezed his hand, and Riordan put his arm around Brynach's hips. "Do it."

Sound slammed into them. Screams, rattles, and the loud noise of officers using a battering ram on the door. It assaulted his senses, but he tried to narrow in on the older woman's voice.

"I'll kill her. If you think I won't, you're out of your fucking mind," she yelled.

It had been a while since they'd seen the disgraced Firinne. She looked awful. Prison had not been kind to her. But Peggy didn't address anyone else after that. Instead, she twisted the knife in Sydney's side and spoke to her. Whatever she said, it made his sister flinch.

The officers finally broke through the door, and a few of the people surrounding Peggy dropped to the ground, hands over their heads. The rest stood firm before the older woman and her hostage. Brynach didn't know where they went from here, but he knew they needed to be fast about it.

One of the officers spoke. "Get on your knees and put your hands behind your heads. It's your last warning before we open fire."

"Open fire," Aisling gasped.

"Rubber bullets," the warden assured her. "But they'll drop you."

Brynach didn't want to see Sydney hit in the crossfire, but it was better than the knife in her side. The officers took careful aim, and a few of the women around Peggy dropped. Her voice called out, but she didn't get down on her knees. Sydney had tears running down her face, but she was staying strong. Brynach was so fucking proud of her.

As the barrier between Peggy and the officers dwindled, he noticed his sister's eyes darting to the side. She was going to move. Fuck. His whole body tensed, and then she burst into action. Sydney ripped her arm away from her mother and threw herself onto the floor while the officers opened fire.

Shields still up and inmates in their cells screaming, they rushed forward to cuff and tase those who still resisted. One officer snagged Sydney and dragged her back. She was out of sight of the cameras, and Brynach was moving.

Behind him, his partners jogged, and the warden screamed after them. Fuck her. Fuck all of this. They hit a locked door, and Brynach stared at the camera in the corner. "Let me through, now!"

There was a buzz, and he ate up ground toward the next door, which also buzzed for him. The officer leading Sydney was visible through a square of glass in the door. He waited impatiently for the door to open and the two to come through.

As soon as the door was closed and locked behind his sister, he ran to her.

Sydney fell into his arms, crying. "Brynach! Goddess, that was scary."

He swept an arm under her legs and glared at the officer. "Infirmary?"

The man shook his head. "Inaccessible. You'll have to take her out of the prison to get looked at."

That's all he had to hear. Riordan and Aisling led the way back through the halls, opening doors as they unlocked. The warden looked at them as they walked past. Peggy was her problem. Right now, he needed Sydney looked at.

As soon as he exited the building, he made his way toward the police. "I need a medic."

The officer pointed toward the edge of the cop cars to an ambulance. Sydney shuffled in his arms. "I can walk, Bry."

"The hell you can," he growled.

"Just let him carry you, Sydney; it's easier that way," Aisling told her.

She sighed. "It's already healing. I can feel it."

He didn't give a damn. He rounded the back of the ambulance. "Hello!" he called when he didn't immediately see someone. The back door opened, and a woman popped out. Brynach wasn't happy to relinquish his sister, but he did so she could get looked at. Just like she'd said, she was already healing, and the EMT didn't anticipate any problems.

"Shouldn't she have scans to check on her organs or something?" This woman was clearly incompetent.

"If she was human, yes. But her body is already doing what it does best. She'll be okay; you have my word." She smiled at him.

"Lady, I don't know you. Your word doesn't mean shit to me," he snarled.

Aisling slapped him on the arm. "Brynach! You apologize right now."

"I'm sorry," he offered. "I'll take her back to her house. You guys, go home. I'll meet you there."

He could see them both about to argue and narrowed his eyes at them until they nodded. Aisling gave his sister a hug, and Riordan patted him on the back before they sifted back home. Brynach turned to his sister and gently pulled her away from the crowd.

"Now, we're going to talk," he told her.

Sydney tilted up her head. "About what?"

Brynach pulled her close and sifted her to the safehouse. "Your mother. What was she saying to you?"

His sister paled and shook her head. "I don't want to think about it. It was nothing to do with you, just more childhood trauma brought to life."

"Did she say anything about Gabriel? Or Brielle? Or Dexter?" Brynach heard himself and cringed. "I'm sorry. That doesn't matter right now. I'm glad you're okay. Get inside and lock up."

"I understand. If it was anything you could use, I'd tell you. I know you need to protect them. Thank you for coming for me." She wrapped her arms around him.

"Always," he promised. Brynach hugged her back and then waited until she was locked away inside. Only then did he run a hand over his face and sift home. Standing alone, Brynach hung his head and let himself take one deep breath. What he wouldn't give to go back to yesterday and the bliss of their bed.

"Bry!" Aisling ran to him, throwing herself into his arms. She took his face and brought his gaze down to hers. "Look at me. Just me. We're okay."

"A stoirin, what the hell are you doing?" Brynach asked and tried to lift his head.

She pulled him tighter to her. "I need you to stay calm for me. Please."

"You're not making that easy. Tell me what's going on." Brynach shook his head free of her hold, and his entire world narrowed to one man.

Just outside the wards that they'd sifted into stood the last person he expected. Riordan was standing entirely too close to them, ward or no ward. Brynach moved forward, pushing Aisling behind him and pulling Riordan back a step.

"Bry, wait a minute. Listen to us," Riordan put a hand on his arm, holding him back. "Look at him."

Gabriel stood, hands out in front of him, eyes wide. He looked awful.

Aisling stood at his side, allowing him to move her behind him again. "Really look at him. He's not Fae. He's human."

Brynach tried to think past the rage screaming for his father's blood. He forced himself to gather magic to him and assess his father. Aisling was right. Gabriel was human.

"So, they lied about him being Fae, so what?" He didn't want to break the ward and allow Gabriel in, but he wanted his hands around the man's throat. "Just means I can end him faster."

"Please, don't," Gabriel croaked. "I know I have no right to be here, but I'm throwing myself at your mercy."

"Where was your mercy when I was a child and you 'taught' me lessons? Where was mercy when Fae begged for their lives?" Brynach snarled. "Fuck mercy."

Gabriel dropped to his knees and raised his hands. "I don't want to die. I know you're looking for me. I thought I could lay low until things died down, but that's not an option anymore. I'm being framed."

Brynach could see the fear in his eyes. But that didn't mean Brynach gave a fuck about him.

"You have two minutes," Brynach said.

The relief in the man's eyes was visceral. "I'm not hurting Brielle. I've been in hiding trying to make it out of this alive, but it's clear someone wants you hunting me."

"Yeah, me," Brynach murmured.

"They're hurting her in my old home, with my weapons, in

my style. But I swear, it's not me." Gabriel was pleading, and it was pathetic.

"And you expect us to do what?" Brynach asked.

Without any sense of irony, Gabriel shrugged. "Keep me safe."

The laughter that erupted from his throat was manic, even to his own ears.

"I heard enough from Aisling and Riordan,"

"Don't you even say their names!" Brynach shouted.

Gabriel nodded and took a step back. "I heard that Peggy got a hold of Sydney. If she does that again, if she gets out, she'll come looking for me. If she finds me human, she'll kill me. If anyone from our court finds me …"

"They'll kill you. I fail to see the problem." Brynach was unmoved.

"Bry," Aisling began, and he closed his eyes. He didn't tell her how to handle her father, but he had a feeling she was about to say something he really wouldn't like. "He might be able to help us."

"How?" Riordan asked.

Aisling moved to his side and stepped in front of him. She forced his eyes down to hers, and he saw the love there. She wasn't doing this to hurt him. She turned, her back to his front, and faced Gabriel.

"Know that I won't hesitate to kill you and that I'll have to fight the two of these men to have the honor," she told his father. "You want protection, and we're in a position to offer it. In return, you will help us build a case against Peggy and Dexter. You will be the nail in their coffins, or this is over before it begins."

"Done," Gabriel answered immediately. "Whatever I know, I'll tell you."

Brynach wasn't surprised. If his father could save his own skin, he would.

"The moment you stop being useful, you're out on your

ass," Brynach said. "And you owe my wife your life."

Gabriel nodded. "Thank you, Aisling, Daughter of Light and Princess of Dark."

"He's not staying here," Riordan said.

Aisling took out her phone and made a call. "Mom, can you come to the house? I have a favor to ask you."

"What are you thinking?" Riordan turned on Aisling. Brynach wondered the same thing. "You can't send him home with your mother!"

Their wife turned to him, hands on her hips. "I can. That house is warded more than any other house I know. It's steeped in a lifetime of magic. My mother is Fae; she can hold her own. And the home office isn't being used because she's too busy with the school and New Fae training facilities. It's perfect. Why would anyone look for him there?"

Brynach ran a hand through his hair and choked on a scream. The whole fucking world was upside down. Nobody would look for him near any of them, but the idea of putting her mother in danger didn't sit well with him. When Lydia sifted to their ward, she cursed, and he guessed she agreed.

"You could have warned me! What's happening here?"

Aisling filled her mother in, and with extreme reluctance, she agreed to take Gabriel captive. There was no other way to phrase it. He wouldn't be free, and Brynach hated the idea of her mother housing him, but at least he'd be under their control.

"What do you know about places Peggy may go to hide?" Aisling asked.

Gabriel looked at her and shook his head. "You think I've been working with her, but I haven't. That woman was obsessed with me, and I bedded her. She was nothing to me. I never kept track of her or her children."

"Fucking useless," Brynach grumbled.

"Tell us fucking something, would you?" Riordan demanded.

"Levinas. He harbored more hate and anger than anyone

realized. He wasn't just a simpering asshole; he was cruel. I caught him watching me torture people more times than I could count." He looked away and shook his head. "Not to mention the number of times the pervert was hard and jerking off watching."

Beside him, Aisling dry heaved and covered her mouth. That's who she'd been locked away with for weeks while they looked for her. Brynach wished he was alive just so he could kill him a second time.

"He's dead now," Riordan reminded him.

Gabriel nodded. "He's dead, but those who worked with him aren't. He never worked alone. He had police in his pocket. Your little friend, for instance." He looked to Aisling.

"Are you talking about Officer Ruiz?" Aisling asked.

Gabriel nodded. "He was working with Levinas. I heard Levinas bragging about scaring you out into a rainstorm for the other man. There were a few murders, informants who saw the officer's true intentions and needed to be taken care of, Levinas practiced on them."

Brynach felt his anger beneath his skin like a breathing entity waiting to break free. He was going to find Dexter and end his life slowly.

"I'm impressed you and that Seelie brat made it out of his clutches unharmed," Gabriel wondered.

Brynach knew neither had. Not really. But he was realizing how lucky he was to have his wife whole by his side. He glared at the man and turned to Mrs. Quinn.

"He so much as looks at you funny and I want you to call me. If you think, even for a split second, that he's a threat, you put him down or call me to do it." He meant every word. He wouldn't put his wife's mother in harm's way.

She nodded. "I can handle myself, Brynach. He doesn't scare me."

"You're not done giving us information. I'll be over soon. Don't forget that you're alive by our sheer good grace. Behave."

Brynach's warning was genuine. Mrs. Quinn smiled at him and then sifted Gabriel away.

Riordan grabbed for his arm. "Bry, if your father isn't the one torturing Brielle, who is?"

CHAPTER 17

Aisling

Riordan's question rang in the silence of their yard. It was a valid question, but she had a more pressing worry at the moment. Gabriel had just confirmed that Dexter was working with Levinas to torment her. Likely, to attempt to push her into his arms. And he was fucking murdering his informants. That asshole. He had to pay.

He was still out, just walking the streets, free to hurt other people.

"Lettie," Aisling whispered. "I have to go to Lettie. The Hive may be able to help. They've seen Dexter before. I want that man locked up!"

Riordan nodded. "You should go."

She pulled out her phone and sent a text. Lettie answered right away that she was at Sean's. "She's at Trent's old place. I won't leave unless I tell you."

The guys nodded, and she reluctantly kissed them before sifting to her childhood home. The idea to send Gabriel home with her mother was a smart one, but that didn't mean she liked it. The least she could do was help strengthen the wards to ensure he stayed put. She stepped onto her mother's porch and ran inside at the sound of raised voices.

"Mom!" she cried out and ran down the hall.

"I'm fine," she called out.

Aisling rounded the corner and saw Nevan glaring at her mother.

"What the fuck are you doing here?"

He spun on her, blonde hair whipping into his face. "Why don't you explain why you sent her home with a murderer?"

"I have no idea what you're talking about," Aisling denied.

"Gabriel is in her basement, Aisling. Don't bother trying to lie to me about it. You think I left you here for decades and didn't put notification wards around the land? I may not be who you want me to be, but I always cared." Nevan threw his hands out. "So, explain yourself."

"Like hell I will." Aisling was just as pissed as she stepped up to her father. "You're not welcome here."

He huffed a laugh. "You know that's not true. If I wasn't welcome, I'd never have gotten through the wards you and your mother put up."

He had her there. Aisling's gaze swung to her mother, and she shrugged. Crap. What was it about the Quinn women that they just never learned when to draw a line with this man?

"He's confined. She's safe. And neither of us is your concern," Aisling reiterated. "You need to leave."

"I'm sorry I hurt you. It was never my intention." Nevan was a good actor. He even looked like he meant it.

"Do you hear yourself? You turned your back on me, and now you want to talk?" Her voice had gotten louder as she spoke, ending in a scream.

"You have to listen to my side," he begged.

"I've given you chance after chance, and where has it gotten me?" There were tears in her eyes now, and she hated herself for it. Her mother moved to her side, and she wasn't ashamed that she leaned on her.

"It's not what it looks like," he started to argue.

Her mother wasn't having it. "You didn't betray her along with the people you trusted to care for her in your absence? On her wedding day? Baring her from the court so she couldn't get closure?"

Nevan shook his head, and Aisling held her breath. She hated herself for it, but she wanted his answer. A part of her hoped he could make it all make sense.

"All of those things happened. Just not for the reasons you think." Her father was still standing with his hands raised, his body rigid. There was nothing he could say that would excuse his behavior.

"Lydia, I needed to keep her away from court. I knew that she wasn't safe there. I was protecting her," Nevan swore.

"If that's true, you could have told me," Aisling whispered. "I'm not a child anymore."

He looked away from her wet eyes. "No, I couldn't. Ellasar has been watching me closely since you became a larger player in Faerie politics. The King and Queen were threatened by you. If I gave them any reason to believe I wasn't theirs, you'd have become a threat they had no choice but to eliminate."

"They did that anyway, Nevan," Aisling reminded him.

"No, they didn't. You're alive. Others who threatened them aren't," he stated with certainty.

"Do they have Brielle? Is it them? I'll kill them myself," she swore.

Nevan shook his head. "If they are to blame for her disappearance and torture, I don't know anything about it."

"You could have left. We'd have helped you stay safe," Aisling said, thinking about Gabriel.

"Aisling, I went to the Seelie court a naive young Fae and, over time, made it my mission to change things. We were close, so close, to the kind of Faerie we'd dreamed of," he said wistfully. "But my brilliant daughter managed to find a way to unite the realms in a move nobody saw coming."

"But the prophecy," Aisling began.

"Wasn't fabricated, of course. Even I can't weave lore that deeply into the culture of Faerie. It became true because you believed it to be. Anyone with the desire, motivation, and skill set could have done it."

Aisling shook her head. "No. I couldn't have done it without Brynach or Riordan. It had to be a combination of us. There's no way it would have worked otherwise."

She wasn't going to let him convince her that what she did was any less miraculous than it had been. A perfect convergence of love, trust, and the desire to fix things. Aisling had been prophesied to do what she did. That was the only reason she'd been able to.

Nevan smiled at her. "Aisling, you are a wonder. What you did was nothing short of amazing, but it had nothing to do with a prophecy."

Her mother was shaking at her side. Aisling reached out and took her hand. As much as she'd misplaced her trust in the man in front of her, her mother had, too.

"This doesn't excuse the way you treated me. You could have confided in me. Told me why you were keeping me at arm's length. I may have understood," she argued.

"And you may have told your Unseelie husband. Or your Ravdi partner. If anyone learned I'd confided in you, they could have used you to get to me, to find out what I was doing," he said.

"They did anyway! I was in danger, regardless. At least I would have known you were there. That you cared." Aisling swiped at her tears. He didn't deserve them.

Nevan took a step forward, and her mother struck. Her hand cracked across his face. Her father stepped back. "Aisling, the danger isn't over. If anything, the Seelie court is more volatile than ever. They made mistakes that cost them their seats of power. They have nothing left to lose."

She shook her head. "Let them burn."

"They won't be the only ones, Aisling." Nevan shook his

head, his eyes softening. "Everything I did, I did to protect you. To help Faerie. To create a better world for you. You have to ..."

Aisling wasn't moved. "Don't tell me what I have to do. There's always a way to justify men's actions, to absolve yourself of blame. They're never good enough."

"Get out, Nevan," her mother said from between clenched teeth. "Now."

The elder Fae nodded. "Forever is a long time, Aisling. Maybe one day." Then, he let himself out.

Aisling fell into her mother's arms. Her throat ached, and her mother whispered in her ear.

"Let it out, honey. Don't hold it in."

Aisling screamed as her mother rocked her. A scream so raw and soul deep she wasn't sure she'd ever stop. Her lungs failed her before her voice did.

"I'm sorry, Aisling. He was never worthy of you, but you've always been worthy of love," Phlyren told her quietly.

"How many times, Rin? How many times did I cry myself to sleep over him? How many times did I ask you why I wasn't enough? How often did I try pretending Alex was my real dad during those years in Faerie? How many?" she yelled to her familiar.

Aisling laughed out loud and then continued the conversation in her head. *"And you warned me. You tried to tell me he didn't matter. That you, and my mom, and Alex and Aindrea were enough. That Brielle and the other kids had it bad, too, and at least I had a mom who loved me. None of it mattered. It was his love I wanted. What broken, sick part of me would crave that kind of disappointment?"*

"You were a child, Aisling. This isn't your fault," he promised.

"How do I stop caring?" Aisling whispered.

"Oh, sweetie, you don't. You have a huge heart, and you're not going to let him change that. But caring doesn't always mean you continue a relationship. Only you can make that decision," her mother told her.

Aisling nodded and stood to get a glass of water. Her mother mirrored her, not letting her go too far from her. After the taste of blood had been purged from her throat, Aisling spoke again.

"I wanted to make sure Gabriel was secured, and you felt safe. I have to talk to Lettie about finding Dexter." Aisling put the glass in the sink and moved toward the door.

"You don't have to go right now, Aisling. You can take a few minutes to let yourself settle." Her mother followed her.

"No, Mom, I can't. I have things that need to be done. Now isn't the time to wallow." Aisling hugged her mother.

"It's not wallowing, sweetie. You're not okay." Her mother framed her face and looked deep into her hazel eyes.

Aisling laughed. "No, I'm not. But I need to keep going anyway."

Her mother didn't argue as Aisling opened the door and walked down the steps, sifting to the street outside Sean's. She didn't bother ringing the bell as she opened the door and made her way up the steps. When she tried the handle that had always been unlocked to her and found it locked, she pushed down the hurt in her chest and knocked.

Lettie answered the door and pulled her inside. "You look awful."

Aisling shook her head. "Thanks, L."

"Hey, what are friends for. How's Syd?"

"She's resting, but she's okay." Aisling turned to Sean. "You were a rockstar. Thank you for helping us get her out of there."

He smiled and ducked his head. "Not gonna lie, it was kinda cool getting permission to hack a prison. Let me tell you, shit is wild in there."

"You're still logged in?" Aisling's eyes went wide.

He blushed. "Um, yeah. I figured it couldn't hurt to keep an eye on Peggy."

Aisling nodded. "Keep us posted."

Lettie pulled her attention. "I assume something else is going on?"

Her friend had black bags under her eyes, and Aisling could see that she'd lost weight. Shame settled heavily on her. She shouldn't be here. Lettie didn't deserve this. But Aisling was selfish enough to do what she needed to.

"We have intel confirming Dexter's involvement in ... well, more than we knew before. I need the Hive to access him. We have to find him, Lettie." Aisling silently begged her friend to understand.

"Yeah, they're watching for him," Lettie told her.

It wasn't enough. If anyone could set intentions and find Dexter, Aisling knew it was Lettie.

"I need to remove the wards and protections on you," Aisling told her. "Just until we find them. You're tied to Riordan and me. You are more motivated than anyone else, and I can assist you. Together, we can find him, L."

Sean moved to Lettie's side. "No. No way. How could you ask that of her?" The way he looked at her made Aisling feel even worse.

"She wouldn't ask if there was another way, Sean," Lettie told him. She smiled up at her boyfriend. "I'll be okay."

"Bullshit! You're not eating or sleeping, and that's with the blockers, Lettie. You can't seriously be considering this." Sean shook his head.

"I'm not considering it, babe." She turned to Aisling. "I'll do it."

"I won't leave until I put the protections back on. If you can't tap into him in an hour, we end it. I'm not here to hurt you, L." Aisling hated herself more than Sean ever could for asking this of her best friend.

"I know." Lettie moved to the bedroom and lay on the bed. "It'll be safer this way. Go ahead and remove the spells."

Aisling didn't correct her. They weren't spells, but to Lettie, they'd be one and the same. Focusing on the magic, Aisling pulled the protective intentions from around her friend. She plucked until there was no barrier between Lettie and the fluid power of the earth. Then Aisling pulled back on her mental wards, telling the universe that Lettie was open to whatever it intended for her. When she opened her eyes, Lettie's were on her, and Aisling gave her a sad smile.

"Now we wait," Aisling said.

Sean sat rigid with Lettie's hand in his and kept a vigilant watch over his girlfriend. Aisling coached Lettie through it. She was no expert on the visions, but she understood intentions and projecting them.

"Let it be known you're open to receiving messages. Focus on Dexter and seeking him to protect others." Aisling kept her voice soft and even, just like Lettie's breathing.

Her phone buzzed in her pocket, and Lettie cracked an eye at her. "I've got this. Go do what you have to do. I'll call you in when I get a message from the great beyond." Her friend was joking, but Aisling knew her well enough to see the fear there. Still, Aisling needed to check her phone and make sure the guys, and her mom, were okay.

She stood and walked into the living room, texting Brynach and Riordan back that she was okay. After a brief recap of her interaction with Nevan, she sat on the sofa.

It must be the day for fathers to
pop in and fuck up our days.

Coulda done without it.

I don't know, I wouldn't mind
if mine popped in.

Ugh, Riordan. Sorry.
Lettie's trying to connect now.
Any sign of him on your end?

Nothing. Liam's looking.

We'll take anything you can give us.

> Sean still has eyes on the inside.
> He'll keep us posted.

Guy is a menace. Love him.

Aisling set the phone down and tapped into the magic surrounding her. She directed the soothing energy toward Sean and Lettie.

"*You're doing the best you can, Aisling. She's an adult. She could have said no if she needed to,*" Rin reminded her.

"*She wouldn't have, though. Not if I needed her. I knew that when I asked.*" Guilt ate at her. She knew how much it drained Lettie to be pulled into these visions.

"*You're being too hard on yourself.*" Her familiar meant well, but Aisling didn't believe him, not when she could hear Lettie thrashing on the bed in the other room. Her Fae senses allowed her to hear Sean's racing heart and the way he cursed her under his breath.

Aisling waited because there was nothing else to do. She didn't mean to cry, but the tears slid down her cheeks all the same. Immediately, she wished one of the guys was there to hold her and let herself recognize that she might be leaning on them too much. She couldn't turn to them every time she struggled. She could handle this.

"Aisling," Lettie called.

She wiped her face and shook out her arms. "You can do this. It'll be worth it in the end." The whispered reminder bolstered her as she walked toward her best friend.

Lettie was sitting up in bed, wrapped in Sean's arms. Her blue eyes were bloodshot. The smile was small, but it was there, and Aisling moved to sit by her side.

"Before you get your hopes up, it's not much," Lettie warned.

"Anything is better than nothing. We appreciate this so much, L." Aisling took her hand.

"He feels like he's ready to go off, Ash. He's got nothing left to lose. He may have been able to walk away from this before, but he knows he fucked himself. The charges and suspicion have eyes on him, and he feels cornered." Lettie shook her head. "He's more dangerous than ever."

Aisling hated to do it, but she pushed a bit more.

"Can you tell me anything about where he is?" Aisling asked.

Lettie sighed. "I really can't. A house. But it looked like any other house. He was alone."

"Okay. Thank you, Lettie. Let's get those wards back up." Aisling moved for her bag.

"No." Lettie stopped her. "Let me see if I can get more. I'll stay here with Sean. I'll be safe. You can come back over before I go to bed and put them back."

Sean started to argue, and she shot him the most Lettie of all looks. Aisling knew enough to recognize she'd made up her mind. If she was a better person, she'd have fought her, but Lettie had the potential to really help. It was selfish, but she was going to let her.

"When this is over, I want it gone, though. You're super strong, and you can strip magic now. I need you to try and get rid of this. I want to be human again." Lettie was resolute.

The idea made her nervous. Lettie wasn't Fae, and her magic wasn't natural. Aisling wasn't sure she could do it. "I can't make any promises, and I won't do it unless I'm certain you won't be hurt. But, of course, I will try."

Lettie nodded and leaned into Sean's arms. There was nothing left for her to do here. "I'll be back by nine to make sure you're good for tonight. Thank you, L."

CHAPTER 18

Riordan

T he fuck do we do?" Riordan asked Brynach when Aisling sifted away.

He ran a hand through his hair. "Hell if I know. But I think a good place to start is your brother. He needs to be updated, and he may have been able to find something. He's the one that's been working on Dexter."

"I should have thought of that. What's wrong with me?"

Brynach reached out and took his chin between his thumb and forefinger, lifting it to his. He didn't make a move to kiss him or immediately say anything. He breathed deep three times, and Riordan felt himself mirror his partner.

Only when the larger Fae felt ready did he speak. "There's not a thing wrong with you. Circumstances lately have been anything but normal, and we're living crisis to crisis. If I hear you talk down to yourself again, I'll punish you the same way I do our wife."

A shiver ran through Riordan's body. Brynach smirked. "You don't hate that idea, do you?"

"Bry, we have to focus." Riordan shook his head. "Let's get to the apartment."

His husband released his chin. "We're talking about that later." Then he took Riordan's hand, and they sifted to Main Street.

Riordan opened the door to Terra Bella and smiled at the once-witch, now-New Fae, and her daughter behind the counter. "She's getting so big!" He rounded the glass case to peak in at Eves. Dawn grinned down at the little girl and then back up at Riordan.

"What are you doing here?" she asked, concern creasing her face. "You never come here anymore."

He tried not to flinch. "Sorry, Dawn. Things have been ... well, things have been."

She shrugged her shoulders. "Yeah, I've been to see Lydia. I'm aware of what things have been like lately. Your brother is up there. He's got company. If I can help, let me know."

Brynach reached out to her, clasping her forearm in a traditional Fae greeting. "Thank you for being there for Mrs. Quinn and keeping our secret."

Dawn rolled her eyes. "So formal. Just go."

They took the stairs two at a time and right into the studio apartment. Liam's face looked up from a screen, and Amber turned from the lumbering Fae she was talking to.

"Riordan?" Liam said and looked back at the monitor. "I should batter ya."

He shot back with his own slang. "Wind your neck in."

Only when his brother shook his head and gave him a small smile did he relax. He knew he'd been a shit brother lately. He should have been taking every moment to spend with Liam before he left for home, but instead, he was avoiding him. A hand settled on his back, and he looked up at Brynach.

"He loves you," he whispered.

"Okay," Riordan said, walking forward. "We need to find Dexter. The police are still dragging their feet on bringing him in, but we have a source with more evidence against him. I want him in custody."

Walker turned to him. "Who's your source? You never mentioned something before."

Brynach stiffened at his side, his hand fisting in Riordan's shirt. There was something going on here, and he didn't like being on the outside of it.

"You know one another?" His voice was low and slow. There was no way to miss the warning there.

Riordan answered, "Not officially, but we've attended some of the same meetings."

Brynach looked quickly at him, and then his eyes were back on the Thor-sized blonde. "Since when are you on any of the security boards?"

The man smirked. "Seems you're not in the loop anymore, Prince."

His partner released his shirt and took a step forward. "I don't trust you, and I don't want you near the people I care about. Not Alex. Not Riordan. Not anyone else in this room. So now would be a great time to explain yourself."

The tension in the room was palpable, and though Riordan didn't understand Brynach's caution, he trusted his partner's judgment. His hand slid to the knife strapped to his belt. Walker tracked his movements, and Riordan shrugged when he brought the blade forward. The other man just shook his head.

"I owe you no explanations. But because there's work to be done and you're being an ass about it, I'm here because Brielle isn't."

Brynach practically growled. "That's not helping your case."

"I don't care. She's not here, and I know she'd want to be, so I'm here instead. Anyone I can spare is searching for her, which is more than I can say for you." Walker didn't break eye contact with Brynach, and Riordan didn't like the silent challenge there.

"Bry, we have to find Dexter. Can this wait?" If he said no, they'd handle this here and now. But there were other things he'd like to prioritize.

The larger man breathed deep, and Riordan felt him pull magic to himself, calming him a little. He nodded, and Riordan addressed the room. "Aisling is with Lettie right now, trying to get eyes on him through the Hive."

"Did it work?" Amber asked.

"Not sure yet. She hasn't checked in. I'm sure she will when she has something," Riordan explained. "But we have to make sure we do this right. If they find him, we should be going with the authorities. I don't want him to have any reason to wiggle out of arrest. We do this by the books."

Even his by-the-rulebook brother groaned. Everyone wanted their pound of flesh from the former cop. Riordan remembered Aisling scared and standing in the rain like it was yesterday when he'd had someone scare her out of the bar. He knew every time he'd pulled her away from them under the guise of work and how manipulative that was. The man deserved the absolute worst. Then again, jail for a cop was.

"When we know something, I'll call them," Liam promised. "He won't get away, Rory."

"What's this new information you're working off of?" Amber wondered.

Riordan breathed through the anger. "He tormented Aisling, manipulated her. Which is enough to make me crave his blood, but we have proof he killed people to hide his crooked-cop scheming."

"Murder. That'll do it," Walker said.

"You'd know," Brynach accused.

The blonde-haired man laughed. "And you didn't snap the neck of a few people this week?"

"How do you—" Brynach started but stopped when Riordan's phone rang.

"It's Ash," he said as he answered. "Aisling, what's going on?"

Her voice was high and breathless. It was clear she was on the move. "Lettie thinks she found Dexter," Aisling told him. He relayed the information to the room. Brynach pulled a handgun from his holster, Walker doing the same. He didn't like the way the blonde's eyes darted to his husband as he checked the chamber.

Liam and Amber shot out of their chairs. Riordan wished his brother was more comfortable with weapons, but his hands were meant for keyboards. Amber, however, cracked her knuckles. She'd be just fine.

"Get your head in the game. I have his scent. Come to me," Valo instructed.

"Valo has his scent. He says he's near the northern outskirts of the Unseelie lands. Can you follow my sift?" Riordan asked the group. "Did you hear that, Ash?"

"Got it. Rin is with Valo. I'll meet you there." She hung up before he could tell her to wait or be careful. "Fuck! She's already sifting. We need to get there." He ran down the stairs and outside of Dawn's wards.

Riordan sifted. His body was reduced to mere cells in space and time. His feet hit the ground and sank into the wet marshland.

"What did Lettie see?" Amber asked as she sifted into existence beside Aisling.

She spoke softly, "Him running through the woods. Something spooked him from wherever he was hiding. He's desperate and dangerous."

"It could be a trap," Brynach commented. "I want everyone on their guard."

Aisling withdrew her throwing knives from her thigh holster and handed one to Amber.

"Try not to lose it," she instructed the New Fae. "This is disgusting," Aisling complained. Her mud-covered shoes made a sucking sound. Together, they ran through the woods, Riordan's familiar guiding them.

"This way!" The urgency in Valo's voice had Riordan turning and running through the marsh. Everyone else followed, mud flinging off their feet.

"Where'd he come from?" he asked the fox.

"I'm embarrassed to say he came from a foxhole. Not a technical one, but he was in tunnels underground. Even more embarrassed that bird-for-brains is the one that spotted the disturbance. Footprints in the mud that I couldn't see from down here. Then I ran in and flushed him out," Valo told him.

"You could have been hurt. You have to be more careful than that, Valo," Riordan scolded.

Riordan scanned the area ahead of him, looking for his familiar. He pointed to the other tracks in the mud, and Brynach caught up to him. "He can't be that far ahead of us. The mud would have resettled."

Liam spoke from behind him, "Where the hell is he?"

Riordan kept looking, but even with his New Fae senses, he wasn't sure.

"He's here. You better hurry," Valo informed Riordan. *"I don't think he's armed."*

"Up there!" Riordan pointed toward the edge of a lake.

The group of them came to rest a respectable distance from the murky waters.

Amber panted beside them, "I don't see anyone."

"Quiet," Liam demanded. "Listen."

Brynach's head swiveled to the high grass. "There."

Riordan turned, and just like that, Dexter, barefoot, muddy, and looking absolutely miserable, appeared. He opened his mouth, not knowing what was going to come out. "Freeze!"

"Really, Rory? Freeze? This isn't a cop drama," Liam mocked. "Give it up, dirtbag! We've got you surrounded." His brother followed up with a yell of his own before pulling out his phone and calling the cops.

Brynach laughed, and Riordan ignored them both. He didn't take his eyes off Dexter as he ran forward. Aisling sifted to the side of him, preventing her ex-pseudo-partner from running in that direction. Brynach sifted and cut off his retreat to the right. Riordan froze when he saw Walker leveling a gun at Dexter's chest.

"Don't even fucking think about it. I'll let Brynach put you down if you so much as put a finger near that trigger," Riordan threatened him.

This was his capture. The once-intimidating cop was gone. He looked worse for the wear. Riordan was used to seeing the slimeball dressed nicely with that smarmy fucking smirk on his face as he looked too hard at Aisling. That's not who he saw in front of him right now. Ruiz looked haggard. His hair was oily and hung down to his ears.

The man's eyes were wild, flicking from him to the rest of the people surrounding him. Dexter knew he was outnumbered.

"You don't stand a chance, man. You could make this easy on yourself," Liam called.

"I'm not going in," Dexter shouted. "Cops don't make it in prison."

"Then you shouldn't have broken the law, asshole," Aisling shouted.

Amber bounced on her heels, and Riordan met her eyes, shaking his head. If he let her, she'd take him out.

"You know there are only two ways out of this," Riordan said. His heart was pounding in his chest as he walked calmly toward the fugitive.

Without knowing what he was doing but desperate to make sure Dexter didn't run, Riordan called on his magic. The mud below the ex-cop's feet softened, and he sank a little deeper. Aisling noticed the pull on the magic and tried to distract Dexter.

"We used to be friends once, Dex." She choked on his nickname. "How could you hurt me and the people I love the way you did?"

Dexter huffed a laugh. "Did you ever consider, for one fucking minute, who I loved?"

"Yourself," Amber said under her breath. The human didn't hear her.

"We had something good before they came poking around, and I was going places. I'd have taken you with me. It's taken two of them to do what I could have alone."

Aisling shook her head as he sank a little deeper. "You weren't going somewhere I'd have followed, Dex. Not with the company you were keeping."

"Have you seen who you're with now?" He nodded toward Brynach. "That guy's a murderer."

Their wife grinned. "Yes, he is. To protect. Not for personal gain."

Riordan saw Brynach's chest puff as their wife defended him.

"Levinas, Dexter? You really threw your hat in the ring with him?" Aisling asked.

The man shrugged. "I hedged my bets. It wasn't just him, Aisling." Riordan didn't miss the way his eyes slid toward Walker. "I'm not sorry. For any of it."

Riordan stared the man down, hatred burning through him. Which is how he noticed when Dexter registered his sinking legs. The man panicked, falling back on his ass and pulling at his legs.

He wasn't going anywhere, no matter how much he struggled. The police were on their way, and they'd handle him. He turned to Aisling and saw her staring at her old partner with disgust.

"The informants, Dex? You really killed the people who were helping you?" Aisling still couldn't wrap her head around the man being so two-faced. Riordan loved that she wanted to see the good in people, but there was none to be had in that man.

"Some people poke around where they shouldn't, and sometimes accidents happen." He tried to shrug, but the way his legs were stuck and the panic in his eyes kept it from looking anywhere close to nonchalant.

Then Riordan felt a surge of magic, and Dexter wrenched

his legs free. He was scrambling away from them as the police approached. Riordan turned to see Loren and a few other officers who looked familiar charging toward them. He snapped back to Dexter, who was making a mad dash in the other direction, desperate to get away.

With his eyes trained on the fleeing man, Riordan hadn't registered Brynach's move. His growl broke through his confusion, and he turned to see his husband with his hand around Walker's throat.

"What the fuck do you think you're doing?" Brynach yelled in the other Fae's face.

Though his face was turning a little red, the other man smiled and spoke. "Making it fun."

Riordan turned back to Dexter and realized he had only one direction to go, and it wasn't a wise one. Of course, that didn't stop him from running full tilt toward it.

Dexter didn't even pause at the lake's edge. He waded in, running through the shallow water until he was hip-deep.

"He's getting away!" Amber charged toward the water, but Aisling held her back.

"Don't," Aisling warned. Riordan ran to them, and Brynach met him there. Liam caught up, and with a quick glance, Riordan saw that Walker had left. Convenient.

The five of them watched as the first ripple formed. Dexter was too caught up in panicking to pay attention to anything but what was right in front of him. Which meant he didn't see the disturbance in the water to the left and right of him. Not until it was too late. That's when the first scream left the man's mouth.

"What?" Amber asked as yet another ripple and splash erupted on the surface of the lake.

"Neapan," Riordan whispered.

"Fuck," Liam cursed. Neither had seen the deadly water sprites, but they were smart enough to fear them. Nobody would be charging after Dexter now. Liam told the officers as much as they joined them, a healthy distance from the lake's edge.

Dexter realized his mistake much too late. Like a pack of piranhas, the neapan tore into him. Even for someone who wanted him dead more than he wanted his next breath, his screams were hard to listen to.

"Help me!" Dexter yelled in a desperate attempt for salvation. It was too late. Blood bubbled in the water around him. There'd be no dramatic rescue today.

Riordan could see the webbed claws leave the water and scrape at Dexter's body. The roiling water was red, and Dexter's cries became louder by the second as more of his body was pulled under.

"Oh fuck," one cop muttered. He drew his gun. "I should put him out of his misery."

Pilson clapped the man on the shoulder. "Don't." Then he turned to Riordan and nodded.

Nobody moved. Amber covered her mouth to muffle a groan, and Brynach put an arm around Aisling. Meanwhile, Liam and Riordan stood unblinking. Watching. Waiting. The screams stopped only when Dexter was dragged entirely underwater. Bubbles broke the surface for a moment, and then there was nothing but blooms of blood and bits of flesh floating to the surface.

"That was—" Amber started.

"Yeah," Liam agreed.

Something was warm against Riordan's leg, and he looked down to see his familiar nuzzled against him. It was strange how much comfort that gave him. Almost as much as his partner's hands on him.

Still, Riordan was numb. He'd just watched a man get ripped to shreds by vicious water nymphs, and he felt ... nothing. Dexter was dead. The man who had undoubtedly played a part in his aunt's death was dead. He should be feeling something.

"*He deserved to suffer more,*" Valo commented and rubbed against Riordan's leg.

Someone put a hand on his shoulder, and when Riordan looked away from the fading red in the water, he met his brother's brown eyes.

"It was a better end than he deserved. It still sucks," he gave voice to Riordan's thoughts.

"Riordan?" Aisling was at his side. "Are you okay?"

He nodded, not looking at her but instead at the still water of the lake. Dexter would live in infamy around the neck of some of Faerie's most vicious creatures. Eaten and bleached by the sun, worn as a trophy.

Riordan turned to his brother, currently being held by his girlfriend. "Liam?"

His older brother turned to him with a shake of his head. "I'm okay. We'll talk later."

Riordan choked down a sob at his brother's departure. Aisling turned to Brynach. "Give me a few minutes to ward Lettie again, okay?"

When she was gone, Riordan let himself cry. He didn't want either of his partners to see him this way, especially Aisling. She'd want to fix what was unfixable. Brynach pulled him into his arms, not saying anything.

"I'm not sorry he's dead," he choked out. "I'm not sure why I'm crying."

Brynach rubbed a large hand along his back and held him even tighter. His silence let Riordan voice his biggest worry.

"He's going to leave me," he whispered.

"I know," his husband cupped the back of his head and held it to his chest. "But you're not alone anymore, Riordan. And you have all the time in the world to see him again."

Riordan sniffed and then pushed away from Brynach a little. His partner brought a large thumb to his cheek and wiped away a tear.

"Can we go home now?" he asked.

Brynach didn't answer, just held him close and sifted. When their feet hit the deck of their home, he zoned out, allowing Brynach to lead him inside and to bed. Riordan wasn't consciously aware of Aisling coming home or of falling asleep. All he knew was that when he woke, he was warm, safe, and cocooned between the two people who made him feel the safest in all the world.

CHAPTER 19

Brynach

H e's really dead," Riordan whispered.

The sun hadn't risen over the horizon yet. Sleep hadn't come easily to any of them, so it was no surprise they were all huddled together, still talking about the events of the last day.

"He is," Brynach assured him.

Aisling shook her head against his chest. "I can't believe it was all about power for him. I don't know why I wanted some bigger evil plan."

"Fucking idiot," Riordan cursed.

Brynach didn't know what to do for his partner. You couldn't fix something like this with muscle. Being rendered useless didn't sit well with him. One of their alarms went off, and a collective groan rose from their sheets.

"Am I allowed to skip adulting today?" Riordan asked as he burrowed his head under a pillow.

Aisling rubbed his back. "Yes, you are. Do you want company?"

The pillow shifted as he shook his head. "No. You both have shit to get done, and I'm going to be miserable company.

You guys go. I'll do laundry and clean ... and then I really have to talk to Liam."

"I don't like the idea of leaving you," Brynach announced, pulling the pillow off his head and moving his hair out of his face. "Isn't there anything I can do?"

Riordan cracked a brown eye at Brynach and managed a small smile. "No, but thank you. I won't be alone. Valo won't go far."

Brynach really couldn't stay home today. He was meant to teach his first class with Semele today. The school had come along fantastically, and some of the courses had already begun, those that couldn't wait. Magic training, familiar relationships, and Fae history.

He pulled himself out from under his partners, ignoring their grumbles. Riordan reached over and pulled Aisling to his side, burying his face in her messy red hair. Goddess, he loved them. He was finishing brushing his hair and teeth when Aisling squeezed in behind him to do the same.

"You think he's going to be okay here alone?" she whispered.

Brynach met her eyes in the mirror and nodded. She frowned, and he gave into the pull to claim her mouth. His large hands cupped her ass and pulled her up his body until she wrapped her legs around his hips.

"We have actual work to do," Aisling reminded him between hungry kisses.

He gave a small growl. "I know." He lowered her reluctantly. What did you wear for your first day as a teacher? He settled on worn-in jeans and a soft t-shirt.

Brynach called out a goodbye to his partners, winking at Aisling as she filled her water bottle. He had to remind himself that phones worked everywhere now. If they needed him, they could reach him. They'd both be okay.

When he sifted to the once Seelie court, he was happy to land outside the gates. The old guards, the stone sentinels, were back in place.

"Submit to the test, or you do not enter," the stone guard requested.

Brynach held his finger out, nonplussed by the stab and tasting of his blood.

"Welcome, Brynach, once-Prince of the Unseelie," it greeted him.

He rolled his eyes. "Can you change that to husband of Aisling and Riordan? Or at least Brynach Campbell?"

They remained silent, as he'd known they would, and Brynach walked through the now open gates. As he neared the palace, he couldn't help but smile at the sight of children playing. Teachers were calling out instructions, the little ones were practicing magic, and familiars lounged in the gardens.

This is the life that Fae children should have, not the ones he, Alex, and Aisling had experienced. Not the neglect and the fear. Hundreds of happy, smiling kids occupied the grounds. He couldn't imagine a better use for the old Seelie court. He'd left enough time to pop in and see Alex before he went to his class. When he found Alex, he was behind his desk, a pen in hand, staring at a stack of papers.

"You look like a tenured professor," he joked.

Alex laughed. "I feel like one. You gave me quite a task."

"One I have confidence you can succeed at, with the right people helping," Brynach said. "Do you have the right people, Alex?"

His friend raised a brow. "What are you asking, Brynach?"

"I'm asking if you're keeping good company, friend. Have you spent more time with Walker? Did you know he let Dexter loose while we waited for the police?" Brynach asked.

Alex shook his head. "And now he's dead. I fail to see how that's a bad thing. I've got things under control," Alex assured him. He looked at his watch and stood.

When had he started wearing that?

"I'd love to chat more, but I have another meeting in five

minutes; I want to look at my notes beforehand. You under-stand," Alex said.

Brynach knew when he was being dismissed. "Yeah. Sure." He made a note to look for Aindrea later and make sure she was okay. He'd never felt the need to check on Alex's wife, but he was worried he was slipping. Brynach wouldn't tolerate that hurting his friend's wife and child.

"You turned up. Wasn't sure you would," Semele said as he walked into the barn.

"Should I be hurt? Of course, I showed up. This is import-ant to me." Brynach knew he'd have to prove himself, and that was okay. He was looking forward to the routine and respon-sibility.

They nodded. "The kids are going to be here soon. I will take half and discuss care. You take the other half, and then we'll switch tomorrow. Longer blocks and reinforced knowl-edge helps it stick."

"You're the expert." Brynach had no problem listening to them.

"And you know how you're going to conduct your classes?" they asked with what sounded like skepticism.

He nodded. "Yup." He wasn't sure why it made him blush to remove the notebook from his back pocket and slap it into his open palm. "I have an outline for the semester and what I'd like the kids to learn. Would you like to see it?"

The smile that split the silver-haired Fae's face was reward enough for the hours he spent debating the order of his les-sons. Before they could continue their talk, the sound of chil-dren coming their way distracted them.

"You ready?" he asked. Without waiting, he turned and exited the barn to greet the waiting horde of children.

Behind the children was an actual menagerie of familiars who'd been instructed to show up for the class as well. Already Brynach could hear the whispers about who had the coolest familiar. He hid a smile, introduced himself, and allowed

Semele to do the same.

"I want all the mammalian-familiar children to my side, everyone else to Mr. Campbell's," Semele instructed, and it took more than a few minutes for the children to rearrange themselves. It wasn't an even split, but it wasn't horribly lopsided. "Alright, any canine familiars with the other group for today. That should even us out."

Brynach nodded and looked at the group of children staring up at him. Birds, foxes, wolves, dogs, snakes, and lizards all stared back at him. He nodded to a large patch of grass further off from the noise of the barn and led the children there.

"Everyone, take a seat," he said and led by example, sitting cross-legged in the grass.

"*Sorry I'm late,*" Kongur said as he strode into the area.

"That large lug is my familiar. He's been my familiar for over two hundred years, and he still doesn't listen to me about what time to show up," he told the kids.

There were giggles through the crowd of children.

"Who here is still making new friends at the school? Learning names?" Brynach asked.

Around him, children raised their hands. He smiled at them.

"I bet a lot of you have siblings," he paused, and heads nodded. "Well, just like with sisters or brothers or cousins and friends, you sometimes argue. It's normal to do that with your familiar, too. For today's lesson, we're going to focus on getting to know one another's names, children and familiars. Then we'll discuss communication. But it's important for you to know I don't expect anyone here to be perfect, and there's no grade in this class from me."

The kids all looked at one another, jaws slack, in shock. He fought to not laugh. He'd debated how he wanted to handle marks for the class, but you can't grade relationships. He knew from personal experience that relationships develop in their own time.

"My name is Brynach, but you can call me Mr. Campbell.

My familiar is Kongur, and he says hello," Brynach began. He gestured to the little boy to his left, and the introductions began.

He did his best to commit the names to memory, hoping that what he forgot Kongur would remember. But he knew his familiar had an awful memory, too. Once they'd made their way around the circle, he had everyone stand.

"We're going to play a game. I want all the kids to stand to my right by the trees. The familiars can go where they want, but they can't be in physical contact with their bonded. I'm going to set out obstacles and trust the kids to keep their eyes closed. Then you'll listen to directions from your familiar to avoid the obstacles and reach me first."

The kids took off for the tree line with excited laughter. The familiars moved to the side, and Brynach ran around the yard, placing cones and boxes around the space.

"Don't get any ideas about cheating. Kongur is going to be keeping an eye on you. So, all eyes closed," he asked with a smile.

"Right!" they chorused.

"Alright. Time to listen to your familiars. Trust that they'll lead you the right way. Good luck." Brynach nodded to the kids and waited for their eyes to close before sifting to the other side.

The exercise took longer than he anticipated, but the kids were laughing, and the familiars were getting competitive. He could tell by the way they chirped and lunged playfully at one another that they were enjoying themselves. Giggles and muffled yelps filled the air, and it made Brynach smile to see everyone having good-hearted fun.

A young girl with a riot of brunette curls grabbed onto his knee, and Brynach called for everyone to open their eyes. There was a mixture of groans and congratulations, and then a bell rang from inside the castle, and the children ran away, waving, to their next class.

Brynach repeated the process three more times before he was done for the day. He'd eaten with the other teachers in the cafeteria at lunch and felt content being a part of it all. He'd run into Mrs. Quinn and snuck in a conversation about her visitor to ensure things were still going well. He checked his phone before heading home and immediately sifted to Sydney's house.

"What's wrong?" he asked, storming in through the front door.

"It's probably nothing, but I knew you'd be upset if I didn't tell you," she began.

Brynach's fists clenched at his side. Her bodyguard moved closer, and Brynach's citrine eyes turned on him, freezing him mid-step.

"I'm no threat to my sister. Sit the fuck down," he told him. "Sydney, talk."

She rolled her shoulders. "There's been some magic thrown at the wards around the safehouse. I don't know if it's our father or someone working with my mother."

"But they held?" Brynach looked around the small house.

"Obviously," her guard sneered.

He turned on the smaller Fae. "Look, buddy, you're still standing because my sister likes you. But run your mouth again, and I'm going to put you on your ass."

To Brynach's relief, Sydney stifled a smile behind her hand. She put her free one on his arm and whispered, "Thank you."

He nodded and then took his fiery glare off her boyfriend. "Do you want Aisling to come reinforce the protections?"

Sydney shook her head. "I already did." Then she looked away from him, and her demeanor shifted.

"Syd," he started.

"Tell him," the smug boyfriend said.

Brynach shot him another look, and he held up his hands and stepped back. When he turned back to his sister, she was biting her lip.

"Victor reached out to me. It was a burner phone. I gave Sean the number, but it's already been ditched," she explained.

"What did he say?" Brynach asked.

"That he had information he'd be willing to exchange for his freedom. He said he had proof that our mother was behind the attack on Riordan's parents. That he'd call from a new number tomorrow night with the details. But he wants us to stop looking for him." Sydney was wringing her hands. "For Riordan's peace of mind, it might be worth it. He's not innocent, Bry, but he's hardly the worst of my brothers."

He rubbed her arm. "If Riordan's okay with it, I'll make sure the police are, too."

His sister nodded. "You'll let me know, right? If you agree, I need cops here with recording equipment to take his statement."

"Do you really think you're safe enough here?"

"We're more than capable of keeping her safe," the guard spoke.

Brynach was on his feet and turned on him. He gripped the man by the neck. "I'm really sick of your voice."

A hand touched his arm. "Bry." He turned and looked to Sydney, who smiled at him with wet eyes. "You have no idea how much it means to me that you're protective of me."

"Still being choked," her boyfriend managed to eke out.

Brynach's hold on him didn't loosen. If anything, he tightened his grip. Sydney laughed.

"Let him go."

At his sister's request, he dropped the man and wiped his hand on his pants. He pulled Sydney into his arms and kissed the top of her head. "Just say the word, and I do it for real," he whispered. He knew the man could hear him, but he was smart enough to stay quiet.

Sydney hugged him right. "Keep me posted on Riordan, please."

He left with one last warning glare at her guard.

Music sounded from inside his home, and he could see Riordan moving around the house through the large windows. His familiar was inside, lounging on the back of their sofa, the sneaky fox. Still, Brynach couldn't help the smile that split his face at the picture they painted.

When he walked inside, the fox scampered out the back door, and Riordan laughed. "You caught him. What brings you back early?"

"Am I?" Brynach asked. It had to be almost six. "Can I help?"

Riordan nodded, and Brynach took the other end of their massive custom-made sheets. As they met in the middle to fold it, Brynach landed a soft kiss on Riordan's smiling lips.

"You're going to be distracting, aren't you?" his partner teased.

"I'd like to be," Brynach admitted. "But, before I can do that, I have something to share with you."

They continued folding as he pushed on. "I saw Sydney. Her brother called her. He has information he wants to trade for the search being called off. He believes what he has to share is worth that much."

"And if it isn't?" Riordan asked.

"Then we don't call off the search," Brynach said.

He took a deep breath. "Did he mention what the information was in reference to?"

Brynach bit his lip, and Riordan's eyes tracked his tongue. "Sydney mentioned solid proof Peggy was involved in your parents' deaths. We need to give her an answer so the police can get recording equipment on her phone before he calls back. You have some time to think about it, though."

His partner dropped the last folded sheet into the hamper and slumped on the sofa. Brynach sat next to him, his large hand on Riordan's thigh, and his thumb rubbed circles on the outside of his leg.

"I should talk to Liam about it," Riordan whispered. He looked at his phone. "I can't make the decision alone. Ironically, he's on his way over to talk."

"Do you want me to leave?" Brynach asked.

Riordan grabbed his hand. "No. Stay."

"Want me to take the edge off your anxiety before he gets here?"

His partner laughed. "We don't have time."

"Get your mind out of the gutter." Brynach turned Riordan and brought his hands up to rub the tight muscles of his shoulders. He swept Riordan's long hair over the opposite shoulder and dug into the knots. He dropped his mouth to the other man's ear. "Do you think I have time to slide my hand into your shorts and stroke that beautiful cock? Maybe taste it? Let you close your eyes and focus on how I make you feel instead of all those swirling thoughts in your head? Grip your thighs and pull you further into my throat while my fingers rim around that pretty asshole of yours?"

He didn't have to look to know that Riordan was hard now. The man's breathing picked up, his pulse beating a wild rhythm in his neck. Brynach placed his tongue over it and licked it before taking the skin loosely in his teeth. He applied pressure, increasing it bit by bit until Riordan moaned at the pain.

"Not so unlike our wife, are you? A little pain feels good, Riordan. I can't wait to show you just how much pleasure I can bring you," Brynach promised.

Riordan didn't just sit there and take it, though. He ground his ass back into Brynach's lap and tilted his face up until he could look into his eyes. "Maybe I make you face the back of the sofa, that tight ass on display for me. Your hands spreading yourself for me while I ready my cock for your ass. Would you like that, husband?"

Brynach groaned. "Fuck. Say it again."

Riordan's tongue snaked out and skated up his jawline. "Husband."

With a growl, Brynach gripped his jaw and kissed him hard. "Yes. Yes, I fucking want that."

A cough caught them off-guard. "I can come back."

Brynach closed his eyes and tried to steady his breathing. Liam had crap timing, but Brynach had done what he intended to and distracted Riordan until Liam arrived.

Riordan pulled away and tugged a decorative pillow over his lap. Brynach smirked and turned to sit, not bothering to hide his erection. Liam's cheeks flushed as he eyed the bulge.

"Hey, eyes here!" Riordan demanded, making Brynach laugh.

"Can you blame a guy?" Liam asked, color staining his pale cheeks.

"That's my husband, perv," Riordan said, but there was laughter in his voice.

Liam shook his head and sat in the large chair opposite them. "It's been a crazy few days. What I just walked in on doesn't even make the top ten."

"It's about to get stranger," Riordan said.

His brother tensed. "Please, no."

"Unfortunately. I know there's still a lot to process with Dexter's death, but we have another issue."

Liam ran a hand over his face and through his shorter hair. "Just say it."

It was Brynach who spoke. "Sydney has been contacted by her brother. He claims to have information that he's willing to trade in exchange for us calling off the search for him so he can live in peace."

Riordan's brother sighed. "We already agreed to let it go. If we can do that and get more evidence against Peggy, I say we do it."

Riordan played with the rings on his necklace. "They'd understand, right? Mom and Da and Maggie?"

Liam nodded. "Yeah, they'd understand, Rory. In fact, I'm sure Da would whoop us for not taking this deal."

Brynach spoke, "He's calling tomorrow night. It will be recorded, but if you want to be there, you can be."

His brother sighed. "I better go and fill Amber in. Text me

the time once you know it."

Riordan stood and went to his brother. "There were other things we had to talk about."

The other man shook his head. "It can wait. This can't. Sorry, Rory."

"Call Sydney and tell her to let the department know. I'll call Aisling and loop her in."

Brynach frowned as his partner walked away from him, his guard back up.

CHAPTER 20

Aisling

Aisling gathered her hair in her hands and tied it in a messy bun. She patted her thighs, letting her fingers caress the ever-present blades Brynach had gifted her. Looking up at the sun, letting the magic around her caress her skin and calm her, she breathed deeply.

"You thinking what I'm thinking?" he asked, his lips skirting her neck.

She sighed and rolled her neck so he could access more of it. "That you're half of a pair of the luckiest men in the world to be married to me," she joked.

"Exactly that." His teeth tugged on her earlobe.

"Stay on course, Bry," Aisling scolded.

"I don't know. I'm with the big guy," Riordan joked.

"We have a job to do tonight, and then we can have some spicy fun times," she reminded them as they neared the safehouse.

There were too many people there, but she'd be damned if she wasn't with Riordan while this happened. They walked inside to absolute chaos. Wires and microphones. More police than she'd seen at a non-crime scene before. Sydney looked like she was ready to be sick to her stomach.

Aisling walked to the kitchen and returned with a seltzer water, cracking it open and handing it to her sister-in-law. "Take small sips."

"Thanks," Sydney murmured.

"What can I do to help?" Aisling asked.

"Can you be near me when I take the call? Use some soothing magic on me?" she requested with hopeful eyes.

"As long as the police say it's okay, yes," Aisling promised.

"Thank you," she whispered.

An officer came over to them and began spewing instructions.

"Wait two rings while we start recording and then answer. He's going to know we're here, so there's no reason to deny it. Keep him talking as long as you can. Get as much information as possible. Ask clarifying questions. Even if we promised not to come for him, we're going to trace the call. He'll know that. He may try and hang up and call back a few times. Try to avoid that if possible."

Sydney nodded like a bobblehead.

"We need him to say his name. We also need him to confirm that he's making an honest statement and that lying during the call is considered perjury," the officer reminded her.

Aisling could see her panicking. "Get a pad of paper and write down the bullet points. Just the essentials," she told the officer.

He nodded and moved to do as asked. Aisling looked up in time to see Liam and Amber move to Riordan's side. Brynach stood behind the sofa where Sydney and Aisling were sitting, protecting them.

"I'm in over my head," Sydney whined.

"You're going to do just fine. Like he said, Victor is smart. He'll know what's going on in here. If you need to, just ask an officer for clarification," Aisling assured her.

They sat in awkward silence, with noise and commotion

around them, until the phone rang and the entire room went silent. An officer pressed a button and nodded to Sydney, who answered the phone.

"Hello, Viktor." Her voice was high with worry.

"Syd. You have the cops with you?" Aisling could hear the man through the earpiece.

"Yes. As long as the information you provide is valuable, they accept your demands. They'll stop looking for you," she assured him.

"Even if the information makes me more guilty?" He double-checked.

Sydney looked to the officer, who nodded. "Even then."

"Good."

When her brother didn't continue, she added. "You're being recorded. It's a necessary part of this. Lying right now is considered perjury. Just tell the truth, Vik."

"And I'm sure they're also trying to trace the call," he muttered. "It won't matter. The information is good."

"Start with your full name and relationship to Peggy, then start talking," Sydney read from the paper in front of her.

"Make sure everything is recording properly. I'm not saying this more than once," he instructed.

The man in front of Sydney nodded, and she confirmed he was good to go. As he spoke, Aisling was very glad Riordan was across the room. She rubbed at her chest unconsciously and raised her eyes to her husband. She saw the question in his eyes and shook her head.

She didn't want to tell him here, not in front of all these people. When she looked at Sydney, the woman had silent tears on her face. She met Aisling's eyes and mouthed, "Go." Aisling gave her hand a squeeze and moved to her partners.

Without speaking, she took their hands. Turning to Liam and Amber, she nodded. "Our house." Then she pulled them from the house. Once outside of the protective wards, they sifted home.

"Aisling, what's going on?" Riordan asked.

Aisling didn't fight the tears that gathered in her eyes.

"You're scaring me a little," Riordan whispered.

"I'm sorry. I love you."

"Love you, too," he promised. He took her hand, and they walked in the front door.

Liam and Amber followed, and she could see the fear in their eyes. She wasn't trying to draw this out any longer than she already had.

"I think everyone should sit down." Around the room, the men listened, but Amber stayed standing, and so did Aisling. She had too much nervous energy, and Brynach had a large hand on their husband's leg. He'd take care of Riordan. Right now, she had to get this out.

"I'm sure there will be more details coming and an official recording from the police, but I heard enough to give you a heads-up," she began.

Riordan and Liam took dual breaths, and she saw them physically brace themselves for the information. Beside her, Amber moved close enough to touch her. It was an uncharacteristically warm action from the other women. She looked to the New Fae and gave her a sad smile, both knowing they'd have hurting partners to comfort after this.

"Sydney had already given us an idea that the Dorcha, and the reasoning for the attack on your parents, had been fabricated. We didn't know by whom or why, but Victor gave some clarity today. I'll preface this by saying I may not have heard everything perfectly, and I don't know how deep it all goes." She looked at both men.

It was Liam who spoke. "Ash, just say it. We won't shoot the messenger. They're gone. They can't get more gone. We'll be okay."

She wasn't so sure, but she nodded. "Before we ever figured it out, Peggy had the idea to try and strip magic from the Veil and see if they could create holes. He doesn't think she was aware she could create drops, but she did think that witches and Ravdi could steal the magic of the Veil for themselves. It was more a bid for power than the unification of two sides. He said their mother was desperate for the power she felt she was owed." Aisling pushed toward the tough part.

"We all know Peggy doesn't like getting her hands dirty if she can help it. Her position at the Firinne allowed her to issue orders to the witches and Ravdi she communicated with. He wasn't sure who else at the Firinne knew, but she didn't act within the organization alone. Being as Ireland is a bright spot for magic, and because the Veil is easier to pierce there, she decided to test a theory with the Carnlough coven. The already strong witches and Ravdi had the best chance at succeeding."

Riordan cursed, and Brynach rubbed soothing circles on his thigh. Amber gave Aisling's arm a final squeeze before she moved to Liam's side.

"She didn't give them enough information to attempt the draw safely. They didn't know what they were actually trying to accomplish, and so they cast a spell that magnified their Ravdis' ability to pull from the magic. Thus, flooding them with too much, with nowhere to put it. They couldn't dump it quick enough, not when they'd been told to keep it and not allow it to refortify the Veil. And the witches didn't know to state their intentions, at least not the right ones. The Goddess didn't react as favorably to their attempt."

Aisling felt the tears on her face and forced herself to keep going. "There was no way they could succeed, not without full knowledge. They couldn't cycle magic, and they couldn't shut down the bonds with the flow that strong. They burnt one another out."

Riordan's voice was raw when he spoke. "They would have suffered. They'd have known there was no way to shut it down, and they just had to endure it. We always thought it was quick."

Liam choked a sob and grabbed for his brother. The two

men hugged while they cried. When they quieted, it was Liam who looked up at her.

"How could they cover that up?" he asked.

Aisling shook her head. "She used her position to convince them to act before asking questions. And as a senior Firinne, she was able to spin a story to cover her tracks and incite fear."

She took a deep breath and shut her eyes before continuing. "When your parents died and that idea failed, she created the curse. It was her attempt at creating a problem she could solve and take credit for. She believed she'd be awarded a higher position if she did."

Brynach finally voiced his thoughts. "All the smaller attacks that were attributed to the Dorcha before the coven's passing? They were all her, too?"

Aisling nodded. "All beginning attempts to harness more magic for herself."

Riordan cried and cursed. It was a sign of how far he'd come that he didn't lash out, didn't demand a drink or storm off. He accepted his brother's embrace and Brynach's comfort. And when Aisling moved to her knees in front of him and rested her head against his chest, his arms circled her. The pain in the room was a living, breathing thing. Together, they cried and mourned.

Eventually, Liam and Amber left, and Aisling and Brynach were left with a worn-out Riordan.

"It shouldn't hurt so much. It's been so long, and I've already mourned them," Riordan murmured.

"Of course, it should," Brynach said as he settled on his other side. "What happened to them has always been wildly unfair, but this changes the context."

"I guess," Riordan said. "There's all this anger inside me, and it scares me. It feels like it's going to consume me."

Aisling kissed his cheek. "That won't happen, Riordan. You're too good for that, and we would pull you back if you went too far. But it's okay to be feeling this right now."

He nodded and rested his head on the back of the sofa. They sat in silence. The emotional toll hit Aisling hard, and her eyelids got heavy. Instead of fighting it, she let her body go loose and light. She was asleep before she realized it.

Immediately, she knew there was something different happening. This wasn't a normal dream. In the darkness, a light shone, and she was shivering cold. Aisling closed her unconscious eyes, and when she opened them again, she was with Brielle. The woman was crying, her face puffy and bruised.

"Don't let him see you," Brielle begged.

"He can't. I don't know how much time we have. Where are you? Help us find you."

She shook her head. "You can't come here. It's what I deserve."

"What are you talking about?"

"A life for a life. This is the Goddess's way of balancing the scales," Brielle said. Her voice was soft, weaker than Aisling had ever heard it.

"You know that's not true, Brielle. Nobody thinks that. It was an accident. You don't deserve this, and whether you like it or not, we're coming for you." Aisling walked to dream Brielle, who, even in her unconscious mind, was horribly abused and maimed. She could have appeared however she wanted, but even here, she was broken.

"Listen, Brielle. I know you want to protect me; you always have. I'm not coming alone, but I am coming. Now, you can either help me be better prepared, or you can let me come blind." Aisling tried to reason with her.

The tears were pouring from between Brielle's swollen eyes. She shook her head hard from side to side. "Fuck, you make me so mad."

"I have to try. Please, tell me something so I can help you," Aisling begged.

"I'm in a garage. It's filthy. I can hear cars, and we're on a flight path. Planes go overhead a few times a day. He knocked me out, so I didn't see anything on the way in. The sun comes in through the windows in the morning and wakes me."

"Who, Brielle," Aisling asked. Her friend shifted her gaze. "Brielle, tell me."

The bloodied blonde sighed. "It's my fault. I fucking trusted him. It's Walker."

Aisling was thrown from the dreamwalk, breathing heavily in Brynach's arms. "Aisling? What happened?"

"I linked with Brielle. Not sure why I was able to dreamwalk now and not before, but I have information about her location." She looked into Brynach's eyes. "I know who has her. Someone named Walker she said she knew."

"That neapan fucker!" Brynach yelled and shot to his feet. "I'll skin him alive."

"We fucking had him. He must have been laughing at us the whole time," Riordan raged and reached for his phone.

"What am I missing? Who are they?" Aisling asked, standing, too.

Brynach pushed his hair back and threw it up into a messy bun, and Riordan mirrored him. Fuck! Okay. She pulled at her wrist, untangling her hair tie from her charm bracelet and throwing her hair up, too. Apparently, it was time to throw down.

"Guys, seriously. What do I not know?" she asked again as she strapped on more weapons alongside the guys.

"He's an asshole mercenary. You met him when we went after Dexter. He's the one who released him from Riordan's leg trap," Brynach explained.

"Who has been attending security meetings and other round tables in Brielle's place," Riordan shared. "I want to hurt him. Bad."

"He got the drop on Brielle. He's clearly planned to be found out. Should we really be the ones going after him?" Aisling pointed out.

Brynach turned on her. "You're right. You stay here."

Her hands went to her hips, and she glared at him. "That's not what I meant."

"It's what I meant. He's unhinged. I can't anticipate what he'll do. You're safer here," Brynach elaborated.

Aisling looked to Riordan for support, and he avoided her gaze. "Riordan? Really?"

He shrugged. "Ash, he's really fucking big. And he's an unknown."

She smirked. "Too bad I'm the only one who knows where she might be."

Both her partner's jaws dropped. "You wouldn't," Brynach said.

She kept her hand on her knives and waited them out. Her husbands shared a look, and she saw when the fight left them. Aisling knew they'd watch her, keep one of them on her to ensure her safety, but at least she'd be there to help save her friend.

Aisling looked to Riordan. "Call Sean."

Riordan didn't argue. He put the phone on speaker, and they waited together for him to answer.

"Sean, we're looking for abandoned houses. She's in a garage along a flight pattern. She couldn't identify the times they flew by, but she said it was regular, and she got morning sun through the garage window. Can you narrow down the search area?" Aisling looked to Brynach. "Start gathering people just outside our wards. By the time they get here, Sean will have something."

She wasn't just tagging along. Aisling could handle this. She tied her boots and then walked through her wards to start welcoming the team. She was unsurprised when Jashana showed up but raised a brow at Breena.

Her sister-in-law looked at her with thinned lips. "Don't you dare. I bet Brynach tried to keep you home, didn't he? And here you are. If you so much as look at me like I shouldn't be here, I'll slap you."

Jashana grinned at her girlfriend. "She will."

Aisling held her hands up. "I won't say a thing. Prepare to slap your brother, though."

"With pleasure," she huffed.

More people showed up, Isaac and some New Fae she recognized from the training ground among them. When her partners came out, she held her breath, waiting to see what Brynach would say. The way Riordan grabbed his arm didn't go unnoticed by either Aisling or Breena, but the larger man didn't say anything.

"Alright, everyone. Nobody searches alone. Ideally, we stay together. Walker is smart, and he's had time to set traps and wards around the space. We don't know what we're walking into, not really. But Brielle is in there, and she needs us," Brynach briefed them.

Aisling took over. "She's in a garage of a house facing East and can hear cars but not people. We're thinking one of the abandoned neighborhoods. Walker was returning when I saw her in a dreamwalk not long ago. We have to assume he'll be there when we show up."

"Walker?" Jashana asked.

Around the group, curses rang and heads shook. Man, people really didn't like that guy. Everyone turned to Riordan, who was staring at his phone, willing it to ring. Dread settled in her stomach. They had to find Brielle, but she wished she wasn't walking into a torture chamber. Not with all that had been happening lately. She was done with bloodshed.

"*Aisling?*" Rin checked in.

"*I'm fine,*" she told her familiar.

"*No, you aren't, and that's okay. You don't have to be strong all the time, Aisling. Nobody is. Nobody can be. You've been pushing yourself too hard,*" her familiar said softly.

"I should be better!" she screamed out loud. Heads turned, but she ignored them. "*I'm so tired. I nearly lost Lettie. I lost Trent. I lost what little I had of my father. I lost my Ravdi bond with Riordan. I lost a career I loved for one I am obligated to. I lost so much so others could gain, and I don't regret that, but I'm allowed to be exhausted and resentful sometimes. But I'm getting my friend, and I'm bringing her home. Then I can lose it. But not right now. Not when I have to prove to the guys I can do this."*

CHAPTER 21

Riordan

When Sean called, it coincided with a series of dropped pins. Riordan put the phone on speaker, and everyone gathered around. "I have narrowed it down to about a half dozen areas. Each one has a few streets of houses facing that direction, but it's somewhere to start. I'm going to review street cam and Ring camera footage and see if I can see the asshole coming and going. If I find something, I'll call back."

Riordan hung up, and Brynach addressed them. "You heard him. It's not that many neighborhoods. We go all together to each one and hit as many houses at once as possible to maintain the element of surprise."

The first neighborhood was eerily quiet. What was once a loud, child-filled block now stood overgrown and still. It was something out of a post-apocalyptic movie. Even if this wasn't where Brielle was, it felt wrong. Using hand signals he'd only seen in Navy Seal movies, they moved along the street and lined up at garage doors. Aisling glared at the larger Fae but stood behind him, weapons at the ready. With Brynach's silent countdown, they all lifted their doors.

Before them, the garage was empty and dust-covered. Heads

swiveling, he saw everyone else shaking their heads, too. A few groups ran quickly to the few unopened doors, but they came up empty. The same process was repeated in two more neighborhoods.

Aisling pulled out her phone. "Sean. We've got nothing on the first three spots. Please tell me you have some video footage. Each time we do this, we're giving him time to leave."

Whatever he said had Aisling holding out her hand for Riordan's phone. She pointed to a pin, and Brynach whistled for everyone to join them.

"You're sure?" she asked. Her red head bobbed as she nodded. "You're the best. Thanks."

After that, everything was a frenzy of activity. Aisling told them the address Sean had seen Walker at, and Fae began sifting at alarming rates. Not wanting to be left behind, Aisling sifted, and Brynach cursed and followed. Riordan quickly folded reality and popped into existence outside the home of a soccer mom.

There was a group of Fae creeping toward the home in question, slowly circling it. Riordan and his partners joined the group, taking the front of the house. He wished for a moment that they didn't have to, but he knew Aisling needed to do this.

"Something feels different," Riordan whispered.

Brynach nodded at his side. "I agree. Watch your back." His eyes traveled to Breena, standing next to Jashana, eyes on the garage door and body leaning forward in anticipation.

He knew without being told that Brynach would be distracted with making sure his sister and Aisling stayed safe, which left Riordan to make sure Brynach stayed safe. Then the garage door went up, and he forgot everything.

It took a while before his brain caught up with his eyes. Magic swirled around the room, none of it particularly bright. Running into the space was probably a bad idea, but fuck, Brielle looked bad. The concrete floor was covered in dark stains, and an unconscious, tiny warrior was chained and hanging from the ceiling by her arms. Her head was on her chest, and her feet just hitting the floor.

What he didn't see was Walker. A shout went up, and then people were charging into the house. Riordan heard Aisling choke on a sob and then rally.

"We need to clear that magic!" she called out. "Nobody goes into that garage until I say so."

Riordan moved closer to her, and they called magic together. He knew how to do this, understood sharing and channeling magic with her. They did it as witch and Ravdi and again for the Veil drops. She could probably do it alone, but he didn't want her straining herself.

"A little help," he called out, and a few more experienced Fae came over. The magic fought them. Riordan had never seen such stubborn magic. Eventually, they'd pulled and redistributed it. The area they'd emptied it into was a barren spot in the grass.

"That would have been ugly," one Fae commented.

With the garage clean of ill intentions, Brynach charged in with Riordan and Aisling at his back. Now that they were in the garage, he could hear shouts from inside. They'd have to handle whatever was going on in there because, Goddess, this was bad.

Brynach lifted the weight of the small Fae and gave the chains slack. Breena was there to unravel and release the woman. Brielle screamed out in pain, and Brynach hurried out of the garage to place her on the grass carefully. Thankfully, she passed out as soon as she was down. All the better, because as soon as the blood flow started back up again, she'd be in horrible pain.

Aisling kneeled next to her and gently checked her breathing. "It's shallow and too wet. She may have a pierced lung or something. Does that make wet noises?"

"I don't know a stoirin," Brynach answered honestly. "We have to get her medical attention as soon as we can move her again."

She was in bad shape. Her pale hair was missing from one whole section of her head. If he had to guess from the random directions they were pointing in, her fingers were broken. Her chest was bare and covered in bruises. If there was any higher power, she'd stay unconscious and sleep off some of this pain.

"Mother-fucking dick-swallowing goat-hoarder," Breena cursed creatively. "He's not here."

They'd given him too much time.

Brynach looked up at Breena and Jashana. "Take whoever is left and find this fucker."

"Consider it done. I'll be in touch," Breena answered.

"Bry," Ash drew his attention. "We have to go. She needs to get to your court for help."

The tears streaming down her face broke Riordan. Carefully, their partner lifted his friend and sifted to the Unseelie court. They submitted to the blood test and hurried to the hospital ward. Rainer had equipped the ward with the best technology, but even they may not be ready for what was about to walk through their door.

As they made their way through the building, word must have spread. As they neared the heavy double doors, Corinna greeted them and opened the door. "Over here." She led them to an empty bed. "Dr. Gardner, we need you!"

From the back door of the room, an old man entered and, upon seeing Brielle, ran to the bed. The white bedding had already turned red under Brielle. The Fae's blood stained Brynach's hands and chest from where he'd held her. Her body would heal, but Riordan knew better than most that psychological damage took much longer to heal.

Aisling was crying at her friend's side, but Brielle still hadn't woken. The doctor began calling out orders for medical supplies and yelling for nurses. Brynach looked at him, and he nodded with his head toward the door. This was going to haunt Aisling for a long time. He didn't want her to see another friend die or suffer.

"Aisling, I think it's best if we let the doctor work," Brynach began. "We can come back tomorrow."

The way she looked at him made even Riordan flinch. He looked to Corinna, who gave him a small smile.

"Aisling, she's going to be out of it for a while. Go. I'll keep you posted. I promise."

Their wife didn't look happy about it at all, but she stood and walked away when the nurses bustled in and nudged her to move. Nobody said anything as they made their way from the palace grounds and sifted home. Nobody said anything as they showered off the blood and grime. Nobody said anything as they climbed into bed. And nobody said anything as Aisling cried herself to sleep. They just loved one another. It was all they could do.

CHAPTER 22

Brynach

He woke before his partners and watched the sun rise onto his wife's and husband's faces. Aisling's eyes were puffy, and her nose was red. Even in her sleep, her chest gave a small hiccup that made him want to keep her in this house, safe, for the rest of eternity. He hated that he couldn't. Every cell in his body wanted to protect her, but Aisling was growing stronger each day, and he had to respect that. Damn Breena and her life lessons.

Brynach wanted to stay like this. Safe in their bed all day long, but he knew they couldn't. They had a maniac to hunt down and a friend to check on. He had a partner to check in on and a class that needed teaching. And more importantly, he had a business partner and damn near-brother who needed an ass-kicking. What the hell was Alex doing talking to Walker? The fact that he'd had any business dealings with that scumbag at all bothered the hell out of him.

Aisling's hand moved against his chest, and Riordan's hips nudged his back as they began to stir. Brynach smiled, waiting for their eyes to open. It was the best part of his day. There was something about seeing the immediate trust and love in their gaze when they saw him. And a joy in being the first thing to greet them into wakefulness.

"Why aren't you sleeping?" Aisling's voice was groggy with sleep still.

He kissed her forehead. "And miss the view? Never."

Her smile made his chest warm. Riordan turned his body toward his, the heat from the other man nestling against his other side. Over his chest, Aisling and Riordan kissed. Goddess, this was perfect.

"You went real still there, big guy," Riordan laughed and ran a hand down Brynach's side to settle at his hip.

Aisling giggled. "I think I know why." The minx wiggled against him. He growled, and the room rang with his partner's laughter. He smiled in response.

"Oh no you don't. We have jobs. Get through your day and the rest of the week, and after our party, you're mine." Brynach gripped Aisling's face gently and angled her head back. The taste of her on his tongue made him groan, and then Riordan's hand was guiding his face back to his waiting lips.

"Old man can't hang," Aisling joked and earned herself a slap to the ass when she stood up. "Is it weak if I don't want to go out there? We have to find Walker, and I have to see Brielle. The press is going to need me. Cathy is already blowing up my phone." She held out the display full of missed texts and calls.

Riordan stretched, naked on their bed. "Bry, you have classes to teach. I'll handle Walker with Sean and Liam, and Aisling can visit Brielle and then the press. Tonight, we can have a family dinner. Sound good?"

Aisling winked. "You look like a meal right now."

Brynach laughed, and Riordan shook his head. "I'm not complaining, but at some point, you should probably discuss with a therapist why stress makes you so horny."

Their wife tossed her hair and walked into the closet to dress. He turned back to the bed and a still-very-naked Riordan. His husband held his hand out to him. "Honestly, we have work to do today."

"And we'll do it. First, come here." Riordan stared at him, waiting. There was no way he was going to deny the man intimacy, not when he was new to, and nervous about, their relationship.

He rested on his side, propped on an elbow over Riordan. "I'm here."

The other man bit his lip. "Yes, you are." He leaned up and captured Brynach's lips in a kiss that heated his blood. It wasn't until they parted, breathless and swollen-lipped, that he asked. "How are you?"

"Hard," Brynach joked.

Riordan locked his fingers in the inky black hair and held his gaze. "Things have been uncertain lately, and I know you don't do well with that. More than that, your best friend has been in closed-door talks with a man who tortured your other friend."

Brynach closed his eyes. "Yeah, that did happen, but nobody has been spared hard days recently."

"No," Riordan agreed. "But most of us don't thrive on complete control the way you do. We love you, big guy. We worry."

He leaned down and captured Riordan's lips. "Don't. I'm okay."

"Would you tell us if you weren't?"

There was worry in his eyes, and Brynach hated it. "Maybe not at one point, but now, yes. You have my word."

Riordan nodded. "Okay. Then get out of this bed and start your day." He popped up and snapped his fingers. "Up, lazy bones."

He was off the bed in a flash, his hand connecting with his husband's naked ass. Riordan gasped, but Brynach watched as his cheeks flushed and he bit his lip. Oh yeah, they were going to test that sooner than later.

Aisling called Cathy long enough to calm her down and promised to come right over as soon as she'd seen Brielle. Brynach had offered to go with her, but she assured him she'd be okay. It upset him how relieved that made him because he had been neglecting his class prep. Luckily, the kids never noticed when he was distracted. Still, Semele had called him on his inability to stick around after class.

"Some kids are shy and come to you afterward for questions. If you're not here, they can't. I suggest setting aside some time to wander the grounds or interact with the children outside of class," they stated. "And I know you're busy; we're all busy. Get over yourself."

Goddess, he liked them. Frankly, he needed the no-bullshit lack of coddling when it came to teaching. He didn't want to mess this up. He had promised them to be around more.

Kongur's voice rang in his head. *The kids are wired today. Game face.*

"Got it. Thank you," Brynach told his familiar. *"Today, we have the rideable familiars. We're going on a trail. We'll be demonstrating the need to discuss safe riding. Meet me at the grounds."*

Semele was still nervous about the kids not using any kind of saddle, but Brynach was sure this was the way to go. Most of the time with familiars, you don't have time to get everything on them, not to mention with communication it was plenty safe without them.

Though maybe they had reason to hesitate, considering the class today would include horses, wolves, a mountain lion, a moose, a grumpy cow, deer, and even a bear. They'd focus on communication, sharing when they were comfortable or needed a break. Recognizing signs of injury. Respecting boundaries and limitations. It would be one of the smaller groups he had, but it was an important lesson to learn. If he concentrated on that, maybe he could make it through the day without throwing up.

"Alright, you heathens. Ben, Diane, Elliot, I need you over here." Brynach waited for the kids and their familiars to join him. He felt Kongur at his back, the kids staring at the large horse. Having him there soothed something in Brynach.

"How many of you have ridden on your familiars?" Around him, hands went up, but a few didn't. He'd suspected as much. "Okay. Check in with your familiar and make sure they're okay continuing with today's lesson. We will be learning to safely communicate and ride our familiars without saddles or assistance."

"*How many fall off?*" Kongur asked.

"*Most of them,*" Brynach answered. But that was okay. They'd learn. Only after the children had gotten confirmation that their familiars were comfortable did Brynach move on with the lesson. They'd stopped by a stream, the familiars getting a drink and the children splashing one another. He sat back and let them have their fun for a few minutes.

As they anticipated, the kids struggled, and more than a few familiars roared or called out their displeasure at hair being pulled or feet digging in painful places. He assured them that was okay and that they'd learn over time to work as a team.

"It's taken me over two hundred years to form the relationship I have with my familiar," Brynach said, stroking Kongur's back. "Nobody expects perfection, but it's important to start your relationship with clear communication. And boundaries, things you are comfortable with or not comfortable with."

"Are there any other questions before we head back and end class?" Brynach asked the group.

A hand raised, and he called on a particularly bright little girl. "Yes, Clara."

Once called on, she bit her lip and looked unsure of herself. Brynach waited her out until she finally spoke. "Sometimes I get scared and don't want to be at home. I feel safer in the woods." She kept a hand on her familiar's side. The female mountain lion purred deep in her chest and rubbed her head on the girl's thigh. "I know it's not okay to run away, but am

I allowed to go with Riva? I'll be so safe. She'll never let anything bad happen to me."

There was something in the girl's eyes, in the protectiveness of her familiar, that gave Brynach pause. If getting out of her house meant safety, he'd never ask her to stay. "Sometimes, I would leave with Kongur and not tell my parents. But I did tell my sister. Or my best friend. Or someone who knew to check in on me. Someone always needs to know where you are. Someone you trust." He waited a moment and then double-checked. "Do you have someone like that?"

Her little head bobbed quickly. "My aunt. She knows I leave sometimes."

Brynach made a mental note to have Semele keep an eye on Clara while he was gone. He instructed the children to get back on their familiars and make their way safely back to the barn. Brynach hung back, waiting to make sure everyone got on their way. The sound of their giggles and shouts as they raced back carried on the wind.

"You're good with them," Kongur said. *"You'll be a great father."*

"Not even a thought in my mind." Not that he hadn't considered having children with Aisling, but they had forever to think about that. *"Come on, let's get back."*

He sat atop his familiar, feeling like everything was right in the world as he saw the children run to their peers and talk about the lesson. Brynach never expected to find such joy in teaching, but he was.

"Get off already," Kongur rumbled. With a pat, he slid down to the ground and walked over to his co-teacher.

Semele had waved him off, saying they didn't need his help in the stables. "I didn't mean right away, Brynach. Go. I am sure you have other things to do after recent events."

"You heard?" he asked.

They tilted their head and squinted their eyes. "Everyone heard."

"Right." He sighed heavily. "Thank you. I do have to talk to someone."

On his way to find Alex, he ran into Aindrea. Joeigh was asleep in a swaddle against her mother's chest, her small fingers in her mouth making soft sucking sounds.

Brynach hugged the woman, careful not to squish the baby. He whispered, "I've missed you."

Aindrea laughed loudly. "She's trained to sleep through anything. She'd have to be, growing up around here, now that I have a few hundred extra kids to care for. Goddess, I miss sleep. This one has decided she likes being awake at night."

Brynach shook his head. "I thought Alex shared nighttime duties."

"He does, but he's been busy lately. I thought I had a lot on my plate, but he's constantly in some meeting or another." Aindrea was smiling, but Brynach knew her well enough to see through it. She was tired and would never say anything bad about Alex, but something was wrong.

"Don't worry, I'll do something about that," Brynach promised. With a quick kiss on Aindrea's cheek, he continued to his friend's office.

He slowed as he reached Alex's closed doors. Voices sounded from inside, muffled but clearly excited. They rose and fell in a conversational rhythm, but Brynach couldn't make out what was being said. Without knocking, he turned the handle and walked into his friend's office. All talking stopped, and heads turned toward him. Theo, Marina, Alex, and Ceiren stared at Brynach like he had two heads.

"Am I interrupting?" He walked further into the room.

Marina flushed, and her hands smoothed down her pants. "Of course not," she answered, obviously lying.

Brynach shot Alex a look, and his friend smiled and shrugged. Turning to the rest of the room, he said, "We'll finish discussing this later."

"Don't stop on my account. I'm sure I'll catch up," Brynach offered.

Alex offered a stiff smile and shook his head, and everyone moved past Brynach. Even Ceiren made an excuse and took off through the stone archway.

"That wasn't awkward at all," Brynach commented.

His friend shrugged. "Yes, well, you did enter during a private meeting."

Brynach's citrine eyes narrowed. "Since when are you having private meetings that I can't attend?"

Alex's smile slipped. "It's not exactly easy running an entire school with over three hundred children, Brynach. I can't possibly pass every decision by you. That's why you left it for me to handle. Right?"

"I thought this was a logical move for you, Alex, but Aindrea says you're losing sleep and family time over this. That was never my intention," Brynach reminded him.

"Don't pander to me, Bry. I'm handling it." He stood, clearly trying to dismiss Brynach. It didn't work.

"Alex, every time I come in here to try to talk, you rush me out. That's not going to fly anymore. Not after yesterday," he said.

His friend opened his mouth, but Brynach held up a hand. "Do not act like you don't know what I'm talking about. I'm serious, Alex."

"Brynach, I know you mean well, but this is larger than you and I. This is about the future of Fae. These children need the best chance at a solid foundation and future. I'm going to do whatever it takes to make sure that happens."

"Even if that means working with a man who tortured and disfigured a woman you helped raise?" His voice rose as he leaned forward in his seat and continued. "She passed out from pain. Her blood soaked through my clothing, Alex. She'll never fly again. Never be free of the memories of that trauma."

"Stop it," Alex barked. "You think I'm okay with Brielle being hurt? I'm not! Goddess, Brynach, who do you think I am?"

"I'm not sure anymore," he admitted. "I certainly didn't

anticipate you talking like that extremist. Whatever it takes, Alex. Really? To what end? At what cost? What's happened to you?"

His friend stood and circled to the other side of the desk. He sat on the edge and crossed his arms. "You put me in power. I'm handling it. If you have something to say, say it. Are you officially challenging me?"

How the hell had it come to this? He didn't want a blood tithe from his best friend, but he did want answers.

"You realize that this behavior, this defensiveness, doesn't look good, right? This is messed up, Alex. I swear, if you bring Aindrea into this. If something happens to Joeigh, or Trixie, or any of the children here because of your bullshit, you'll pay." Brynach did stand then.

"Do not threaten my family," Alex yelled.

"I never thought I'd see the day where I felt the need to protect them from you, Alex. Figure your shit out!" Brynach didn't wait for a response before he walked out. Before he could exit the palace, a hand shot out and dragged him into an empty classroom.

He spun with his knife already in his hand.

Ceiren held his hands up. "Sorry. Didn't want anyone to see me talking to you."

"What is with everyone being weird as fuck?" Brynach wondered out loud.

His brother arched an expressive brow, a genetic trait their mother passed along. "Glad you caught on. I thought this was going to be a tough sell. But your friend has gone off the rails!"

Brynach shook his head. "You've been spending too much time with the New Fae. You talk like one of them now. Now, tell me what you know so I can get to the bottom of this."

"He's been taking meetings, a lot of them, and not letting us in on them. The people going into those meetings, Brynach, they're not good people." Ceiren looked worried.

Brynach pulled out his phone and sent Aisling a text. She answered back right away.

Need a favor

Anything

Can you ask Phlyren if he'd
be willing to spy for me?

He's on his way & I'm intrigued!
What am I telling him to do?

Listen in on Alex's meetings.
I need to know who he sees
and what they talk about.
Tell him I said thank you.

He said not to worry.
Gotta go. They're calling me.

Love you! Good luck.

"Okay. I'm listening," Brynach promised. "Just so you know, I already confronted him and got stonewalled. He really tried to stare at me and deny he was being shady."

Ceiren nodded. "I want you to know I'm not innocent in all this. I've been working for decades to upset the power balance of Faerie. My role with the Unaligned allowed me to plant seeds of distrust for the courts. I have never believed in Light and Dark. We're one people. I still believe that."

"Change is hard, and something drastic had to happen to force it," he agreed.

"Right." Ceiren ran a hand through his hair in an action so like his own that Brynach felt an immediate kinship to his half-sibling.

His brother continued, "Over the years, I've worked with Alex. Not just to place children but because he believed, like me, that we might be better off without the court's control. I know I have a reputation around the palace for being soft. I'm not like Levinas was, or even Rainer, and certainly not you and Breena. I believe that good comes to good people."

Brynach felt his patience slipping. "I know you, Ceiren. I am not questioning your actions. Tell me why you're questioning Alex's."

"A little while back, right after you started discussing the possibility that Aisling may bring down the Veil, Alex had a shift in his mindset. I thought at the time it was Joeigh and new parenthood making him worry more. But, time passed, and more change happened in the world, and his views kept getting more..." Ceiren struggled for the right word.

Brynach offered a few suggestions. "Enthusiastic. Intense."

"Extreme. Radical," Ceiren corrected. "I know our history is tense, and we're not close, but I don't say this to hurt you."

He hung his head. "What do I do?"

Ceiren frowned. "I can't tell you that, but I do know until we know more about his motivation, he's a danger."

"Fuck," Brynach pulled at his hair. "Theo? Marina? Have they been in the meetings?"

His brother shook his head. "No. Theo is an ass, and Marina is a bit naive, but they haven't been involved."

"Well, at least that's something. Let's keep our eyes open. I want documentation. I'm not doing anything without proof." Brynach looked up at his brother. "You have my permission to move on him if a child so much as appears hurt. Understood?"

Only after getting his brother's promise did he reach out to his familiar. *"Want to ride?"*

"On my way," he answered.

Brynach walked out to the front lawn of the Seelie court and grinned at how changed it was. Children, Fae children, swarmed. He'd never seen such potential for the future of Fae in all his long life. Knowing that these children would benefit from health and longevity healed some of the broken parts of his own traumas.

"*And you say you don't want children,*" Kongur mocked when he pulled up beside him.

"*I never said I didn't want them. I just don't think we're ready for them right now.*" Brynach loved the idea of children. Of filling Aisling up with Riordan and being surrounded by the cries and squeals of kids. But their wife hadn't mentioned children yet, and after the childhood she had, she might not want them. He'd respect that. There was no timeline for starting a family, not for them, not anymore.

Brynach swung up onto the Percheron's back, and Kongur took off, racing across what once was Faerie but now housed human homes, roads, and buildings. They ignored the stares when they couldn't stick strictly to wooded or more remote paths on the way to the computer hub that was Sean's place. It would have been faster and easier to sift, but he'd missed this time with his familiar.

"*You're getting awful sappy up there,*" Kongur commented.

"*You know you've missed me too,*" Brynach countered. His large hand stroked the neck of the horse as they skirted around a car. His familiar didn't argue. Instead, they lost themselves in the stretch of muscles and the rush of the wind.

Sean and Liam were leading the behind-the-scenes search for Walker. Nobody monitored street cams and hacked into systems like Sean did. He didn't want to even consider what it would look like if he'd used that genius brain for the other side. Brynach was glad they were friends. Once he knew where the search was, he'd sift to Jashana and the others. When that fucker was brought down, he wanted to be there.

Any night that he laid down with his partners and that man wasn't dead or behind bars was an uneasy one. Who the fuck could torture a friend that way, and for what? That's what he needed to know. They pulled up to the building, and Brynach thanked his familiar before leaping down to whistles.

"Damn, Wyatt Earp," Sean laughed from his window. "I

thought I heard you clopping your way here."

"*I don't clop!*" Kongur argued. "*I'm too majestic for that.*"

Brynach laughed and walked up the stairs and into the already open door. "If you're staring wistfully out the window for me, I assume all the work is done."

Sean rolled his eyes, and Lettie stood with her hands on her hips. "He hasn't slept at all. I don't understand an eighth of what he's looking at, but he's rubbing his eyes constantly. The doctor told him he has to look long distances every now and then to give his eyes a break."

"Sorry, Lettie. You're right. Thank you, Sean." Brynach was sincere in his gratitude. Lettie seemed appeased by his apology. He couldn't stop the way his eyes slid to the computers.

Sean laughed. "Come on, I'll show you."

Brynach followed the pale, lanky man to his comfort zone, a large cushioned chair and a hub of monitors. Just like Lettie, he had no idea what he was looking at. Sean's fingers moved over the keyboards and clicked into tabs and live feeds faster than Brynach's brain could process. Which was saying something with Fae senses.

"You're a master," he commented.

Sean shrugged his shoulders. "So, this is a feed from three in the morning. He's aware of where most obvious cameras are, but people don't consider just how many lenses are on them at any given time. This was from a corner security camera and a nosy neighbor spying on the girl across the street. Walker avoided the bank camera and the clear doorbell camera, but he didn't avoid these two." Sean pointed at the large man.

"You can't see his face," Brynach commented.

Sean nodded. "Yeah, I know. But I have the computer looking for the size and gait length of Walker along with facial features and hair. This pinged because ..." He clicked another button. "Right here, a block later, a camera facing the other direction caught his face and hair under the hoodie before he ducked his head."

"Fuck. That's scary but impressive," Brynach wondered.

Lettie sighed. "I really wish I didn't know all this. I'm paranoid all the damn time now."

Sean turned to her. "I've got you, baby. Nobody can hack into your stuff. I have control of anything near your home."

"Not exactly comforting." She rolled her eyes but dropped a kiss on the man's cheek.

He turned back to the screens. "I reported it to Jashana, but the thing about a lack of Veil is that he can sift away immediately. If we can't get him locked into a location and warded, he'll just keep jumping away from them. It's a fucking frustrating game of cat and mouse."

Sean pointed to a monitor to his left. "See here. He sifted out and was pinged on this car dealership camera about thirty minutes later. By the time the coordinates were relayed, he was gone again."

"So, what do we do?" Brynach asked.

"Liam is helping. I've got a live feed of my pings going straight to him, and he's developed a program that will triangulate and trace everywhere we see him. We're looking for patterns or a central location he moves around. But that takes time that we don't really want to give him to plan a true escape." Sean answered.

Brynach asked the real question. "Why hasn't he left the area?"

Sean finally looked away from the screens and up at the large Fae. "My guess? He's not done."

He hated that he knew Sean was right. Which meant that someone else was in danger of being taken by that maniac.

"Will we be safe tomorrow night?" Lettie asked.

Brynach smiled at her. "Nowhere safer. But you do what feels right for you. Aisling will understand."

His wife's friend straightened her spine. "I'm not living in fear of anyone or anything anymore."

CHAPTER 23

Aisling

"Why are we doing this again instead of massages and sex?" Riordan asked.

Music played from the speakers around the home, and sparkling lights danced within the tree limbs. Aisling had planned a get-together for the full moon. It felt like a good time to clean out negative energies, set intentions, and see her friends. Aisling needed a night to drink and dance and forget how much things had been sucking lately. And maybe that was indulgent, but she realized she really didn't care.

"Because we deserve to celebrate with friends, and you know damn well we're having sex later anyway." She winked at her husband. "And all you have to do is wince a little, and Bry will schedule the massages."

Dexter was dead. Brynach's murderous human father was hiding away at her mother's house. Alex was a possible scumbag. Her father was a tool. Shit was hitting the fan left and right, and she had to leave town again soon. So tonight, they were going to forget all that and enjoy themselves.

They were calling it a late wedding reception for their handfasting and a full moon party. Or just a "hey, come get drunk and eat" gathering. Either way, she was looking forward to the night. Riordan took her hand and raised it over their heads, palming her hip and spinning her. She laughed and then came to rest against his chest.

She wrapped her arms around him. "How did we get this lucky?"

"Is that what we're calling it?" he teased.

She kissed his lips. "What else could we be to have one another through all this?"

Aisling ran her hands through his long hair and reminded herself to tell the guys they were never allowed to cut it without telling her first. "I love you," she whispered as she rested her forehead against his.

"Unhand my brother," Liam said, sifting in nearby.

Aisling laughed and kissed Riordan one more time before turning to say hello to Liam and Amber. It wasn't long before Sean, Lettie, Tara, and Kara arrived. Between the six of them, they had a cake, booze, and a bowl of crystals to charge. Aisling hugged them before leading them to the drink table.

Brynach had arranged for Sydney to attend, but only after her boyfriend-bodyguard had scoped out the wards around the house. Aisling smiled at Sydney as she settled into a deck chair and Brynach handed her a water.

"I'm totally fine! I'm Fae, for Goddess' sake. Stop hovering," Sydney scolded, but Aisling saw the way she smiled at her brother. She liked having someone worry about her.

Breena had sifted in with Jashana in time to hear their sister's comment. "Yeah, tell me how that goes. I've been trying for hundreds of years. Best to just get used to it."

Sydney smiled and shrugged. "We have to keep trying, right?"

Breena gave them the finger and moved to the booze, filling a glass with vodka and the smallest splash of cranberry juice. If Aisling heard correctly, she muttered something that sounded a lot like "fucking urinary tract." She covered her mouth and fought the laughter. Oh, to be human.

Jashana seemed to be fighting the same smile and shook her head at her lover. Her mother and Dawn sifted in, and Aisling ran over to say hello. She hugged her mother tight before moving to Dawn.

The New Fae was grinning ear to ear. "Loren has Eves, and Mama is going to party!"

"Everything's good at home?" Aisling asked but was looking at her mother, who nodded.

"Amazing. Though my husband is a smidge moody about being the only human in the house now," Dawn commented.

"Mom?" she asked. Nobody had checked in on Gabriel in far too long. But her mother just smiled and nodded.

"All good."

Aisling pointed the women to the snacks and drinks. Brynach approached and took her face in his large hands, stroking his thumbs along her cheeks. He kissed her softly, and she melted into his large body.

"Can you change the music to something a bit more dance-worthy?"

He backed away from her and bowed. "As you command, my princess."

She laughed at him pulling out his phone to change the play-list. As she watched him, or mainly his ass, Riordan approached her with a cup in his hand. Kareem and Russell were mingling behind him, with Cait attached to her boyfriend's side.

"It's sangria made with Fae wine. Be careful; the fruit has a kick." He kissed her. "Figured tonight was a night for getting buzzed."

"Yes, please." She brought the cup to her mouth and took a large sip. The music and mood were light, and laughter floated in the air. "I've missed this."

Riordan moved behind her, his hips swayed, and her body matched him. She felt his breath on her neck, and she stifled a groan when his lips met her skin. Brynach joined them, his body pressing to her other side.

"We have a surprise for you, a stoirin. Follow us," Brynach instructed.

"The party," she started.

"Now." The dominance in his voice was impossible to miss. Heat pooled low in her belly, and she nodded before following the two men.

Once inside, they led her to the bathroom. She looked around, nervous that they'd be seen, but Brynach growled, and she hurried inside.

There was plenty of room for the three of them in the large bathroom, but her husband crowded her. Aisling fought to not squirm under his gaze. Her eyes shot to Riordan, but he just smiled and shook his head.

"Eyes here, Aisling," Brynach called her attention back to him. When she met his gaze, he grinned at her. "The other night has us addicted to you. Do you think you can handle us both tonight?"

Aisling's whole body trembled. She pressed her thighs together and whimpered. "Goddess, yes."

"But," she started.

"Butt, indeed," Riordan joked. "I can't wait to see Brynach inside it."

"Wait! Bry?" She wanted it, of course she did, but he was too big.

Brynach leaned under the bathroom cabinet and came up with two items. A butt plug she'd never seen before and a bottle of lube. Which was saying something because recently, they'd acquired plenty of toys. Her eyes went wide, and he smirked at her.

"We need you nice and prepped for me when everyone goes home," he said. She watched as he opened the package and cleaned the black plug.

"You want me to wear that during the party?"

"Yes, we do," Riordan answered.

Brynach looked at her, daring her to argue. She wouldn't.

"Hands on the sink and pull up your skirt so I can see that pretty ass, Aisling," Brynach ordered.

She turned toward the mirror and stared at her flushed face. It was impossible to ignore the way her chest rose and fell in quick jolts. Brynach's large hand hit her lower back, forcing her to arch more. Once he had her where he wanted her, he kicked her legs open, and Aisling held the position. She relaxed her body and prepared for the cool sensation of lube and the warm stretch of the plug.

Her husbands watched her face as Brynach spread the lubricant around her asshole. Then he held up the toy and showed her how he was preparing it for her. Aisling bit her lip, and this time she didn't stop the moan from leaving her lips.

Slowly, he applied pressure, pulsing against her until she pushed back on him. Their laughter made her cheeks redden, but she knew they were proud of her.

"That's it. Take it, Princess," Brynach encouraged.

Aisling slid herself back and carefully fucked herself with the plug, pushing in and easing out a few times until, with Brynach's gentle push, her ass welcomed it. It was big enough that she couldn't ignore it, but it wasn't uncomfortable. Brynach straightened her underwear, and Riordan helped her rise from her position. He pulled her to him and kissed her. Aisling leaned against his chest, her hands holding him right. Then her body lit up. Her partner's smile was evident against her mouth.

"What?" she gasped as the toy came to life inside her. Aisling gripped Riordan's arms.

Brynach held up his cell phone and smirked. "Remote-controlled, my heart."

She wanted to protest, but then the plug came alive, and pleasure nearly brought her to her knees. Suddenly, she couldn't find the energy to be upset. Aisling knew she could stop it all with one word, but she didn't want to. Instead, she took another deep sip of her drink and kissed Brynach before moving past them. Their laughter followed her as she entered the yard and her group of friends.

Lettie hugged her tightly. "About time you got your ass down here. They see you all the time. I swear, those men are so selfish."

Aisling squeezed her friend tighter and laughed, "You have no idea."

"I can't believe you have two husbands, and this one still won't put a ring on it," Tara nudged Kara's shoulder with her own. It was so nice seeing them, but Aisling still felt guilty for how small their handfasting had been and said as much.

Kara shrugged. "Small and intimate is the way to go. That's what we're going to have."

Tara blushed and changed the subject. "We left a gift inside when we got here."

"You didn't have to," Aisling told them. "You guys aren't drinking the sangria, are you?" She pointed to the dark liquid in their glasses.

"The drinks are clearly labeled for Fae and non-Fae. This is the regular sangria," Kareem answered. "Although, I wouldn't mind getting Fae levels of fucked up."

"One glass, and you'd be hallucinating," Aisling teased. "We're looking to have fun, not blackout."

"Speak for yourself," Amber said, joining the group with Liam.

"Why so desperate for escape?" Sean asked.

Amber looked to Liam and then surged on with the conversation. "Deciding to up and leave your country for another one is a pretty big decision."

"You're going back with Liam?" Lettie asked, clearly surprised.

The New Fae nodded. "I'm a sucker for the nerd."

"I wanna dance!" Lettie crowed, and Aisling followed her to a patch of grass lit by hanging lanterns.

The two moved together like they had so many times, twirling and laughing. Under the stars and a full moon, Aisling could convince herself this was the old Lettie. She looked happy and healthy, and it struck her that despite all the changes in their lives, her spirit was the same. She had the same laugh and a smile that Aisling loved. What initially drew Aisling to Lettie still existed.

The others joined them, forming a large circle of women holding hands and dancing under the full moon. She'd never felt more witchy. Or at least she did until other feelings overrode that and made her gasp.

"What's wrong?" her friend asked.

Her face was hot. "Pulled a muscle." She wasn't about to tell her friend that her butt plug was vibrating. She clenched her legs together and tried to mimic dancing while she turned and glared at Brynach. The large Fae held up his hands and winked at her. When she found Riordan in the crowd, he held up the phone and blew her a kiss. Those fools.

Lettie called her attention. "You mean to tell me you're some strong Fae now, and a little dancing has you pulling muscles? I don't buy it."

Aisling didn't answer. Instead, she took another sip of her drink, and when the vibrations stopped, she began dancing again.

"You didn't tell me Riordan had a hot new friend." Lettie nodded over my shoulder toward Isaac. She'd never really looked at him that way, but she supposed he was handsome.

Aisling laughed. "He's a good guy. Sean's better."

Her friend rolled her eyes. "It's annoying, right? He's so good to me it's gross."

Lettie turned to find said boyfriend, and Aisling watched after her until the buzzing started again. She cursed Brynach as he wiggled his fingers in a ridiculous wave. She was going to kill him. Aisling turned when she heard loud voices singing, only to see Dawn and her mother, drinks in hand, dancing in a circle around the bonfire Brynach had started. The full moon party was in full swing.

Aisling called to anyone who brought crystals to join her in the stream. Then she led them through the cleansing. After they'd purged the crystals of negativity, they set new intentions. They placed the crystals on a rock in the moonlight. As a part of her de-stressing, she'd made herb bundles for love, money, and protection. Each of her friends was encouraged to take one.

Unsurprisingly, when the official full moon worship was over, Lettie and Amber stripped down to their underwear and frolicked in the shallow stream.

"We can get rid of negative energy from ourselves, too," Lettie called out.

For a multitude of reasons, Aisling would not be joining them. But she did refill her drink and move to her partners to enjoy the show. A few of the guys stripped to their boxers and joined them. She caught Lettie's eye as Isaac joined and laughed.

"They had no interest in the crystals and intentions, but half-naked full-moon stream frolicking is a go," she joked.

"Why aren't you joining them?" Riordan winked.

"You're evil," she responded.

Brynach leaned down and whispered in her ear, "And you love it."

She leaned into him and agreed, "Now, how quickly can we end this thing and go upstairs?"

Riordan tsk'd her, "That's not very hospitable of you."

"I'm going to remember this, Riordan. One day this thing will be inside you to prep you for Brynach," she reminded him.

She watched his body tense and then lean into their partner. Brynach put an arm around him and held him close.

"Aisling is right. I can't wait." Brynach let his voice dip.

Riordan cursed. "Excuse me while I stick my head in the ice bucket to get rid of this hard-on."

They laughed as he walked away and got himself a beer. It took only another hour for Aisling's mother to sift her drunk friend back to her husband and daughter. Lettie and Amber had put their clothes back on and were by the fire warming up. Kara and Tara were practicing their tarot card skills with Russell, Cait, and Kareem.

Aisling made her way to where Breena was swaying against a sober Jashana.

"Having fun?" Aisling asked.

"I'm fucking trashed," Breena answered. "How come nobody told me it was this fun?"

Jashana grumbled, "Fun for who?"

"Me, you big idiot," Breena playfully swatted at her girl-friend.

"You watch that mouth," Jashana warned.

"I'm going to watch it, and so are you, when I'm dining on that—" Breena got cut off.

"That's enough of that! Time to go," Jashana declared.

"Hey, no! It's early. I want to drink more," she complained.

The warrior wasn't having it. She lifted Breena up onto her shoulder and slapped her ass. "Thanks for having us," Jashana said before sifting.

Aisling was still laughing when Lettie called her back down to dance. Russell and Kareem danced, too, while the other guys sat on the deck with the outdoor gaming setup. Except instead of a controller, Brynach was playing with his phone, and Aisling was spastically writhing on the lawn.

She was sweaty and tipsy. "Is anyone else really hot?" She ripped a hairband from her wrist, tying her long red waves up onto a messy bun as she continued to dance. Lettie fell into Sean with a laugh, and Aisling could tell he was supporting a decent portion of her weight.

"I think it's time to get someone home," Sean declared.

Tara turned to Kara and said quietly, "If they're heading out, I think I'd like to get you home, too."

Her girlfriend nodded. Kara wouldn't argue with whatever made Tara feel better. The adjustment to the new world hadn't been easy for either of them. She called up to Brynach to get everyone home, and Kareem and Russell gathered up the girl's crystals. A look at her phone told her it was past one in the morning. Aisling thanked everyone for coming, and then people started walking past where the Veil used to exist and climbed in their cars.

She'd started to clean up the yard before Riordan grabbed her and pulled her close. "The rest of this can wait until tomorrow."

"Tomorrow, I don't want to be able to walk. It's better to get it done now." Aisling laughed at the shocked look on his face, but he helped her finish cleaning.

"You're lucky I don't have Bry's phone," he threatened.

"Did you hear me complaining?" Aisling asked.

"No, I suppose I didn't." He moved closer to her, running his hand up her thigh. "You're dripping, Ash."

She refused to be embarrassed. "You're surprised? You two have been fucking with me all night."

Brynach sifted back, and Aisling noticed his posture. Head high, shoulders back, chest wide and commanding. His eyes were locked on her. She was being hunted. She wanted to run, but she'd learned her lesson. Aisling held her breath as he stalked closer, paying so much attention to him that she forgot about Riordan until he cupped her sex.

She gasped as he squeezed her and then moaned as Brynach's hand circled her throat. Aisling leaned into his hold and rolled her hips against Riordan's palm. Her tongue slid out to lick her lips, letting the feel of her lovers crawl over her. Aisling rested her weight back on Riordan, and Brynach leaned in further, hand still circling her throat and a fire in his eyes.

Brynach ran his hand down and palmed her breast, his fingers plucked at her nipple while Riordan moved her panties to the side and plunged two of his fingers into her. She ground down on his hand and mewled out a complaint when Brynach grabbed her hips and held her still. Aisling was so primed; she was near the edge already.

Then Brynach's hand circled her while Riordan's thumb strummed against her clit. The large Fae's fingers found her ass, squeezing and shaking her cheeks before he landed on the plug. He pulsed his fingers against it, making her whole body clench and strain for release.

Riordan groaned, and she felt him rock against her. "He's teasing you while the back of his hand rubs my hard-on."

"You don't get off unless it's on our cocks," Brynach growled into her ear as his teeth found purchase on her neck. She cried out, damn close to coming. Aisling fought to move Riordan's hand away from her clit, but Brynach held her tight, letting the other man torture her.

"Please," she cried out. Her chest rose and fell against Brynach's as he leaned into her. "I need ..."

"And you'll get," Riordan promised, but his fingers didn't still.

Her legs were shaking, and she was barely clinging to sanity. She wasn't going to be able to hold off her orgasm much longer. Brynach pulled her close, and Riordan reluctantly pulled his fingers out of her. He reached over her shoulder to Brynach, who took the other man's fingers in his mouth and tasted her. Riordan moaned in her ear. Then she was in Brynach's arms, and he was carrying her up to their bed.

Together her two beautiful men stripped her of clothing before Riordan slapped her on the ass, making her moan and clench around the toy. Her fingers hurried to get their shirts off and see their beautiful bodies.

Aisling allowed herself a moment to appreciate how much labor and battle had sculpted her lovers. Their stomachs were stepping stones of muscles, and their legs thicker and stronger than ever. She bit her lip, and then her breath left her as Brynach growled and lunged at her. She turned for the bed but wasn't fast enough. Before she knew it, she was pinned under him.

"You can't look at me that way, a stoirin. It makes me want to sink myself into you until you know nothing but the feel of me," he told her.

"Do it. Please," she begged.

With a quick thrust of his hips, Brynach sank deep into her pussy. Aisling couldn't contain her throaty cry. The toy in her ass and her partner's thick cock left her feeling warm and deliciously full. Riordan turned her face so his mouth could swallow her cries. She lifted a hand to his face, running her fingertips over the textured scruff, and groaned.

Brynach's hips pressed her down into the mattress, held her so she couldn't move against him even though she was dying to. Forgetting whose mouth was on hers, she bit down on a lip, and Riordan cried out.

"Damn it, man. What are you doing to her?" Riordan asked.

Aisling's hand ran down Riordan's body until she found his cock. She wrapped her fingers around him and squeezed before stroking him and easing their kiss.

"Never mind. Continue," Riordan rasped, making Brynach chuckle.

His deep shallow thrusts could be felt throughout her whole body. His cock bottomed out inside her in a way that was as painful as it was pleasurable. Riordan broke their kiss, and she continued to stroke him.

As she watched, Riordan wound his hand into Brynach's hair and crushed their mouths together. Brynach's thrusting stuttered, and his cock jumped inside her. She slid under him, moving him in and out of her while she watched them make out.

Brynach's large hand pressed down on her hip, holding her still before he ended the kiss and flipped them over. Aisling took immediate advantage, riding Brynach in a desperate search for her orgasm. Riordan leaned over, taking her breast in his mouth while the large Fae took hold of her hips and held her still while he thrust into her roughly.

"I'm going to come. Please. Please." She was close. So close. Just like that, she was lifted off Brynach's cock and left empty. The guys chuckled as they switched roles. Riordan splayed himself out on the bed and pulled her onto his lap. Aisling sank down on him eagerly.

"Ready, my wife?" Brynach asked.

She nodded and swallowed hard. She wanted this. Her body could do this. Aisling felt Brynach at her back, and then his fingers were on the plug, pulling slowly and letting it stretch her tight hole as it exited. She missed the fullness immediately.

Brynach leaned down and kissed her, his hands along her back and his tongue coaxing a moan from her body. He soothed her, treating her like a cherished thing. There was the cool slide of lubricant on her ass, and her breath caught.

"Shhh. You're ready, Aisling." Riordan's strong hands worked over her body, his cock seated deep inside her.

Brynach ran a hand over her neck, and then his cock pushed against her.

"Let him in, Aisling. Let us love you together," Riordan encouraged.

Aisling nodded against his chest and breathed through the discomfort of such a large cock seeking a home in her body.

Brynach groaned, "So fucking tight with him inside you."

It was too much. She needed a different pain to distract her from the stretch and burn of both the men. "Spank me. Bite me. Pull my hair. Something!"

Brynach's large hand came down on her ass as Riordan's teeth sank into her neck. She cried out and begged. "Please. Please, just get inside me."

"You're doing so good, a stoirin."

She gasped. "Fuck!"

Brynach slid in slowly. Aisling panted, tears gathering. The pleasure would override the pain if she could just move. She braced her hands on the bed above Riordan's head and thrust her body back into Brynach.

Both men cursed, and Aisling screamed as her body strained to accommodate two well-endowed men. She moved through the pain, seeking the pleasure she knew would come. They held still while she fucked herself on their cocks, letting her body adapt to the sensations.

She fell onto Riordan's chest and rested her head there for a moment. Riordan gathered her wrists and pressed them behind her. He held her body up, arms pinned, and slammed up into her.

"Oh, Goddess!" Aisling cried.

"Fuck our Princess, Riordan," Brynach growled as he rode her ass.

"You're impossibly tight like this," Riordan ground out. Brynach took control of her arms and used them as leverage to thrust into her body. Riordan bracketed one large hand around her throat and continued to fuck her.

Eyes locked on Riordan's, jaw clenched and body tight, Aisling's orgasm slammed into her. She cried out and shook. They'd said she had to finish on their cocks. She'd listened. The men both cursed as they rode out her spasming. Her body pulled at them in a way that nearly sent her spiraling into another orgasm, but she held out. Aisling didn't want this to end. She never wanted it to end.

Riordan punished her pussy while Brynach made love to her ass more cautiously. She wanted to tell him to stop being so careful, but it was probably best that he was. As it was, she'd be sore later.

"Worth it," she said out loud.

"What was, wife?" Brynach asked.

"All of the heartache that led to this. Worth it. All of it," she gasped, ignoring the burning in her shoulders and the hand at her neck.

Riordan sat up to kiss her, forcing her back on Brynach's

cock at a new angle that had her crying out. The shift pushed them harder together inside her, and Brynach cursed as he pulled her down on their cocks.

"Get up," he ordered.

Riordan slid out of her, and she missed him immediately. Brynach stood with her legs resting on his forearms. He moved until his ass was pressed to the window. Riordan stepped in front of her, and Aisling used his shoulders to find leverage to fuck herself on Brynach's cock. On one particularly hard downward slide, Riordan slid back into her pussy.

"Fuck!" she gasped.

Brynach lifted and lowered her onto their combined cocks. She didn't know how they were standing when she could hardly form rational thoughts. It was too much. So, when Riordan's hand dipped down to flick her clit, she came hard.

The sound that left her was animalistic as the two men used her body for their pleasure.

"Please," she begged. "Please."

She wasn't sure what she was begging for, but then Brynach thrust hard into her and came with a growl. He filled her, staying in her ass, and holding her for Riordan to thrust up into. Carefully, Brynach slid from her body and with more room to move, Riordan went feral. Her head fell against Brynach's shoulder, and his mouth found her. He kissed, licked, and murmured how wonderful she was. How powerful. How beautiful. How perfect.

When Riordan came it was with a curse and a prayer, both in the form of her name. Aisling saw stars as she came around his cock a third time. Her body limp, sweaty, and used.

"I love you," she managed between gasping breaths.

CHAPTER 24

Riordan

The spell Aisling wove over their world with the full moon party shattered the moment they woke. She flew off to the next drop even though Brynach was anxious about it. Walker was still unaccounted for and the idea of Aisling being far from them bothered them both. Riordan gently reminded the big guy that their wife was both trained to fight, Fae, and surrounded by press too often to be a good target.

Brynach was distracting himself with teaching and Riordan had abandoned the training grounds to work with Liam for the day. Both because he needed to be a part of bringing this asshole to heel and because time with his brother was limited now that he had a return flight booked. They only had two weeks before he and Amber packed up and took off.

That didn't mean he stopped thinking about the New Fae, though.

"Everything good?" Riordan asked when Isaac answered his call. He could hear the sounds of the gun range in the background.

"Yup. Have the seasoned New Fae at training today. The greenies are with magic, and everything is running smoothly.

Don't jinx us by worrying," his friend assured him before hanging up.

When he turned, Liam was watching. "What?"

His brother shook his head. "You're really going to be okay, aren't you?"

Riordan nodded. "I'm not alone here anymore. It felt that way at first, after Aunt Maggie, but it hasn't felt that way in a long time." Riordan didn't want him feeling guilty for doing what was right for him. "I'll miss you, but you don't have to worry about me." He moved to his brother and pulled him into a hug.

"I love you, Rory." Liam held him tight.

"I know. Now you get to go back home as the hero who took part in breaking the world," Riordan joked.

"Bettering, not breaking. Though, I am looking forward to Stanley getting his full magic." Liam flushed red. "I still have hope this will get easier for me once he's New Fae, too."

Riordan understood. "Aisling really thinks it will, but even if it doesn't, you have time to practice now, brother."

Liam waved him off. "Enough. Come on, I have shit to share."

They moved to the computers and his brother pointed out the pins on a map. "This is everywhere we've seen Walker so far. New locations come in almost non-stop. The fucker is making me dizzy."

"We'll find him," Riordan promised.

"Before or after he takes someone else?" Liam asked. "He's dangerous."

"We are doing all we can. Now, let's see if we can make sense of this," Riordan said. Behind Liam was a giant white board and with the help of a projector, Riordan traced a map and marked everywhere they'd seen Walker. Seeing it large helped them triangulate a central point to the majority of the spottings. There were outliers, but the majority seemed to be within a five-mile radius.

"I'll call Jashana," Riordan said. Before he could dial, his phone rang. "It's Sean."

"Where are you?" his friend asked.

"The studio," he answered.

"Stay there. I'm on my way." Sean hung up and Riordan turned to Liam.

"That can't be good." He dialed Jashana. When she answered he gave her the search zone to target and told her to stay tuned for whatever Sean was about to unleash on them. Riordan's fingers went to the chain around his neck. He hadn't been wearing it often, but today he'd put it on. As he worried the rings, he was glad for it.

There was a commotion downstairs and then Sean was running up the stairs, a laptop in his hands. He didn't stop for hellos. Instead, he ran to Liam's computers and connected to it with a cord. They gathered around behind him unsure what they were seeing.

"Sean, you gotta talk to us, buddy," Liam prompted.

"Just look," he said and pointed to the screen. The grainy black and white footage was clearly inside a jail.

"Is this the cell block break?" Riordan asked.

"Two weeks before it," Sean clarified. "I was curious about the events leading up to it. I looked into the visitor log the week of but had a gut feeling to check a little deeper in my spare time."

Riordan rolled his eyes. The man had no free time, he just never slept. As they watched a man walked with his back to the camera and sat down at a table. His fingers drummed the table for a few minutes until a visitor was walked into the room and sat opposite him.

"That's Peggy!" Liam exclaimed.

"Keep watching." Sean was excited. Together they watched while the two spoke, unable to hear anything being said. Then the man stood to leave, and the woman mirrored him, tripping a little, and Sean screamed. "There! See!"

He didn't.

"Uh, no." Liam was squinting at the screen. "I don't see anything but his back."

Sean groaned and rewound the footage. "Watch his right hand as he stands. He angles himself so his left side blocks the right from the camera, but you can see his elbow move forward."

This time, knowing where to watch, Riordan saw the man reach toward the woman as she stood up. "He's reaching for her before she stumbles."

"She stumbled to cover it," Sean agreed. "He passed her something. Watch as I go forward, and she reaches to pull up her pants."

He played the tape forward and sure enough Peggy slid something into her waistband. Played fast and at a casual glance, it doesn't look like the two ever touch. There'd be no reason to look closer at the footage. Not unless two weeks later that same woman stabbed her daughter with a knife that was most definitely not prison made.

Sean turned to them and hit play again. Riordan's eyes are on his friend, who nodded his head toward the screen. He braced himself with a deep breath and then looked in time to see the visitor turn. What he saw had a stone weight falling in his stomach.

"Son of a bitch," he cursed. Liam's hand rested on his shoulder, and Riordan shook his head. "It's going to kill him."

Riordan looked between Sean and Liam and made them swear they'd let him break the news. They both agreed, and he gathered up his things. "I have to make a stop and then I'll go to him. Just ... fuck, just keep me posted, okay?"

"Will do," Sean promised.

Riordan left the two of them talking and sifted to the only other person who might know what the fuck was going on. The wards parted for him, and Aisling's soft wash of magic falling over him was familiar and welcome.

"*Are you sure this is a good idea?*" Valo's voice sounded in his head.

"*It's a choice. Whether it's good remains to be seen. It's worth checking before I break his heart,*" Riordan answered.

"*Just be careful,*" the fox told him. "*I'll keep an eye out.*"

"*Thanks,*" Riordan said and took out his keyring. The lock opened with a combination of magical recognition and metal turning mechanisms. Inside the office turned holding cell, Gabriel stood facing the door.

"And here I thought you'd all just leave me to wither and die," he complained.

"Three squares and a cot, that's all you get," he reminded the man. "Sit down. I have some questions for you."

Gabriel was in no position to argue and knew it. He sat and waited.

"What do you know about an Unaligned Fae named Walker?" Riordan asked. He watched the other man's face closely for recognition. There was a spark of something in his eyes, he was sure of it.

"Nothing on a personal level, but I've heard of him. He was never a threat to me, but I know others feared him," Gabriel answered.

"Why?"

The man scowled. "Sometimes that's how things move forward. You have a goal, a mission, and those that stand in your way either move or get moved. He wasn't afraid to do the moving."

"He killed people?" Riordan clarified.

"Of course he did," Gabriel said.

"Only Fae?"

"I doubt it mattered to him. If he killed Fae, a human would mean nothing to him," Gabriel said like it was the most obvious thing.

"Right. And who did he work for?" Riordan asked.

Brynach's sire laughed. "For? Nobody. That man didn't take orders."

"If not for then with?"

He shook his head. "Can't say I ever paid much attention to him."

"Bullshit," Riordan roared. "You know something."

Gabriel stared him down but said nothing. Riordan stood, and when he sat back down, the older man was sporting a cut on his lip and cheek from his ring. Gabriel licked at his cut lip and scowled.

"I bet you've been waiting to do that," he said.

Riordan had been. It was a fraction of what he deserved for the fear he'd instilled in a young Brynach. For making him feel vulnerable and unwanted. His jaw ticked as he swallowed the urge to hit him again.

"You're here, protected, only because you promised information. I suggest you share it, because I know your daughter would love to visit." Riordan smirked. He didn't miss the way Gabriel tensed at the mention of Breena.

"I told you I didn't pay much attention to him. But I did see him with people from time to time," he said. As he spoke, blood spilled from his lip. "I saw him with a tall tattooed Fae. I believe he was a friend of yours."

"Ollie?" Riordan asked, and the other man nodded. "What did they do together?"

"How the hell would I know that?" Gabriel argued.

Riordan swallowed down the nerves and asked what he'd come for. "Did you ever see either of them with Alex?"

"Brynach's friend?" Gabriel sat back. "Can't say that I did."

"And Peggy?"

"Did I see Peggy with Alex?" Gabriel asked with a laugh. "That woman was cold-hearted, but she was loyal to me. I don't think I ever saw her talk to another Fae that wasn't a servant in my house."

Riordan nodded, stood, and turned for the door. He didn't say a thing to the other man as he turned and locked him back in. Once outside the wards, Riordan sifted home. He paused on their steps long enough that Brynach came out.

"You going to stand out here forever?" he joked.

"Nope." Riordan smiled and jogged up the steps. As soon as he reached the top, Brynach took him in his arms and hugged him.

"What's wrong?"

"How do you know something's wrong?" Riordan asked.

"You're tense, and you smell like blood." Brynach frowned.

He tried to keep his face neutral but failed. "I, um, stopped in to see your father and got a little heated."

"That's my father's blood?" Brynach's eyebrows shot up into his hairline.

Riordan shrugged and his husband laughed. Relieved he wasn't upset, they moved inside. His phone pinged with the still-shot images of the grainy video Sean had shared earlier. He'd requested them to show Brynach, knowing he'd argue against facts. Not that Riordan blamed him. When he moved to the sofa and took a seat, Brynach joined him.

"You're scaring me."

"I don't mean to. But earlier, Sean stopped in to see me and Liam at the studio. He brought surveillance video from the prison of the person who smuggled the knife to Peggy. The one she used to attack Sydney." Riordan pulled off the meta-phorical Band-Aid instead of drawing it out.

"It was Alex."

Brynach shook his head and laughed. "Yeah, right. I know he's acting shady, but there's no way he helped Peggy. He doesn't even know her."

Riordan handed him the phone and watched him scroll through the images and the short video. Watched the hurt and betrayal crease his face and hated that he was the one to cause it.

"How could he?" Brynach whispered.

"I don't know. I went to Gabriel, but he didn't know of any connection between Alex and Peggy." Riordan put a hand on

Brynach's bouncing knee. "I don't know what it means, but the video wasn't tampered with. Sean would know if it was."

His husband cursed. "How did I miss this? Did I ignore it because I care for him? Is this my fault?"

"No!" Riordan assured him. "The fault is his. And I'm not sure you missed anything. There are a lot of people in your life that respect Alex. I don't think any of you saw this coming."

"I need to talk to Ash. She's got Rin watching him. Ceiren is, too. Once I gather all the information, I will act. No amount of loyalty excuses this. She fucking stabbed my sister with the knife he provided her. What is he thinking?" Brynach pushed his hands through his hair and pulled at it.

"Hey, don't do that, Bry. His faults aren't yours. We'll figure this out," Riordan promised, even though he wasn't sure that was true. What he did know was there was nothing they could do right that minute. "Pizza and a video game? Take your mind off it for a bit?"

He nodded his head, and Riordan pulled up an app to place an order. Once that was done, he got up to get beer for them.

"I miss her," Brynach said.

"Has she called yet?"

Brynach checked his phone. "Not since she got there. I know she's fine; I'm just on edge."

Riordan answered as he stood from the fridge. "Sean and Liam have Walker locked down. He's not going anywhere without being identified, and he's still local. Ash is okay."

When he rounded the sofa, Brynach didn't have the game loaded. Instead, he had a guitar on his lap.

"You've never played for me." Warm citrine eyes smiled at him.

Heat crept up his neck as he accepted his instrument. He didn't bother with the amp. He let his fingers travel the strings, tuned it a little, and looked at Brynach.

"Any requests?"

"Surprise me."

His smile set something fluttering in Riordan's belly. Since when did he get nervous playing for someone? His partner needed him, so he pushed it aside. Riordan closed his eyes and cleared his mind before giving his hands permission to play whatever they wanted. He was part way through the song before he opened his eyes. Brynach was lounging, legs spread and hand resting on his thigh as his gaze swept from Riordan's mouth to his fingers and back up again.

He fumbled a note, and Brynach smirked. Damn that man. When the chorus came Riordan locked eyes and let his voice sing the words.

"What would you say if I took those words away? Then you couldn't make things ..." he began.

By the time the song was over, Brynach had shifted position. Slowly, he reached forward and cupped the back of Riordan's neck, pulling him close.

"No words, then," he whispered.

The kiss wasn't rough or hurried. Brynach's tongue played at Riordan's lips until he opened for him. He sighed into the kiss, tangling his fingers in the other man's hair before running them over his jaw. Brynach tipped Riordan's head back so his tongue could stroke into the other man's mouth. When he pulled back, it was to place gentle kisses on Riordan's lips.

"That was beautiful. Another?" Brynach asked.

Riordan nodded. "Okay." He lost himself in the music he'd ignored far too long. It felt nice to connect with it again. Even better that he was sharing a moment like this with a man so strong he terrified most people but who allowed himself to be soft with Riordan. The fact that Brynach was turning to him for comfort right now set something alight inside him.

By the time he was ready to set the guitar aside, Brynach had stopped staring at him like he was an anomaly. He didn't get it. Fae were known for the arts. Music wasn't something new to Brynach. When he said as much, the other man shook his head.

"Music is about emotion and passion. It's always beautiful, but never more so than when you can connect with it personally. Hearing you create it feels like every note is being played across my body." Brynach placed a hand on Riordan's leg. "It's about you, Riordan, not the music. Though that was beautiful, too."

"Bry," Riordan breathed. "You can't say stuff like that to me."

"Why not?" Brynach stood and held out his hand. "You're my husband, aren't you?"

What kind of trick question was that? Of course, he was. Riordan placed his hand in Brynach's and let himself be pulled to his feet.

"Yes, you are," Riordan, heart hammering, answered.

Long black hair fell across his partner's face as he smiled down at him. Riordan reached up to brush it behind his ear. With a gentle tug on his hand, Brynach led him up the stairs to their bedroom. Once up there, Brynach sank to his knees at the edge of the bed and started working on Riordan's jeans.

"Bry?" His voice shook.

The larger man looked up at him. "I want you to make love to me tonight. Only if you feel ready."

Was he? The erection Brynach pulled from his boxers and kissed was on board. Riordan knew this was inevitable, but he hadn't given thought to how it would play out. What if he wasn't good? All logical thought stopped as his cock was swallowed down to the root. His head fell back on a groan.

"Brynach. Fuck, that feels good," Riordan encouraged.

He hummed around his length and licked around his head. Large hands moved up Riordan's stomach, pushing his shirt up until Riordan took it off. All the while, Brynach worked magic with his mouth. If he kept that up, this would be over too soon. He could do this. He wanted to do this.

With a gentle hand, Riordan lifted Brynach's face and moved him onto the edge of the bed. Then he helped the larger man undress.

"I should be prepping you. It's me who should be making you feel good before I fuck you." He knew better than to learn from porn, but that much had been consistent. The one receiving always got spoiled first.

"Should?" Brynach asked as he lifted his hips so Riordan could remove his underwear. "There's no should, Riordan. What do you want to do?"

"Make you feel good." The answer was immediate. So was Brynach's smile.

"You will. You do." Brynach turned his body to crawl up the bed. What Riordan saw stopped him dead in his tracks.

"Brynach!" Riordan moaned.

Black hair splayed across his bare back and shoulder as he turned his head and winked. His smile just as bright as the jeweled butt plug he was wearing. The fucker had planned this. This was happening. Thank the Goddess, this was happening.

Riordan climbed onto the bed and into the circle of his arms. They kissed, hands wandering one another's bodies until each man held the other's cock and stroked it. Their breath mingled as their foreheads touched, and they let themselves be together in the moment.

"I love you," Brynach whispered, and Riordan returned the words. Both verbally and in action. He pushed himself up and kissed Brynach's jaw, his neck, his chest, and the muscles of his stomach and hips. Riordan's teeth scraped and nipped as he went, causing the other man's marble-carved body to tremble with need.

Riordan stroked Brynach's cock and then lowered his mouth to it. His hand rose to meet his lips, doing his best to take Brynach's length but knowing he couldn't manage it all. Then, like he'd seen Brynach do to Aisling many times, he pulsed a finger on the end of the plug.

Hips rose. Moans escaped the Fae's lips. Riordan felt high on them. Brynach twisted his body, Riordan's mouth and hand moving with him. A bottle was handed down and placed next to his hips, but he didn't rush to finish. He wanted Brynach on the edge. Needed him turned on, because he didn't know how long he would last once he got inside the other man. It wasn't fear of being judged but rather wanting it to be good for his partner that kept his mouth moving and his fingers exploring.

With a gentle tug, he pulled the plug to the edge of the ring of muscle before spitting on the toy and sliding it back in. Brynach cursed, and Riordan looked up, meeting the other man's eyes as his mouth lowered to him once more.

"I need you now," Brynach pleaded.

Riordan opened the bottle of lube and let some fall onto his waiting cock while Brynach used a pillow to lift his ass. The large man pulled his knees up to his chest, opening himself to Riordan, who pushed one leg to the side and leaned down to kiss Brynach.

"If I do something wrong, you'll tell me." Riordan wasn't asking, but Brynach nodded.

"You won't," he promised.

Carefully, he removed the plug and set it aside before moving the head of his cock to Brynach's ass. He braced one hand on Brynach's thigh, pushing his leg down and out while the other rested on his chest. Slowly, he pressed his cock inside that tight ring. He was used to the feel, the squeeze, and the snugness of Aisling's body like this. But here, now, looking down into Brynach's face. This was different. Not because it was a man but because this strong, guarded man was letting Riordan make love to him.

"Riordan? Are you okay?" Brynach's hand reached up to his face.

"Yes, just taking it all in."

"Actually, that's what I'm doing." Brynach smiled at him. "Give me more, husband."

"Fuck, I get it now. That's sexy," Riordan growled and slid deeper into Brynach. Out of extreme caution, he used more lube and then slid all the way home. "Just give me a second."

"Come here." Brynach pulled him down for a kiss, groaning when it pulled Riordan deeper into his body. Brynach rocked gently as they kissed, and Riordan swiftly lost control.

He pulled back and began fucking into Brynach rougher, trusting the other man to tell him if it was too much. Though if the way he growled and stroked his own cock was any indicator, he was just fine.

"When you finish, I want it on my stomach along with my load," Brynach purred, and Riordan nearly nutted.

All he could do was nod and thrust into this warm, firm body. Riordan held Brynach's finely-haired leg under his hand and watched him for signs that he was doing okay.

"You're fucking me so good, Riordan. Making me feel so good. Tilt me back a bit more. Put your weight on me. Force me to feel you." Brynach's mouth ran as Riordan did all he could to make this last.

He listened, though, using his full weight to lean onto his legs and pin them to Brynach's chest. He knew the moment he stroked into the other man's prostate. Come leaked from Brynach's cock, and he screamed.

"Fuck. Just like that." Brynach held his breath, and Riordan read his cues.

He moved one hand to rest around his throat, squeezing at the sides as he thrust into Brynach. They hadn't been gentle with Aisling, and she'd been fine. He didn't need to be soft with this man. He could weather his lust.

He stared down at Brynach, meeting his unflinching gaze. "Stroke your cock and come for me. I'm close," Riordan groaned. He drove himself into his partner's body, praying he got him to the finish line because there was no stopping this orgasm.

He pulled out and stroked himself, crying out Brynach's name as they took turns spilling themselves onto his stomach. Brynach lowered his legs and pulled Riordan down to him, kissing him softly and holding him close. Their come now coated both their bodies, and Riordan didn't care.

Eventually, they'd get up and shower. But for right now, they stayed like that, sweaty, sticky, and perfect.

CHAPTER 25

Aisling

D on't forget to stay in view of the camera," Cathy instructed for about the tenth time.

Aisling nodded. "This isn't my first time, Cathy. I've got this."

"We have a room set up for you to meet the local Firinne representative before the drop. They want to know a little more before they go on camera." Cathy lowered her voice. "Turns out they're not the strongest of witches, and they don't want to make a fool of themselves on global television."

It wouldn't matter. The collective would be strong enough to hide their lack of ability. Having done her research, Aisling knew that the witch in question was an actress with a movie about to release. Given the way her last role was received, she really couldn't afford the negative press. Aisling would make sure they looked good.

Cathy led her to a room with a very nervous-looking actress. The door closed, leaving her alone with a woman at least ten years her senior, who nervously twisted the bracelet on her wrist.

"Aisling Quinn, right?" She held out her hand. "I'm Prudence; nice to meet you."

There was no need for the woman to introduce herself. Aisling shook her hand and sat down, encouraging her to do the same. "It's Aisling Campbell now." At the woman's look of embarrassment, Aisling waved her off. "It's new. It's nice to meet you, as well. I hear you have some questions for me."

The woman began, "My agent told me not to do this. They said it looked like a desperate attempt at garnering publicity. I swear it's not a PR stunt. This is important, and I want to be a part of it. But I'm not looking to jeopardize my career, either."

That hadn't been what Aisling expected. Immediately, her opinion of the actress shifted. "There's no need to worry. This is a collective effort and not dependent on any one witch or bonded pair. You will aid in the larger spell work, but nobody will be able to pinpoint your personal signature unless they're trained and familiar with it. I can place you near a stronger witch if it eases your mind."

Prudence took a deep breath. "I don't want to get any special treatment, but I think our PR people wanted me close to you."

Aisling nodded. "That's fine with me. Obviously, the cameras will be trained on us the whole time, but you're used to that."

"I've been keeping up with the news. There have been red carpets with less media coverage than some of your drops." She smiled. "How do you do it?"

"I could ask you the same thing," Aisling commented.

The actress shrugged. "It's my job. I chose it. You didn't choose this."

Cathy poked her head into the room. "All set?"

Aisling stood and ran a hand down her pants. "As we'll ever be. Prudence is sticking with me."

"Please, call me Pru," the actress encouraged.

The smile on Cathy's face was genuine. "Lovely. We'll be

walking you through the barricades to the front. It's getting a little rowdy, so just push through until you're behind the police lines."

Prudence's eyes went wide. "Are we in actual danger?"

Aisling tried to reassure her, "There's always a risk at public appearances, right? They're just being cautious. I'm sure it's nothing more than you're used to."

Cathy opened the door, and a corridor of security led them through a line of police. It was bright. It was loud. It was positively electric. There was a buzz of magic in the air so strong she felt like she could reach out and touch it. The hair on her arms rose in response. Once they reached an opening far beyond the screaming fans and protestors, they stopped.

"Is it always like this?" the actress asked, rubbing her arms.

"No," Aisling admitted, mildly unnerved. She turned to the local organizer. "Where are the Ravdi?"

They pointed to the large group, and Aisling walked over, flanked by the actress and their security. When she approached, they quieted.

"Mrs. Campbell, it's an honor to meet you. Is Riordan here?" The man looked behind her, hopeful.

"Sorry, he couldn't make this one." She smiled her apology.

The man's face fell. "That's a shame. It would have been nice to have him here."

"I agree," Aisling said. "I came over to ask about the Veil. Do you see an unusually large concentration of magic, disturbances, or castings over the area?"

The Ravdi shook his head. "No more than I'd expect with this many magic workers in one area."

Prudence commented as they walked away. "I may not be the strongest, but I've checked, and I don't see obvious spell work, at least not dark."

It was the largest chunk of the Veil to drop since Birchwood Falls, so it stood to reason the magic would be stronger here. She scanned the area, her senses overloaded by the screaming, the bright sun, the press of magic, and the strange feeling of being watched.

Cathy called out to her, and Aisling stepped up onto the makeshift stage. As the representative for the local witches, Prudence joined her. She tapped the mic and began speaking.

"Thank you for joining us for this momentous drop." She paused for the cheers and ignored the screams of protests. "We have come together today to right the wrongs of centuries past and unite the two realms, returning the magic owed to witches and Ravdi. Change is essential for growth, and right now, we need to work together to ensure the safe transition of the New Fae. Today will be the first day of forever in many of your lives or the lives of your loved ones. It's a day of celebration but also a day to recognize what was taken from us, kept from us, and all we sacrifice in order to move forward as our truest selves."

She paused to look around the crowd, not burdened by a teleprompter. Cathy had forced her to memorize the speech. The cameras and lights were on her, but she only saw the witches and Ravdi gathered. Their lives really would change today. The gravity of that wasn't lost on her.

Beside her, Prudence cleared her throat, and Aisling smiled. "I am thrilled to be here with Prudence on this historic day. I'm sure she has some words for you."

The actress grinned and stepped up to the microphone. "On behalf of the witches and Ravdi who will be working to unite the realms, I ask that you support them with your thoughts. Energy of unity and wholeness are appreciated. What we put out into the universe, the universe returns to us." She smiled at the crowd.

"Fucking cunt witch!" someone screamed, and Aisling turned to see security drag them away.

Prudence paled, but Aisling stepped forward, taking the woman's hand. "As we begin, please remember that this is a serious undertaking. Please stay behind the barricades for your safety and the safety of those working."

Aisling backed away from the mic. It only took a few bad apples to turn a crowd, and she knew enough to get the hell off stage before that happened. Her leaving the mic was the cue to the magic workers to get ready. Things would happen quickly now.

Prudence turned to her. "You're a natural." She fell into step with Aisling and Cathy as they made their way for the Veil.

"Yeah, well, there wasn't much room for a learning curve." Aisling turned to the actress with a conspiratorial wink.

They joined the witches who stood with the Ravdi at their backs. The work had already begun, but it was Aisling's job to bolster them.

"You're doing great," she called out. "Remember that intention matters. We are here to heal what's been broken and return the balance of the world. As you pull on the magic, focus your intent on mending. The last bit will fight you. I'll be here to pluck it out."

Around her, heads nodded. Prudence hadn't started her work yet. "How? How do you grab onto the last of it?"

"I'm not sure," Aisling admitted. "I believe I connect to Kailyn, or the Goddess, but I'm not sure if it's real. I see the last bit of raw magic. I promise to heal it, and then I just pull."

Prudence looked at her, and then Aisling felt her begin to funnel magic into the greater world. She wasn't the strongest, but she had more power than she'd lead Aisling to believe.

She turned to watch the woman work. Which is how she saw the sun flash off something. Her brain acknowledged the danger before her eyes fully understood what they were seeing.

Security shouted, "Shooter!"

Aisling knew they were too far away to do anything. She had a moment to decide what to do. She could sift away, but nobody else could. Which meant a bullet intended for her would hit someone else. Decision made, Aisling pushed Prudence to the ground.

She wasn't fast enough.

She sent a silent prayer to the Universe that Riordan and Brynach weren't watching as white-hot pain brought her to her knees.

If she'd thought, for even a moment, that getting stabbed had been painful, she'd been wrong. Getting shot was far worse. The sheer force of the bullet as it burrowed into her body was unlike anything she'd ever felt. She felt every second as it clawed its way into her.

Screams rang out, and she vaguely registered hearing someone yell that the shooter had been disarmed.

Prudence stirred under her. Once she'd pushed herself up and saw the blood, she joined the screaming. "Goddess. Fuck. Holy fucking crap! Is that real blood?"

Aisling groaned. "Pretty sure."

"What do I do?" She panicked, hands fluttering in the air over Aisling.

"Finish the drop, but only if it's safe," Aisling directed her. The actress was terrified, but Aisling saw the moment the mask dropped and she began acting. Resolve settled in her shoulders as she stood.

"We're not stopping! Keep pulling," Prudence called to the remaining witches and Ravdi.

Aisling closed her eyes. Either they'd make it work, or they wouldn't, but she didn't have the strength to help. She started to push up off the ground.

"Oh no you don't." Cathy leaned over to her.

"I can get up, Cath. It hurts, but I'm not going to die." Aisling made to get up again.

The woman's voice dipped. "I'm glad you're not going to die, but nobody else needs to know that. You just saved a celebrity's life, and you're bleeding. You look awful. Let the cameras get that for a bit."

Really? This woman was too much. An officer dropped next to her. "How you doing, Mrs. Campbell? Nasty looking hole you got there."

"Funny." She rolled her eyes. Turning to Cathy, she threatened, "I'm going to need you to get me out of here, or I swear by all things holy, my husbands will hunt you down and make you pay for that bullshit comment."

The officer reached for her. "Right. Of course. The thing is, you have a mighty large hole in your chest, and, uh, I don't think I should move you."

Chest? She thought it was her shoulder. Chest sounded way scarier. She took silent stock of her body and acknowledged that her head felt like she'd been kicked by Kongur.

"The shooter was taken into custody. Nobody else was hurt. Television crews caught it all," he informed her.

"Yay for ratings. You said the TV crews caught it all?" At the man's nod, she said, "Do me a favor and count to five for me."

The man looked at her funny but did as she asked. He hadn't even reached three when Brynach and Riordan sifted to the chaotic scene. Leave it to her men to find her before the security on site could get their heads out of their asses.

Brynach's voice boomed over the distant sirens and sounds of the crowd, "Aisling! Where are you?"

She stared at where her partners were and opened her mouth to answer, but Riordan turned and saw her. He paled, reached for Brynach's hand, and pulled him. They reached her together.

"A stoirin." Brynach kneeled next to her, his hands pressed on her wound.

Riordan was at her head, stroking her cheek. "Had to go and get shot, huh? You know I hate blood."

Aisling chuffed out a laugh and then cursed. "That hurts."

Her husband glared at Riordan and then looked down at her. "Can you move your toes?"

Could she? She hadn't tried. She wiggled them in her shoes

and nodded. "I'm not broken."

Brynach closed his eyes in what looked like a silent prayer. Riordan kissed her forehead. "He worries too much."

Brynach growled, and Aisling smiled. "Calm down. It's obviously not life-threatening. I'm fine."

She stared up at them, their worried eyes staring back at her. The sky beyond them swirled, their faces getting sucked up in a strange cyclone of stars.

"Or not," she tried to say, but her tongue was too thick to get the words right.

"Damn it!" Brynach called, and then she was floating. She tried to stay awake; really, she did.

She failed.

W hat the fuck happened? How did they get past the security screening for the event?" Brynach's voice was loud. She loved the man, but it would be great if he shut up.

"I don't care that he's in custody. Don't come at me with that 'they took him down swiftly with no other injuries' bullshit. There shouldn't have been any injuries at all. My wife almost died," he continued.

Aisling tried to open her eyes, but they were so heavy. "Shhh," she managed to whisper and winced at the searing pain in her throat.

"She's awake!" Riordan called. The touch on her arm tightened. She couldn't help the yelp that escaped her lips. "What hurts? Aisling, what hurts?" He grabbed tighter to her hand.

"You're screaming, and my head is pounding," she cried out, her eyes shooting open. It was bright, so bright, and she blinked away the intrusive light. The pressure on her arm disappeared, and she saw Riordan cover his mouth.

"I'm so sorry!" he cried.

She murmured, "It's too loud, too bright, too everything." The sounds outside her door were violently rattling in her brain.

Brynach ran for the wall and shut the light. "Better?" His voice was a whisper.

Aisling nodded.

Riordan stood next to her, looking like a kicked puppy. She looked down at herself and saw bandages wrapped around her chest.

"How bad?" she asked.

Riordan murmured so softly she almost didn't hear him. "The bullet was a hollow point that shattered. Your body tried to heal itself too quick. They had to put you under to reopen the wound and clean out the shrapnel. It required a tonic to negate your Fae healing while they worked, so recovery has been slow."

"I'm okay now?" she asked.

"Yes," Brynach reassured her. "The bullet is out. Your wounds have healed."

"Do Fae get migraines?" Aisling asked.

Riordan's shoulders shook. Brynach put a hand on his back. "Anyone would feel crappy after what your body just went through. I'll get you aspirin."

She noticed Riordan's eyes were red, his whole body bent in on itself. He looked exhausted.

"How long was I out?" she croaked.

"We're on day two," Riordan answered.

Aisling's eyes went wide. For a Fae, that was unheard of. She coughed, and Riordan lurched for a glass of water, then held the straw to her lips. She drank greedily.

When Brynach returned, she swallowed the aspirin and closed her eyes. "Who was it?"

"We still don't know." Her husband ran a hand through his hair.

"It wasn't Walker?" He seemed like a logical suspect to Aisling.

Riordan shook his head. "Sean and Liam had eyes on him somewhere else. It wasn't him."

"Don't you dare do that again. I lost feathers worrying," Rin complained.

"I'm sorry, my oldest friend. I'll do my best to avoid being shot in the future." She sent him love alongside her sarcasm.

A nurse came in to check her vitals now that she was awake. The light they used to test her eyes was wildly painful to endure. Damn it, that Fae healing needed to kick in a whole lot stronger.

"Please notify her doctor that she's awake. We need her released as soon as possible," Brynach instructed.

The nurse nodded as they wrote in Aisling's chart. "I'll see what we can do."

Aisling saw Brynach open his mouth to complain and reached out to take his hand, squeezing it to silence him. They were doing their job, and he was doing his. She understood he wanted her home, but the way she felt, she didn't need to rush leaving.

When the nurse was gone, Riordan spoke. "We can't protect the hospital the way we can our home. We haven't slept in days," he explained.

"I don't feel so hot, guys. Maybe it's better I'm here for a bit longer." She watched worry crease their faces and closed her eyes.

T he dim light was tolerable when her eyes blinked open next.

"There you are." Brynach's smile.

"Been gone long?" she wondered out loud.

Brynach brought her attention back to him. "A few hours. Riordan went to get us food."

Aisling tried to sit up but quickly gave up on that idea. Brynach pushed a button on the bed and raised her to sitting up. Even with the mechanical aid, she couldn't help the wince.

"Are you in pain?" Brynach asked.

"Just stiff. I take it I'm not going home yet?" Aisling hated that she was relieved by that. She reached out with her good arm to smooth the wrinkle between her husband's eyes. He snagged her hand and kissed it.

"A stoirin, you're so strong, but that bullet tore through you. The scans, the images I've seen. The damage was significant, and your body tried to heal so quick. They had to break bones to extract pieces, reopen wounds, and slow your magic to do it. Your body went through a lot in the last few days. You're doing amazing. If you hadn't already been Fae ..." Brynach couldn't finish his thought.

"But I am, and I'll be okay. How is my mom?" Aisling asked.

"A mess," he answered. "She's been over a few times, but with the school and Gabriel at her place, and Alex. Well, she knew we had you covered, so she went back to work."

"What do you mean with Alex?" Aisling asked.

Brynach frowned. "I don't want to talk about it right now. We have time to get into that later. Right now, let's just focus on getting you home."

"Suppose it's a good thing I brought food, then," Riordan said as he entered with full hands and a grin.

Aisling forced a smile and ate the food but couldn't keep the worry from gnawing at her gut.

CHAPTER 26

Brynach

Brynach knew his wife. He could tell she was physically uncomfortable and that she was worrying. But he held his tongue for Riordan's sake as they ate. Watching Riordan almost lose someone else he loved had been unbearably painful. He'd done all he could to keep it together for the other man, but Brynach had been terrified, too. He never wanted to feel like that again.

Riordan had been on the sofa watching Aisling and Brynach had been in the kitchen grabbing a drink when the shots rang out. Two of them. Riordan had screamed, Brynach had spun, and their world had turned upside down. They couldn't sift to the site because the Veil hadn't dropped yet. Instead, they had to sift as close as they could and then make small jumps toward her. It had taken entirely too long.

Aisling got full fast, and Brynach offered his phone so she could video chat with her mother while they finished eating.

"Thank you for getting this," Brynach said around a bite of his burger.

Riordan shrugged. "I had to do something. Before we leave here, we have to get the paperwork for medical emergencies.

They tried giving me shit about coming up again."

Brynach agreed. The number of hoops he had to go through and the threats he needed to make just to make decisions for Aisling while she was unconscious had been ridiculous. Brynach was cleaning up their dinner when Aisling's doctor checked on her.

"It's past discharge time, but we'll aim to have you home by lunch tomorrow. How does that sound?" he asked.

"Sounds good to me," Aisling answered. "Am I cleared to stand on my own and shower?"

"I don't want you on your feet that long. You'll need help. I can get a nurse," he told her.

"We've got her," Brynach assured him.

He smiled at them. The guy was nice and had taken Riordan and Brynach both in stride. "I'm sure you do. You'll have some follow-up appointments, and I'd like a little physical therapy, too. I know you're Fae, but your body still had a serious amount of trauma."

"Whatever she needs, we'll make sure she's there," Riordan promised.

Aisling nailed both men with a hard look before smiling at the doctor. "She's right here. Thank you, Doctor. I promise to be a good patient."

He was laughing as he left the room. Their wife turned on them, but Brynach held up a hand.

"You don't get to be angry at us for worrying. Not after you threw yourself in front of a bullet. So, bite your tongue, or as soon as you're well enough, I'll make your ass so red you can't sit." Brynach meant every word.

She stuck out her tongue at him. "Promises promises. Who's helping me shower?"

Brynach gestured to Riordan. "I'll get out the clothes we brought from home for when you get out."

The other man gave him a smile, and Aisling brightened. "You have my clothes?"

Brynach cupped her cheek and kissed her. "Go get cleaned up."

He busied himself cleaning up the room and packing away what they wouldn't need before going home. Then he pulled out a clean pair of underwear and an oversized t-shirt of his that Aisling liked sleeping in and laid them on the bed. Brynach walked out into the hall.

"Hi, I was wondering if I could get some clean bedding for my wife's bed while she showers?" he asked the nurse at the desk.

"Of course. I'll be right in to remake it." She stood and moved for a closet.

"I'm happy to do it for you. Really. Sit." Brynach gestured to her chair, and when she shook her head, he reassured her. "Honestly, I just want to feel like I'm doing something to help her. Please."

"Alright. Just holler if you need anything else," she said and sat with a smile. "She's one lucky woman."

He shook his long black hair, which was in need of a wash, too. "No. We're the lucky ones."

His response just made the nurse blush as she said, "Like I said."

Brynach moved away with his arms full. He stripped the bed, placing the old sheets in the soiled linen bin, and put on the new ones. When Aisling exited and saw him fluffing pillows on the fresh bed, she tilted her head and smiled at him.

He helped her sit on the edge of the bed and used a second towel to dry her legs, placing socks on each foot. Before he put the shirt on, he used the hairbrush they'd brought to detangle her long hair and braid it.

"This is embarrassing," Aisling complained.

"A stoirin, I don't like that I have to take care of you, but I love being the one to do it all the same," he promised.

Riordan finished her hair, and Brynach maneuvered her arms through the holes of the shirt. By the time they were done, Aisling looked exhausted.

"Back in bed," he ordered. He nodded to Riordan. "You, too. Both of you, sleep."

There's just one problem with loving a woman as independent as Aisling, and that's feeling incapable of protecting her. No matter how dominant, how insistent he was, there was no telling her what to do. It was one of the things he loved most about her and one of the qualities that made him want to rip his hair out. Not only was she not resting, but she was giving press conferences and interviews. Granted, he'd demanded that she gave them from their living room via webcam, but still.

This morning he'd left her to teach after being absent most of the week at work. Today, after seeing Alex duck down a hallway when they locked eyes, he was pretty sure he was right where he needed to be. Sean had stopped by with Lettie to see Aisling and brought him the recording device he wanted. No whir. No hum. Nothing to give it away. Even Brynach couldn't hear it or sense it. Today he'd be planting it in his friend's office. He hated everything about this, but he couldn't deny that Alex was involved in something he'd never support. What he needed was finite proof.

He took out his phone and texted his wife.

Can you check in with Rin?
Is the coast clear?

Yeah, he's in the dormitory.
Staff and kids in cafeteria.
You should be clear.

Thanks.

Be careful. Keep us posted.

Her familiar's report when they'd left the hospital hadn't been positive. The word of a bird wouldn't hold up, but Brynach knew now that Alex was at least tangentially involved with Walker in a more official capacity. Poor Aisling had learned about her father figure's betrayal and been heartbroken.

Brynach made his way through the halls, smiling and nodding at the teachers and children he saw. Rin was right, the cafeteria was busy, but nobody paid him much attention. Not like it would be strange to go into his friend's office anyway. He'd thought it through and gotten everything ready. The bug was linked to an app on his phone, and he confirmed it was working before he left. He had a note he could leave as an alibi if someone walked in on him. But he could do this.

Except, when he entered the office, he was faced with Alex's familiar. The bobcat was tame and posed no threat, but it made his job harder. Crap. He was giving Phlyren hell for this when he got home.

"Hey there, where's your bonded? That man is hard to nail down," Brynach said and petted the cat gently. Luckily the note would get him over to his friend's desk, and the tracker was nestled alongside the note so he could hide it as he took the letter out. The bobcat rested its head back on its paws and closed its eyes, ignoring Brynach.

He didn't believe for a second that Alex didn't now know he was in there or that the cat wasn't listening still. He removed the letter and shuffled around to find the best place to leave it on the desk, deciding on dead center. In the shuffle, he dropped a pen and bent to pick it up, sliding the bug under the desk in a small knot of the natural wood. Brynach was back up in a second and used the retrieved pen to add a postscript to the note before walking out.

Brynach held on to a small piece of hope that something they captured would make sense of all this. He understood, logically, that the chance was slim, but he wished for it all the same.

His phone buzzed in his pocket, and what he read had a growl building in his chest. He immediately called Riordan.

"The hell does that mean?"

From somewhere not far from Riordan, Aisling yelled, "It means you can't hold me captive anymore. I'm leaving tonight, and you are both staying put."

"Like hell you are," he yelled, knowing she could hear him.

"Hello, ears, right here," Riordan complained.

For the past few nights back at the house, they'd snuggled and played card games. The days had ended in gentle kisses and cuddles. Aisling had given no signs she was ready for anything more. A part of Brynach craved the roughness of their love-making to really prove she was okay. How had she gone from tired and complacent to demanding so quickly?

Aisling called out, "Don't be a brute! I promised the girls a sleepover, and I'm going to the condo to have it. I'll be with plenty of people."

"Who?" Brynach asked.

"Lettie, Kara, Tara, Sydney, Breena, Jashana, Amber, Corinna, and Brielle. It's a going-away party." He could hear the challenge in her voice daring him to argue with her.

With Jashana and Breena there, she'd be safe enough. Hell, Aisling was almost back to fighting shape, too. He had absolutely no leg to stand on here. The condo was warded, and Aisling needed her freedom. Fuck, he hated it still.

Riordan whispered into the phone, "She's gloating."

Damn that woman.

CHAPTER 27

Riordan

We can't keep doing this," Riordan commented after they settled Aisling into the condo and made sure all the ladies had all the food and drinks they'd need. Absolutely no reason to open a door, go out, or let anyone in. "I can't keep watching her get hurt."

Brynach and he sifted back to the house. "We won't. Things will settle down. We'll be okay."

Would they? Over and over, they'd seen Aisling fucking hurt, kidnapped, and bloody and been unable to stop it. He'd seen Brynach with bullet wounds. Hell, he'd been shot. He'd lost friends. He had watched Dexter get eaten alive. Over and over, he lost people. Over and over, he was exposed to death and dying.

Riordan loved Brynach, but he was wrong, and Riordan didn't want to be placated right now. Anger boiled in him until it was too big to contain. He knew it wasn't the right thing to do, knew it was falling on old traits, but he wanted to hurt someone.

If he was a better man, he'd feel bad about what he was about to unleash, but he wasn't. Neither of them was okay, and he was fucking tired of pretending that they were. He let go of Brynach's arm and braced his legs.

"I'm sick of this, Bry. It stops now." Riordan dared him to deny something was wrong. "I am not your sisters. I'm not Aisling. I don't need to be babied or protected."

He felt his face and neck go red. "Nothing to say?"

"Seems to me like you were the one who needed to talk." Brynach stood with his hands in his pockets.

Riordan wasn't sure why that pissed him off, but it fucking did. He didn't think. He sprung. His punch landed on Brynach's jaw, and damn, it felt good. Riordan wasn't naive enough to think he'd bested the other man. He stood, hands still in his pockets.

"Would you fucking react?" Riordan screamed in his face and punched him again.

Brynach turned his face back to him, his tongue flicking out to soothe his fat lip. "Feel better?"

"No, you giant stone asshole." Riordan hit him again, looking for a reaction, any reaction at all.

"That's the last one I'm giving you. I love you, but I have limits," Brynach warned.

"Maybe then you'd show some fucking emotion," Riordan said and swung. The other man ducked and landed a punch to his ribs.

"Are you out of your fucking mind?" His growl was positively feral.

Riordan swung a leg out and tried to kick Brynach. It was a glancing blow. He dropped to the ground and tried to scissor his legs on either side of Brynach's and trip him up. But Brynach dropped to kneel beside him.

"Riordan, what are you doing?" His husband asked. His voice was angry, but his face was concerned. It pissed Riordan off even more.

He didn't answer with words; instead, his fist came from the side and connected with Brynach's kidney.

"Damn it. Stop," Brynach snarled, pinning Riordan's hands next to his head. "You can't actually believe that I'm not upset."

"You sure as shit aren't showing it," Riordan fought against Brynach's hold. He jerked his hips up, trying to get room to maneuver himself. "You went mad after Aisling was hurt or went missing. But then, nothing. Numb. You didn't care about me. It was easy for you to leave me. You left me behind to search Faerie without a backward glance."

Fuck, he hadn't meant to say that. Brynach stilled on top of him.

"Leaving you was so fucking hard, Riordan. I thought about you, wanted you with me, the entire time. It was a mistake. I made a mistake," Brynach cursed.

Riordan tried to get the larger man off of him. Again, he failed. "You think I'm weak. That I can't handle things. And now you're trying to coddle me into believing things will be okay even though there's no evidence, at all, that it will."

"What do you want from me? You need me to fall apart to prove I'm terrified?" Brynach pressed his hips into Riordan, holding him down.

"Yes!" Riordan snarled and turned his head, biting into Brynach's wrist.

"Fuck!" Brynach didn't let go. "Would you stop throwing a tantrum and just talk to me?"

"I'm sick of talking. All you do is lie to my face. She'll be fine. We'll be able to protect her. As long as we're together, everything will be okay," Riordan listed. "We're not fine! We *can't* keep her safe! We're not okay. Stop telling me we are."

"You want me to tell you that she's probably going to nearly die a hundred more times in our lifetime? Do you want me to whine that I can't stand the thought of you losing anyone else you love? That it would kill me to lose her as much as it would kill me to see you in pain?" Brynach was screaming now. His red face was inches from Riordan's, and his weight on Riordan's wrists was painful now.

"I'm supposed to be your equal. We're supposed to be partners, and you're sheltering me like you do your siblings." He brought his legs up, trying to get leverage and fight back with more than words.

The large Fae wasn't having it. His hips drove into Riordan, and he stilled. "I know who you are. And I think we both know I have never, will never, think of you in the same light as my siblings."

The erection stabbing Riordan's stomach was proof of that. His breath caught as Brynach ground himself against his stomach. He resisted the urge to roll his hips into Brynach, not to drive him away but to beg him closer.

"If you need reminding, I'll fucking provide it." The threat was followed by the violent crush of Brynach's mouth on his. He bit and demanded access to Riordan's mouth.

He could have granted it, but he was still angry. Instead, he continued to try and buck the larger man while denying that the kiss was shredding his resolve. When he opened his mouth to scream, Brynach took advantage. Riordan couldn't help the moan at being claimed by him.

"Fuck you," Riordan panted between kisses. He wasn't done being angry. The glint in the other man's eyes spiked adrenaline and fear through him.

"I tried my words. I tried being patient. If you need reminding that I'm not a robot, I'll happily give it to you," Brynach leaned down and bit into Riordan's neck, no doubt leaving a mark. "What will it take to convince you?"

The way he arched into his partner pissed him off. He didn't want to respond this way. Not right now.

"Get off me!" Riordan yelled, even though he hoped the other man stayed where he was. He needed Brynach to fight for him.

"You want to be stubborn; that's fine. I know how to tame brats." Brynach followed through with his threat by flipping Riordan onto his stomach so fast his head swam. Then the large Fae was pressed against his back, body to body, his mouth at Riordan's ear. "Maybe fucking your ass will prove to you that I know you're a man. My equal. My heart. This way, you'll know for sure how I feel instead of assuming. You'll be fucking feeling it for days."

Riordan's body shook, and the shame of his need ate at him. They shouldn't be doing this right now. That didn't stop him from being rock-hard and wanting exactly what Brynach was offering.

"I'd have preferred something sweeter for your first time, Riordan. I'd have given you that. I still will if you tell me to stop. You remember your safeword?" Brynach's voice was raw in his ear.

He'd figure out another time why he needed this. Why Brynach's angry lust made him feel safe and wanted. Here it was, Brynach's terrifying focus on him. Claiming him. Finally. But the words lodged in his throat. Instead, he rolled his body under Brynach and cursed him again.

Brynach leaned back just long enough to pull Riordan's pants down over his ass and do the same to his own. The hot press of his cock made Riordan groan.

The sharp slap to his ass made him gasp, "The fuck?"

Brynach continued to rain down on his ass, his flesh stung, and sweat broke out on his forehead as he fought to not cry out. Riordan didn't know what number he was on when it switched from pain to a blissful connection with Brynach instead.

"Act like a brat, and you get treated like one. Now suck on these fingers so I can stretch this pretty asshole for my cock," Brynach's words shot straight to Riordan's groin.

Without hesitation, he opened his mouth and messily let Brynach fuck his mouth with his fingers, coating them in saliva.

"I want both my hands prepping you. Don't you dare fucking move." The threat would have follow-through; he knew that. Riordan stayed where he was when Brynach's weight came off him. "Better. Ass up for me."

Riordan didn't complain because it meant freeing his cock from digging into the dirt. He let Brynach kick his knees open and spread his ass cheeks, spitting between them in a way that made him feel filthy. He loved it. Riordan hadn't realized how much he craved Brynach's loss of control. He couldn't handle being treated like something expendable or breakable.

The other man's first finger slid in easily, but the second required a little more relaxation as he slowed his breathing. More of Brynach's spit slid down his crack, and another knuckle slid inside him. One hand smoothed over his back while the other thrust inside him, curling to reach that ball of nerves and stroke it.

"Enough!" Riordan bit back. It was going to be uncomfortable no matter how much Brynach prepped him. He needed to fucking feel something right now.

Brynach slid a hand up Riordan's spine and grabbed his hair at the root, tugging viciously. He ripped his head around for a kiss that was both demanding and loving. How did he walk that line so well? Before he could come up with an answer, Brynach was using his hold on his hair to shove his face into the grass.

"Head down, chest flat, and keep that ass up for me," he instructed.

Riordan followed orders, putting his newly muscled body into a very unnatural position. He cursed when Brynach pushed down on the small of his back, forcing him to arch further.

"So fucking pretty for me," Brynach commented as his cock pushed gently on Riordan's asshole. "I love you, but I don't appreciate you questioning my devotion to you. We're going to talk about that later, but first, I'm going to take what's mine."

He eased himself in, and Riordan hissed at the burn. Brynach stilled, and rage burned in Riordan's chest. If Brynach paused, if he worried about hurting Riordan, he'd ruin this.

"Don't you dare stop," Riordan hissed. "Spit on your cock and fuck me."

Brynach used his free hand to pull Riordan's hips back until his stomach was flushed against his ass. He couldn't help the strangled cry he let loose into the earth beneath his face.

"Riordan," his name was a curse and a prayer on Brynach's tongue. "Are you okay?"

"I don't want your caution." He was gasping as he rocked back into his husband. "Take me."

Brynach's hand squeezed his neck. "Remember you asked for this." Then Brynach was fucking him. Tears swelled in Riordan's eyes. His partner was huge, and the sensation was overwhelming. It hurt, sure it did, but he'd never felt closer to Brynach. Riordan forced himself to relax and breathe through the pain.

"Tell me who's inside you," Brynach instructed as he rode Riordan's ass.

He shook his head. He wouldn't say it. He was giving himself to Brynach; that was enough.

Brynach reached over his body, forcing his cock deep, and then teeth were on his neck. "You're mine, damn it. Say it."

Other than panting and animalistic moans, Riordan gave him nothing. A growl was his only warning before Brynach pulled out of his body completely. Riordan was about to complain when Brynach breached his body again. He didn't go deep; he felt his fat tip right inside and continued to pull it out and push it in. The sensation of being stretched and owned repeated over and over until Riordan was ready to beg him to stroke deep inside him. He gripped the grass, pulling out large clumps.

"Please!" He begged. His legs shook, and Brynach gripped his hips hard, holding him still as he quaked.

"Who is fucking you, Riordan? Let me hear you say it?" Brynach demanded.

"No," he panted.

The other man's hand wound around his hip and gripped his cock tight. He gave it one rough stroke and then another while he bottomed out inside of Riordan.

"Brynach!" he cried out. "Fuck. You are, Brynach."

The purr from behind him was hedonistic. "Was that so hard? Would you like to come, Riordan?"

"Yes." He wasn't going to last. Not with Brynach stroking him while he drove into his body.

"Hmmm." Brynach licked his neck. "You know what I want you to call me if you want to finish."

Riordan did. It was the same thing he demanded of Aisling. Not because he needed to own them, but because in saying it, they claimed the large Fae. He needed it as much as Riordan needed to finish.

He fucked Riordan harder. The feeling was so intense, but he didn't know how to let go. His back arched, his body shook, and he bit his lip so hard he tasted blood.

"Stop fighting me, Riordan. Get out of your head and remember who you're with. I can't protect you from everything, but I can keep you safe when you're in my arms. I won't let you fight me on that." Brynach's voice was hoarse.

"Are you close?" Riordan panted.

"Yes, damn it. How can I not be with your tight ass squeezing the life out of me? I've waited so long to see you under me like this, to feel myself inside you. And you're so fucking strong. So brave. So beautiful. I'm fighting to not lose it. Now stop being so stubborn and finish for me. I want to feel you make a mess of my hand." Brynach kissed along his back as he spoke.

Riordan nodded against the ground. "Yes, husband. For you."

Brynach cried out behind him and drove himself into Riordan. His hand continued to stroke Riordan as he came. His back arched hard enough that he was sure it would break. Riordan's entire body shook with the force of his release. Brynach didn't relent. He drove deep into his body, his hand still stroking him.

"Say it again," Brynach moaned.

Riordan panted, weak and rung out. "I love you, husband."

Brynach lost the smooth rhythm of his fucking and came with a ragged moan. Riordan couldn't move. Couldn't think. He was lost in his own body until Brynach pulled out of him and gathered him up. Riordan's head was cradled against Brynach's chest as the larger man curled around him.

"You're perfect. Strong, fierce, and mine. I don't keep my sadness from you because I think you're weak, Riordan. I keep it from you because I'm afraid of what will happen if I let myself fall into that grief. All you had to do was talk to me." Brynach ran a hand through Riordan's hair and down his side. He held him tight and kissed his shoulder. "Don't ever do that to me again."

Riordan shook from the adrenaline crash. He hated himself for it, but the tears began to fall.

"A chuisle? Did I hurt you? I shouldn't have been so rough," he stammered.

"You didn't hurt me. I'm just ... I'm scared, Bry."

"I am, too." Brynach pulled Riordan's pants up before righting his own. "Come on. I want to take care of you."

"Don't start with that again," Riordan said, but he was only kidding. He understood that aftercare was important for Brynach, and he was beginning to think he needed it, too. As he stood, he could feel Brynach's come leaking out of his ass. Fuck, that was a new feeling.

"I need a bath. You fucking wrecked me." Riordan smiled and leaned up to kiss Brynach. He winced when he saw his husband's face. "Sorry I hit you."

"It wasn't my favorite part of the day, but I understand acting out in anger and hurt. That won't happen again, will it?" Brynach took his face in his hands. "I'm not sorry I fucked you, Riordan. But I'm sorry it wasn't something ... more."

He kissed his husband and took his hand, pulling him

toward their home. "I didn't give you much choice, did I?"

Brynach laughed beside him. "What did I do to deserve two brats?"

He smiled up at his husband. "Aisling is going to have so much fun with this."

CHAPTER 28

Brynach

When the bath went cold, they dried off and climbed into bed. Riordan ran his fingers through Brynach's hair as he lay with his head in Riordan's lap, reading a book. He felt relaxed, but there was something missing.

"You think she's doing okay?" Riordan voiced what he'd been thinking.

Brynach smiled up at him. "If she wasn't, we'd know. I have a solid dozen people watching over that condo."

Riordan shook his head. "Of course you do."

There was no way he could leave his wife at the house without extra protection. Especially not with Walker still unaccounted for. Sean was keeping an eye on the place with surveillance regardless because Lettie was there. Nobody was getting near the girls. And since he didn't have to worry about her, it gave him plenty of time to worry about Riordan.

How had he messed up so badly? He'd somehow missed all the signs that Riordan was feeling alone in his grief. Brynach hated that he'd made the other man feel isolated or weak. A part of him knew it wasn't his responsibility to be every single thing for his partners, but he prided himself on being in tune with their needs. That had been a large one to overlook.

"You're thinking pretty loud, big guy," Riordan commented. "You haven't turned a page in five minutes."

"A lot on my mind, and I'm trying not to remember how much I love seeing you under me." He laughed as Riordan's neck and chest flushed red at the comment.

"You're a menace." Riordan shifted. "My ass still stings, and I heal fast now, so that's saying something." His fingers still played in Brynach's hair as he thought out loud. "I get why Ash likes the pain. It was cathartic. It took my hurts and turned it into a pain I wanted, craved even."

Brynach loved providing that for them. "You know I don't want to actually hurt you. Ever. I've had this discussion with Aisling, but what gets me off isn't hurting you. Your tears, your pain, that's not what I crave."

"What do you get out of it, then?" Riordan asked.

Brynach thought for a moment. "Your submission. Your trust. I like knowing you place your body and heart in my care. That I provide something you need that nobody else can."

Riordan tugged at his hair lightly. "Seems like it's a good thing you landed yourself two brats, then, doesn't it?"

He rolled his eyes and moved off Riordan's lap. "Let's get to sleep. The sooner we do, the sooner we wake up and Aisling comes home."

Without protesting, Riordan snuggled up against Brynach and closed his eyes. It took Brynach a little longer to drift off, and when he did, it wasn't into a regular dream. He was surprised to find himself in his childhood glen. Even more so to realize he wasn't alone.

"Alex?" Brynach asked and moved toward his friend. "What are you doing?"

His friend huffed. "I could ask you the same thing. I found it, you know. Tricky, but the device wasn't undetectable."

Panic lanced through Brynach. Before he could speak, Alex held up a hand. "I'm sure you've already listened to what you did get. I'll admit, it took me longer to realize it was there than I'm proud of."

Brynach wasn't about to admit that he hadn't listened to anything yet. "I don't understand how we got here, Alex. What happened to you?"

"Nothing happened to me, Brynach. You never understood what it was like, not really." Alex shrugged and sat on a large boulder. "You may have been neglected and abused, but you still lived in a palace with guards, food, and at least one sibling who had your back. I had all the abuse and none of the same benefits. I won't let kids grow up the way I did."

"That's what the school is for, Alex. That's what we're doing. It doesn't require any of the back-alley deals you're making. Why are you even associating with Walker?" Brynach asked.

"He gets things done, Bry. Things I need done but can't do myself. I have no stomach for violence, you know that," Alex said. "But the kind of change we need doesn't come without some bloodshed."

Brynach wanted to understand. "What kind of change is that?"

"The school is fantastic, but it's not going to solve our issues. Those young kids are getting a good start, but what will the world look like as they age? How long do you think it will be before the courts find a way to claw their way back to power? It's not enough to unseat them. They need to be destroyed."

"That's my family you're talking about," Brynach pointed out.

Alex shook his head. "Some family. You hate them."

"No, I don't. They were subject to the same horrors I was. Some more than others. Not everyone came out of it a bad person. Rainer, Corinna, the future of the courts, they aren't so bad, Alex." Brynach ran a hand through his hair. "But that's hardly the point. You can't actually be trying to eradicate entire families."

"Eradicate, no. Invalidate, yes." Alex waved a hand. "I didn't come here to defend my actions. You'll never understand. I came here to tell you to stop digging, Bry."

"I can't do that," he answered.

"You can and you will. For all your posturing, you don't like getting your hands dirty. I need you to step back." Alex stared him down.

"Is that a threat?" Brynach was stunned.

"It doesn't have to be," his friend answered. "I've taken a holiday. Aindrea and Joeigh are at the school still. I'll come back when you have calmed down, but I have eyes. I have ears. Let it go, Brynach. I mean it."

Before he could argue with his friend, he was tossed from the dreamwalk. He woke hurt and angry in the arms of his husband, who stared at him with a worried expression.

"You had a nightmare," Riordan said.

Tears stung his eyes. "No. It was much worse than that."

"Do you want to talk about it?"

He appreciated that Riordan gave him the option. His partner knew how hard it was for him to open up at times. If he could trust Brynach with his body, then he could do the same with his feelings. Riordan had asked that he not hold himself back anymore, and he'd honor that.

"Alex dreamwalked with me," Brynach began. "He found the recording device, and I'm pretty sure he threatened me if I don't stop digging into what he's doing."

"He what?" Riordan was immediately alert.

"I don't know what's gotten into him. He said he left and won't come back until things die down. Alex made it clear that he's still got people at the school but that it's in my best inter-est to not ask any more questions."

"That's horse shit." He could hear Riordan's heart racing. "I'll fucking clock him myself. How could he say something like that to you?"

Brynach shrugged. "I don't know. That wasn't the man I know. He said he wanted to eradicate the courts."

"What does that entail?" Riordan wondered. "Sounds unhinged to me."

"Me, too," Brynach agreed. He reached for his phone and breathed a sigh of relief to see Aisling hadn't messaged, nor had any of her security.

"She's okay, Bry." Riordan ran a hand over his arm.

"I know. I had wanted to send them breakfast. Want to help me put together a delivery for them? Bagels, breakfast sandwiches, or waffles?" Brynach gestured to his screen.

"All of it. And mimosa fixings if they do booze." Riordan grinned. "You're going to score us a lot of brownie points."

He laughed. "Hardly the point, but I imagine I will."

After he placed the order, he messaged Aisling the delivery time so she'd know it was okay to answer the door. He also alerted the team around the condo. She sent back heart emojis, and Brynach sent back kissy faces, like the lovestruck idiot he was.

"I need to stay busy. I'm going to cook for us," he announced.

"Not going to argue," Riordan answered and stretched lazily on the bed.

Brynach constructed hearty breakfast sandwiches for his husband, who came downstairs, sweatpants low around his hips and rocking bed head. He was stunning.

They'd started to eat before Riordan addressed the elephant in the room. "He ran because he thought you'd already listened to the tape. We have to see what's on there, Bry."

"*Uh, buddy. We have a situation.*" Kongur's voice interrupted their conversation.

"What kind of a situation?" he asked.

"*Jashana got word about Walker. Sydney sifted fast enough to ward him in. Breena refuses to stay behind and wants in on the capture. Your girl is incoming,*" his familiar informed him.

"Fuck. Stay with her!" Brynach instructed. He turned to Riordan. "Get dressed."

While they dressed and strapped on their weapons, he

filled his husband in. "So, all the girls are there, and we're the last to know? Hate that," he commented.

"You and me both. Let's go!" Brynach moved for the door and was surprised to see Aisling running up the steps.

"Want my weapons," she called, and he tossed her the holster with her throwing knives already strapped in.

Kongur was thundering his way. *"Phlyren is already ahead with Valo. We need to catch up."*

"Can you handle all three of us?" Brynach asked his familiar. He knew it was asking a lot.

"Don't insult me. I won't be as fast, but I can more than manage," he answered as he came to a grinding halt on their lawn.

The three of them ran down to meet him. Aisling dutifully placed a foot into his hand and let him heft her up onto the horse's back. Riordan groaned but took Aisling's hand and swung himself onto Kongur.

Brynach quickly lifted his wife and repositioned her. "I love you, a stoirin, but Riordan is too skittish for you to keep a hold of. Besides, your weight closer to Kongur's neck is better than his. He'll ride in the middle," Brynach informed them. Then Kongur was flying toward the action.

"Fuck," Riordan yelped. "I forgot how much I hated this."

Aisling's laugh was pure joy as her hair whipped back. Riordan made quick work of braiding it as best he could on a moving horse and tying it with a hairband from his wrist. Brynach was certain he heard him grumble about lacerations to his eyes.

"Oh, hush. It's not that bad." Aisling chided. "If you can handle the motorcycle, you can handle this. Enjoy the ride."

"Bullshit. It's nothing like my motorcycle," he argued.

"Rin says to head east," Aisling called out.

Kongur responded immediately, veering to the left. It was impossible to miss the way Riordan was trying to hold himself up off the rampaging horse's back. Brynach's lips quirked up at the memory of the last time he rode this fast with Riordan.

"You okay back there, big guy?" Riordan turned his head.

"Yeah, why?"

Riordan shifted in front of him. "Your dick is digging into my ass."

Aisling lets loose a loud laugh. "I love you two."

Brynach shrugged. "I'm remembering another time riding with you."

"We never speak of it, Bry! Never," Riordan gasped.

His wife turned around so fast he was surprised she didn't get whiplash. "Never speak of what? I want to know," she whined.

"What part of 'never speak of it' was unclear?" Riordan asked.

"We have sex now, Riordan. I don't think we need to keep it a secret anymore," Brynach commented.

"Never!"

"*We're coming up on them*," Kongur alerted.

"We're here," Brynach announced.

Aisling whined as Kongur slowed. "I want to know!"

Brynach threw himself to the ground. He reached up for Riordan, but both he and Aisling had already dismounted and were straightening themselves. They stared at the house in the woods surrounded by people.

He moved to his sisters' sides. "You two don't need to be here."

Breena got in his face and poked his chest. "Don't you fucking dare, Brynach!" She shoved him, and he took a step back.

Jashana took her by the arm and pulled her away. He wasn't surprised by her outburst, but he couldn't deny his shock when his sister allowed herself to be held by the other woman.

"It's bullshit," she mumbled into Jashana's chest. The Fae glared at Brynach.

"You know better," she said.

Aisling moved to Brynach's side, but he shook his head.

His sister was right.

"The way I'm treating you is based on my fear, not your ability to protect yourself," he admitted.

Breena rolled her eyes but relented. "I still don't understand why we're here when it's clear Gabriel hurt Brielle, not this douche."

"He didn't," Brynach assured her. "You've talked to her. You know she saw the man who attacked her."

"A glamour," Breena said.

"I know you want it to be him, but it's not," Brynach promised.

"How can you be so sure?" Breena pinned him with a glare.

Aisling and Riordan moved to his sides. "I know because he's currently being held in a safe space after turning his very human self in for protection in exchange for information."

His sister slapped him. He nodded. "I deserved that."

"Yeah, you did," she yelled. "You fucker."

Riordan spoke up. "Look, what's done is done, but right now we should be focused on Walker."

Jashana spoke. "One small roadblock. When Syd locked him in there, he wasn't alone. He's got a hostage."

"We don't negotiate by giving him anyone else in exchange for whoever is inside." Brynach looked them over. "Is that clear?"

Jashana frowned. "We didn't know who it was in there, but, um."

She paused and looked between Breena and Brynach. "My familiar made their way inside."

"Who is it?" Breena asked. Her voice was cold, but Brynach knew she wasn't heartless. She didn't want anyone hurt.

"I need you both to stay calm. Do you understand?" Jashana asked.

"You're freaking them out," Aisling said. "Who is it?"

Jashana bit her lip before nodding. "It's Trixie."

The world slowed and a hum began in his ears. Beside

him, Aisling gasped and covered her mouth, Riordan cursed, and Breena took an angry step toward the house before her girlfriend stopped her. Brynach blinked before turning to Jashana.

"You're sure?"

She nodded.

"Okay. Okay. This doesn't change our approach," he started.

"Like hell it doesn't," Breena cursed. "That's our niece!"

"I know who it is, Breena, but we handle it the same. If we get emotional, we lose our edge. We need our heads clear," he said.

It was pure happenstance that he had been reading a book on hostage negotiation. He wasn't prepared for this. Especially not where emotion was involved. If anything happened to Trixie, he'd never forgive himself.

"Nobody makes a move without us. Jashana, make sure everyone knows to stand down for the moment. We need a plan," Brynach said.

Jashana walked off, and Aisling put a hand on his arm. "She's going to be okay."

Brynach pushed the images of Brielle bruised and broken from his mind. No way that happened to Trixie. Rainer and Ceiren sifted in, and Breena ran to them. His brother's broken voice rang through the space. His twin quickly pulled them away, and Aisling squeezed his arm before going to them.

"Bry," Riordan started. "We need eyes. A sharpshooter. He's not coming out alive or unharmed. We know that. He's going to fight. We need to be ready. Magic workers and weapons trained and ready. The woods benefit us. This isn't impossible."

He nodded. "Right. Okay. I want thermal imaging immediately. I want to know the heat signatures inside the building. Right where he is and where Trixie is. He'll keep her close. Contact Pilson for the equipment if we don't have access to it."

Riordan pulled out his phone and began acting. The decision-making helped Brynach; it unfroze his body. He walked to a large group of Brielle's colleagues. "Are you prepared to put him down?"

"Fuck yes, we are," one answered. "For Brielle."

"There's a child in there. He took her from the school," Brynach told them and saw one of the men flinch. "We use an overabundance of caution. No wild shooting or magic work. No charging a door and hoping he doesn't fire. You wait for the signal to move. Is that understood?"

"Yes, sir," a woman responded. "The only person getting hurt today is Walker."

Brynach nodded. "Does anyone have negotiation training?"

Around him heads shook. "Not really our style."

Well, fuck. Until the police got there, he was their best shot. He wanted Walker engaged sooner rather than later. The longer they waited, the longer they remained in the dark about what was going on inside. If he could move the man toward a part of the house with a clearer line of vision, it would help a lot.

Don't piss him off. Keep him talking but not defensive. Stay calm. Don't escalate the situation. He moved to Riordan who was speaking to Pilson. He nodded to the officer.

"Thanks for coming so quickly."

"The perks of officers who can sift," the man answered. "I understand your niece is inside?"

"Yes," Brynach choked on the word.

"I brought our hostage negotiator. I think we should use him." He waited for Brynach to argue.

Everything in him was screaming to stay in control, to be the one to talk to Walker. But Brynach could admit he wasn't an expert and Trixie needed the best right now. The best wasn't him. Not right now.

"Okay."

Riordan's hand on his back soothed him a little.

The older man frowned. "I know the father is here, and other family members. I can't dictate your actions, but I want to strongly suggest that you sit back and let others who aren't emotionally distracted handle this. The men I brought aren't new to these situations."

Aisling showed at his side, her eyes begging him to listen to the other man. Riordan's fist against his back was both supportive and cautionary. Panic rang through him at the thought of letting anyone else run this.

"Fine, but if I think you're fucking it up, I'm stepping in." It was the best he could do.

Pilson nodded and went to talk to his men.

CHAPTER 29

Aisling

She was still in shock that Brynach had agreed to stand down. Together, she and Riordan moved with their partner toward his siblings. Sydney had joined Rainer and Ceiren, and Brielle accompanied them. Aisling had tried to keep her friend from coming, but once she heard they had Walker pinned down, she'd demanded to come.

The girls' night had been everything she wanted it to be. They'd laughed and eaten too much junk food while having fruity drinks and watching movies. Aisling could honestly say she'd never anticipated Jashana, Breena, Brielle, and Corinna cuddling up with Lettie, Tara, and Kara on a giant mass of mattresses in the living room to have a slumber party, but that's what they'd done. And somehow, it had been seamless, natural. Right up until Sean had called Jashana, and she'd put him on speakerphone.

The warrior had shot to her feet and the rest of the Fae joined her. Voices rang out in unison.

"I'm coming," Breena demanded.

"Sift with me. I'll ward him in." Sydney was already pulling on shoes.

Brielle stifled a groan as she moved. "I'm going. I need to see this for myself."

Aisling wasn't going to argue with any of them. "Lettie, have Sean call Bry and let him know. I'm heading back there for my weapons, and then I'll meet you there."

She locked eyes with Brynach's sisters. "If Sydney can't get him locked in, you leave. No heroics."

Both gave her a look that said they'd do no such thing. Aisling knew they were capable women, but her husband had started to rub off on her. She wanted to make sure they were safe. She held up her hands and turned to Tara, Kara, and Lettie as the three women exited her wards and sifted.

"You're all welcome to stay here, if you want. You'll be safe within the wards," she told them.

Tara looked at her girlfriend. "Will we be safe if we go home? No offense, but we're probably safer somewhere they won't look for you."

She nodded. "Yeah, you're fine. Lettie, what will you do?"

"I'll be with Sean. Go!" Lettie waved her off. "Be careful."

Aisling ran down the stairs and sifted home. It hadn't surprised her to see the guys strapped up and ready for her to show. But watching Brynach stand with his siblings while SWAT moved toward the house where an unhinged man held Trixie astounded her. She was grateful he wasn't putting himself in harm's way, but the fact that any of them were standing here baffled her.

"If they don't kill that sorry son of a bitch, I will," Rainer cursed. "I've done all I can to protect Trixie, and then this happens." He turned on Brynach. "I've talked to Ceiren enough to know Alex could be behind this. I'll kill him, too."

She wanted to tell him he was out of his mind and Alex would never hurt Trixie, but she couldn't anymore.

"If he had a part in this, I'll kill him before you get the chance to," Brynach answered.

Aisling watched Riordan flank their husband and put a

firm hand on his arm. She leaned her head against his other side and felt him release a little tension. Breena was pacing behind them, angry that she'd been told to stand aside, but she couldn't argue when Jashana was there, too.

From closer to the house, a man started talking through a bullhorn to Walker. They listened, but no response came.

"*Rin, what can you see?*" Aisling asked her familiar.

"*There's a skylight in the living room that's not covered but he closed the windows. I can't see much. I don't see him or Trixie, though,*" he answered. "*I'll let you know if that changes.*"

Aisling turned to Riordan. "Any intel from Vola?"

Her husband stilled for a moment. "He can hear them moving around inside. Said he hears Trixie talking."

"What's she saying? Is she hurt?" Rainer demanded.

"He doesn't think so. She doesn't even seem to be restrained or scared. She recognizes Walker as someone Alex knows. She trusted him and still thinks this could be a game," Riordan answered. "That's good. It will keep her from panicking and potentially causing him to spiral."

"Not with that bullhorn going," Ceiren answered. "She'll know now."

Aisling started when someone called her name. She turned to see Corinna, pale lavender wings tucked tight to her back, walk toward them.

"Come to gloat, Princess?" Rainer asked with venom in his voice.

She spared him only a moment's glance. "I came because I want to help."

"I'm not sure that's a good idea," Aisling said. "If the people trained in combat are sitting it out, I think it's safe to say you should, too."

Corinna shook her head. "Not everything is about muscle." She gestured with her head to her shoulder and the small field mouse that sat there. "Caspian can get inside."

Brynach nodded. "Thank you. Let's go talk to the police."

He led the princess toward the front line and straight to Loren. The large officer nodded, and Corinna set her familiar on the ground and climbed into the back of a tactical truck.

"You okay?" Riordan asked quietly. Together, they watched their husband guard the open door, protecting Corinna. Riordan looped his arm around Aisling's waist and pulled her tight.

"No, not really. I just want this over. I want Trixie safely in her father's arms." Aisling's stomach felt sick at the idea of her niece hurt or scared.

There was nothing to do but wait while Corinna's familiar got inside and relayed information to the police. Around the building, men and women stood in armor and held massive weapons. The idea of them running in and scooping up a now-scared Trixie made her sick.

Suddenly, there was a flurry of activity, of hand motions and movement. Rainer tensed next to her.

"What the fuck is going on?"

"Looks like they're making a move," Jashana answered.

Ceiren held Breena close and Aisling held her breath as a canister flew through the window, and smoke began to billow out. They all heard a child scream, and then chaos broke out. Aisling turned to see Rainer shoot away from their group. Ceiren shouted for him, but his brother kept running.

Shots rang from inside the house toward the police and most took cover behind vehicles. Brynach shot them a quick glance and then jumped in the back of the truck and closed the bulletproof door around him, Corinna, and whoever was manning operations inside.

Riordan had grabbed her hand. "What do we do?"

Someone kicked in the front door and ran inside. Movement from the back of the house drew their eyes, and Aisling gasped to see Rainer running with Trixie in his arms. She pulled her knives, and Riordan pulled his gun, and they ran for the front line. With a war cry, Breena followed, and Jashana was forced to do the same.

Brynach was going to kill them for not staying put, but Trixie was safe. A body charged out of the house, and it took a moment to register that it wasn't a cop. The large blonde man took an officer by surprise and was able to get an arm around their neck. Using the other person's body as a shield, they started screaming.

"Drop the ward!" Walker demanded.

Sydney and the other Fae feeding the ward didn't waver.

"I mean it. Drop it, or I snap this man's neck." His wild eyes darted around the area.

Aisling and Riordan came to a stop behind the door of a vehicle. She really didn't want to draw his attention to them, but she also needed to make space for that man to get away. Of course, there were probably people better trained for that.

"Maybe we shouldn't," she said to Riordan.

He looked around the area. "They're not doing anything, Ash. They can't; legal red tape won't let them. They can't lose their jobs. We have nothing to lose and everything to gain. What do you want to do?"

She assessed the situation again. "I can get a knife in his hand, no problem. That man's tactical gear will protect him. A one-two shot with my knives, and he should drop his hand and shift his position."

Riordan nodded. "Then I'll take the shot."

"You sure?" she asked him.

He nodded. "On the count of three?"

Aisling took a deep breath, and then her partner began counting. His words were whisper-soft against her cheek.

One.

Two.

He paused, leveling his weapon as Aisling eyed her target. She could do this. Regulate her breathing. Control the release. This was just like target practice.

Three.

She let the knife fly, the second following just a moment

later. The first one buried itself in the forearm wrapped around the officer's neck. The officer's eyes went wide as a second knife struck a little higher on the man's arm. Walker cursed and pulled his arm away, letting the other man take a step to the side. Aisling's ears rang as two shots sounded next to her head, one after the other. The hot casing bounced off her cheek and the acrid smell of gunpowder wafted over her.

Then people were moving. The officer Walker had held was on his knees, pulling the Fae's hands behind his back. Brynach was charging at them, face red with rage until he reached them. His arms circled them, and he growled.

"You idiots. I swear to the Goddess…"

Aisling stood frozen in his arms. The last few seconds too much to register. "Is he dead?"

Riordan turned his head and stared toward the building. He shook his head. "No. I didn't go for kill shots. He'll live."

"Still so angry with you. And so proud. Don't you ever do anything like that again," Brynach yelled.

"Oh, stop. They did great, Brynach," Breena scolded. "I mean, I'm angry I didn't get a chance to do anything fun, but that was impressive."

Aisling offered her a small smile, but it fell when she saw Pilson bearing down on them. Brynach wasn't the only one upset with them right now. She pulled away from Brynach.

"Go check on Trixie. I think Riordan and I are going to have some explaining to do," Aisling told him. "We'll holler if we need you. Give her a hug for me."

Brynach looked at the older man as he approached and then nodded. "Come on, Breena."

Pilson shook his head. "That was a stupid move. Brave but stupid," he told her. "Do you have any idea the nightmare of paperwork I'll have to deal with?"

Riordan spoke, "Was it, or was it not, easier to have someone else take him out?"

"Technically and off the record?" Pilson nodded. "Let's not

make a habit of it, okay? It's bad enough when Brynach takes out vigilantes. At least this one is still alive."

"I want my knives back when you're done cataloging them or whatever you have to do with them. They were wedding gifts." Aisling demanded.

Pilson shook his head. "You'll get them back. I want you both down at the precinct tomorrow to give statements. Mr. Campbell, I need that firearm. You'll get it back when we're done with it."

Riordan slid the magazine out and removed the chambered bullet and hung it on the pen that was being held out to him. The older man frowned and looked at her. "I'm impressed and proud, but please, for my sake, don't do that again."

"Cross my heart," Aisling answered. "Are we free to go?"

"Yes, but like I said, I want to see you tomorrow before noon." The officer turned and walked away, already barking out orders for evidence bags.

Riordan reached for her hand, and they walked toward their husband and his family. Trixie was cradled between them all, squirming.

"I'm fine," she complained for what Aisling was sure was not the first time. "Tell them girls are strong, Aunt Aisling."

"Yes, we are," she said and kissed her niece's cheek. "We're proud of you."

Rainer smiled at Aisling before turning back to his daughter. "Yes, we are. But no more leaving school or palace grounds with anyone, at all, ever, unless I tell you it's okay."

She bowed her head and nodded. "Okay, Daddy."

He kissed the top of her blonde curls and held her even tighter. With a few more quick words, Rainer, Ceiren, Jashana, and Breena left for the Unseelie court. Brielle stood with them, and together they watched Corinna make her way over to them.

"That was ... intense," the princess said. "I'm glad I could help, but that was ridiculous. You guys just do that all the time?"

Aisling laughed. "Not quite all the time."

Her purple hair shook. "Still. No, thank you." She turned to Brielle. "I think that's enough action for one day for you. Let's get back home."

It surprised everyone when Brielle nodded and took the other woman's hand to sift away. Riordan turned to her and lifted a brow. "They're friends now?"

"Trauma bonding," Brynach answered. "It's a thing."

"I know what it is, big guy. Just seemed like an unlikely pairing is all." Riordan shrugged. "Think we can go home, too? I'd really like to put this day behind us."

Aisling didn't get a chance to answer as Brynach gathered them in his arms and sifted them to their lawn. They were quiet as they walked into the house, and Aisling pulled cold pizza from the refrigerator. They settled on the sofa, box on the table, and ate while they processed.

"How are you feeling?" Brynach asked when the leftovers were gone.

"Fine. I think," she answered honestly.

"I shot a dude," Riordan whispered. "Twice."

She could see her partners' minds whirling. Brynach with worry and anger, Riordan with fear and mixed emotions. Aisling understood that sex wasn't always the answer, but it had been too long since they'd been together. Since before her attack. They needed to reconnect right now.

She sat up and met her husband's gaze. "I need you to stop my racing thoughts. I miss you. Both of you."

Brynach's entire demeanor changed. The switch flipped, and finally, he had an outlet for his recent worries and anger. A safe one.

His hand fisted in Aisling's hair, and he tugged her toward his body. "You think you're healed enough to handle me. Handle us?"

"Yes," Aisling bit her lips as a shiver ran down her spine.

Brynach kissed her hard. "Good. I've been waiting to hear

that. We have a certain flogger I have been waiting to use on both of you."

"Both?" Aisling asked, looking to Riordan. He was flushed.

Her other husband nodded. "Both. After that bullshit stunt you pulled, most definitely both. Upstairs. Now," Brynach ordered.

Riordan took her hand and pulled her up. "Come on, beautiful."

She took deep, grounding breaths, and Brynach cupped her ass from behind. She leaned into Riordan and let him undress her. Once she was naked, she stood, hands behind her back, waiting for Brynach to tell her where he wanted her. It surprised her when she realized Riordan was doing the same thing. Before she could question what was going on, Brynach called their attention.

"You know I love you," Brynach began. "And you'll use your safeword if you need to."

"Yes."

Brynach nodded. "Riordan, get the wedge."

Once the triangle pillow was set at the end of the bed, Brynach positioned Aisling over it, her ass high in the air. She turned her head to see Riordan naked and in the same position over a pile of pillows. There was a question in her eyes as he reached over and took her hand.

At the end of the bed, the larger Fae slapped the flogger he'd bought her for their handfasting against his thigh, and Aisling moaned.

"Eyes on me, Aisling," Riordan told her. "Who takes care of you?"

"My husbands," she answered and ended on a scream as Brynach kissed her ass with the braids of the flogger. "Thank you."

Brynach growled and gripped her smarting ass. "You'll count and thank me after each one."

"One. Thank you, husband," Aisling cried.

She waited for the next blow, but when she heard the

sound of falls on flesh, she felt no sting. Riordan's grip on her fingers tightened, and he cursed.

Behind them Brynach waited, and Aisling nodded at Riordan.

"One. Thank you, husband."

"Fuck, I like that." Brynach sounded absolutely feral. "I'm going to paint you red."

The tails came down hard and fast on her ass, and she cried out with each strike. Riordan tugged on her hair until her mouth met his. Brynach growled his approval from behind her.

"Still with us, my toys?" he asked.

"Here, husband," she answered. "Please. I need more."

Brynach's thick fingers dragged along her core, and he cursed. "So wet for us. Do you like when I make your ass red?"

"Yes, husband. Thank you," she responded. Then the tails came down again, again, again. For each of hers, Riordan got one, too. Aisling could see Riordan change from pleasure to pain and the way he fought to not call a stop to things. She was about to do it for him when Brynach told Riordan to turn over and sit on his raw ass. Of course, he'd seen it, too.

"Do you understand how angry I am with both of you for putting yourself in danger?" Brynach asked. "I don't care that you're Fae. You're not to take risks with your lives. Mine means nothing without you. Do you understand?"

She watched Riordan gaze up at their husband with love in his red eyes. "Yes, we do."

"Good." Brynach ran a hand over her ass. "Where are you at, a stoirin?"

"More. Please," she begged. She was close to coming; she just needed that last push.

That's when Riordan's hand snaked down her belly and his thumb pressed on her clit as Brynach landed a particularly hard strike. She fell apart, sobbing her release. As she settled, Riordan pulled her into his lap.

Aisling looked up at him. "You let Brynach spank you."

He laughed at her. "I did."

"We've also made love," Brynach added.

She looked between the two of them, sitting side by side, watching her for her reaction. There was no denying she was a little jealous she hadn't known right away. And maybe disappointed she hadn't been a part of it. She took a moment to acknowledge those emotions and then let them go. Their relationship was their own, and she was so happy for them.

Aisling took both their faces in turn and kissed them. "Will you ... can you show me?"

Riordan winked at her. "You want to watch me fuck Brynach?"

Heat pooled in her, and she clenched her thighs together as her pussy pulsed. "Very much."

Brynach was kissing his way down her body, his mouth moving to her core. He tugged her, her raw ass burning against their sheets. Then his arms were under her, lifting her to his mouth and devouring her.

"Fuck!" She threw her head back. She closed her eyes and moved herself over Brynach's tongue.

"Eyes open, Ash. You asked for a show," Riordan's voice was husky. When she looked up, she realized why.

"Tell me," Aisling encouraged as she moved beneath them.

"He's got a finger in me. Fuck, two." Brynach ground out as he licked at her.

"You have a safeword, Brynach?" Riordan asked and kissed his shoulder.

Not a single chance in hell Aisling thought he'd use it.

"Prince."

Riordan stilled behind him, but neither of them commented. Aisling let out a strangled whine when her husband lost focus and stopped licking her. Brynach snarled into her pussy as Riordan added another finger and stroked into his body. Aisling's hands went to her breasts, pulling at her nipples, but her eyes never left Riordan's hand.

"You like this?" Riordan asked as he dripped lube onto his cock.

"Stop teasing," Brynach called to Riordan. "Tell him how much you like this, Princess."

"It's so hot. You're both so fucking sexy," she panted. Then Brynach pushed down on her pelvis and sucked her clit, hard, and she fell apart. She shook in his arms and cried out his name. As her body settled, she watched Riordan stroke his cock and begin to slide into Brynach.

Aisling scrambled up on her knees in front of Brynach and watched as Riordan guided himself inside her husband. She cursed and leaned down to taste Brynach's moans. As Riordan stroked into him, she drank down his grunts.

Her hand snaked down to grip his cock and stroke him as Riordan rode his ass. It wasn't soft. It wasn't gentle. It was raw need between the three of them. Brynach bit her lip, and she gasped into his mouth.

"Pause," he called to Riordan and immediately, he did. "I want to fuck you while Riordan fucks me."

Aisling nodded. "Yes. Goddess, yes."

He lifted himself up on his hands, and Aisling slid under his body, using one of the pillows to prop her hips up. Then she took Brynach's cock again and slid him inside her. She rolled her hips and fucked up onto his cock while Riordan slid into him.

She looked over Brynach's shoulder. "I want to feel you fucking us both, Riordan. Want you to drive into him so hard it pushes him deeper than ever inside me."

Riordan's hand pressed on Brynach's back. "Arch for me, Bry."

"Fuck!" Brynach cried out and leaned down to kiss Aisling. She bit his lip as Riordan bottomed out inside him.

"So tight. Damn it, Bry," Riordan cursed.

"We're not going to last, Princess. You are going to be a good girl and finish for us again. We won't until you do." Brynach braced his hands by her head. "Rub that clit for me."

She snuck a hand between them and stroked herself. How

could she possibly concentrate on her own pleasure when she was busy watching her two men?

Brynach's back bowed further, and his body pulled off Aisling's, allowing her more room to strum her clit. She clenched around him, so fucking close to losing it.

"You're both so amazing," Riordan called out, his hands gripping Aisling by Brynach's hips.

She looked up into his warm brown eyes and then Brynach's citrine eyes and felt so safe. Aisling pulled Brynach's full weight down onto her and let Riordan drive him in and out of her pussy with his own thrusts. He breathed hard against her mouth.

"I love you." It sounded like a prayer on his lips. "So much. I'd be lost without you."

She kissed him over and over. "I'm right here. We're right here. I love you."

"Forever, Brynach," Riordan promised. "So close. Please tell me you're close."

Together they nodded, and the Brynach moved his hips back, and Riordan stilled so he could stroke into Aisling until she cried out their names and came beneath them. She quivered around Brynach's cock, clawing at his back until Riordan lifted her hand.

Riordan licked Brynach's neck, then pushed until Brynach was flush against Aisling's chest.

"Grab his ass, Aisling. Spread him for me," Riordan's voice was a growl. When had he become the dirty talker?

"I'm not going to last, big guy. Fill our girl." Riordan grabbed Brynach's hips, pulling him back on each of his forward thrusts.

Brynach's hands fisted in the sheets next to Aisling's head, and he met her eyes. She was panting and flushed. She looked up at him and mouthed that she loved him. He came with a jagged cry, spilling into Aisling as Riordan rode him hard.

"Inside me," Brynach moaned.

Riordan cursed, and Brynach rested on Aisling as she held

him close, hands moving from his ass to his back and then his face. The sounds of their bodies nearly made her finish again as Riordan tensed and jerked behind him.

"Fuck." His hands on Brynach's hips clenched.

"Thank you," she whispered. Riordan kissed Brynach and then her over their husband's shoulder.

"Shhh, little one." Brynach kissed her neck. "We've got you."

CHAPTER 30

Riordan

You have everything? Dawn has her keys? You checked in with the groundskeeper at the house so they know you're coming today?" Riordan asked for the hundredth time.

Liam laughed at his side. "Yes. Yes. And yes. I've got it under control, Rory. Don't worry so much."

Aisling turned from her seat in the front of Brynach's truck. She smiled at Amber. "You ready for this?"

She nodded. "As I'll ever be. Nothing keeping me here, and I love a good adventure. Plus, I hear the Irish love to fight. I'll fit right in."

Liam groaned. "Don't even."

"Boxing, babe. I want to box." She bounced in the seat between him and his brother.

"We're going to come visit," Brynach promised.

"You better. It's going to be okay, Rory. This isn't like last time," Liam reminded him as Brynach pulled up to the departure gate.

The larger Fae pulled the bags from the bed of the truck while Aisling hugged Amber and Liam embraced Riordan.

"I'm damn proud of you. You know that, right?" Liam said,

holding Riordan's face in his hands. "I love you."

Riordan was trapped, staring at the raw emotion in his brother's eyes. "I know, Liam. I love you, too. Go unite Ireland. You've got a lot of work ahead of you."

"Ugh, don't remind us," Amber groaned and hugged Riordan.

Brynach snagged all four of them in his massive embrace, and their laughter was loud enough to draw attention. The big guy didn't care.

"Be safe, both of you. Let us know when you land." Brynach released the group of them, and Liam and Amber gave excited waves as they wheeled their luggage into the airport.

Riordan's partners took his hands and led him into the truck. Aisling sat in the back so he wasn't alone with his thoughts. Which was good because he desperately needed a distraction. Hell, they all needed a distraction,

"Sydney said they have Walker in a warded cell, but they want me down there to strip him today. They don't want to rely on the magic to keep him there." Aisling said.

"And I can't ignore those tapes any longer. I have to figure out what Alex has going on. Then I need to bring his ass back here and kick it," Brynach said.

Riordan groaned. "Bry, you're teaching today. I took the day off. I'll go with Aisling to the prison, and then we'll listen to the tapes."

Brynach shook his head. "That's my job. It'll bore you."

Aisling reached forward and put a hand on his arm. "Bry, you know you're putting it off because you're not ready to hear what's on there. Let us take care of it."

They were pulling into town before Brynach caved. "I don't like it. It should be me, but you're right. You have time right now, I don't, and we need to listen."

Reluctantly, he left them at the prison gates. He was out of the truck and rounding the back to embrace them before their feet hit the ground. Brynach kissed Aisling until she was limp in his arms before giving Riordan a much tamer version.

"Keep each other safe," he instructed. "I hate the idea of you in there." Worry creased his forehead.

Aisling reached out to smooth the lines. "We're going to be okay. Riordan will have my back, and I'll ask for extra guards."

Riordan could see that the big guy didn't like it, but with a look at his watch, he didn't argue. He kissed them one last time before he climbed into the truck. Aisling paused and stared up at the intimidating building. The male prison was loud and run-down. Not that the female one they had experience with was any better.

"Come on," she said and walked toward the guest door. Once inside, she gave her name, and they were taken down a plain, painted hallway to a room to wait. Neither of them was surprised when the Regional Director and warden of the female facility entered.

"You two are a PR nightmare. It had to be you?" she asked.

"Just make sure we're safe and nothing goes wrong, and you'll be fine," Riordan reminded her. His hand gripped Aisling's, and his thumb ran along the inside of her wrist.

"I want extra guards. Armed guards. I don't care what it takes; I don't want to be alone and unprotected with that man," Aisling demanded.

"Already done," the woman promised. "I have a total of five guards, and all will have live weapons."

Riordan nodded. "I want to see the feed, but while she's in there, I need to talk to you."

Aisling knew he had to show the woman the footage of Alex smuggling Peggy the knife. He didn't know how the hell Alex had snuck it inside, but it had to be addressed. As the Regional Director, she oversaw several prisons, including the one Peggy was in.

She smiled at him and nodded.

"I'm ready."

The guards and the prison's Associate Warden accompanied her down the hallway to the magicked holding cell. Riordan followed her movements on the screen as she entered new sections of the prison.

The woman next to him sighed. "Once they straighten out the new world laws, this will never fly. Stripping him of his magic before a trial will be unheard of. I can't believe we're getting away with it as it is."

Riordan didn't give a fuck how it was happening, so long as it was. On the screen, a black-and-white Aisling approached the prisoner. As promised, there were weapons pointed at him while Aisling set up. Without being able to hear her or sense the magic she'd use to strip him, there was no real way to tell when she began. That is until Walker began screaming.

He turned away. "I have something you need to see."

The woman pulled her eyes from the screen and raised a brow. "More important than that." She nodded toward the monitor.

"If having insufficient screening for prison visitors is more important, then yes," Riordan answered and pulled up the video. Unlike him, she saw the issue right away.

"Motherfucker," she cursed. "Who is that?"

Riordan didn't want to tell her, but she'd find out on her own anyway. "Alex. Hell if I know his last name. Fae. He skipped town, and we're looking for him. The real question is how did he get in with that weapon? Or why wasn't Peggy searched after her visit?"

She frowned. "I'll address it. Thank you for providing this. Can you send it to me?"

He nodded and did as asked. Then all attention was back on Aisling, who was already wrapping up the magical castration, as it were. As she was turning her back, he saw Walker lunge for the bars of his cell. He let loose a scream and moved to the monitor, as if it would do anything. There was no need. A shot rang out, and Walker went down. The warden went running from the room as Aisling was hurried away.

Riordan ran out into the hall and opened his arms for his wife as she breached the door closest to him. "The fuck was that?"

"I don't know." She shook as she clung to him. "I'm fine. Just scared me a bit."

"Non-lethal ammunition, ma'am." The guard informed her.

Riordan glared at him and then walked away with Aisling. "Let's get out of here."

As soon as they exited the prison, Aisling's steps stuttered. "Crap."

Cathy was walking up the sidewalk toward them with a determined gait. "Aisling Campbell, how many times have I told you to notify us if you're doing something like this?"

Aisling bristled. "I don't owe you shit, Cathy. I give you a lot of room to make demands, but if you keep pushing, I'm going to give you absolutely nothing. Is that understood?"

The other woman paused and pulled her neck back. "Aisling, this is your job. You can be mad about it, but unless you resign, this is a part of the deal."

Riordan put a hand on Aisling's back. She was heated, and he understood. "Is there something you needed?"

Cathy nodded. "You need to come with me and do a press conference. There are questions about prison safety for non-Fae and Fae alike. We need to address it, and we want your face to do it."

Aisling's back stiffened. "You get an hour. That's it." She turned back to Riordan. "Go home. Start the tapes. I'll meet you there."

He didn't like the idea of being separated, but she didn't need a chaperone all day. He was no good at a press confer-ence, anyway. "Press conference and then right home. And she has security escort her," Riordan insisted.

His wife rolled her eyes. Walker was taken care of, Gabriel was nullified, Dexter was dead, and he had no reason to be that cautious, but the extra measures made him feel less anxious. Luckily, Aisling seemed to recognize that and didn't fight him. She kissed him and then walked off with Cathy, and he sifted to their home.

Inside, the house was quiet enough to be mildly unsettling. Riordan pulled up the audio recordings from Alex's office on Brynach's laptop and sat down to start listening. No sense putting off the inevitable. No matter what he heard on here, it was going to upset Brynach. Afterall, it had been enough to send Alex running.

Riordan picked up a notebook and pen to write time stamps down and started listening. It began with Brynach rustling around on the desk and then leaving and closing the door. Then there was the sound of heavy footsteps and the door opening. Alex addressed his familiar and then got closer to the desk and read the note.

"And he didn't say anything? Or look at anything else?" Alex spoke, Riordan assumed, to his familiar, whose response obviously couldn't be heard.

"Why won't he leave it alone?" Alex wondered aloud, and then Riordan heard a chair pull out and papers shuffle.

After that, it was a boring budget meeting, an interview with a cleaning crew, and a visit from the school board members. Theo and Marina knocked to discuss enrollment and expansion. At one point, Riordan thought he heard Aindrea, but Alex moved her out of the office and earshot before talking. Then it was the background noise of the cafeteria while Alex was out doing whatever it was he did during the day.

Before thirty minutes were up, Riordan's skin began to itch. He couldn't sit and listen any longer. Instead, he synced up his earbuds and swept and mopped the floors. Then he dusted shelves, sanitized counters, and cleaned bathrooms while he listened to the boring ins and outs of a school. He had a casual conversation with Valo while taking out the trash and came inside to hear Alex in his office, talking to someone. Fuck. What had he missed? He went to the laptop and rewound the recording.

"What does that mean?"

It was Alex's voice, but Riordan didn't hear anyone else talking. Was he on the phone, or was he talking to his familiar?

"Will he talk?" Alex asked. There was a large exhale, another curse, and then a loud slam. He wasn't sure if the man had punched something, kicked the desk, or what, but it was loud enough to make Riordan wince.

He rewound the audio again, but Alex never said the name of who he was talking to. When Alex entered in the morning, Riordan began listening again. Most of what he heard was mundane, but then he got a phone call, and this time, he addressed Walker by name.

"I didn't tell you to hurt her. You did the same shit at the training grounds. Nobody was supposed to die. You gotta rein it in. Don't prove yourself to be a liability," Alex threatened.

Riordan groaned. "Fuck!" Of all the things he believed Brynach's friend to be capable of, attacking a training ground of New Fae wasn't one of them. Hell, Brynach had been shot there. Twice. What possible reason could he have for targeting them?

He stopped cleaning when he heard another voice join them.

"You've gone too far. This has gotten out of hand. This one has drawn too much attention," he complained.

Walker cursed him out, and Alex interrupted.

"Whoever controls the kids controls the future of Fae. I know what I'm doing," Alex assured the other man. "They may not understand right away, but they'll see the logic later. That's always how these things work. The ends will justify the means."

He was straightening the bedroom when his phone rang, and he ran for it. Sydney's name lit the screen, and he picked up quickly.

"Hey, Syd."

"Riordan, thank the Goddess." She sounded out of breath.

"What's wrong?" He was immediately on edge.

"I'm not sure. Um, I tried calling Brynach, but he's not answering, and my security isn't here. They were supposed to be getting groceries, and one was supposed to be here, but I can't see them." She rambled.

"Okay. Deep breath. You're alone in the house?"

"Yes. I thought I heard something outside, and someone for sure tested the wards, but I didn't go out and look," she explained.

"Good. Don't. Stay inside. I'll be right there. Don't open the door until I tell you to."

"Wait! Code word. What if someone has you at gunpoint or something?" Sydney said.

"You watch too many cop dramas," he said, but she had a point. "Um, SpongeBob."

Riordan hung up the phone, pulled on his shoes, grabbed a weapon, and sifted. If Brynach didn't answer for his sister, there was no point trying him as well. He'd see the messages after classes were over. Besides, it might be nothing.

"So help me, Riordan. You be careful." Vola was not thrilled with his risk-taking as of late.

"I'll be fine," Riordan assured him.

"They'll kill you if you die doing something stupid." His familiar was pissed.

"And you know you could be helping me right now instead of, I don't know, distracting me!" Riordan pointed out. *"Check the other side of the house, would you?"*

"Fine, but if I get hurt, I'm biting you," he promised.

Riordan waited while he let his vision slip, let the magic of the land enter him, and searched for anyone else in the area. His weapon would be useless if someone attacked him with magic. He needed to be ready. The rain from the prior day still sat below the surface of the ground, and Riordan drew it to him, holding a ball of water in his hand. He was getting really good at potentially dry-drowning people if need be. Again, he was reminded he needed to practice more with the other elements.

"*Nothing,*" Valo confirmed what Riordan already suspected. Whoever was here was gone now.

"*I'm going to circle the house before I go in,*" Riordan informed him. "*Keep an eye on my back.*"

The magical signature wasn't familiar, and it wasn't friendly, but it was nowhere as nasty as someone like Peggy. He told Valo to keep watch and then stepped up to the porch.

"Sydney, it's me," he called. "You can open the door."

From the other side came a shaky voice. "How do I know it's you?"

He grinned. "SpongeBob."

The door opened, and a hand shot out and grabbed his arm. He was pulled inside, and then Sydney slammed the door shut and locked it. Good. He was glad she was being cautious. Riordan took out his phone and sent Brynach a text message to let him know he was with Sydney and she was okay. He'd be worried when he finished class and saw that many missed calls. The next message was to Aisling, to tell her he wasn't at home but to go right there.

"What's going on out there?" Sydney asked, her hands twisting.

"I'm not sure. There's nobody there now, but there is a signature. It's not too dark, but it's not great. Not one I recognize," Riordan told her. "I'm more concerned with where your protection is."

"You and me both." Sydney was still in witness protection until the trial was over. "I called my contact and told them my detail was MIA. They're sending someone out."

"Good." Riordan pulled his phone out again and made a call. "Sean. Hey, man. I hate to keep doing this to you, but I need eyes on the safehouse. Someone tested Syd's wards. Can you prioritize it?"

"I don't get paid enough," Sean complained. Riordan laughed.

The guy got paid plenty. He'd bill the department, without a doubt.

He hung up and turned to Sydney. "Turn on the television. I want to see how Aisling is."

Sydney reached for the remote and searched until they saw his wife's face. She was already accepting questions, which meant she was almost done.

"What are the current statistics on the prison reformation recently implemented?" a reporter asked.

Aisling smiled and answered with ease. "I don't have those exact numbers, but we're positive that, with time, we'll see the positive financial effects of our changes. The prison system simply wasn't meant to house inmates for hundreds of years. Stripping Fae with life sentences of their magic and putting them in human prisons eliminates the need to magically ward more buildings. Fae with lesser sentences can be housed in magical holdings. We're seeing positive proof that this was the right move, but time will tell."

She deflected a few objections and walked from the podium. Riordan couldn't help but smile at the way she handled herself.

"Aisling is really good at that," Sydney commented.

Riordan nodded. "She is."

There was a knock on the door, and Riordan moved toward it, weapon drawn, after having Sydney hide. He checked a side window and saw a large man, also with a weapon, scanning the area. Riordan immediately recognized him as the man Sydney was dating. He moved to the door and flung it open, weapon down at his side.

"You didn't even fucking check to see who it was!" he yelled and marched inside.

"Like hell I didn't. You realize you were standing within sight of that window right there, asshat." He pointed to the left of the man.

"Oh." He didn't apologize. Riordan was unsurprised. "Where's Sydney?"

"Hall closet," Riordan answered as the man moved to it, opened it, and welcomed Sydney into his arms.

While he got her settled, Riordan answered Brynach and Aisling both. His wife refused to go home and instead came to the safehouse. Their partner was doing the same. They were there within a few minutes of one another, both going to Sydney to comfort her.

Brynach got on the phone with Jashana and arranged an extra detail, much to her boyfriend's protest. "I don't give a flying neapan fart what you want, buddy. I'm going to protect my sister since you clearly can't."

Riordan stepped in front of the other man and put a solid hand on his chest. "Don't." One word. It was enough of a warning. Riordan shook his head, and the other man took a deep breath before stepping back.

When his phone rang, everyone went still. "Sean, whatcha got?"

"You won't like it," he said. "Put me on speaker."

With a click, Riordan gave him the go-ahead. "You're on."

"I checked local cameras and hacked the government streams around the house," Sean said in a nonchalant way. Sydney's detail noticeably stiffened in discomfort. "There was only one person I caught around the time of the disturbance. It wasn't on the property; they were next door, but I think they were testing the wards all the same."

"Who was it, Sean?" Brynach demanded.

"You know who it was," he answered softly.

Riordan cursed, and Brynach turned and punched a wall. Aisling moved to him, taking his hand and kissing his split knuckles. Now wasn't the time to tell him what he'd heard on the recording.

"Enough's enough," Brynach barked. "We find him. Now."

Sydney made an offhand comment. "We need to do a location spell. Who knows a witch?"

There were a few chuckles, but Riordan saw Aisling's eyes light up.

"Ash?"

She ran her hand through her hair. "I'm an idiot!"

"I was kidding," Sydney said.

"I'm not," Aisling answered. "I need to talk to Dawn."

She made for the door, and Brynach growled. "Walk out that door, and I'll leave marks on your ass that even Fae healing won't be able to handle."

CHAPTER 31

Aisling

S he spun on her husband. "Then come with me, but I'm leaving." Brynach followed after her.

"You're too rash," he complained.

Aisling sifted, dragging him along with her. As they exited on Main Street, they got a few stares. She ignored them and moved toward Terra Bella. The bells over the door chimed as she walked in.

"It's about time you came to visit, Aisling," Dawn said from behind the counter. She was wearing baby Eves on her chest in a sling and stilled when she saw Aisling's face. "The energy you're giving off is ... something. What's wrong?"

She moved toward her friend and mentor. "I need your help. I want to do a location spell, and I don't know enough to do it safely. Can I look at your books and raid your herbs?"

Dawn nodded. "Of course, but you don't need a book. I can show you. Turn my sign and lock the door, Brynach. Aisling, follow me."

The one-time earth witch moved into her back room and started pulling things from her shelf. A crystal pendulum, a sprig of dried rosemary, a laminated map of the town, and four candles.

"You need to lay out the map and light a candle at the north, south, east, and west locations. Then focus on who you're looking for, tune into their magic and signature, and start the pendulum swinging in clockwise circles. If you have something of theirs to strengthen the spell, you can tie it to the pendulum or anoint the candles with it," Dawn said as she laid everything out. "You can burn the rosemary while you do this."

"And that will work?" Brynach asked with obvious doubt in his voice.

The New Fae looked at him. "I know it's not the kind of magic you're used to, but that doesn't make it less powerful. This is how Aisling and I were trained. We are in tune with a magic that you never had to know. We adapted. We became powerful in our own right. You're a smart enough man to know there's more than one way toward a goal."

He nodded, appropriately scolded, and Aisling took his hand, so he knew she understood. She thanked Dawn, dropped a kiss on Eves' little head, and then gathered all the tools in a bag.

"Sorry we can't stay longer. Time is of the essence," Aisling explained.

Dawn waved her away. "Go."

Aisling walked out the door and turned to Brynach. "Have Riordan meet us at home. We don't need an audience, and I think I'm going to need quiet for this. I'd rather do it inside my own wards."

Her husband nodded and lifted his phone while Aisling sifted to their home. Truth be told, she was nervous about trying the spell. Not because she was afraid she couldn't do it, but because she was afraid it would locate Alex.

After her father, Alex's betrayal felt even worse, and poor Brynach was miserable over it. Her husbands joined her after a few minutes. She was setting a circle on the floor in front of her altar in the living room when they walked in.

"Ash, can we put a pause on that?" Riordan asked. He glanced between Aisling and Brynach and then around the room. He shook his head and then spoke. "I listened to the tape."

Aisling froze. If he had waited until they were alone to bring this up, it wasn't good. Beside her, Brynach was leaning forward, excited. She closed her eyes and cursed. This wasn't going to go well.

"I swear, if you don't start speaking, I'll put you over my knee," Brynach threatened.

"You should really look into the whole spanking thing, big guy," Riordan joked. "It's not good, but I think you need to know before we jump in and look for him."

He walked to the laptop and cued up a piece of the audio. "One last warning, this is about as bad as it gets."

"It's not like he's murdering people," Brynach said. "Just play it."

But Aisling saw Riordan's face while their husband was staring at the laptop. He'd flinched. He kept his eyes on her while he hit play, the sounds not really registering for Aisling. Brynach gasped, and Riordan closed his eyes. Only then did she focus on what Alex was saying.

Aisling's ears rang, and her vision narrowed. Riordan was there in a heartbeat, arms around her, easing her into a chair. Brynach was still staring at the laptop when she put her head between her knees and tried to regulate her breathing.

She'd heard wrong. She had to have heard wrong. But then the audio paused and restarted, and there was Alex all over again, claiming responsibility for the training ground attack. The attack had resulted in both her men getting shot. Brynach listened to it one more time while Aisling rubbed a hand over her chest and tried to ease the pain.

"Ash?" Riordan's voice sounded panicked. How many times had he called her name? She looked up at him, and his hand cupped the side of her face. "Okay. You sit right there. Don't move."

She didn't answer, and she didn't move. Her head was still spinning, and when her eyes lifted and found Brynach, the tears spilled over. He looked broken. She pushed up from the chair to go to him, and Riordan's arms wrapped around her stomach and tugged her back.

"Hey, I said don't move," Riordan scolded. He handed her a bottle of water. "Drink it."

"Bry," she started.

"Is on his feet and rightfully pissed off. Your pupils are blown out, and you're in shock and shaking. Sit. Down." Riordan wasn't going to take no for an answer.

Aisling lifted the bottle of water to her lips and drank, but her stomach turned, and she stopped. The last thing she needed to do was get sick. She kept her eyes on Brynach until he turned and saw her. He quickly moved to her side and knelt at her feet.

"A stoirin, are you okay?" He took her face in his hand and wiped at her tears.

"No," she whispered. "No, I'm not. You aren't either. None of us are. How could he do this? You and Riordan could have been killed. Maybe he didn't know you'd be there, or I'd be there, but he knew Riordan would be, and he still ..." She couldn't finish.

He cursed and took his hands away from her, balling them into fists at his side. "I'm going to kill him. If he were anyone else, I'd have stopped this bullshit sooner. I just couldn't believe he was actually involved. Not to this degree."

Brynach pulled Riordan closer. "I'm sorry. I put you both at risk by staying blind to his behavior and allowing you near him."

Riordan pulled his arm away. "Cut the crap. You didn't do anything, and I'm not going to let you think you did. At no point did you force us to interact with him. He had us all fooled. This isn't your fault."

"I put all those kids in danger," he groaned.

"Even if his motives for the school are fucked, the results haven't changed. It's still a safe place for the kids, Bry. It's still a good thing you did," Riordan assured him.

"We don't know how deep this goes. Who it spreads to. How do we move forward with the school? Who do we trust?" the Dark Fae wondered out loud.

"I recognize the other voice. It's Ellasar. So, we have some idea who not to trust, though we already figured out the Seelie are shit bags." Aisling put a hand on his arm. Aisling swallowed more water and then set it aside. She forced her voice to remain steady. "We have to find him."

She stood and moved to the circle she'd already constructed and sat. Aisling looked up at her partners. "I could use help."

Without question, they sat with her. She laid out the map, placed the candles, and asked for a bowl for burning the rosemary. Riordan hurried off and returned with one and a lighter from the kitchen. The smell of rosemary was pungent, and one she could have done without, but what was good for the spell was good for her.

"Visualize Alex in your mind's eye." Aisling closed her eyes and started the crystal swinging.

When she opened them, the crystal still moved clockwise, the tip swaying but not focused in any one spot. She willed it to pause, to stutter or sway. It didn't. Exasperated, she sighed and set it down.

"Maybe I can't do it." She slumped against Brynach's shoulder. "I couldn't do it before; I guess I can't do it now."

"Don't be silly. Of course, you can. Dawn said if we had something of his, we could anoint the candles or tie it to the pendulum," Brynach reminded her.

"I can't think of anything I have," she answered.

Brynach stood and moved to their closet, returning with a tie. "This was his. He loaned it to me forever ago, but it might work." He tore at the fabric and handed a strip to Aisling.

She wrapped it around the chain, and they refocused. There

was a good chance this wasn't working because, not so secretly, she didn't want to find Alex. When she did, Brynach would sift out to try and bring him in. Once they found him, he'd have to face his best friend's betrayal, and she knew how much that hurt.

"Ash," Riordan whispered. Her eyes opened, and she stifled a scream. Without realizing it, the crystal had settled down onto the map. The chain was limp between her hand, but the crystal stood straight up, quivering on its point.

"Holy shit," she gasped.

Brynach was staring so hard at the map she was surprised it didn't catch fire.

"Get Isaac and whoever else can be trusted. This isn't a friend we're going to try and find," Aisling said. "We're doing this legally. We meet at the precinct."

Brynach nodded. "We find him and bring him in no matter what it takes." Then he paled and tore at his hair. "Aindrea and Joeigh. We have to make sure they're cared for. There's no way she was involved."

Aisling promised, "We will. Nobody will abandon them."

Riordan picked up his phone and called Sean and gave him the location. He immediately got to work, looking at video surveillance. She listened to them call in the cavalry, and she picked up her phone to call Pilson. This wasn't a vigilante mission. When they found him, they had proof of his involvement in the attacks. He'd be held without question.

They both moved to the weapons locker. Aisling's knives still hadn't been returned to her after they'd been embedded in Walker. She paused behind Brynach and Riordan.

"You don't have to come, Aisling," Brynach offered.

She shook her head. "I do. We do this together."

Riordan tucked his knife into the holster and checked his gun. "You're not obligated to do shit. We've been through a lot, all of us. You can sit this out."

Aisling stood and tied her hair back, picking up a pair

of throwing knives that she'd be fine with. She strapped her holsters to her thighs and tucked them in. "I'm going, but we ward ourselves. We use body armor. I know we think we know him, but we clearly don't."

Brynach grumbled but eventually agreed. "We treat this the same as Walker. We don't get involved unless we have to. We're too close to it."

Immediately, Aisling felt better. She nodded, Riordan agreed, and they left for the precinct. The vibe was energetic, if not a little nervous. She reminded herself that this couldn't be worse than apprehending Walker. Alex may have fooled them all into thinking he was gentle, but he didn't get his own hands dirty. No, he simply hired others to do his dirty work. The thought still made Aisling sick, but at least they'd be safe on this particular trip.

She saw Fae officers armed with magicked cuffs, and most of the people there were wearing some kind of protective charms. Riordan split off to talk to Isaac, and Brynach moved to the chief to make sure they understood who they were dealing with.

"Aisling!"

The voice broke through the noise, and Aisling sighed. Of course Cathy had shown up. The woman had been drooling over a chance to see Aisling and her husbands in action. She wasn't going to even question how Cathy'd heard about it. She was waving a camera crew toward her, and Aisling walked to meet her.

"What do you think you're doing? This isn't some PR stunt," Aisling accused.

Cathy shook a hand at her. "Please. This is an easy grab, and you can't keep telling me no. We need this footage."

Aisling looked at the cameraman. "You know what you're signing up for?"

He looked at the armed police around him and nodded. "Not my first rodeo, darlin'."

Before she could yell at the guy, Cathy did it for her. "Talk to her like that again, and you won't have a job with us anymore."

"Yes, ma'am," he answered, but Aisling saw him roll his eyes.

The guys walked back over, and the cameraman had the grace to look intimidated as they each put an arm around her. "Cathy," Brynach greeted her. "To what do we owe the pleasure?"

"I'm cashing in on my live footage of the three of you in action." She had her hands on her hips, just daring him to argue.

Riordan clearly loved the idea as much as he loved a migraine, but he didn't say anything. Instead, he squeezed her and said, "We're ready to go. Everyone's been briefed. You ready, big guy?"

Brynach gave a quick look to the camera and then back to them. "Yeah. I'm ready, but we stay behind the first line. Understood?"

There was a shout, and then the first line of the police sifted to the location the spell identified. Brynach looked back at them. Aisling nodded. "Let's go."

She reached out and grabbed Cathy's arm while Riordan pulled the cameraman into the sift. Immediately, it was clear they'd misjudged the situation. The first wave of police were kicking down the door, and immediately, they were thrown back.

"What the fuck," the cameraman cursed while retching.

"Get that damn camera up!" Cathy yelled.

Aisling gathered magic to her and used wind to stop the fall of some of the officers. Beside her, Riordan and Brynach moved toward the building.

"We stay back!" Aisling cried out. Both men stilled and turned back to her. She was staring at the door, her magic still assisting the officers as they scurried back behind cover. "We don't go in!"

A second group of officers, those armed with magic, charged

the now-open door. From inside, there were shouts and clear sounds of a fight, but no firearms, which was something.

Her phone rang, and she hurried to answer. "Lettie?"

"Ash! Are you there? He's not alone!" Lettie screamed.

"What are you talking about?" Aisling put the phone on speaker.

"Sean said he's not alone. There's more than one person in that building." Lettie's voice was high and fast.

Aisling stared at the small Fae dwelling. "Yeah, I know, L. Our people are in there now."

"No! Before they got there. Alex isn't alone!"

Brynach's eyes went wide. "Aindrea!" He turned and charged for the house.

Riordan looked between Aisling and their husband for a second before turning and following him. "Fuck!" Aisling hung up and hurried after the guys. This was not a part of the damn plan, but if Aindrea and Joeigh were inside and in danger, she wasn't leaving them.

The house opened up to a large room that was scarily empty. Where the hell was everyone? The guys were at the back of the room, Riordan looking down a hallway and Brynach scanning the yard through a window.

"What the hell is going on?" Riordan asked and turned to her. His eyes went wide a second before Aisling felt the arm band around her and a knife plunged into her side. She screamed before she got a handle on the pain. Fuck, that hurt.

"Weapons down," Ellasar ordered.

She'd never liked this man, but how in the hell had he wound up working with Alex? No way their end goals were the same.

"I don't know about that. They're not that different. I don't want that whiny bitch and her pushover husband in power, and Alex was happy to help make sure they never are again." Ellasar answered something she hadn't realized she'd said out loud.

"Where is he?" Brynach asked.

Aisling flinched at his first words not being about protecting her, but then she straightened her spine. He trusted her to get out of this. She would. Although standing straighter with a knife in your side was probably a bad move. Aisling hissed through her teeth, and Riordan cursed.

Brynach growled low in his throat, and Riordan lost all color. Aisling was helpless to do anything but watch them process the situation. She couldn't drop her weight, couldn't twist and escape his grip, not with the knife lodged between her lowest ribs. There was no telling how long the blade was, but it sure as shit felt long enough. Adrenaline kept her on her feet, eyes trained on her husbands.

Ellasar was stiff at her back; his free arm went around her neck. "Nobody comes back from a broken neck. Don't move."

She kept her eyes on Riordan, mouthing an apology. He shook his head. Aisling hated that he was seeing her hurt again. "I'm not moving. They're not moving. We just need to know where Alex is, and we need to communicate out there to not come in. Okay? They don't know you're here. You can get out of here, still."

He laughed. "Oh, child, I'm not going anywhere. Not until I've purged this world of some filth. Alex is in the other room with the officers who ran inside. They were dead; he may not be yet. He served his purpose. I had no use for him anymore."

Brynach cursed and shifted.

"Uh uh." Ellasar drove the blade up, and she screamed. "Stay where you are. He lives or dies by the grace of the Goddess. Now, be a good boy, and call out there to stand down."

Her husband closed his eyes and opened his mouth. "Stay where you are! Nobody else come in."

"Ellasar, you slimy bastard, you let them go!"

Aisling's eyes went wide in disbelief. Nevan was here.

The man holding her didn't bother turning his head when he yelled out, which meant he shouted into her ear. "I knew you were a rat, Nevan. Like always, you're too late to do anything about it. I've got your bitch of a daughter, and I won't hesitate to slit her throat. You know I won't."

What the hell was he thinking? Ellasar hated him. No way was he going to make things any better by opening his mouth. One thing was certain, they were on their own in here. The issue now became how to get out of it. Aisling looked at Riordan and saw the sweat beading on his forehead. He was hyperventilating. His eyes were hyper-focused on the knife in her side, the blood she could feel wetting her leg. Aisling could handle this. This wasn't the end. Aisling could talk him down; she knew she could.

"How do you see this playing out, Ellie?" she asked.

His hand jerked the blade. The scream that ripped from her throat was unstoppable. Fuck, that hurt. Brynach growled and clenched his fists. Okay, not the best idea to mock the man. Noted.

"You have to know this isn't going to end with you in power," Aisling pointed out.

Behind her, Ellasar hummed. Okay. She could put this together. "And the way the King and Queen fight. You've been slowly working your way into Branwyn's head ... and bed."

Another chuckle from behind her. What the fuck was she supposed to do now? The man was clearly unhinged.

Brynach decided for her. "Ellasar, you didn't do all this to not enjoy the payoff. Don't be stupid. You don't make it out of here alive, or with your magic, if you don't let her go. You don't want to do this. Think before you do something you can't come back from."

Riordan swayed and fell back into the wall. He was clearly terrified and about to pass out. That poor guy really hated blood. They had to figure something out quickly. She was focused on him and almost missed Brynach shifting. It was slight, but she saw as his hand slid behind him, and Aisling immediately knew what he'd done.

"Riordan, babe. Look at me." She called for his attention. "Picture yourself in the cool water behind the house. Breathe and think of the water."

Aisling widened her eyes and ignored the white-hot pain in her side. Brynach took a step forward, and Ellasar yanked her back. She wanted to yell at him to stop, but the closer he got to her, the more he blocked what was behind him.

"Listen to her, a chuisle." Brynach stilled, hands up when Ellasar tightened around her neck.

Slowly, she saw him take a deep breath, and she winced when she tried to mirror it. He looked at her, and she nodded. "Think of calming things. Running water, the sound of it, the feel of it."

"Oh, shut up!" Ellasar growled.

She saw when Riordan understood. Brynach looked at her, and she took as deep a breath as she could before closing her eyes and opening them slowly. It was as good as a nod. This was going to fucking suck. Aisling forced herself to not tense up, it would only make it worse.

While Ellasar was distracted by Brynach moving for his weapon, Riordan pulled on the water Brynach had turned on and directed it at the older Fae. With both his hands occupied and his focus on Brynach, Riordan was able to circle his head with the sphere. On instinct, he grabbed for his face instead of using his magic.

Which meant he wrenched the knife up into Aisling's side. She pulled away with a strangled scream. Then, everything moved in slow motion. Brynach pulled his gun free and took aim at Ellasar. There was the violently loud crack of a bullet ripping through the space. But there was something else, too. Ellasar was staring at the hole in his chest, teeth bared and snarling through a ball of water. The combination might kill him, but not before he fought back. Even now, Aisling could feel him pulling on magic.

But Ellasar was too busy to notice what Aisling had seen. Behind him, through the window, a large vine prepared to launch through the glass. Before Brynach could fire again, glass shattered, and the large vine broke through. Aisling stared, slack-jawed, with a hand over the wound on her side, as she looked up at Ellasar. Riordan gagged from the other side of the room, and the water sloshed to the floor. She didn't blame him. The vine that had broken through the glass was wrapped around the Fae's neck, and tendrils climbed up and through his eye sockets. Ellasar was seizing as another thin vine slid down his throat and out through the front of his neck.

There was the distinct sound of gurgling blood as he drew his last breaths, and then he went limp. The vines that had caused his demise were all that kept him upright. The sight was grotesque. The magicked plant withdrew, and she heard shouts from outside. What the hell was that? When Aisling closed her eyes, the image of the Seelie's brain leaking out through his eyes remained.

CHAPTER 32

Brynach

B rynach!" Riordan's voice called his attention away from the hallway he was staring down. He wanted to go to Alex, make sure he was alive, if only so he could kill him himself. When he turned and saw Aisling slumped on the ground, his world tilted, and he ran to her.

He knelt next to Aisling. "A stoirin, are you okay?"

"Nope," she groaned. "Most definitely not."

"She's bleeding, a lot!" Riordan was panicking.

"She's going to be okay, but we need to get her to a medic." Brynach decided as police stormed the building. Aisling closed her eyes, her features pinched.

His hands went to Aisling's side, lifting her shirt. He ground his teeth hard when he saw the wound. Blood still flowed from the jagged cut and into the pool of blood under her. "Hospital. Unseelie court."

He sifted and trusted that Riordan would follow him. Brynach was already through the gate, Aisling moaning in his arms. When he kicked the door open, eyes shifted to him, and when they saw the blood dripping from his wife, they hurried over. He placed her gently on a bed and knelt at her side.

"What happened!" Corinna cried out.

Riordan moved to Aisling's head and stroked her hair back. Brynach didn't miss how pale his partner looked. "Hey, no fainting. I'm serious. I can't have you both down and out."

"I'll do my best, big guy. No promises." He shook his head and didn't look away from Aisling.

"Knife wound to the side," Brynach told the doctor when he ran over with the nurse. "Fuck!" His scream echoed in the small room, and Aisling started to cry.

"Hey, knock it off. Come on. You need to clean up. She's in good hands." Riordan took his hand. "I can't stand seeing her blood on you. Please."

Brynach nodded, and Riordan brought him to a sink. He stood still while his partner cleaned him with wet paper towels. "How did we get here, again? How could I let her get hurt, again?"

"You didn't let anything happen, Bry. Something happened. It's not like it needed your permission. It was fucked up, and I hate it just as much as you do, but it's not your fault." Riordan cleaned his fingernails.

"I keep letting you down. I have one fucking job. Keep the people I love safe. And I can't do it." Brynach hung his head.

Riordan went still in front of him long enough that Brynach lifted his head. He expected anger, resentment, and disappointment. What he hadn't expected were tears. When his partner turned from him and walked out the door, Brynach was left confused.

"You're really fucking it up," Corinna commented.

"Thanks. That helps," Brynach muttered.

She shrugged. "The way you view yourself isn't how they view you, idiot. That man loves you. He was trying to care for you, and do you know what you did?"

"Enlighten me." Brynach had zero expectation of her actually knowing what she was talking about. The woman had as much life experience as he did in his pinky.

"You just told him that he was failing at loving you."

He shook his head. "Like hell I did. I've never been more loved."

The look Corinna gave him made it clear she thought he was clueless. "By telling him your only job is to protect them, you're telling him he hasn't loved you well enough to prove to you that you're so much more than that. That he hasn't loved you enough that you understand what you can do for them isn't why they love you."

Brynach stilled. Is that what he'd done?

"The way you view yourself, your hang-ups, they're hurting the people who love you." She lifted a shoulder. "But what do I know?"

Brynach turned and walked out the door. It wasn't hard to find Riordan. He hadn't gone far. He was slumped on the floor against the wall, head in his hands. Brynach lowered himself next to him.

"I'm sorry." Brynach didn't know if he should try to hold Riordan. He kept his hands in his lap. "Me being hard on myself isn't a reflection of how I think you view me."

"Isn't it?" Riordan asked. "Over and over, we've tried to show you how nuanced you are, and still you say shit like that."

It was obvious how hurt his husband was. How had he missed the way he was making them feel? Now he did take Riordan in his arms.

"I'll do better, I promise. It's just taking longer to let myself believe who you see is who I really am." Brynach buried his face in the other man's hair. "Are we okay?"

Riordan shook his head. "No, but we can talk about this later. Let's go make sure our girl is okay."

That was as good as he was going to get right now, and probably all he deserved. Riordan stood and offered him a hand. Brynach took it and held onto it as they walked back into the hospital ward.

"Misters Campbell," the doctor addressed them, and Riordan chuckled. "Your wife has internal damage but was lucky.

The knife missed most organs, only nicking her lung and liver. Nothing she shouldn't be able to heal."

"Great, more work for me," Aisling joked. That woman was a fucking goddess. The way she'd handled herself was nothing short of amazing. Which was good, because he'd absolutely froze.

Riordan wavered a little on his feet.

"Hey, it's not so bad. Has anyone checked on Alex?" Aisling asked, quickly changing the subject to give Riordan something else to focus on.

Brynach was embarrassed to realize he hadn't even thought about the tense situation they'd left. Now, both he and Riordan dug for their phones. There were texts and a voicemail on his phone, and he had no idea how he hadn't felt it vibrate in his pocket. Riordan scrolled through much of the same.

"He's alive and in custody," Riordan confirmed.

"Good." Aisling closed her eyes and took a deep breath. "That's real good."

"Um, that's not all, though," Brynach said, but Aisling was breathing heavy. "We'll tell her later."

Riordan looked at their wife and then nodded.

By the time they'd sifted home, they were all itching from the dried blood on their bodies. They wearily went to shower, all without speaking. When he'd finished washing himself, too afraid of Aisling's wounds to even touch her, he grabbed a towel and walked away. He heard them call out for him and ignored them.

He was no good for them right now. He needed to snap the fuck out of it. But today he'd let his partner do his dirty work because he couldn't face his best friend being shady. He'd watched his wife get hurt, again, and did nothing to stop it. Once more, he'd somehow managed to let everyone down and render himself useless. What was he supposed to do with that? How could he look at them right now?

Aisling needed rest. Riordan needed some mental and physical reassurance that she was okay. They'd go up to bed and cuddle, and when they were done napping, they'd feel better, and he'd have had time to think through his bullshit. That's what needed to happen. It didn't matter that they didn't blame him, he couldn't stop blaming himself. He just wouldn't show them anymore.

The water turned off and he heard his wife whisper. "I should go talk to him."

"Let me." Riordan was going to take this one for the team, he guessed. Fuck. He didn't want to do this. But he knew he couldn't refuse to talk to them without hurting them more. Why couldn't they, just for right now, love him less?

"You know we love you, Bry. Neither of us are okay with you beating yourself up. Today was hard on everyone, for a lot of different reasons, but everyone we love is okay. It wasn't a bad day," Riordan told him.

Brynach cursed. "Just because neither of you died doesn't make today a win, damn it. Neither of you should have been in harm's way to begin with. You had to watch her get hurt all over again."

"We're not asking you to fix everything. That's not why we love you," Riordan argued.

Brynach was opening his mouth when Riordan shook his head. "No. You shut up for a minute and listen because nobody has the energy to keep saying this to you. You have a massive heart, and we love that, but our safety and happiness are not your responsibility. By taking that on, you are sending the message that we're incapable of providing that for ourselves. We are, all of us, complete people. I get that you have trauma responses that confuse your usefulness with your worth, but you need to work that shit out. That's too much pressure to put on us."

He heard Aisling approach and braced for her reprimand.

Aisling came up the steps. She ran her nails down his arm until she reached his hand. She took it and brought it to her still-bare breast. "Feel that?"

Brynach fought to not curl his fingers over her warm flesh. He wanted to punish her for putting herself in danger, as if it was her fault. He didn't trust himself to be touching her right now. Aisling forced his eyes to hers.

"I'm here. I'm fine. Riordan is fine. And Bry, you're fine, too. Today sucked, but we're home, together. Right now, things are okay."

"I could have lost you," Brynach whispered.

"You didn't." Aisling kissed his jaw. "I'm right here."

Riordan softened his voice. "You're gentle and honest. You're kind and caring. You would do anything to keep us happy and smiling, and you care for us in all the ways we need."

Aisling took his face in her hands. "It's time to let that go and figure out who you are for yourself. What you want, not what you think you should be."

Brynach tried to keep his voice from breaking. "What if I don't know?"

"Then we'll help you figure it out," Riordan promised. He looked at Aisling, and she nodded. "But for right now, why don't you take care of us?"

The other man's voice had dipped, deepening with a lust Brynach was becoming addicted to. He looked at his wife and didn't miss the way she bit her lip or pressed her legs together. Brynach tugged her lip from between her teeth and ran his thumb over the wetness she'd left behind.

"You're hurt." The words were weak.

Aisling showed him her side, the wound already pink and healing. "I'm okay, Brynach. Take care of us. Not because it's all you're good for, but because we need you."

He knew he could make it good for them. Knew it would help him turn his own racing thoughts off to focus on them and them alone. They need the connection.

"Get your ass on the bed, Princess," Brynach ordered with a bark.

Aisling scrambled next to Riordan with a giggle. Brynach reached out and wrapped a hand around Riordan's ankle before pulling him to the edge of the bed.

"Ride his face, a stoirin. Let's see how long he can hold his breath." Brynach instructed, and Aisling scurried into position after grabbing Riordan a pillow.

Riordan wrapped his arms around her hips and pulled her down onto his face with a moan. Brynach met her heavy-lidded gaze and kissed her hard. She whined into his mouth as Riordan licked at her. When the kiss broke, Brynach leaned down and kissed Riordan's stomach.

His hand traveled the man's chest, tweaking his nipples before making their way to his cock. He stroked him a few times while he watched Riordan's tongue disappear between Aisling's folds. Their husband moaned her name, and she closed her eyes, head thrown back.

"Fuck," Aisling cried out as Riordan made unabashedly loud noises, devouring her.

Brynach winked at her before sliding to his knees and taking Riordan in his mouth. Aisling raised herself long enough for him to drag in a desperate breath and moan their names. Brynach was about to scold her, tell her to sit the fuck back down, but she moved on her own. He hummed his approval around Riordan's length.

Watching the two of them was enough to make him thrust against the edge of the bed like a horny teenager.

"So close," Aisling moaned as she ground herself down on Riordan's tongue. She slid across him, allowing him to breathe every so often. Brynach may have had Riordan's cock in his mouth, but his eyes were locked on Aisling.

"Don't let him breathe until you finish, Princess." Brynach rededicated himself to Riordan's cock after issuing his order.

Aisling leaned forward, gripped Brynach's hair, and pushed

down on his head. She used him to rock on Riordan's face. Fuck if it wasn't one of the hottest things he'd ever experienced. Brynach relaxed his throat, taking Riordan deep like his girl wanted him to. He reached down and stroked himself as Aisling moaned.

"You look so sexy swallowing his cock. Yes, like that, Riordan!" Aisling cried as she fell apart. When she came down, she let go of her grip on Brynach's hair, and he pulled off Riordan's cock. He gathered Aisling to him, and Riordan took a shaky breath.

"Damn. That was—" Riordan began.

"Just the beginning," Brynach finished when he released Aisling from their kiss.

He laid Aisling out and took a breast in his mouth. She arched into him and accepted Riordan's kiss when his mouth lowered to hers.

"Someone, fill me," she begged and rolled her hips.

"I've got you, Ash," Riordan promised and nudged her legs. He splayed her open, dragging his cock through her wetness until she was whimpering.

"Riordan," Brynach met his eyes. "You both finish before I do, and I really want to finish."

He moved to the bottom of the bed, behind Riordan, while he stroked into Aisling's sweet pussy. Brynach stroked the other man's back and ass. He squeezed and then delivered a few well-timed slaps, reddening his cheeks. Riordan cursed and drove into their wife.

"Bry, I need you," Aisling's voice was a siren song calling him up on the bed. He pulled pillows up under her, lifting her head.

When her mouth fell open and she turned those hazel eyes on him, Brynach nearly lost it. He dipped his fingers into her mouth and slid them over her tongue. Her eyes never wavered. "If it becomes too much, three taps on my thigh."

She nodded. "I understand."

If Aisling didn't want to be treated like she was breakable, she'd get it rough. The need to drive into her mouth rode him hard. She stuck her tongue out and he purred.

"Good girl. Now keep that mouth nice and wet while I fuck it," Brynach instructed.

Riordan moaned as Brynach's length slid into their wife's mouth. He couldn't get as deep as he wanted to with her mouth like this, but he couldn't bend her back over the bed, not when it would pull at her side. For now, stroking against her warm, wet tongue, was all he needed to ground him.

He reached over and stroked her clit, making her moan around his cock. Riordan cursed. "She's squeezing me."

"That's because she's a needy slut for us, husband." Brynach kept the bass in his voice as he talked to them. "You fuck that pussy hard while I take her mouth. Let's show her just how strong she really is."

Riordan drove into her, the sound of his body slapping against hers almost as loud as his moan. Their wife had turned her head and swallowed down another inch of him.

"Fuck, beautiful. You're so good for us. Never going to stop fucking you. We'll never stop wanting you like this," Brynach praised her.

She quaked as she came, her throat constricting on a scream as Riordan fucked her through the aftershocks. They weren't done yet. Not by a longshot.

"Come here." His command was for Riordan, who pulled out of Aisling and moved toward Brynach. He nodded his head, and Riordan stood on the bed next to him. "Need to taste her on you."

He leaned forward, tasting the rich flavor of Aisling on his husband's cock. He felt himself twitch in Aisling's mouth as she sucked him hard. Riordan groaned, and Brynach came up off his sensitive cock. His hand went to Aisling's hollowed-out cheek and stroked it before giving it a light slap. Her eyes rolled back in her head, and Brynach's hand moved to her clit.

He wanted one more, just one, before he finished.

She was slick with come and her own arousal and primed to burst. Riordan winked at him and slid down her body, his tongue sliding against her core and down to her ass. Brynach cursed, Aisling's body jumped off the mattress, forcing Riordan to pin her down.

She never stopped working Brynach over, though. Her tongue played with him, her fingers pressing on that sensitive area between his balls and ass until her finger was toying there. Fuck. He wasn't going to last.

When his orgasm hit, his whole body went rigid, and Aisling drank him down like he knew she would. He pulled out of her abused mouth and gazed into her eyes as she finished, and her body went limp.

W hy do people hate us?" Riordan grumbled as the third bang on their front door sounded.

"I'm not getting up." Aisling shoved her head under a pillow.

Brynach fumbled for a pair of shorts. "I'm coming!" he screamed down below. "We are going away soon. Somewhere nobody can find us." The combined affirmatives from the bed made him smile as he jogged downstairs.

Breena stood outside, alone. He stepped out and closed the door behind him. "Breena?" He looked her over.

She gave him a slow smile. "I went to see him."

"Him?" Brynach asked, though he had a sinking feeling he understood exactly who she meant. But she wasn't bloody or carrying a weapon. "How'd you find out?"

His twin glared at him. "You really think you're the only one with connections? You think I don't care enough about the people you love to make sure they're safe. That Aisling's mother wasn't on Jashana's rounds?"

Brynach shook his head. "I didn't know."

"I'm hurt. How could you hide him from me, Brynach?" Breena asked.

"I was afraid of what you'd do. You hate him so much, and you're human, and he's still ... him," Brynach admitted. "And I also felt weak for not wanting him dead."

"I didn't kill him. The saggy ball sac is human. Let him wither and die. He can live out the rest of his life knowing he's fragile. That's worse than anything I can do to him." Breena shrugged.

Brynach stared at his sister. "Fuck. You really have grown."

His twin gave him a sad smile and took a deep breath. "I'm leaving. Not for a vacation. I'm just ... going."

"What do you mean?" He moved to her, but she shook her head.

"I can't be who anyone wants me to be. I'm not sure who I am as a human yet, but I know I don't have forever to figure it out. I want to travel. I want to make the most of this one life I have. I can't stay here and be reminded of all I lost, of who I used to be." Breena's chin wobbled, and Brynach took her in his arms.

"Breena," he said, kissing her head.

"I know, but it has to be this way." She pushed back. "I'll never figure out who I am in the shadow of who I was. You have your life, and I need to have mine. I won't be alone." She blushed. "Jashana is coming with me. So, you know, I'll be safe."

"And loved." Brynach smiled at his sister.

Breena nodded. "Maybe I'll come back one day all grey and hunched to say goodbye."

Pain lanced through him, and air failed to fill his lungs. The idea of his sister dying, of not being near her, hurt so much. He tried not to let it show. She needed this, and he had to let go.

His sister nodded. "I know, brother. I wish things had worked out differently. I'd have happily spent a lifetime fighting by your side and ruining my lovers for others," she laughed.

"But this is where I am, and I'm trying to make the most of it."

Brynach gave her a sad smile. "For the record, I hate it."

Breena pulled something out of her pocket. "Jashana forced this on me. So, at least we can stay in touch. The wonders of technology with no Veil."

It was a small concession, but he stored her new number. "When do you leave?"

"Now. It won't get any easier the longer I wait." She shuffled her feet. "I love you, you know that, right?"

Brynach shook his head. "Don't be ridiculous. Of course, I do. Look, I know I was overbearing, Breena. It's just that—" How could he put it into words? "You were my safe place. I couldn't lose you. You were all I had."

"But I'm not anymore. They love you, Bry, and you are deserving of that. Stop fighting so damn hard." Breena hugged him.

"It took becoming human to become wise?" Brynach laughed.

"Nah." Breena stepped away from him. "Always was, just couldn't let anyone know. We don't have to be those tough kids anymore."

She looked up at the house. "You'll say goodbye to them for me? I can't handle any more of these." She gestured between the two of them.

Brynach nodded and fought the urge to gather her in his arms again. "Want me to sift you back to her?"

Breena waved him off. "I could use the walk. It's really fucking annoying that calories don't burn themselves anymore. Never forget the privilege of Fae metabolism, brother."

She laughed and turned away. Brynach waited until she was out of sight, but she never looked back.

Good for her.

CHAPTER 33

Aisling

Dinner was nothing like their quiet nights in their cozy cabin home. The Moore household never was, and Aisling loved it. Lettie had her arm around Sean's waist, and her hand in Aisling's as they watched Mr. Moore and Brynach chatting by the grill. Riordan was engaged in a cutthroat game of chess with the twins, who played as one.

Cait and Kareem were cozied up on the sofa while the other kids ran around. Aisling had just gotten free of Gracie's death grip of a hug. Mrs. Moore wiped away her tears long enough to get back to her kitchen.

"I'm going to steal Lettie for a bit," Aisling told Sean and pulled her to the front porch. She sat on the porch swing, and Lettie cozied up to her side.

"What's up?" her best friend asked.

Aisling nodded. "You still want your magic gone, right?"

Lettie met Aisling's gaze. "The people I love are human, present company excluded, and I want to feel like myself again."

"I can do it now if you're ready," Aisling offered.

"I am!" Lettie's genuine joy made Aisling smile. "Will it hurt?"

"Nope," she reassured her friend. "But it may feel a little strange. You trust me?"

"Duh." Lettie rolled her eyes. "Okay. Do it."

Aisling took her hands even though it wasn't necessary. She closed her eyes and felt for the threads of magic within her friend. It was there, thrumming inside her, woven into parts of Lettie that worried her. Aisling always pictured her magic in her core, her heart and soul, but Lettie's resided in her brain. Maybe this wasn't such a great idea.

"Um, Ash? I don't feel anything," Lettie commented.

"Yeah, L. Just getting the lay of the land. It's very ... brain-centric. I want to make sure I don't yank your synapses." Aisling joked.

"Not comforting," Lettie said, her hand tightening on Aisling's.

"I wouldn't be doing it if I didn't think I could. Just let me know if it doesn't feel right."

"How the hell should I know if it feels right?" Lettie cried. "Fuck it. Just do it. We won't have much time before someone comes bursting out here, and I'd like you focused for this."

Aisling closed her eyes and re-centered herself. She found the first thread and pulled, bringing the magic into herself. Lettie didn't cry out, so that was a start. Slowly, Aisling continued her work, tugging one thread at a time instead of gathering it in one fell swoop.

The magic felt wrong inside her, but Aisling managed not to squirm as she looked through Lettie. The signature was strange, the soot black of Peggy and some of Sydney's unique green hue. There were other threads, maybe her brothers, but they all wove individually through Lettie's mind. Connected in ways that Aisling had to unknot and gently remove.

Inside, someone called Lettie's name, and she stirred. "We doing okay, Ash?"

"Mhmm. Just a little more."

Lettie took a deep breath, and Aisling did another check. She was confident she had it all stored in her. She didn't want to release any of it, scared it would target Lettie without focused direction.

She opened her eyes and saw Lettie crying.

"It's okay, L. Good as new," Aisling promised, and brushed away her friend's tears.

"Really?" The hopeful lilt in her voice was clear.

"Really." Aisling hugged her and stood. She moved down the steps, eager to be rid of this magic. She stopped by the driveway, sinking her hands into the dirt by a bush Mrs. Moore always complained about. Good thing she didn't like it, because as Aisling let the magic go, she could feel the roots wither. It wouldn't live long.

"Are you okay?" Lettie asked.

"Yup." Aisling smiled. "How do you feel?"

Lettie thought for a moment. "Not any different, really." They turned when Mrs. Moore called everyone to the table. "Thank goodness, I'm hungry!"

Aisling shouldn't have been surprised at how easily Riordan and Brynach fit in amongst the Moores. The kids looked a little star-struck, and even Mr. Moore looked taken with Brynach. It made Aisling proud. The ribs and chicken were passed. The potato salad and coleslaw made their rounds. Everyone tucked into their food, and Riordan groaned his approval upon the first bite of cornbread.

Mrs. Moore beamed, and Aisling laughed. "Good, huh?"

"Otherworldly," Riordan exclaimed.

Conversation started up and eventually circled to Aisling.

"Sweetie, I thought you were supposed to be gone right now. Isn't there a big drop tomorrow? I was surprised when Lettie said you could come today." Mrs. Moore observed. "I don't mean to talk business at the table, but is everything okay?"

Was it? Aisling wasn't so sure. The idea of being away from Brynach and Riordan had sent her into a tailspin. Recent events had triggered her anxiety, and it was worse than ever.

Her mother had assured her it was totally normal. Still, Aisling was glad that Prudence had stepped into the spotlight.

The actress had accepted invitations to other drops, promoting her movie while working to drop smaller sections of the Veil. Aisling had taken a leave of absence.

"We're taking a vacation," Brynach answered when she didn't. "My bride and husband deserve a honeymoon."

Mrs. Moore blushed and put a hand over her heart. "How romantic. Do you know where you're going?"

Aisling answered, "Ireland and a stop in Scotland. I figure it's about time I see my home there."

Lettie choked back a small sob. "That's perfect. You'll Facetime, right? I want to see it."

"Of course," Aisling promised.

"Gotta show these two my old home." Riordan was beyond excited to share with them the country he loved. Liam had been excited to learn about their visit.

"It's nice to know that Aisling is being taken care of. One less kid to worry about." Mr. Moore winked at her.

Dinner conversation turned to other topics, which was good because Aisling was near tears. Mr. Moore had always felt like a father to her, and his words meant a lot. She was pretty sure the guys earned extra brownie points when they sent the kids outside to play and cleared the table.

Mrs. Moore took her to the side. "They're amazing, sweetie."

"I'm very lucky," Aisling confirmed.

With a conspiratorial smile, Mrs. Moore said, "More power to any woman who can handle two men. But it's not luck, sweetie. You fought for this happiness."

Aisling blinked away tears and let Mrs. Moore hug her. Brynach walked up to her and dropped a kiss on her head. "All cleaned up, Mrs. Moore. If it's not too forward of me, I thought I smelled dessert."

Her husband was really putting on the charm. Mrs. Moore blushed and grabbed his arm, letting him walk her back to the kitchen.

"As if you need to be sweeter," she teased. "I made my famous brownie cake and a lemon blueberry poundcake."

"One slice of each, please." Brynach grinned back at Aisling.

They were sitting outside on the porch with their plates, watching the kids run around, when Lettie spoke.

"Aisling took away my visions," Lettie told her parents.

"We know, darling. It's wonderful of her to make sure you are warded and safe," Mrs. Moore said, reaching over and squeezing Aisling's hand.

"No, Ma. She took them away entirely. I was stripped of the magic," Lettie clarified.

The Moores looked between Aisling and Lettie, and the surprise on their faces was clear.

"Charlotte, dear, what are you saying?" Mr. Moore asked.

"I'm saying that the magic that lingered in me was just like any other. Ash stripped it away like she does with the Veil." Lettie smiled.

Mrs. Moore had tears in her eyes as she stood and pulled her daughter into her arms and rocked her.

Aisling smiled. "I'm sorry it took me so long, but I had to be sure I could do it without hurting her."

It was Mr. Moore who reached her first and lifted Aisling into a bear hug. His wife followed suit. Then they were back crying over Lettie. Riordan moved to Aisling's side and held her close.

"You did good," he whispered.

"Mr. and Mrs. Moore, thank you for the warm welcome and the delicious dinner. We promise to repay the kindness as soon as we return from our trip. I should really get these two moving, though. We have another stop to make before we can start packing." Brynach was smooth, she'd give him that.

After another round of hugs, they were piling into Brynach's truck. They drove the familiar streets to Aisling's childhood home. The woods surrounding it had become home to a troop of sprites. Her mom loved the help they were giving the garden and said the wisps made the backyard glow.

"You might want to warn Riordan that there are some alates here who want to speak to him," Rin cautioned.

"I think Vola already has," Aisling answered when she noticed Riordan nervously playing with the rings on his necklace.

"Riordan?" She took his hand as they pulled into the driveway.

"You two head in. I should do this alone," he answered.

"Do what alone?" Brynach looked confused. Aisling kissed Riordan and pulled Brynach inside by the hand.

"Mom," Aisling called out.

"In here," came her mother's response from the family room. When she saw Brynach, her eyes lit. "Are those brownies from Mrs. Moore?"

The large Fae laughed and handed her the plate. She peeled back the foil and sighed. "This almost makes up for the fact that you're taking my baby away from me for weeks."

Brynach laughed, "You know, honeymoons are a pretty common thing. We won't be gone forever."

"Where's Riordan?" her mother asked around a bite of brownie, effectively ignoring Brynach's rational response.

"Outside. There are alates that wanted to talk to him," Aisling answered.

Brynach shot her an angry glare before turning to the door. "Can't believe you left him out there alone!"

Her mother patted the sofa next to her. Aisling tucked her head into her mom's shoulder. "I've been wondering lately. Do you think I'm making a mistake not talking to Nevan?"

"Sweetie, we make the best decisions we can with the information and feelings we have in the moment. Sometimes we fuck up, and other times we surprise ourselves and get it right. There's no handbook, but you've made it work so far," her mother said. "You have an eternity to decide how you feel about him. But for the record, no, I don't think you're wrong. I think anyone in your life has to earn the right to be there. He hasn't."

An eternity was a long time. Maybe one day she'd have the answers, but for right now, she leaned into the uncertainty. Brynach came back inside, a red-cheeked Riordan in tow. They sat in chairs to the sides of the sofa.

"I'm jealous. I can't remember the last time I took a vacation," her mother said.

"Honeymoon," Aisling corrected.

"Or one of those." She smiled at the guys. "But I'm glad you'll be getting away. It's time for the new world to figure out how it works without my girl leading the charge."

Aisling agreed.

"Seems like Sydney can fill a role or two," her mother commented.

Brynach grinned. "It'll be nice to have her around, especially now that Breena is off exploring." He'd already video-chatted with his sister, or he'd likely be a lot more sensitive about the topic.

Mrs. Quinn agreed, "Her job with the police department and moving into the loft at Terra Bella will be good for her."

Her husbands looked at her mother. It was Brynach who spoke. "Speaking of moves. We can't keep Gabriel here anymore. We're letting him go. Today. Now."

Her mother nodded. "I won't be sorry to see him go. I'll reinforce the wards so he can't get back in as soon as he leaves."

Mrs. Quinn nodded. "Peggy's trial starts soon. You're okay leaving during it?"

Riordan shrugged. "If that bitch can join virtually, I can, too. My testimony is on record, and she's not getting off this time. I refuse to let her steal another moment of my peace."

"I'm proud of you," her mother said. "I know it's not easy to let go of the desire for revenge. You deserve to go enjoy yourself."

"You'll be alone," Aisling worried.

"Dawn has Loren checking in on me while he's on patrol. And it's not your job to worry about me. I'll be just fine." She kissed Aisling's cheek.

Aisling frowned. "And Patrick, he's really just, gone?"

Mrs. Quinn nodded. "I know it seemed sudden to you, but it was a long time coming. I'm a bit proud you never saw the cracks, to be honest. It didn't hurt nearly as much as it should have. All those trips he took got me used to him being gone. Somewhere along the way, I just stopped feeling for him the way I used to. I think a large part of me staying with him was so you'd have a father figure."

"I never needed anyone but you." Aisling hugged her mother tightly. "I love you."

"Love you too, kiddo." She wiped at her face. "Now, out, all of you. I have brownies to finish, and you have bags to pack."

She stood and hugged and kissed the three of them, making them promise to call often, before ushering them out the door. They made their way around the side of the house. Aisling stopped Brynach before he opened her mom's office door.

"You don't have to go in there. We can do this if you can't," she told him.

"No. I need this closure. Come on." He pushed inside.

Gabriel rose to his feet quickly. "Brynach."

"Sit down. I'm going to talk. You're going to listen." Brynach pointed at the chair, and Gabriel sat. "I don't for a second believe you have the capability of being a good person. I'm telling you right now, you had better do your best to be a decent one, though. You get this one chance. If you step out of line, if I have even a suspicion that you're going back to your old ways, I'll end you myself. Do you understand?"

His father nodded. Aisling couldn't help but notice how gaunt he was. His hair had lost its shine, his muscles suddenly not as intimidating as they'd once seemed. If he tried to go back to his old ways, someone would end him. Brynach would never have to worry about carrying out his threat, and they all knew it. Most of all, she could see Gabriel knew it, too.

"I just want to stay alive. I'm not courting trouble," he promised.

Brynach nodded. "We're letting you go. I don't want to see you again. Don't come back here, and don't show up on my radar."

"I won't. You'll never see me again, I swear it." Gabriel hurried to his feet, and it looked for a moment like he was going to approach Brynach.

Aisling walked over to him and put an arm around his hips in silent support. Riordan walked to his other side and slid his hand in Brynach's back pocket. Damn it, that was cute. Gabriel, wisely, stilled his trajectory. Brynach shifted them, giving his father access to the door.

"Goodbye, Gabriel," he said as the other man walked away.

As soon as he was out of sight, the tension left his body, and he gathered the two of them into his arms. They held him until he stopped shaking.

CHAPTER 34

Riordan

Once they were inside their home, Riordan knew he couldn't put off talking to his partners. He'd managed to finish up his conversation with the sprites before Brynach had stormed out with fire in his eyes.

"Are you going to tell us what they said?" she asked.

Riordan nodded. "Yeah, it's something we should talk about."

He sat down and took a deep breath. "Bry, if you had to say if sprites were Seelie or Unseelie, Light or Dark, what would you say?"

"They're neither. They predate the division of courts. They were around before Fae," Brynach answered.

Aisling nodded. "They're impartial, but like anything, they can lean into their positive or negative attributes."

Riordan sat back. "Right. Well, the alates that wanted to speak to me needed to reiterate that. Seems that some of my messages from them were purely guidance, while others were from a select few who had taken up with less-than-savory Fae."

"We knew that, didn't we?" Brynach asked.

"Yes and no," Riordan said. "I assumed all the messages were from the same entities. But a lot of what I was warned against was to spare my heartache. They saw me bonding with Aisling. Saw me weaving magic into my life in a way that would put me in danger. I think they even saw us working to bring down the Veil."

He took a deep breath. "When I first got here, that's the very last thing I'd have wanted. I think they were trying to help. Even the sprites who warned me when Maggie was murdered, they weren't necessarily bad. They knew about the explosives and were warning me while staying impartial."

"Oh, Riordan." Aisling moved closer to him.

"No, it's okay. I'm okay. It was easier to have someone to blame, but I can see it now. They weren't purposefully cruel. That's their nature. Expecting them to act with human compassion isn't logical," he explained.

"Doesn't make any of it hurt less," Brynach said.

"No, it doesn't." Riordan accepted Brynach's warm hand. "But it's nice to know there isn't a larger conspiracy against me and my happiness. I think I can let that particular chip fall from my shoulders."

Aisling kissed him, and he felt himself get physically lighter. Brynach's hand stroked his hair, and Riordan leaned into the other man. Letting them soothe some of his hurt felt nice. When he parted from Aisling's sweet mouth, he accepted Brynach's.

"There's another elephant in the room," Brynach said when they parted. "Before we leave, I have to see Alex."

"Do you want us to come with you?" she asked.

"No. I need to do this alone, if that's okay." Brynach answered.

Riordan nodded. "Yeah, that's okay."

Aisling bit her lip. "I want to go see Corinna. I want to pick her brain about Ellasar." She paused and admitted, "I think I want to talk to Nevan."

Brynach looked at Riordan, and they knew it was past time they told her. "A stoirin. You know we love you and would do anything to protect you."

She looked between them with suspicion. Rightfully so. "You're freaking me out."

"Do you remember when Ellasar was skewered by vines?" Brynach began.

"Are you serious? It's kinda hard to forget." Aisling cringed.

Riordan still felt sick to his stomach remembering it. But the next part, oh fuck, she was going to be so pissed.

"We got the news when you were in the Unseelie hospital ward. You were healing, and then—" Brynach shook his head. "No excuses, Aisling. I just didn't want to tell you. I didn't want to upset you or confuse you."

"Just tell me," she said, her fingers worrying over her rings.

Brynach took a deep breath. "The Fae who sent that magic, who killed Ellasar. It was your father."

Aisling gasped. "How did he ... Wait. He killed Ellasar? I don't understand."

Riordan took her hand. "We don't either, Ash. We haven't gone to see him, but Pilson confirmed it. He asked the officers to stand down. Remember when we were making out and your magic went wild and the jasmine bloomed like crazy? I think he felt so strongly about you being in danger that his magic acted out. He killed Ellasar with the vines that grew from his strong emotion."

He watched Aisling process the information and all the emotions that flittered across her features. The one thing he didn't see was anger, and for that he was grateful.

"A stoirin?" Brynach lifted her chin. "I'm sorry. We should have told you."

She shook her head. "It doesn't matter. I mean, it does, but it's okay. I need to talk to him, though. I know I don't owe him anything, but I want to."

Brynach gave her a small smile. "I don't want you to go alone. Can Riordan go with you?"

When she nodded, he looked at Riordan. "Yeah, big guy, I

can do that. Go talk to Alex, I'll take her to the Unseelie court, and we'll meet back here."

The two of them were in for some pretty rough conversations, and all he could do was help them weather it. They were only a few days from their trip, and then he'd be back in Ireland. He'd be with his brother and some of his old friends. Riordan would get to share the country he loved with the people he loved. First, they needed to put this last chunk of hardship behind them.

Brynach got himself ready to leave and kissed them both. Aisling held onto him a little longer. "You don't owe him your forgiveness. You don't have to stay or fix anything. If it becomes too much, leave."

He pulled her into a tighter hug. "I will."

Aisling got herself ready to go, and Riordan watched her closely. After last night, he was worried about her healing, but she didn't seem stiff in her movements. Instead of assuming, though, he asked, "Do you feel okay?"

"I'm confused and a little nervous," she answered.

"No, Ash. I mean, I care about how you're feeling, but I meant physically. Your side."

She blushed and pulled up her shirt. "Yeah. All better."

There was still a pink line down her side, so she wasn't completely healed, but she certainly wasn't in any danger. Relief surged through him. Aisling must have seen the way he reacted, and she closed the distance between them.

"Have I mentioned that I'm sorry you had to go through that? I know it wasn't easy for you. I could see how hard it was. I'm proud of you for gathering yourself and helping me." She kissed him softly.

"I'm sorry I didn't think of it sooner. I kinda locked up," Riordan admitted.

"Anyone would have." Aisling pushed his hair back.

"You didn't," he commented.

His wife shook her head. "I was terrified; I just also happened to be uniquely motivated to not be a pincushion anymore. It tends to force you to act."

Riordan felt his stomach flip. "Please don't bring that up again. You ready?"

She laughed and the two of them stepped out of the house. Rin came swooping down out of the trees and dive-bombed Aisling. She ducked him and held up her hands.

"I'm sorry! I know I promised no more injuries. It wasn't my fault," she argued with her familiar while playfully swatting at him.

He watched them with a smile and then took her hand to sift to the court. He held his hand out for the snake stones statues to test his blood. Aisling did the same, and then the gates swung open. They quickly made their way into the palace.

"It's going to be strange not seeing Breena and Jashana," she whispered.

Riordan agreed. The idea of not having them around still felt strange to him, but he was proud of Brynach's sister. He took Aisling's hand, and they walked up the stairs and into the Unseelie court. They didn't have to find Corinna; she came running toward them.

"Thank goodness you're here. I was just about to call for you," she said, taking Aisling's hand and pulling her down the hall.

"Hey, easy! She's still healing," Riordan said.

"Oh, she's fine." Corinna waved her free hand. "Come on!"

The deeper they got into the Unseelie court, the louder the voices became. Riordan's New Fae hearing allowed him to decipher a word here or there, but it was hard to focus around the sound of their feet slamming the marble floor and his heart thundering. What the hell was going on? He was sick of surprises.

But that's what he got. Corinna shoved her way through an unguarded door and into what could only be described as a mockery of a high school debate team. One side of the room had angry Seelie, the other angry Unseelie, around them New and Unaligned Fae, and in the middle of it all were Brielle and Nevan trying to calm everyone.

Aisling's wide hazel eyes swung to him and then back to the scene in front of them quickly. Then the room took notice of them, and the yelling was directed their way. More than a few of them took steps toward them, and Riordan shoved himself in front of his wife.

"Calm down. Nobody's going to hurt her," Brielle assured him.

He liked Brielle, was glad to see her up on her feet and feisty, but he didn't trust that statement at all. Corinna let go of Aisling's hand and grinned at them. Riordan squeezed her hand harder, and she moved to his side. The arguing started back up at a lower scale, and Aisling turned to Brielle.

"What the hell is going on?"

The smaller Fae shrugged. "Turns out the Unseelie Queen didn't appreciate her Regent killing their Advisor and her lover. The King is less than pleased that his wife is a bitch and told her as much."

Aisling bit her lip but didn't hide the smile. "I'm sorry I missed that."

Brielle laughed. "Yeah, well, then Rainer wanted to bring charges against Branwyn for crimes against Fae, and she wanted Kyteler to back her up, and he straight up said he agreed."

Riordan assessed the screaming Fae. "Where are we now?"

"Undecided," Corinna answered.

This was an absolute shit show. And he didn't see why Aisling needed to be a part of the discussion.

"Daughter, please come here," Nevan called to her.

"Corinna," Kyteler beckoned.

Riordan moved alongside the two of them to stand between the two lines of court Fae. Both looked to their respective parents.

Nevan addressed his daughter. "Aisling, you are owed a blood tithe from the Seelie court and their late Advisor both."

Kyteler broke in, "Corinna, knowing what we do now about both your mother and Ellasar's motives, you are also owed a blood tithe from the Seelie court."

An Unaligned spoke up, "Brielle is also owed a blood tithe from the Seelie court."

The three women stood side by side, the attention of everyone on them. That was a lot of weight and responsibility, but more than that, a lot of political bullshit on their shoulders. Riordan stayed quiet; this wasn't his decision.

Brielle was the first to speak. "My tithe has been satisfied with the stripping of Walker and the death of Ellasar."

Riordan saw her back flex, the wings she no longer had still trying to move. His heart broke for her, but again, he was struck by her strength. Corinna spoke next.

"My attacker is dead, and that woman is no mother to me. I don't want a blood tithe," she answered.

Heads turned to Aisling, and he didn't like at all that the weight of this decision was on her. To her credit, his wife didn't wither under the weight of their gazes.

"The blood tithes owed me have been executed already by either myself, my partners, or my father. I want no further tithe." As soon as her words died off, the screams began anew.

Rainer's voice was the one to silence them this time. "Well, mine hasn't been. I want that bitch's blood for the kidnapping of my daughter at the request of her lover."

"He did no such thing. Talk to your brother's friend for that tithe," Branwyn declared.

"I'll have it from you, hag," Rainer demanded.

Shouts rang out, and though Riordan expected it, Kyteler didn't move to stand with his wife. In fact, she very much stood by herself.

Nevan spoke over them. "The lack of power in the courts is punishment enough for Kyteler. As for Branwyn, I suggest banishment from Fae areas in exchange for retaining your magic."

The woman scoffed, hand to her chest. "You can't."

Brynach's brother stepped forward. "It's too good a deal for you. However, to not have to look at your face every day, I'll settle for it. If I ever see you again, though, I'll have my blood."

"We need a vote," Corinna said. When heads snapped toward her, she shrugged. "Isn't that what we do now? Vote?"

There were sounds of agreement, and absolutely nobody was surprised when Nevan's suggestion of the Queen's banishment passed unanimously. The guards moved to her and took her by both arms. Branwyn didn't go peacefully; she called her magic, flames bursting from her and leaping to the guards. Riordan swiftly called water from the fountain outside the open window and put it out.

"Don't make this harder on yourself, my dear," Kyteler said with clear sarcasm. "Perhaps you can join Moura in her country home."

"You bastard," she screamed. "You'll all regret this."

She was pulled from the room, and Corinna turned to Aisling. "Well, that was fun. See why I was so excited? I'm not ready to talk to my father again, but maybe you should talk to yours? Yeah?"

Aisling nodded. "I'll talk to you later."

The younger Fae nodded and left with Brielle. The room emptied for the most part, small groups breaking off to talk to one another. Rainer made his way to them, and he spoke to Riordan while Aisling moved to her father's side. He looked over the other man's shoulder, eyes tracking his wife.

"She's fine. She's safe here." Rainer shook his head. "At least now she is."

"We think. She always felt safe with Branwyn. And with Alex, for that matter. Forgive me if I don't trust anyone with her anymore," Riordan countered.

"Fair point. But now she's Fae and trained to handle herself. Come on, we need to talk." Rainer put a hand on Riordan's arm and maneuvered him to the door.

"You get me to the wall, that's it. I'm not leaving this room." Riordan wasn't leaving her with Nevan even if the man did save her. "What do you want, Rainer?"

"I've been an idiot. I never thought they'd target Trixie. I really thought I had eyes everywhere and knew what I was up against," he started.

"Why are you telling me this? Seems like something you need to talk to Brynach about," Riordan interrupted.

"Probably is. Maybe I'm just weak, but I hate that I put my daughter in harm's way. He warned me, you know? It's not easy to admit I'm wrong, but here we are. The three of you changed the world, and instead of accepting it, I resisted change. I'm done. The courts are gone. The crown means nothing." Rainer looked around the throne room. "I'm walking away. However Fae decide to govern themselves, it doesn't matter to me. Only she does. She's all I have left of my wife. I've taken too much for granted."

Riordan was deeply uncomfortable. "Um, thanks? Again, not really sure what you want me to say here?"

Rainer smiled. "I didn't expect anything. Everything I said is true, but as a father who had to face the reality of almost losing my daughter, I wanted to give Nevan the benefit of talking to his alone."

His eyes shot to where Aisling was. "You sneaky bastard."

The once-king laughed. "She's fine. But you would have hovered and listened in. Give them a few minutes, okay?"

Riordan didn't look away from Aisling but nodded. Rainer reached over and patted his shoulder before walking out. Every second he spent not walking across the throne room floor to Aisling felt like a second too long. The fact that his wife never looked his way was the only reason he stayed where he was.

In the nearly empty room, Riordan overheard enough to know his wife was thanking Nevan but not absolving him of his past mistakes. Her father pleaded his case by saying he did what he had to in order to continue to trace the corruption inside the palace. He had already expelled a dozen other Fae who had worked with Ellasar from both the school and the Unseelie palace.

The ends didn't justify the means, not when Aisling's feelings were at stake. But Riordan couldn't deny he was glad to have someone with knowledge of how deep the bad seeds were planted. Sheer force of will kept his feet planted where they were until Aisling turned and walked to him.

"You okay?" he asked as he opened his arms. Aisling stepped into them, resting her forehead against his.

"Yeah. I'm good." She closed her eyes and breathed with him for a moment. "Can we go home?"

"Ask and you shall receive," he answered. They walked out of the large room and down crowded halls, stopping only so Aisling could say goodbye to Corinna and hug Brielle. Then they were outside the palace gates and sifting home.

"Is it okay if I don't talk about it right now?" Aisling asked.

"You never have to talk about it, Ash. I would imagine it's complicated. Give yourself some time to process, and know whatever you want to do, we're behind you." Riordan took her hand.

"*Bring her to the water,*" Valo's voice sounded in his head.

"*Good idea,*" Riordan agreed. "Come on," he said to Aisling. He tugged her to the stream at the back of their yard.

"What are you doing?" Aisling asked as he leaned over to take his boots off.

"I figure now is as good as time as any for a cleansing," he said as he pulled his socks off. "Come on, beautiful. Give me that free foot content."

She laughed and toed off her sneakers before peeling off her socks. The water was as much a comfort to him as it was his wife. It always had been. He stepped into the stream, careful of the moss-covered rocks under the waterline. He held out his hand, and Aisling stepped in with him. Riordan pulled on it, letting it swirl around them and slightly up their calves.

"Do you remember our first date?" She kicked her feet in the water.

"Is that what it was?" Riordan laughed. "You took me on a wild goose chase through a glen."

Aisling's smile was bright as she leaned in and kissed him. "You loved it."

"Then we went up to the stream and got caught in the rain. I've never wanted to kiss someone more in all my life," Riordan admitted.

"I wish you had...I think that's when I knew what I felt for you wasn't just our bond. The way you felt about water, the way I felt seen by you, it meant something even then." She leaned into him.

"I wanted to be so angry about our bond, but you made it impossible. You were so excited about it and so damn beautiful it made it hard to breathe," Riordan said. "I never stood a chance. I still can't believe you're my wife. That this is my life."

Aisling kissed him softly. "We have a lifetime to get used to it."

He breathed against her hair. A lifetime of this sounded like perfection. "Come on. Let's get rid of this bad juju."

He leaned down, filling his hands with the running water and splashing it over his face and arms. Like Aisling had taught him countless times while a witch, he set intentions and let go of all negative feelings as he cleansed himself. Riordan was a little lost in the process when a stream of water was magically lifted and thrown at his chest. Aisling's laughter followed.

"Oh, you're in so much trouble!"

CHAPTER 35

Brynach

Brynach had never experienced a cavity or needed to have a tooth pulled, but he imagined it felt something like leaving Aisling and Riordan that morning. The fact that he had to do so only to go face his once-best friend didn't make it any better. He had no idea how he'd feel when he saw Alex.

Angry he'd put lives at risk, his own, his family's, and his partners' included.

Relieved that he wasn't dead.

Confused as to how his friend had progressed to that level at all, let alone without him realizing it.

Hurt. So fucking hurt.

Betrayed.

They'd agreed to let Brynach talk to him through the magicked cell he was in. No visitation rooms. No access to touching him. He'd agreed without hesitation. He needed to do this. Had to find out why he'd helped Peggy hurt Sydney. Why he'd hired Walker to hurt people and kidnap Trixie. Why he'd thrown his hat in the ring with a man like Ellasar. Knowing full well that nothing he said was going to justify what he'd done. Brynach would never understand it.

No amount of preparing himself to see the other man was enough, though. Alex looked awful. His hair was knotted, with his orange outfit shockingly bright against his pale skin. But it was the anger on his face that gave Brynach pause. The only time he'd ever seen that look was when Brynach had turned up black and blue or Alex had sifted into their hiding space with tears on his face.

"You shouldn't have come," Alex said and turned away from him.

"You shouldn't be here," Brynach countered. "What were you thinking, Alex? How could you do this?"

The other man shook his head. "You'll never understand, Brynach. You never could. I told you the other night you couldn't. I asked you to stop looking for me."

"You knew I couldn't do that, Alex. I was never going to just forget, not even for you." Brynach frowned. "But I would like to understand."

Anger flashed over his face. "And I've told you that you can't. You won't. I'm not going to stand here and make some ridiculous villain monologue. Not going to give them ammunition against me. You think I'm going to make a case for Aisling to strip me by opening my mouth?"

"She fucking should, Alex. You stood for me at my damn wedding. You helped raise that girl, and then you nearly had her killed. And for what? For Ellasar to turn on you? For Walker to go AWOL and end up killing Fae? For Trixie to get kidnapped? For your wife and daughter to now have to live without you?"

"You leave them out of it!" Alex roared.

"You think everyone else will? That they won't suffer for your actions? The families of people convicted of treason and murder are rarely treated well," Brynach pointed out.

Alex paled even more than usual. "You'll watch out for her, right? I know you hate me, but you couldn't hate her."

"No, I couldn't. You know I will, but for her and Joeigh, never for you," Brynach answered.

"Don't care why or for who as long as you do." He turned and sat on his cot. "It wasn't supposed to be like this. You want the truth? The truth is it all got away from me. Got bigger than I anticipated, and I was in over my head. I brought people in because I knew I was out of my depths."

"You could have just stopped. Called an end to it all," Brynach pointed out. "It would have sorted itself out. We were already doing amazing things, Alex. It didn't have to end like this."

"Maybe not, but it's where we are all the same. No amount of magic reverses time." He hung his head. "I need you to leave. It'll just be harder seeing you. Tell Aindrea not to come. I don't want her to see me here. I'll serve whatever time they tell me to. I'll accept the blame I deserve. I can at least be man enough to do that."

Brynach shook his head. "You should have come to me. I could have helped you before it went this far. I'll tell her, but that's all. I'm not ordering your wife around."

"It's more than I have a right to ask for. Thank you," he said.

"Again, not for you, for her. I don't want her seeing you like this either." Brynach stood close to the bars, but not touching. "You really have nothing else to say, Alex?"

The other man looked up at Brynach and sighed. "What do you want to hear? That I'm sorry? I'm sure you would have done things differently, Bry, but I did what I felt I had to. I'm not sorry about that. Am I sorry people got hurt in the process, yeah. But if it had gotten me where I needed to be, even if it pushed us in that direction, it was worth it."

"What direction, Alex? That's what I don't get. What could possible turn you into ... this." Brynach waved at the cell.

His friend stared at the floor before lifting his eyes. "I told you in the dreamwalk, Bry. My answer hasn't changed. The courts and any other body trying to gain power needed to be nullified. Fae don't need control any more than the humans do. We should be free to do as we see fit."

"That's what we were doing, Alex! That was already happening. They'd have all gotten there without the violence. Reason, Alex. Words. We never fell back on violence, not us." Brynach fought to keep the emotion at bay. "You should have come to me. I could have helped you make sense of things before you acted irrationally."

"It wasn't irrational, and that's why I didn't bring it to you," Alex said.

"That's how we're leaving this?" Brynach asked, a tear breaking free.

Alex's shoulders rose and then fell. "There's nothing left to say."

With a frown and a nod, Brynach turned his back on a man he'd considered a brother and forced himself not to look back when he heard broken sobs from the cell. He kept his cool until he was out of the building and had sifted to the glen that he had considered a sanctuary for so many years. Once there, he thrust his hands into his hair and screamed so loud birds took flight.

There was a rustle in the woods, and Kongur walked out, large black eyes on Brynach. "*I figured you'd come here.*"

"*And you came to save me, like always, old friend,*" Brynach rested his head on the horse's long nose. "*It hurts.*"

"*Of course, it does. And like so many other times, I wish I could take that pain away.*"

They stood like that, silent and pressed against one another, until Brynach could pull in air without his chest feeling like it was on fire. His familiar's coat was wet with his tears. He wasn't sure how to move past this. All he knew, in this moment, was it hurt. And that he didn't want to bring this hurt home.

"*They'll love you through it. They want to support you, Brynach,*" Kongur reminded him.

"*I know. It's not about showing weakness, not really. It's just that I don't want to feel like a burden.*"

"Loving someone is not a burden. Have their problems ever felt like a burden to you? Has loving them through the hard times felt like a chore?"

"Never!" Brynach answered with heat.

"Well then? Why are you or yours any different?"

"I'll thank you not to bring logic into this discussion."

Kongur made a rough laughing noise and nudged Brynach's shoulder. *"Come on. Aindrea could use a friend."*

Brynach jumped up onto the Percheron's shoulders, and Kongur took off. There was no thought, just joyous freedom as he rode toward what he knew would be a very hard conversation. All too soon, Kongur was stopping outside the Seelie gates and Brynach was submitting to the bloodletting. Only when they'd identified him did he walk inside with Kongur beside him.

"I'm going to go check on the stables and Semele. Call me when you're ready to leave," Kongur requested.

He walked through the Seelie court toward the rooms Alex and his family had claimed, but he was surprised to see them empty.

"Are you looking for Aindrea?" a Fae he didn't recognize asked from behind him.

"Um, yes, I am."

"I suspect you'll find her up in the dorms or the nurse's office. That's where she spends most of her time." They turned away before Brynach could thank them.

She was working? How could she stand to? He went first to the nurse's office, which was good, because that's where he found her. She was leaning over a watery-eyed child, hand in their hair, soothing them. He waited in the doorway, watching her until she stood and saw him. Only then did her smile slip and sadness crept into her eyes.

He nodded toward the hall, and she held up a finger. Brynach walked out and found himself nervous. When had he ever been nervous to talk to Aindrea? Suddenly, he felt like this was an awful idea. Nothing he said was going to matter.

"No, you big lug. You don't have to fix everything. Just be there for her," he muttered low to himself.

"You're not a lug," Aindrea said, coming up behind him. "But you're right; you don't have to fix everything. You can't fix this."

He gathered her into his arms, and she let out a groan as he squeezed her tight. "Sorry," he said as he set her back on her feet. "I'm so sorry. I should have ..."

"Should have what? Seen something that even I didn't when I was the one living with him? Loving him? Building a future with him?" Aindrea shook her head. "I'm hurt, Brynach. So angry and broken. Not just for me but our daughter. She'll never know her father. Never know the man I fell in love with, only the one who made awful decisions and justified it with her future."

"She'll have me. You'll always both have me," he swore.

She smiled up at him, her purple cheeks flushing a darker violet. "You'll have your own children to care for one day, Brynach. You already have your own partners who need you. We're not your responsibility."

"No," he agreed. "You're my family. Nothing changes that."

Aindrea swiped at the tears. "And you're mine. We love you, and I never thought you'd turn away from us. But we're going to be okay. I have the school. I have a home and things to keep me busy. I'll rebuild our name, make it something to be proud of."

Brynach looked around the halls and the children walking through them. "It's going to be okay, isn't it? We'll keep doing good here."

The woman nodded. "Of course we will. That Lydia means business. I see where Aisling gets it from. Even Ceiren has impressed me lately. He'll say he doesn't want to help, but I think he likes it."

He wanted to let it go, to never bring him up again, but I'd do him this one last favor. "He asked you not to visit him. He doesn't want you to see him like that."

Aindrea laughed. "As if I would try. That man, whoever he is, isn't the man I love. Don't you worry about me, Brynach. I won't be going."

Brynach kissed the shorter woman on the top of the head. "You're a marvel."

"Always were a sweet-talker. Go." She waved him away. "I have sick children to tend to. I'll see you when you're back from your honeymoon. I assume you'll resume teaching?"

He smiled. "Absolutely. I love it."

She nodded. "Good." She didn't wait for him to leave; she turned her back and left.

Why were so many people doing that to him lately?

CHAPTER 36

Riordan

Aisling bounced as she fastened her lap belt, and it was all Riordan could do to stay in his seat and not rush to kiss her. She was adorable.

Riordan turned to Brynach, but the big guy was definitely not bouncing with excitement. "Uh, Bry, you okay?"

"Mhmm, sure." He checked his lap belt for no less than the fifth time. "Is the air thinner in here?"

Aisling put her hand on his leg. "Hey, look at me. I know it feels strange. There's a disconnect from the land, and the air feels different, but we're going to be okay. Planes take off and land safely thousands of times a day. Yeah?"

His black hair moved as he nodded. "I'm rethinking that anxiety pill you offered before."

Riordan laughed. "You'd burn through it too fast, anyway. We'll watch a movie, and you'll forget all about it."

"Doubtful," Brynach murmured.

They'd sprung for first class, so Aisling was sitting next to Brynach, Riordan across the aisle from her. The booze certainly helped Brynach take the edge off, especially now that the airline started keeping Fae wine stocked. They all indulged in a glass, or two, before night fell on the flight. Seat reclined and blanket over her, Aisling snored softly. The two men shared a look over her.

"Still can't believe this is my life," Riordan wondered.

Brynach smiled at him and nodded. "Get some rest. You're going to need it. I have big plans for us once we get to the hotel."

Adjusting his hardening cock without alerting the older man resting to his right was downright difficult. Brynach chuckled and closed his eyes. Riordan tried to relax, but his thoughts were racing. This wasn't just a honeymoon, and as excited as he was to share Ireland with his partners, he was nervous. He played with his wedding band instead of the rings around his neck. The person heading toward Ireland wasn't the same one who left years ago.

Coming home as a man deeply embedded in a world of magic, the very opposite of who he'd wanted to be, scared him. Would it feel the same? Look the same? Had he changed too much to feel at home in Ireland now? It was one thing living this new life in a new country, but how did who he was now merge with the place and person he used to know?

He looked over at Aisling and Brynach and knew, deep in his soul, that no matter what, he'd already found home.

D on't judge too harshly. Dublin isn't all Ireland has to offer. Once we get into the country, you'll see why we love it. And the ocean, oh, I can't wait to take you home," Riordan shared as he drove their rental away from the airport and toward their first hotel.

Aisling rolled down the window and took a deep breath of the city air. "It's perfect already. I didn't realize how badly I needed to get away from home."

Brynach huffed, "We did."

Riordan drove and let them gaze through the windows.

"The Veil," he started.

"It's weird, right?" Aisling finished. "Every time I go to a drop, it hits me that this is what it used to be like. I don't miss it."

"Me either," Brynach answered. "Though, while I'm not sure what Vola and Rin are saying, Kongur is downright pissed that he's not joining us on the trip. That guy is a straight-up grump."

Riordan laughed. "Vola has no desire to travel in a carrier or leave the woods." His familiar's voice was softer in his head, but there all the same. Having eyes back home felt nice, safe.

"I hope they don't regret lowering the Veil here," Aisling said.

"Everyone after us is making an informed decision. How they feel is not our responsibility. All we can do is support them," Brynach reassured her.

"Ash, the sprites, the Fae, they were much more integrated here. It wasn't like Birchwood Falls. I doubt some people will even notice," Riordan told her.

When he reached the outskirts of the city proper and located their hotel, Brynach grabbed their bags, and Riordan checked in.

"No elevators and narrow hallways. This building is so cool," Aisling commented as they made their way to their suite.

"Speak for yourself," Brynach grumbled, trying to get their bags and his broad shoulders through the small hallways.

Riordan couldn't help the smile that broke across his face at the image he created. He looked like a Gandalf in a hobbit's home. As soon as the door shut behind them, Aisling stripped off her clothes and turned for the bathroom.

"I was going to check out the view from the balcony, but I think I prefer the one in the bathroom," Brynach joked and started removing his clothing.

With a laugh, Riordan did the same. The shower wasn't their usual large one; it was a basin tub, and the three of them weren't exactly comfortable as they navigated getting clean. He probably should have waited and showered after them, but they made it work. Aisling moaned as Brynach massaged her tight shoulders and rubbed her lower back.

"Oh, that's nice," she sighed. "But no frisky shit. I mean it. I want food first."

Riordan shook his head at her attempt at a stern voice. "There's a pub just down the street. Genuine Guinness and fish and chips. Though, I'd wait until we're closer to the shore for that. Still, there'll probably be some live music."

Brynach hummed his approval. "Sounds perfect."

Riordan dressed comfortably in jeans and a t-shirt and Brynach mirrored him. Aisling pulled on ripped jeans and a tank top along with her brown leather jacket.

"Feels a little strange not strapping on my knives," she said, tapping her thighs. "But it's kinda a relief."

The guys agreed. The three of them held hands as they walked through the lobby and down the street.

Aisling was the first to notice the stares and whispers. "I forgot we're not at home, and this may not be as accepted."

Riordan held her hand tighter and was sure Brynach did the same. "We're in tourist areas still, Ash. This country is one of the most inclusive of Fae and their lifestyles. In most areas, this wouldn't cause a stir, but in areas like this, it may."

As they strolled the streets, wisps approached them. The air sprites had never paid him much mind when he'd lived here. And maybe before his talk with the elementals at home, their attention may have alarmed him, but he greeted them kindly.

They circled him, his hair lifted, and a chill settled over his skin. He waited, unsure what they wanted from him. A spiny alate joined them and hovered in front of his face. Beside him, he felt Aisling draw magic to her and Brynach move closer.

"Riordan Campbell, we welcome you home. May the protection of the Goddess surround you," the alate spoke before they all flew away.

"Well, that was … something," Aisling said.

"Right?" Riordan added. "Is it strange that it made me feel better?"

Brynach clapped a hand on his shoulder. "I don't think so. Come on, I'm hungry."

Once seated at a bar top at the pub, Riordan ordered three Guinness and a Smithwick's just in case Aisling hated the heavy stout. They were passed their drinks along with a bar menu.

"Order what you think we'd like," Brynach told Riordan.

Riordan grinned and ordered four plates for them to share. Aisling turned her back to the bar to face the band. She swayed as she took a sip of her Guinness. Her face immediately screwed up before she swallowed. As he watched, she let the taste settle on her tongue and shrugged.

"It's not bad." She took another sip.

Riordan felt a surge of pride. Brynach took a large draw of the heavy beer and patted Riordan on the back. "When we get to your hometown, I think we both want to see our very own broody musician in his element."

They ate while the pub around them joined in singing along with the musicians. A few women and one man got up to dance. It was nothing more than he'd expect from a night in a pub. But seeing Aisling's pure joy at experiencing it for the first time was amazing. Seeing his old home through his partner's eyes was surreal.

Riordan stood and pulled Aisling into an open space. He taught her some dance steps, slowly and patiently. She could move her body with the best of them, but the choreographing and structured dance didn't come as naturally to her. Still, she picked it up relatively well for her first time. Around them, a few people clapped, and a woman grabbed her arm and swung her around to dance with the larger group. She let loose a booming laugh and spun, her hair flying as she danced.

He'd never been more in love.

Brynach came up to him and placed a hand in his back pocket. "She's stunning," Riordan whispered.

"So are you," Brynach countered. "You okay?"

"Perfect," Riordan assured him. He wasn't lying. Things felt different, yes, but not in a bad way. He'd expected grief to slap him in the face when he'd landed, and it hadn't.

"I miss it sometimes, our bond," Brynach said, turning Riordan to him. "Miss being inside that brain of yours." The large man's hands framed his face, and he rubbed his fingers over Riordan's temples.

With a smile, he leaned into Brynach's touch. "I promise I'm okay. I was afraid things would feel off, but it's wonderful. I miss it, too, you know. You have my word; if you ask, I'll answer honestly. It's not the same, but I won't hide from you."

Brynach's citrine eyes caught the light as he leaned down to kiss Riordan. He lost himself in the Guinness-rich kiss until hooting pulled him to his senses.

The band finished their song and called out, "Welcome home, Riordan Campbell and partners. Let's raise a glass to the liberators of the Fae."

Before Riordan had left Ireland, his face had been plastered everywhere, alongside his dead parents. He didn't look the same anymore, he'd bulked with his New Fae training, but his face was recognizable all the same. It wasn't like the three of them could fly under the radar after all their media attention.

They were handed fresh drinks, on the pub, to join the toast. Brynach looked wildly uncomfortable, but all three drank with the room and accepted handshakes and hugs.

By the time the buzz died down, they were more than ready to head back to the hotel. They took their time walking back, enjoying the sounds of a night in Ireland. There was music and laughter, the loud voices of people talking sports, and shops closing up.

As they got back to the room, Aisling yawned, and Brynach

flopped into bed.

"All those promises of ruining us when we reached the hotel are spinning down the drain," she teased.

Riordan shook his head. "We're all too tired. We'll rock your world after a good night of sleep in an actual bed."

Aisling nodded. "Deal."

When they fell asleep, it was with the windows open and the air or Ireland rolling over their naked bodies. He'd never been happier. At least, that's what he'd thought. Over the following week, he'd learned that watching Aisling experience Ireland was like watching a kid on Christmas morning. Pure joy and magic. Each memory they created more magnificent than the last.

She fell in love with Kylemore Abbey and Galway. An appreciation for both Irish folk music and Guinness grew in her with each leg of their tour. Riordan didn't skimp on any of the tourist spots or the unknown gems and ruined castles to explore.

Riordan thanked her Fae immortality as he watched her scale the sea-spray-slick stones at Giant's Causeway and the Carrick-a-Rede rope bridge. Brynach sipped on whiskey, and they catered to her every whim. It was perfect.

The closer they got to Carnlough, to seeing Liam and Amber, the more he couldn't put off facing one of his biggest fears. For the first time since their funeral, Riordan was going to honor his parents.

They dropped their bags at the famous Londonderry Arms, where they'd be spending the night, grabbed a drink in the stylish bar inside the hotel, and walked down to the water. Aisling had sneakily plucked some flowers from the hotel planters to bring to the water.

Together, they passed around the sea wall down to the rock-covered beach. This wasn't where his parents died, but it was the first time he was ready to enter the waters off the coast of Ireland. And it was close enough, as close as he could get without having a panic attack.

Aisling pushed off her shoes, and Brynach and Riordan mimicked her. She let out a small yelp as her feet were covered in the cold water. Riordan couldn't help the smile that split his face.

"We're a hearty people, love." He came up behind her and hugged her. "You'll get used to it."

Brynach joined at their side, and Aisling handed them each a small bunch of flowers. They held hands in the surf, and Riordan knew he should say something, but the words stuck in his throat.

"We honor Calyssa and Finnegan Campbell with these offerings and acknowledge their sacrifice for the witches, Ravdi, and Fae who came before and after them." Aisling dropped the flowers into the waves. "You'd be so proud of the man Riordan is today. The way he supports those he loves and the control he has over his magic are unrivaled. He's a good man with a big heart and has earned the respect of many. Thank you for gifting him to the Universe so that he could find me."

Riordan's throat burned as he tried to fight back tears. Aisling wound her arm around his hips and rested her head on his shoulder.

"Calyssa and Finnegan Campbell have become names synonymous with selflessness and power. You should know that Riordan's has joined yours. But more than that, I know you raised him in love, and the amount he shares with others is a marvel. I am constantly unsure I deserve it, but he gives it to me anyway. I can only imagine how the example you set with your own relationship has molded him. If you loved one another half as hard as Riordan loves us, I know you rest together, forever bonded. Know that he's found pieces of his soul in two people who would burn the world down for him," Brynach spoke softly while holding Riordan's hand tight to his chest. He let his flowers drop into the white-crested waves that washed over their legs.

Riordan stopped pretending not to be crying. His partners held him together as he tried to form words. "Mum, Da, I was a stubborn arse. I'm sorry for every ounce of grief I gave you, but I want you to know I understand now. I understand that sacrifice isn't a burden; it's a gift to those you love. I wish you were here to meet Aisling and Brynach, to see the man I am today because of and in spite of your passing. I'd give anything to have you back, but thank you for your own sacrifice so that I can be where I am today. I love you."

He dropped the flowers into the water and broke. His shoulders shook as he cried, but then Aisling and Brynach surrounded him.

"We've got you, a chuisle. Let it go," Brynach whispered against his hair.

When his throat was raw, Brynach gently lifted him, and Aisling walked beside them back to their room.

That night they ate in their room and talked about how far they'd all come and where they hoped to go. They cared for one another with quiet promises and soft touches. And in the morning, after they'd filled themselves on yet another traditional Irish breakfast, they got in the car for the last leg of their Ireland tour.

As they pulled up to the familiar house, Riordan felt a lightness in his chest. He'd let go of so much pain yesterday, and he was glad he'd have this reunion with his brother with a happier heart.

He'd expected Liam to embrace him first, but it was Aisling he scooped up. Aisling threw herself into her brother-in-law's open arms and then hugged Amber, too. Brynach's phone rang, and he shared a look with Riordan before turning and taking it. Aisling walked away, arm in arm with Amber talking about how much they loved Ireland.

"So, things are going well?" Riordan asked.

Liam looked after his girlfriend. "She still scares me. She started training at the boxing gym here. The girl has a taste for blood."

Riordan laughed. "I know the feeling."

When his brother looked at him, Riordan recognized the gleam in his eyes.

"I'm going to marry her, Rory," Liam announced. "I haven't asked her yet, kinda afraid she might clock me when I do, but I think she'll say yes."

"She will." Of that much, Riordan was sure. He might not know the New Fae nearly as well as his brother, but even he could see she was in love with him. "And things have been okay here? The drops?"

Riordan couldn't help but notice that, with the windows and doors open, sprites freely came and went from the house. Liam seemed at ease with them.

Liam shrugged. "You know how it is. The witches and Ravdi here have always been more Fae, more attached to magic. They're adapting better."

"And you? It got better for you?" Riordan still worried about his brother.

"A lot changed after Stanley became Fae. I'm happy, Rory. Don't worry about me," Liam said. He pulled him close and brought him to the kitchen where he pulled out a few beers. "How has the trip been so far?"

"Fantastic. Lots of free beer once people realize who we are," Riordan joked.

"I bet. The same happens to me, and I'm not nearly as recognizable as you are." Liam tapped his bottle against Riordan's and took a sip. "I heard from the States."

"What? Nobody's contacted me."

Liam shrugged. "I think they're trying to give you space."

Riordan was immediately alarmed. "What does that mean? What happened?"

Liam shook his head. "Nothing to worry about." They walked out to the small garden where Amber and Aisling were, and Brynach came through the house a moment later to join them. "The trial is going well. The proof against her is irrefutable.

She'll be spending life behind bars, Riordan. They're sure of it."

Brynach made a small humming sound as he joined the conversation. "That was Sydney on the phone. Apparently, they tacked on additional charges, including perjury. Peggy is sitting on the stand, blatantly lying."

Riordan shrugged. "Doesn't matter. That's going to add all of nothing to the sentence. That's not what I want her held accountable for."

Amber moved to Liam's side, and Aisling added, "But each time she does something like that, it further proves to a jury that she's guilty. That's good for us."

"Can we forget about it for a little bit? I just want to enjoy being here with everyone?" Riordan requested.

Around him, heads nodded. It was Brynach who broke the tension.

"I know we just got here, but we were promised a hometown pub and a rockstar husband." The wink he sent Riordan made his stomach flip.

His brother laughed, and Amber nodded. "Hell yes! Let's go."

Luckily, his brother lived close enough to town to walk. Riordan had a guitar slung across his body, hanging at his back, and Aisling's hand in his as they walked through familiar streets. The chance that Riordan would see a few old friends at the pub was high. In fact, it would likely be packed with people he knew. The idea of being there with Aisling and Brynach filled him with pride.

Liam and Amber entered first to a few friendly calls, but when Riordan entered, the place went feral. He was surrounded, and calls for drinks were shouted. Aisling was at Brynach's side, laughing, when he turned to find them. With wide eyes, he gestured them closer, but she shook him off.

"Have fun," she mouthed.

Riordan turned to his friend Seamus and nodded toward

his wife and husband. "Go get them for me."

With a grin, one of his oldest friends moved across the bar and took Aisling's hand. Brave man putting a hand on her in front of Brynach. If Riordan hadn't have sent him over, things may have ended differently. As it was, Brynach let the other man pull Aisling through the crowd and followed behind them.

A beer was thrust into both their hands as Riordan was moved to the stage. He saw them settle against the wall to the right of him, massive grins on their faces. He'd promised them music, and that's what he gave them.

The lights stayed high, the noise in the room no less boisterous as he began to strum on the strings and sing. But the voices quickly turned to accompanying harmonies. The walls shook with their raised voices, and Riordan's heart soared.

When he looked out at the pub and saw familiar faces smiling back at him, his wife and husband among them as they were pulled to dance, he felt a sense of peace. This. This is what he'd been missing. Even if it didn't last, even if they didn't stay long, this is what he needed.

Riordan closed his eyes and sang until his throat was raw and the smile made his cheeks hurt.

CHAPTER 37

Brynach

The ferry ride was peaceful. For once, he could enjoy the ocean and not fear sea monsters. Without the old borders, with whole new oceans to explore, they'd gone deep into hiding. He'd thought that Faerie was beautiful, and it was, but there was no denying that Ireland was magic. It crackled in the air there, the hillsides ripe with Fae and old magic. The trip so far had been more than worth the discomfort of the flight. Not just because his partners were smiling, relaxed, and well-fucked, but because he was, too.

Brynach couldn't remember a time he had been this at peace. It worried him how he could be this happy, given what had happened directly preceding this trip. Alex's betrayal had left a hole inside him that was still raw, but here, with them, it was healing.

He'd checked in a few times already. Enough to know the school was doing okay. Marina and Mrs. Quinn were leading the school for now, which Brynach preferred to Theo. Aindrea had been offered space at the new school and had happily accepted. She was determined to see Alex and Brynach's original vision of the school come to life.

So now Brynach was traveling with his partners and trying to reconcile that hurt with the fact that he was happy. Turns out, it's just as hard to admit that things are good as it is to live through times that are bad. But he'd find a way to adapt because this was too good to pass up.

Now that they had some road time under their belt, Brynach took over driving. Scotland was just as stunning as Ireland, and Brynach felt the same call to the land. The rugged nature spoke to him. They'd decided to take the trip from Cairnryan up through Scotland and back down to Edinburgh and the home Trent had left to Aisling.

The drive through the countryside was pleasant, and they'd already hit a few touristy places, but Trent had wanted to be away from prying eyes. His house was tucked away from the already-quiet road. The gate opened to a stone home that sat off a bricked courtyard. There was no grass to be seen in front of the house; instead, it was cobbled stones to the front door.

Aisling stood, staring up at it. There was no denying that it was beautiful.

"Guess this is it. No more putting it off." She straightened her spine. "This is good. I need the closure."

"Who are you trying to convince, Princess?" Brynach asked, purposefully using her bedroom name.

Her eyes swung to his, mischief in them. A small smile crept across her face, which is all he'd wanted. Aisling took a deep breath before she turned the key and swung the door open.

Brynach wasn't sure what he'd been expecting, but it wasn't what he saw. He'd been in Trent's apartment, and it was nothing like this. Where that was modern and clean, this was rich dark wood, sage green walls, and throw pillows on vintage furniture. Actual honest-to-goddess throw pillows on a settee by the door they could sit on to take their shoes off.

"Oh, wow," Aisling exclaimed. She wandered through the rooms, each more impressive than the next. She stopped, wiping her tears, in a library that housed titles even Brynach knew.

An archway separated the stairs from the hall, and Aisling took them slowly. The bedrooms were smaller than American ones but no less beautiful. Brynach nearly wept at the giant claw-foot tub they found in the master bathroom. It was angled to face a floor-to-ceiling window overlooking a lush backyard. He'd missed their baths together. There were fireplaces every-where, but as they made their way down a back staircase, it was the room off the kitchen that had them all slack-jawed.

It was a glass atrium with the most comfortable-looking furniture, guitars, and small lights strung around the ceiling. The view was magical. Rich gardens, mature trees, and a cas-tle-like turret stood at the edge of the property. And past that, a river ran lazily by.

"Can we move here?" Riordan asked.

Brynach nodded his head. He'd do it in a heartbeat.

Aisling mused. "This is it, the last of him."

Riordan took her hand. "You still have his letter. And you'll always have this home."

She shook her head. "I brought it with me. It felt right to read it here. I thought it would hurt more, but it feels nice. He was happy here. I can feel it."

Quietly, Aisling opened the door to the sunroom and walked into the yard. Brynach grabbed the bags from the car and dropped them in the master bedroom. It wasn't ideal for them. The bed was too small even though the room was the largest. Through the window, he saw Aisling walking barefoot with Riordan. He grinned down at her picking flowers from the garden. He pushed open the windows and aired out the house. Then he began rearranging.

His phone rang, and he dropped the mattress he was car-rying to dig in his pocket. He'd already spoken to Sydney, and Aisling's mother had checked in about the counselors at the school, so there weren't many people who'd be calling him ... unless something had gone wrong.

When he saw who the video call was from, he grinned and answered.

"If it isn't my wanderlust sister," Brynach said.

Breena grinned, tanned and healthy-looking, from a hammock by the water. "It's not my fault you went to damp-ass places, and I'm living it up on Bora Bora with my sexy-ass girlfriend."

Off-camera, he could hear Jashana laugh. "I'm glad you're happy. Where to next?"

She shrugged a shoulder. "Not sure. We might stay here for a while. Everything is dirt cheap, and I look my best in as little clothing as possible."

Brynach laughed and rolled his eyes. "Well don't forget to wear sunscreen. You wouldn't want to end up with age spots and wrinkles."

Breena gasped and gave him the finger. "Not cool!"

"Love you! I gotta go. I'll check in later," Brynach said. He had to get back to work.

"Whatever. I'm going to go bang my girlfriend in a waterfall. Have fun eating sheep intestines." She hung up. That woman would never change. He loved that about her.

Brynach continued his interior design plans for their room. Before Riordan and Aisling were back inside, calling up about heading out for food, Brynach had brought a second queen-sized bed in from another bedroom and created a super-king. There was a small gap between them, but until they got a larger bed, this would keep them all in the same room.

"Oh, Bry!" Aisling cried and flung herself into his arms. "You're the greatest. Thank you."

Riordan smiled at him, and Brynach glowed under their praise. Maybe one day, the way they looked at him wouldn't surprise him, but today was not that day. Aisling pushed on his shoulders until he was sitting on the bed and climbed into his lap.

"I could be swayed against going for food right away if you fed me a snack." She kissed the corner of his mouth.

"Ash, that man is more than a snack," Riordan joked and

pulled down her leggings. "But I doubt we will ruin our appetites."

Brynach took control, not just because he liked to, but because Aisling was emotionally overwhelmed right now. Once they were naked, he arranged them like a Twister game. Brynach laid himself out, head on a pillow and Riordan kneeling by his face, feeding him his cock. Aisling was on her knees, her mouth on Brynach's length while her ass was up and facing Riordan, showing off her wet sex.

Riordan used his magic fingers on her pussy. Nothing about the way they were fucking one another was graceful, it was raw and needy. It was groans, moans, bruising fingers, and gentle teeth.

Brynach raised his hand and slapped Aisling's ass, causing her to hum around his cock, which was a happy bonus. He landed another strike, all while hollowing his cheeks and sucking Riordan deep. Their joining was frantic, and the goal was most definitely the finish line.

Aisling thrust back on Riordan's fingers, and her mouth rose and fell on his cock in tandem. Her body made wet sucking sounds. Riordan groaned, and his cock twitched in Brynach's mouth.

"She's going to fucking squirt for us, Bry," Riordan crooned and picked up Aisling's hips. She straddled Brynach's chest, leaving their partner to finger-fuck her over his body. Brynach was going to punish Riordan for that later, even if the idea of being soaked with Aisling's release made him wild with want.

"Riordan!" She came off Brynach's cock but continued stroking him. Brynach turned his head just enough to watch while still sucking Riordan. He saw his partner thrust down toward the front of Aisling's pelvic wall while curling his fingers every few thrusts.

"Soak us, Ash," Riordan coaxed.

Brynach wanted to praise her, tell her how beautiful she was, and how much he desired her. He'd never get enough of her. But he wouldn't dream of letting Riordan go untouched. Her legs shook as she came.

Her juices sprayed Riordan and Brynach. Both men groaned as Aisling lay shaking. Her hand on Brynach's cock had slowed, but it didn't matter. He came in hot ropes across her back and part of his stomach. Riordan followed shortly, the taste of Aisling dripping down his stomach and onto his cock, coating Brynach's tongue as Riordan finished.

"Fuck," Brynach moaned when his mouth was free. "If I'd known all I had to do was make a bigger bed this whole trip, I'd have done it much sooner."

Aisling laughed, "Not just anywhere, our home. Crap, I don't think my legs work anymore."

"We've got you, Princess," Brynach said, but made no move to get up. It was Riordan who pulled her into his arms and walked her to the shower. Brynach followed, eyeing the tub that would have to wait.

"Let's get clean, change those sheets, and go eat. I'm ravenous." Riordan stepped under the steamy spray.

They were masters at efficient cleaning and dressing, especially when food was the reward. As they dressed, Aisling seemed a little off. When he asked her if she was okay, she turned to them.

"I think I'm ready to read his letter," Aisling admitted. "Somehow, it doesn't feel as daunting here." She gestured around the house.

"What do you need from us?" Riordan asked.

She looked away and then back again. "Sit with me?"

Without questioning her, they sat on either side of her on a dark-green velvet sofa. She curled herself up to them and ran her nail under the seam of the envelope. Aisling carefully unfolded the letter and began to read. Brynach didn't want to pry, but as he glanced down, the letter was shorter than he'd anticipated.

Under his arm, Aisling laughed. She looked up at them.

"He's such an ass. He never could let me have the last word. Apparently, him sleeping with a grandpa has nothing on me marrying a man over two hundred years old."

Brynach chuckled.

"The rest is mushy. I miss him so much." Aisling's voice broke as tears fell down her face. "He said he knew I'd read this here. Said I was too type-A to resist the full circle of it all. Apparently, he left something for me in the tower. Want to go check it out?"

She stood, and they followed her through the atrium and into the yard. The wooden door to the tower by the stream creaked as it opened. It was lit inside by only the sunlight through the windows, but there was a round table in the middle of the space, chairs all around it like some medieval meeting place. On the table was a piece of clothing.

Aisling's laughter rang against the stones as she lifted it. Brynach didn't understand why the denim jacket made her smile the way she was, but he liked seeing it all the same. His wife shrugged off her brown leather and slid her arms into the jacket. The rhinestones caught the light and bounced off the interior of the tower.

Quietly, his wife whispered, "Top that."

With a laugh and a shake of her head, she walked out, and the guys followed her. Brynach locked the house, and they walked into the town center with a smiling Aisling. Her eyes lit up when she saw an Indian restaurant, and they made their way over to ask for a table outside. It was too beautiful a night to sit inside, and Aisling much preferred to kick off her shoes and sit in the fresh air.

Brynach took a foot in his lap and rubbed it once drinks were ordered. "I like you without shoes."

"I like not feeling like I need to wear them in case I have to run off to an emergency," she stated. "I know we were kidding earlier, but honestly, I'm not sure I want to go back."

Riordan took her hand. "Ash, we have a literal eternity. We

don't have to do anything we don't want to do."

She shook her head. "Lettie doesn't. Sean doesn't. Maybe one day, but I want to spend time with them while I can, and while they still want to spend it with me."

"So, we'll pay to bring them here, a stoirin," Brynach offered. When Aisling opened her mouth to argue he held up a hand. "I'm not saying that's what we have to do, just that we have options. Let's not take anything off the table just yet."

After that, they dropped the topic and dug into their meal. Sharing food, drinks, and laughter with them after an emotional day just felt nice. The sun was starting to set when Aisling answered a video call, and they waved to Lettie and Sean.

"Aisling Campbell, what are you wearing?" Lettie gasped.

Their wife split into a teary smile and handed Riordan the phone so she could showcase the jacket. Through the speaker, they heard Lettie's teary laughter. Then Aisling took the phone back, turned the camera around, and walked them through town to the house before going to give them a tour. Brynach pulled out two of the beers they'd bought on the way back and settled into a chair with Riordan in the glass room off the back of the house.

"She's smiling more. The real ones," Riordan commented. "I know you questioned this trip."

"I did not," Brynach started to argue.

"Yes, you did, Bry. You hated that you walked away from the school. You still worry about Sydney and Breena. I get it. But, like you said, it will all be there later." Riordan brushed Brynach's hair behind his ear. "You're happier, too, you know? I can tell."

"How?" Brynach questioned.

"You have less growl to you," Riordan laughed. "I'm not sure I've ever seen you truly relaxed. Even when you were happy at home with us, you were vigilant. Alert." Riordan gripped the back of Brynach's neck.

"Less growl, huh?" Brynach was teasing now. "I could always add some back if it makes you more comfortable, a chuisle."

Riordan's laughter rang loud enough that Aisling turned from the lawn and smiled at them. Brynach's heart thudded in his chest.

"How do you feel about the Isle of Skye? I hear it's pretty magical," Brynach commented. "We could extend the trip and visit for a little."

"Think she'll go for it?" Riordan asked.

Brynach pulled out his phone and started looking up places to stay. "I think this is one of those situations where it's going to be easier to ask for forgiveness than permission. She wants the extra time, but she's having a hard time believing she deserves it."

"Well, we can't have that. Sign me up. But let's give her time here. And don't forget about the games," Riordan joked. "I still plan to kick your ass."

CHAPTER 38

Aisling

Aisling, a little help would be nice!"

"I'm going to chafe. I know it."

The grin that split Aisling's face was so wide it was borderline painful. She was dressed in a tartan skirt and white tank top as she strode across the green field toward Riordan and Brynach.

Riordan's kilt was struggling to stay aloft on his hips meanwhile Brynach was squatting down to "unstick" things. Or at least that's what he mumbled as she approached. Aisling approached Riordan first, moving his hands away and taking over. She stood in front of him, Brynach at his rear, while she unwrapped him from the piece of fabric and then brought it around again.

"Hold," she instructed as she brought the belt around from behind him and fastened it tightly. "There, good to go."

"Ash, I'm all for living in the moment, but you do realize that my goods are just out there, right? And that caber ... I mean, there's a good chance people see it all." Riordan blushed.

She stroked up his bare chest to his face. "Oh, I know. It's my gift to the people of Scotland."

Brynach put a hand on Riordan's shoulder and lowered his face to his ear. "Whoever throws the caber the furthest gets to fuck Aisling first."

Riordan's eyes went wide, and he started to stretch in an exaggerated way. Aisling's laugh was genuine as was the lust that curled low in her belly. She was still tender from the night before. They'd had more sex on this trip than in the entirety of their relationship to date. But of course, Brynach wouldn't miss an opportunity to make it a competition for her pussy.

She winked at the men, turned, and flicked up the back of her skirt. Unlike the guys, she was wearing underwear, but the thong covered nothing. Their dual groans put an extra sway in her hips.

"I don't care who wins, we make her pay for that," Brynach said, his voice deep.

"I can hear you," she threw over her shoulder. "And just so you know, if I win, I'm pegging one of you."

She heard them curse behind her as she walked away. She'd left most of her things tucked away in a tent they were sleeping in on the grounds for the night. There were children playing at the carnival games and running races around the track. Grown men and women were riding bikes on grass, which was a sight to see. But Aisling was paying a lot more attention to the tests of strength. The caber toss, the barrels and atlas stone-lifting were where it was at.

She found a pleasant patch of grass and took a seat. Aisling was careful to cross her legs and smooth down her skirt as she lay back in the grass and stared up at the clouds. "Wish you were here, Trent," she whispered to herself.

Aisling closed her eyes and pulled up Trent's face. His smile, the way he chewed on his lip ring when he was about to say something that would annoy her. She'd been afraid his letter was going to break her, but it had been sweet. It was a hits list of all his favorite moments with her. Road trips, make-overs, listening to stories about Faerie, forcing Lettie to sneak out, or getting drunk and sleeping in Ash's den as teens. The time he got them fake IDs to get into a gay club and danced until the sun came up. Then he'd given her a replica of the jean jacket from *Teen Witch*. Not only was it hilarious, but how long had Trent been holding onto it? Did he regularly move it around each year when he updated his will until she found it? The commitment to having the last word was commendable.

She sat up and watched as Brynach and Riordan took their places. Both men sized up their competition. To be honest, she didn't care which one won, she was just happy to be there with them.

Aisling hadn't told them she signed herself up for an event. She sure-as-shit wouldn't be participating in the caber toss. Instead, she had signed herself up for the ax-throwing competition. She had time before her event, so she sat back and watched her men pick up large poles and toss them. Before coming to Scotland, she hadn't understood the appeal of the events, but now, surrounded by beautiful, accented men and women all showing off for one another while still laughing and enjoying themselves, she got it. The combination of eye candy and genuine comradery was fantastic. Everyone was so nice, and she found she didn't mind being called lass one bit. Even more so when Riordan said it with his renewed Irish accent.

Riordan ran over while Brynach moved toward his caber. He knelt carefully, and Aisling grinned and lifted the front of his kilt.

"Hey! Don't get cheeky. I need a good luck kiss." He tilted his head. "And if you wanna make it good enough to distract Bry, that'd be awesome."

Aisling laughed. "I'm not getting in the middle."

"You didn't mind being in the middle last night," Riordan teased.

She blushed and blamed it on the sun. He took her hand and lifted her to her feet. She jumped into his arms, and Riordan cupped her ass. Aisling liked to think he was covering her from mooning everyone, but more than likely, he just wanted a handful of cheek. He kissed her with a hand in her red locks. Fuck, it was good. Good enough that around them, whistles and cheers rang out. Aisling assumed they were for the games until Riordan pulled back and let her slide down his body and she looked around. Yeah, no, they'd gathered a crowd of onlookers.

Brynach was among them. He quirked one wickedly black brow and licked his teeth. Oh, they were in trouble. A shiver ran through her, and she slapped Riordan's ass as he walked back to the group waiting for their turn. Aisling fixed her skirt and was trying to ignore the people still staring at her.

"Those men are dedicated to you," a plump, freckled brunette commented as she nudged Aisling's hip. "I'm jealous. So are most of the other women here, and a few of the men. I'm Tilly." She pointed across the field to a burly red-headed man in a kilt, boots, and nothing else. His chest was broad, and he had what could only be described as a Viking dad bod. "That one is mine. Fergus, and yes, I know it's a laughably Scottish name."

"Good on you. He's something. I'm Aisling. You're from here?" Aisling asked.

"Can't escape it, and don't want to. Your beau is Irish, yeah? And the other, I can't place." She was fishing for information, but Aisling never minded bragging a bit.

"Unseelie Prince and my husband," Aisling answered. "They're both my husbands."

"Princess, huh?" She nodded. "I like it. You participating?"

"Ax-throwing right after I watch my guys," Aisling answered.

"Me too. I'd wish you good luck, but I think you've already won." With a friendly smile and a wink, Tilly walked away. With some more time here, Aisling knew they could be friends.

Aisling turned in time to see Brynach blow her a kiss and then pick up his caber. The toss was both graceful and not. I mean, it's hard to be suave while hurling a 175-pound pole across a field. The other Fae clapped for him, and Brynach accepted a few slaps on the back. Riordan was next, and Brynach was sweet enough to give him a slap on the ass to cheer him on.

She couldn't tear her eyes off Riordan as he hefted the large pole. Not too long ago, her sensitive musician couldn't have physically handled it. Her New Fae husband was muscled and battle-worn now. It was a wonder to her how different he was when his heart, what made Riordan himself, had remained the same. But there he was, leg muscles strong and arms ripped, tossing the caber with little more than a grunt.

Watching the two of them laugh with the other participants, cheering and clapping for them as they took their turns, it was impossible not to be grateful for the moment. Her phone rang, and she picked up, turning the camera toward her guys.

"Oh my gosh, is that Riordan and Brynach in kilts?" her mother laughed. "Tell me they're going traditional."

"Oh, they are," Aisling confirmed. "You just missed their caber tosses." She kept the phone pointed their way until her mother got the chance to watch another toss, then flipped it so she could give her a smile.

"You're enjoying yourself?" her mother asked.

"Like you wouldn't believe. I miss home ..."

"But," she prompted.

"It's amazing. We are extending the trip a bit. Brynach really wants to visit the Isle of Skye, and we're here, so you know." Aisling paused. "I may have mentioned to the guys that I'd really like to see Greece. It's a quick flight and then maybe a cruise of the islands."

Her mother sighed. "Will you ever come home?"

Aisling knew she was joking, but the truth was Aisling wasn't sure. "I think I am home, Mom. Not here in Scotland, though the house here does feel like our cabin does. I mean, with Riordan and Brynach. They're my home."

"I miss you like crazy, baby, but I'm so happy for you.

You're right, you know. You're already over there. You might as well travel as much as you can."

Arms circled Aisling, and she cried out as her feet lifted off the ground. "Hello, Mrs. Quinn," Riordan crowed. "We both lost. Isn't that great? No pegging."

"No what now?" Mrs. Quinn squeaked.

Aisling smacked Riordan on the shoulder and turned to her mother. "Gotta go, Mom. Love you."

"Some guy named Fergus came over to us and offered us a drink from his flask. Shit was strong. Anyway, fuck, that was fun." Riordan grabbed her hand, and Aisling let him pull her to Brynach.

It was loud; the sound of grunts and shouts rang through the air. So did the laughter and the cheers. The smell of food and a vague fog of smoke from one of the vendors rolled over the green grass. Someone ran in front of them, nearly knocking them over.

Aisling reached for the knife strapped to her thigh. Only, it wasn't. Her thigh was bare, and she felt a moment of panic before Brynach took her hand.

"You don't need it, a stoirin," he reminded her.

Nobody was targeting her. There were no reporters to dodge or bullets to worry about. Unlike a drop, nobody was protesting her being here. The screams that surrounded her right now were happy ones. In a small patch of grass, alates taught children how to weave flower crowns. A Fae was sifting people from one side of the fairgrounds to the other.

Riordan snagged her hips and turned her toward him. His mouth lowered, and Brynach covered her back while their partners' hands slid under her skirt. She let herself be cradled between the two men who loved her, kissed, and kept safe.

"Aisling! Stop kissing those men long enough to get over here so I can kick that sweet ass," Tilly yelled, and Fergus laughed beside her.

"Who is that?" Riordan asked when he released her.

She grinned and pulled away from the guys. She laughed as she ran across the field.

THE END

If you enjoyed this story, please consider leaving a review on Goodreads, Amazon, The StoryGraph, or the bookseller where you purchased *A Destiny in Ash*. Reviews help authors more than you know.

For updates on future books by Julie, please sign up for her newsletter.
Visit JulieZee.com/newsletter and sign up today!

You can also find Julie on social media:
Instagram: https://www.instagram.com/according2jewls/
Twitter: https://twitter.com/According2Jewls
YouTube: https://www.youtube.com/pagesandpens

ACKNOWLEDGMENTS

I can't believe I'm sitting down to write the final acknowledgments for the *In Ash* series!

Throughout this process, I've repeatedly asked myself why I felt it was wise to begin my writing career with a trilogy. It's been one of the most difficult and rewarding endeavors. I've questioned my sanity and skill a million times over.

I'm lucky. Aisling, Brynach, Riordan, and the rest of my characters continue to live rent-free in my head. I've been asked in countless interviews, book club chats, and discussions with readers if this is the end for them. It's not. And it won't be for you, either. I promise that at some point in the future, I will publish novellas featuring some of your favorites. There is so much I still want to explore inside this world. But for now, they're going to live their lives without us.

There was a small part of me that wanted to dedicate this book to myself. Those who know me know I work tirelessly and loathe failure. I have spent so many sleepless nights worrying over whether this was a fitting end to my story. Alas, I couldn't dedicate this book to myself. Well, I could, but it seemed in bad taste since I didn't write this in a bubble.

As always, I had my writerly friends surrounding me. Their feedback was as invaluable as their support. To Katlyn Duncan, Amber McManus, Jessica Williamson, and my entire Sunday Night Sprint Fam, I give you my heartfelt thanks.

To my ARC readers, you are truly deserving of all Brynach's love (I know it's the one you're hoping for). I couldn't ask for a better street team or a more devoted group of readers.

For Melanie and the Unplugged Book Box team for making all my author dreams come true and providing me the opportunity to have exclusive editions of my book and bookish merch for the *In Ash* series.

To all local indie bookstores, but most especially, Main Point Books in Wayne, PA, and Cupboard Maker Books in Enola, PA. Your support and dedication to authors is unmatched. If you're ever in the area, please visit them; they're fantastic.

To the team at Atmosphere Press for three years of support and encouragement. My fantastic developmental editor Megan Turner, to whom you owe your thanks, because she encouraged more sexy time scenes. Thank you for strengthening my stories and encouraging me to dig a little deeper. To Kevin Stone for three fantastically photographic covers—I'll stare at them for years to come with the same awe I did upon first sight. For Alex and Cam, who walked me through the publication and post-publication process. Thank you for your patience and continued excitement about the opportunities I have to market the books and grow my readership. I can't believe this is the end of our journey, but I'm grateful for your company along the way.

All my appreciation for those of you creating fan art, taking stunning bookstagram pictures, leaving thoughtful reviews, choosing the *In Ash* series for your book club, asking me to join your discussions, or otherwise talking about and hyping this series. It has nothing to do with sales numbers and everything to do with your love of the characters I've spent nearly ten years getting to know so I could transfer them from my imagination into your hands and hearts. If you choose to talk about this book or any of the others, be sure to use #InAshSeries and tag @according2jewls.

For my family, who dutifully purchase my books but probably don't open them, let alone read this far ... I still love the heck out of you.

Prior books have been for my sisters and parents—this one is for my nieces and nephews. To Charlie, Ava, Carter, Edie, Shyanne, Atticus, Lochlan, and *insert any future love bugs here*. I'm pretty sure it's agreed upon that, despite being the oldest of your aunts, Juju is the coolest. You amaze me constantly with your kind hearts, ridiculous senses of humor, and brilliance. If you are our future, the future is in good hands. No matter what, remember I love you the mostest.

And because I have no idea when I'll have your undivided attention like this again, this is my reminder to everyone that growth is hard-earned, not just in my books, but in real life. I have always, and will always, advocate for mental health. It's taken me far too long to accept that I'm deserving of happiness. I know how that sounds, but putting myself first isn't easy for me. I want you to know you're worthy, too. Of love, safety, healthy boundaries, saying no, and welcoming joy without worrying about the other shoe dropping. So, I suppose this is where I thank Autumn for the past year-plus of therapy. Ten out of ten, I do recommend doing whatever it takes to ensure your own mental health. The time to destigmatize seeking/ needing help has long since passed.

Thank you, once again, for making this author's dreams a reality. I hope you'll always remember fondly your time spent between the pages of this series. It's been quite the adventure, but just like Aisling, Riordan, and Brynach, I'm off to new ones. I hope you'll join me wherever they take me by staying in touch at JulieZee.com and @according2jewls on Instagram and Twitter.

All my deepest heartfelt love!
Julie

ABOUT ATMOSPHERE PRESS

Founded in 2015, Atmosphere Press was built on the principles of Honesty, Transparency, Professionalism, Kindness, and Making Your Book Awesome. As an ethical and author-friendly hybrid press, we stay true to that founding mission today.

If you're a reader, enter our giveaway for a free book here:

SCAN TO ENTER
BOOK GIVEAWAY

If you're a writer, submit your manuscript for consideration here:

SCAN TO SUBMIT
MANUSCRIPT

And always feel free to visit Atmosphere Press and our authors online at atmospherepress.com. See you there soon!

ABOUT THE AUTHOR

Julie Zantopoulos grew up in the suburbs of Philadelphia but spent weekends and summers in the Pocono Mountains where she wandered the woods and daydreamed of the world beyond the Veil. She's been obsessed with the written word as long as she can remember. She reads voraciously and widely and credits that, and her degree in Psychology, with her love of creating rich characters and worlds.

When she's not writing she's running her YouTube channel, hosting writing sprints to encourage the online writing community, or reading. If all else fails, you'll find her enjoying "bad" SyFy-Channel made-for-television movies or snuggling with her senior rescue cat, Jasmine.

Find her online at JulieZee.com, Pages and Pens on You-Tube, and @according2jewls on Instagram and Twitter.